GW00501806

Reviews o
by E..... ......

A DREAM DEFERRED

'*A Dream Deferred* is particularly convincing on the corrupting effect of power on sexuality.' – *Times Literary Supplement*

'Carim's style can encompass action, psychology and a certain kind of prophetic analysis with great persuasiveness.' – *New Statesman*

'An impressively powerful and stylish novel... written as well with sympathy, understanding and even tenderness...' – *Sunday Express*

'I liked the book for its unsentimental quality and its realism. A formidable novel...One of the outstanding titles of the year.' – *Sunday Times*

THE GOLDEN CITY

'Takes the reader on a penetrating journey through the shadows of a city unparalleled in any other book except perhaps *The Autobiography of Malcom X.*' – *Los Angeles Herald-Examiner*

'Bubbles with vital juices in spite of all the searing bitterness.' – *New York Times Book Review*

AIDS: THE DEADLY EPIDEMIC

'Arguably the most complete and concise overview yet written... Essential public-affairs reading.' – *Booklist, USA*

'A passionate book, forceful in its message and persuasive in its arguments.' – *Nursing Times*

Also by Enver Carim

The Price of an Education

A Dream Deferred

The Golden City

AIDS: The Deadly Epidemic
(with Graham Hancock)

Third World Development,
in three volumes (as editor)

the trouble with
Sophie Gresham
love in the genetic revolution

Enver Carim

To Tom Vossen

This souvenir of our long
friendship

From Enver
27 November 2014

SilverWood

Published in 2014 by SilverWood Books

SilverWood Books Ltd
30 Queen Charlotte Street, Bristol, BS1 4HJ
www.silverwoodbooks.co.uk

ISBN 978-1-78132-290-1 (paperback)
ISBN 978-1-78132-291-8 (ebook)

British Library Cataloguing in Publication Data
A CIP catalogue record for this book is available from
the British Library

Set in Bembo by SilverWood Books
Printed on responsibly sourced paper

For the kind, industrious and lovely Ruth Florence

And for the distinctive sisters Fiona, Rachel,
Lara and Maria with love and admiration

Author's Note

Whilst researching a non-fiction book on the Aids epidemic which I co-wrote with a friend and which *Booklist* in the US described as 'essential public-affairs reading', I met in their labs some of the world's leading virologists, immunologists and gene-transfer specialists. I discovered that despite their arcane professional work, research scientists are just as human as the rest of us. They too have hopes, fears and disappointments; they too have conflicting emotions to contend with and relationships that are sometimes fraught.

The inner lives of scientists are so complex that I felt a book which encompassed all the issues in an integrated way had to have that boundary-less coherence one tends to find only in works of fiction. Hence this novel. It's a 21st-century love story against the background of attempts in labs around the world to scotch inherited diseases at source, including breast cancer, Down syndrome, muscular dystrophy, in order to end the epic saga of human suffering by means of genetic enhancement and synthetic biology.

I offer this book as an entertainment to people with a secular cast of mind who are appalled by the violent behaviour of religious zealots denigrating, imprisoning and slaughtering communities all over the world who reject their obscurantist beliefs, especially intelligent, assertive females and gay people who are vilified to the nth degree. This story is also a celebration of the cultural upliftment which science and technology have afforded humanity throughout history, not least in cures for killer diseases.

Disclaimer

This book is a work of fiction. Except for individuals and institutions clearly in the public domain, all the characters are invented and any resemblance between them and real persons, living or dead, is purely coincidental. This work is intended for free-thinking people with inquiring minds who are open to the new biological future now being ushered in.

Now I am ready to tell how bodies are changed
Into different bodies…
You think heaven is safe?
We have a population of demi-gods…
Ted Hughes, *Tales from Ovid*

John ap Rice says, 'Reason cannot win against these people.
You try to open their eyes. But ranged against you are the
statues of the virgin that weep tears of blood.'
Hilary Mantel, *Bring Up The Bodies*

I like the dreams of the future better than the history of
the past.
Thomas Jefferson, third President of the United States

1

Sophie Gresham slept with me seven hours after she graduated from Cambridge University, seven hours after I met her by chance whilst looking for someone else in a hall full of students with mortarboards on their heads and black gowns draped over their shoulders. She had promised herself that she would lose her virginity if she got a double first in the final exams; she would embark on her sex life as a reward for achieving her academic objective.

I wasn't one of the new graduates in the hubbub of that crowded hall where waiters wearing bow ties and white gloves were carrying trays and distributing glasses of wine and professors were wishing individuals well in their future endeavours. I was already working full time in a genetics lab. My colleagues and I were searching at the molecular level for the causes of inherited diseases and seeing if there were ways to slow down the ageing process. I was a research scientist in an international team exploring synthetic biology, how genes from other species might boost the human genome.

A week after she ended my sexual famine, Sophie told me she'd booked two seats on a flight and a hotel room in Paris and asked if I spoke any French. I said I didn't and that the only time I had travelled outside the United States was when I came to England.

'It doesn't matter,' she said. 'I'll do the talking and be your guide.'

From Charles de Gaulle Airport we went by taxi straight to Montmartre in the 18th *arrondissement* where, from the sloping gardens of the Sacre-Coeur perched on its hill, we had a clear, sweeping view of the rooftops of Paris; the golden dome of the Hôtel des Invalides rose like a beacon on the south side of the river. Sophie pointed out the general direction of the places we'd be visiting, including Notre Dame Cathedral, La Dèfense, and the Centre Pompidou where, she said, quite a few Picassos were being exhibited. We'd also be going for a boat ride along the Seine, she said, so that I could see the historic buildings on either side and pass under about twenty of Paris's three dozen bridges.

We then drove to the Latin Quarter on the Left Bank of the Seine. Sophie asked the driver to take us round the Jardin du Luxembourg, along the Boulevard St Michel, and up the short street that leads to the Sorbonne where students were milling about in front of the bookshops and cafés. A while later we were moving slowly over the cobblestones surrounding the Panthéon, a neo-classical edifice with columns and pediment in the ancient Greek style. We got out of the taxi and Sophie led me into that building and down a steep flight of stone steps to the basement 'basilica' part; it was a cold, sepulchral place where our voices echoed and where, Sophie said, something called 'the spirit of France' was personified.

In the dim light we saw heroes of French history lying in stone sarcophagi in narrow cell-like rooms, the remains of individuals such as Voltaire, Victor Hugo, Jean-Jacques Rousseau, Emile Zola, Braille, and quite a few others, their wigs, too, in a state of dusty decay on the faded cushions under their embalmed, emaciated heads. It was interesting, I guess, but a tad too necrophilic for my taste, and I was glad to get back up those steps to the ground floor and proper daylight. The Panthéon at that level did have the look of a classical temple, the airy space dominated by a sculpture of 'Immortality', a voluptuous woman whom a forest of outstretched arms were straining to reach.

In the busy Boulevard St Germain humming with

traffic Sophie asked the driver to pull over opposite the Eglise St Germain des Prés and wait for her in front of a florist's shop where a display of flowers and plants vivified the sidewalk. She hopped out, entered the shop and got back into the car a few minutes later with a large floral bouquet.

'Smell these,' she said, lifting the beribboned bouquet to my nose.

I inhaled. 'They're fragrant, so lovely and fresh. Are they for me?' I asked, thinking the crimson and creamy-white carnations were a gift to confirm our relationship. We'd only known each other one week.

'No. They're for someone else.'

'Someone else? Who would that be?'

'Wait and see.'

'D'you know someone here in Paris?'

'Yes.'

'Someone special?' I asked, feeling a sudden rush of embarrassment heating my head and a corrosive emptiness filling my heart.

Sophie must have noticed my unease, the surge of jealousy, because she smiled warmly at me, slid across the seat pressing her thigh against mine, and kissed me reassuringly on the cheek.

'These flowers are for an old friend whom I love and respect, someone I first met when I was about nine.'

'Long before you met me.'

'Of course.'

'D'you still love him?'

She looked into my eyes. 'Stop worrying, Charlie Venn,' she said. 'It's nothing to be concerned about. You give me what he has never been able to give, even though he taught me to cherish the pleasure when it did finally come along.'

'Come again? I'm not sure I understood that. He taught you to cherish the pleasure – when you were *nine*?'

'Yes. I was about nine years old when the lessons began.'

'The lessons?'

'Uh-huh,' Sophie nodded, a far-away look coming into her eyes. 'Lessons which *I* controlled – to suit my mood, my curiosity.'

'What was this guy – some kind of paedophile?'

Sophie grinned. 'I don't think so – that never occurred to me. He made me feel good, even though he confused me somewhat. He made me feel wise in a warm, sensuous sort of way.'

'Wise when you were nine?'

'Sounds silly, doesn't it?'

'Who is he?'

'I said – wait and see.'

Sophie held on to the bouquet and told the driver to head for a destination I didn't quite catch because my knowledge of the French language was less than elementary; all I caught were the words 'Montparnasse' and 'Boulevard Edgar Quinet'. She had obviously been there before. The driver was wearing a beret. He looked over his shoulder at Sophie, glanced at me, mumbled '*d'accord*' and steered the car back into the traffic.

I love Sophie dearly. She's now a successful writer and through her I've come into contact with a species of people I would probably not have met otherwise: authors of novels and short stories. They're an interesting set of specimens. The ones I've encountered are volatile and introspective at the same time, dreamers who count their royalty cash carefully. From the awkward conversations I've had with them, which nearly always end abruptly on a sarcastic or derogatory note, leaving me feeling patronised and pitied, I've come to the conclusion that novelists aren't necessarily keen on engaging the real world but prefer to construct alternative realms in tune with their own preferences. Perhaps if they weren't so jealous and resentful of my work; if they weren't so inclined to cast aspersions about DNA manipulation and synthetic biology, I might discover what mysterious power it is that enables them blithely to float over life's rough edges and to inhabit the more amenable milieux of their imaginings.

There's nothing mysterious or mystical about *me*, however. As a research scientist, I am totally empirical; I'm steeped in the ways of reason and the millennial logic of molecules. My mind abhors the sort of medieval guile that relies on incense and incantation to win over followers by mesmerising them and suppressing their critical faculties. (Incidentally, incense sticks, when lit, emit carcinogens.)

I was amazed, therefore, to find myself getting out of the taxi, crossing the sidewalk and following Sophie through the black gates of a graveyard. We passed an office on the left-hand side where a glass case on the wall displayed the *Plan du Cimetière*, a map, but Sophie barely glanced at it. We seemed to be on some sort of pilgrimage. I strode beside her along the tarmac walkways that divided the cemetery into geometric sections. Sophie took me round to the double-tomb of shiny mottled-grey stone where Samuel Beckett and his French wife were interred together. This tomb had no religious words or symbols and was simply inscribed:

Suzanne Beckett née Dechevaux-Dumesnil 1900–1989
Samuel Beckett 1906–1989

Sophie read the names and dates aloud, paused for a pensive moment, then led me between the headstones to the grave of the philosopher/novelist Jean-Paul Sartre near the perimeter fence and the plot where his lover/companion, the proto-feminist Simone de Beauvoir, lay buried alongside him. He had died in 1980, she in 1986.

'It was Sartre who declared that "hell is other people" and that "*Si tu veux être philosophe, ecrivez romans*" – if you want to be a philosopher, write novels. They insisted on occupying separate spaces in death,' Sophie said, waving her hand from his grave to hers, 'just as they had in life, to avoid falling into what he'd famously called *mauvaise fois* – bad faith. They never crowded each other when they were alive and didn't intend to do so afterwards.'

I didn't know what to make of this arcane information. I didn't think anyone intended *anything* once they were buried.

Sophie started to move away, then turned back to Simone de Beauvoir's grave and said: 'It was in the memoir she wrote of her mother's last days called *Une mort très douce* – *A Very Easy Death* – that she declared, "bourgeois marriage is an unnatural institution". She'd come to that conclusion from what she'd seen of her parents' relationship. Her father had had affairs with other women which everyone knew about except her mother. The wedding-ring on her mother's finger, she said, had "authorised her to become acquainted with pleasure". But when her mother was thirty-five and in her prime, her father more or less stopped making love to her. Simone writes very movingly that her mother Françoise lay in bed for years on end with the husband she still loved, hoping, waiting, pining – in vain.'

We moved on again, stepping carefully between the graves, me following Sophie, until a few minutes later I was gazing at a worn headstone roughly rectangular in shape and inscribed in French with words to the effect that the poet Charles Baudelaire died in Paris at the age of 46 on 31 August 1867.

The sky had been overcast when the plane landed at the airport and now it began to rain. I could feel the drizzle soaking my jacket and collar and seeping down my neck and I felt ridiculous. Sophie's hair became soggy. Her dress, too, was soon drenched, but she didn't seem to mind. Her mind was clearly elsewhere, her face serene as she placed on the tomb the bouquet of crimson and creamy-white carnations and paid homage to this star in her literary firmament. There is no place in the world she would rather have been at that particular moment, despite the weather.

We stood in the midst of the rows of closely packed graves under the steady rain, the only visitors there on that inclement day, looking at the tomb alongside the much larger monument to one Charles Sapey, *senateur, grand officier de la Légion d'Honneur*, who had died on 5 May 1857.

On Baudelaire's flat, rectangular, marble-like tombstone where Sophie had placed her flowers there was already a broken flower-pot and two pieces of handwriting in ink on sheets of white paper. One of the writings, a poem, was kept down by a shell with a stone on it, the other by a lump of masonry. The rain was beginning to render the handwritings illegible, splattering and smudging the ink and making it run irrationally across the two sheets of paper.

Sophie bent forward and read aloud one of the writings:

'Glory and praise to you, Satan, up there in Heaven, where you used to reign, and deep down in Hell where, conquered, you dream in silence! Grant that my soul may one day rest in you, under the Tree of Knowledge, at the time when over your brow, like a new Temple, its branches are once again spread.'

'What's that about?' I asked.

'Someone's prose translation, a bad translation, of Baudelaire's poem called "Prayer",' Sophie said as she straightened up. 'Baudelaire is incomparable. As well as finding beauty in decadence and evil in his first book of verse *Les Fleurs du mal* – Flowers of Evil – and exploring the powers of love in exquisitely beautiful language, he also sussed out God's vulnerability to learning and new knowledge, why God felt threatened and took refuge in wrath and promised to punish people whose devotion was to anything other than himself.'

'He was a jealous god, you mean?'

'Exactly – as God himself says in the Bible, in Exodus, Deuteronomy and elsewhere.'

'Only *he* was to be worshipped? *He* was the reigning icon of the universe. Is that what you're saying, Sophie? Only *his* explanations were valid, even though they were based almost entirely on punishment, cruelty and threats of suffering?'

Sophie nodded. 'It was Baudelaire,' she said, 'who translated the work of your compatriot Edgar Allan Poe long before it became famous and hugely influential in American literature.'

'Really? Poe was known in France?'

'He was, and elsewhere in Europe too. His gothic tales and grisly stories have inspired more than a hundred film and television adaptations. I think it's sad,' Sophie added, shaking her head, 'that Poe died penniless, destitute, despite pretty much inventing the detective-story genre. Sir Arthur Conan Doyle thought highly of him. So did H.G. Wells for his science fiction.' She bent forward again and began reading the other poem, in a different handwriting:

'*Charles*
  je veux votre âme
  a jamais elle m'effroie…'

and then stopped. The raindrops were obliterating the words, making it impossible to read farther.

'What does it mean,' I asked, 'what you've just read?'

'Something like "I want your soul ever to inspire me with awe".'

'I wonder who wrote it. Who would place a message on the grave of someone who's been dead for a hundred-and-twenty-eight years?'

'A lover of rhythmic cadences, most likely, and of dark

erotica,' Sophie replied. 'A citizen of this city of light, perhaps.'

She turned her head absently. Rain water was dripping from her hair and nose and chin, but there was a faraway look in her eyes, something supernal and blissful. She stepped closer to me, curled an arm around my neck, pulled me to her and kissed me hard and long on the lips. She pushed her tongue into my mouth and flicked it about, deploying her other hand below my belt. The fragrance of her perfume at such close quarters had a rousing effect. In the driving rain in that French cemetery so full of tombstones streaming with water gurgling into the furrow under our feet, I felt happy to be alive and vigorous.

We dried ourselves in the taxi as best we could with my handkerchiefs and Sophie then took us, bedraggled, across a bridge called Pont d'Austerlitz to Victor Hugo's house in the Place des Vosges near the site of the notorious Bastille.

The house, on several floors, is now a museum and a focal point of France's cultural heritage. I noticed again how Sophie's demeanour changed to something resembling veneration. This man Hugo was French, a poet of distinction as well as a novelist, dramatist, essayist and statesman who'd been elected to the *Académie Française* in 1841; his novels include *Les Misérables* and *Notre-Dame de Paris*. He had died in 1885, according to the tourist information, one-hundred-and-ten years ago, yet here was this Englishwoman, this new girlfriend of mine who couldn't seem to get enough of me in bed, who was still exploring different positions in which to make love, beaming at me the while – here she was carrying on as though she were at a religious shrine, genuflecting almost, as if there were invisible angels in the place whose fluttering wings were wafting some essence of the writer's spirit towards her face so that she could inhale it and be inspired to...to...what? Produce an uplifting poem? Write a superior kind of prose?

The beatification was baffling. A wan, virginal expression

permeated her countenance. At one point as we stepped from room to room looking at the framed pictures, the period furniture, the actual table on which Victor Hugo used to write, the delicate *chinoiserie*, and Rodin's massive bust of the author on a tapering wooden plinth, Sophie smiled at me and her smile was that of a maidenly madonna conscious anew of her goodness and of the superiority of her chosen *métier*.

The vibes coming off her were curious, uncanny.

They were other-worldly, those vibes. I couldn't read them, didn't understand them. I felt sure they had nothing to do with being in France or with the French language, and I realised there was a whole side to Sophie that was opaque. This woman was ethereal, it suddenly occurred to me. She was enlivening to be with; her low voice was a delight whenever she spoke, and to embrace her was the prelude to purest pleasure. Nevertheless, I had a distinct sense that I might turn out to be too shallow for her. I might well not be astral, not spiritual, enough.

What was it with Sophie Gresham and dead writers that made her go weak at the knees and become deferential?

2

My colleagues and I at the Institute of Molecular and Neural Genetics in Cambridge are moving closer to scotching inherited diseases at source including breast cancer, Down syndrome, muscular dystrophy and to slowing down the ageing process by manipulating the human genome in very precise ways. I've been analysing particular chromosomes in the lab. It's intensive work. The equipment we use includes electron microscopes, DNA sequencing cells, electrophoresis apparatus, high-speed centrifuges, flasks of liquid nitrogen, Petrie dishes, hybridisation ovens and other gear. The CRISPR genome editing tool enables us to delete, insert or replace any particular DNA sequence at a specific location in the genome; this technique has enabled us to create mouse models of human diseases far more rapidly than was previously possible. We are making progress, slow but sure. We're closing in on our objectives, but problems in my private life have begun to affect my concentration. I haven't been sleeping well. I've been waking up tired. A bad dream keeps me tossing and turning and sweating in bed. It is detailed, complex, deeply disturbing, a proper nightmare. I'm a research scientist at the cutting edge of molecular medicine, not a street thug cutting people's faces, so why am I being assailed by this dreadful dream? Perhaps it's because I'm an American in England that this nightly assault has a transatlantic aura; it is full of my country's iconography.

I dream I'm a mobster in control of rackets that include bootleg liquor, gambling and extortion. On my say-so hoods who encroach on my turf get bumped off and disappear without trace. The police are in my pocket. Corrupt mayors take my money and look the other way. I'm a version of Lucky Luciano, legendary head of the Mafia's Genovese family in New York and boss of the Cosa Nostra syndicate, acknowledged founder of organised crime in the United States. I'm immaculately dressed in tuxedo and black bow tie, expensive rings glittering on my fingers. The shine of my slicked-down hair vies with the sheen of the white silk scarf hanging elegantly from my shoulders. I'm *nouveau riche* and vulgar and love every minute of it. All the broads come to my parties: they know the booze flows like water and that I book the very best bands in town, not only at the Cotton Club where Duke Ellington swings. If a pianist won't play at one of my places, I have his fingers broken. If a trumpeter won't gig for me, he won't gig for anyone else: with a punctured lung he won't have the necessary puff.

I open the door to the master bedroom and see that Sophie, my woman of ten years, has been two-timing me all along. Sophie's heart has been elsewhere. I see her pelvis pushing up and down, up and down, and wonder if she's forgotten the words of the song we've sung together more than once about not going to strangers when we're in the mood for love but coming to each other for pleasure. I open the door of the main bedroom in my penthouse apartment and Sophie is crying out in ecstasy. A guy is lying between her smooth thighs, fucking her as if there is no tomorrow, thrusting vigorously.

The bed is rocking under their naked bodies.

Their clothes are scattered on the floor.

A food-trolley with champagne bottle and two glasses is reflected in the dressing-table mirror. Smoochy music's coming from the sound system fitted into the wood panelling.

They keep heaving and grunting, Sophie and this unknown guy, unaware of me standing in the doorway.

Her legs are wrapped around his back, her nails dug into his flesh. His hairy butt is rising and falling furiously, banging the hell out of her.

She cries out again in rapture, eyes shut. The guy's thrusting movements suddenly stop, his orgasm makes his backside judder and a long sigh rises from the pillow into which his face is pressed. The salty smell of sex hangs in the room like an invisible fog.

Only when he withdraws from her, when he rolls off her body and lies beside her on the quilt, his slack dick shining with the wetness of semen, only then does the guy become aware of a presence in the doorway and turn his head on the pillow.

'Had enough, have you?'

My voice makes Sophie's head jerk up. She looks across her lover at me standing in the doorway wearing a tuxedo, black bow tie and white silk scarf.

'Screws well, does he?'

Her face goes red.

Her hair is loose, down to her shoulders. The embarrassment makes her cover her breasts with her arms. She has no other defence. The thought must be flashing through her mind that she'll soon be dead, her body rolled up in a carpet and thrown into a dumpster on some back street.

'Answer me,' I tell her. 'He's a good fucker, is he? Better than me?'

She can't speak. Her mouth is suddenly dry, tongue seized up. That sort of thing happens to people who cross Charlie Venn when he brings them justice. She knows about my temper under the calm exterior.

She shakes her head. She pleads with her eyes. There are no words in the world to get her out of this fix.

Fear makes her stupid. She pushes herself up into a kneeling position on the bed and arches her back to show her nipples to best effect, those tits I've often told her are the best I've seen in years. She hopes desperately that I'll spare her because of the beauty of her body.

'How much did he pay you?'

She shakes her head.

'How much?'

Croaking sounds escape her lips: 'Nothing, Charlie.'

'Nothing? That adds insult to injury. I give you two grand a month spending money – cash in hand. I give you this penthouse with views across the city, a brand-new Jag to run around in, food on my tab at any restaurant you like – and you screw this shit for nothing? It makes a monkey of me.'

I step into the room, closer to the bed, and look down at lover-boy's naked body. A silver cross linked to a chain around his neck is resting on his hairy chest. His legs are long, stomach flat, skin white like hers. I notice how shrivelled his dick is; it is shrunk into creamy creases of moist skin, almost hidden in the hair. I wonder if Sophie has told him about our love rag under the pillow.

'Strange,' I say. 'Your manhood seems to have disappeared.'

I hate being humiliated, hate being shafted, made a fool of. I have a reputation to protect; my street soldiers would lose respect if they heard some john from the burbs was poking my piece. I push my hand under my tuxedo and draw my weapon from its shoulder-holster; it's a Walther P38 9mm pistol. Then I turn my head and look down into the eyes of the guy who's just been banging *my* woman, in *my* bed, in *my* apartment.

'What's she like?' I ask. 'How would you rate her, out of ten?'

The soft brown eyes looking up at me from the pillow are surrounded by pools of white. The bony face is bloodless, gone pale from shock. Hair's grey, eyebrows thick, both his lips twitching.

'I asked you a question – don't dare ignore me again,' I glare at him and brandish the pistol. 'How would you rate her, out of ten?'

His lips part, the Adam's apple bobs in his throat, but only a hoarse sound emerges.

'Don't be secretive. There's no one else in the apartment to hear what a fool you've made of me. Speak up, man. Give me your honest opinion.'

'She's wonderful,' he says in a dry, frightened voice, his eyes wide.

'How wonderful?'

'Ten out of ten.'

'The best piece you've ever had?'

'Yes.'

'How many times have you had her? How many times have you sneaked behind my back and banged my woman?'

'Only once, I swear. This is the first time.'

'You think it was worth it – what's gonna happen to you?'

'Please, Charlie,' Sophie pleads. 'It's not his fault.'

'It's not his fault?' I glance at her kneeling on the bed beyond her lover and point a finger downwards. 'Whose dick is that, then? Mine or his?'

The blood that rushed to her face is gone. She's pale and drawn, like a stiff on a mortuary slab before an autopsy.

I move my arm and touch the muzzle of the pistol to the guy's forehead.

'You've got about a minute of your life left, so you might as well tell the truth. This is your last conversation – make it count. What's your name?'

'Please. Please don't kill me,' he says hoarsely. 'Please. I've never harmed anyone.'

'You've never harmed anyone? Strange perception you have. I catch you inside my woman, violating the sanctity of relationships, humiliating me – and you say you've never harmed anyone. Get real. What are people gonna say about me when they hear of this?'

'They won't hear of it, I swear. I'll never mention it.'

'The people who knew you were coming here – they'll be laughing at me.'

'No one knew I was coming here – truly. I didn't mention it to anyone.'

'Are you gonna tell me your name or not?'

'Robert Paige.'

'Page as in book?'

'No – P-A-I-G-E. Rob Paige.'

'What's your job, Rob? What d'you do?'

'I look after people's souls.'

'You a shoemaker, a cobbler?'

'No. Not that sort of sole.'

'What sort then?'

'The sort that is the essence of people, what pagans call the psyche.'

'You a priest, are you saying?'

'Yes, I am – a bishop, if truth be told. God has been my vocation since I was at high school.'

'This gun is loaded, Robert Paige. Are you pulling my leg?'

'Not at all. I'm Anglo-Catholic, high church, properly baptised. That's my identity.'

'Your identity?'

'The core of me. The click of rosary beads, the smell of incense, statues of the Virgin Mary and Jesus holding the sacred heart – those are the accoutrements of my communion with God.'

'They allow you to fuck other men's women, do they?'

He shuts his eyes briefly. I notice his chest expanding as he inhales. 'Thanks to my good work,' he says in a superb non-sequitur, 'and God's will, I'm going to be listed in the next edition of *Crockford's*.'

'Really? Despite boning someone else's partner? Following the example of other bishops, are you – traumatising little boys in a global pandemic of child rape and cover-up? Being dragged to court because you have no sense of right and wrong. So tell me, Rob Paige: where'd you meet Sophie? She doesn't go to church, as far as I know.'

'At the swimming pool in the leisure centre, not far from where you and she play squash.'

'She told you about me?'

'She said that although she liked the game, it was getting to be a bit of a bore.'

'Really? She said that about the squash we play?'

'She did.'

'I find it hard to believe.'

'You have a gun to my head,' he says, still hoarse, swallowing, his eyes dilated. 'I'm in the presence of my maker – why would I lie?'

I glance at Sophie kneeling on the bed beyond him. Our eyes meet and she blushes again. It's a shock to me that Sophie finds a priest attractive despite all the derogatory things she's said over the years about organised religion, its rigid dogma, built-in hypocrisy, hard-heartedness, encouraging pogroms, burning people at the stake, vilifying gays. Despite all her criticisms of religion, she is evidently still seduced by it. It offers a kind of comfort, not a challenge, pre-chewed mouthfuls ready to be swallowed, something that is free of charge and doesn't have to be earned.

I look down at Rob Paige and tap his forehead with the muzzle of the pistol. He winces and turns his head away.

'You met her at the swimming pool, you say. Were you in the water with her?'

He turns his head back and his eyes meet mine. 'On several occasions. I showed her some strokes.'

'Did you, reverend? Which strokes did you show her?'

'How to do backstroke.'

27

'And breaststroke?'

'That too.'

'And yet Sophie's a good swimmer. She's known all the strokes since she was a kid.'

'Then she pretended not to know the strokes.'

'So you and Sophie became friends?'

'We did.'

'What did you like about her, Rob, apart from her lovely figure and face – and her soul, of course?'

'I liked her deep voice,' he says. 'I liked her friendly smile. It turned out she'd read some of the books I'd read. We talked about books.'

'Very cultured. You in your swimming trunks and she in her bikini – you talked about books at the side of the pool?'

'That's right. At one of the tables, sipping Diet Coke.'

'With other people walking by dripping water, you talked with my woman at the side of the pool?'

'I did.'

'Did you notice the gold ring on her wedding-finger?'

'Yes, I did.'

'It cost me a packet, that ring – I paid full whack. Gold encrusted with diamonds to show my love. Products are proof of feelings – the more expensive the product, the deeper one's love. Ain't that so?' He doesn't reply. His eyes are huge petrified orbs. 'So what did the ring mean? As a bishop, you'd've known what the ring meant, wouldn't you?'

'It meant she was a married woman.'

'So you know that a wedding-ring sends a signal to all and sundry?'

'I do.'

'What does the signal say, Rob?'

'It says keep off the grass.'

'And what does that actually *mean*?'

'It means…it means…'

'Say it, man. I can't stand here all day. I'm warning you, don't keep me waiting again,' I hit his head with the pistol.

He winces, baring his teeth, then says: 'It means she's not available.'

'Not available for what?'

'For sex.'

'Why not?'

'Because someone else is her partner. Someone else is… you know…her partner – legally and in the sight of God.'

'Yet you, a bishop, kept talking to her.'

'I did.'

'Even though she was wearing a wedding-ring. Did her husband come up in the conversation?'

'He did, but not at first.'

'Who mentioned him first – you or she?'

'She did.'

'What did she say about me?'

'She said you were a nice guy, a generous lover – you were free with money. She said she loved your hazel-green eyes and hairstyle. She didn't mind the jagged birthmark on your left cheek – it never bothered her, she said. And it didn't matter at first that you were a scientist who worked in a lab.'

'Did she say what sort of scientist I was?'

'A molecular biologist, she said – a gene-transfer specialist. Something like that.'

'Did she say what that involved?'

'Manipulating genes, she said, analysing the chemistry of molecules. She said you referred to it as the chemistry of love. She said you were on the wave of the future. She said you and your colleagues in labs around the world were involved in a war between the sacred and profane. You were going to re-make mankind in a post-human image. You were going to strip out the mistakes and errors that were part of God's image – the in-built diseases, the pus and diarrhoea, the disabilities and rancour that rise up from nowhere and bring so much pain and suffering. You were going to get rid of them at source, the inherited diseases, at the molecular level, you and your colleagues on every continent, along with the hatred, selfishness and violent greed that have characterised human nature hitherto. That's what Sophie told me, anyway – more or less. Your project was to liberate men and women from the excruciating bonds of their bodies, from unnecessarily early ageing, loss of vigour, so they can soar up to a heaven of their own making.'

'Not a bad summary, reverend. You grasped the essentials. And what did you think of the project?'

'It reminded me of the eugenics movement in the early 20th century,' he says, frowning, 'that vain attempt to improve God's handiwork which not even angels can improve. I thought it hubristic, sensationally arrogant. You scientists are again reaching too high, trying to play God.'

'You would say that, wouldn't you – because you're jealous. You're *jealous*,' I shout at him with the pistol touching his head and hear my voice echoing in the room *jealous, jealous, jealous*. 'You religious lot hate the idea of people really being born again a bit more divine – because it *isn't you* making it happen. It *isn't you* juggling the genes, re-arranging the nucleotides. Genes were little more than a notion in the early 20th century. Rosalind Franklin at King's College London hadn't yet sent a beam of X-rays through a crystal and allowed the scattered beam to hit a photographic plate – it showed for the first time ever the double-helix structure of DNA. Ask Mensa – it's people with the highest IQs in the world, with fresh, clear, inquiring minds, who know we have to be self-reliant, who know that religion is deeply degrading. You're redundant, bishop. Your time has passed. You had your chance and used it to burn people at the stake, burn them alive, hear them screaming – such exquisite cruelty.'

I suddenly dislike him intensely and press the muzzle of the pistol harder into his forehead. 'So you told Sophie my work was arrogant?'

He has guts, he has nerve – I'll give him that.

'I did,' he says, straining to push his head deeper down into the pillow away from the tip of the pistol. 'I told her it reminded me of a line of Nietzsche's: "All gods are dead – now we want the superman to live, *die Übermensch*".'

'He will live, believe me, born of knowledge – precisely the knowledge your god forbade Adam and Eve to have in the Garden of Eden. You worship icons that never change, like your certainties. Your beliefs are stagnant and you know it. You're stuck in ignorance, rooting for idiocy, and you know it. Your jealous god has no DNA, no means of transformation. That's why you lot are resentful, always demanding punishment and death – even for qualified doctors who help women in distress. You think you're the moral majority, but you are nothing of the kind. You are the *jealous* majority, forever furious and frothing at the mouth.'

I realise as I press the pistol into his head that the anger welling in me is beginning to make *me* froth. I scrape the muzzle across his eyebrows; he bites his lower lip. 'What else did Sophie say about me?'

'She said something I couldn't understand at first. She said her love life was marvellous. She described you as…,' he watches my eyes with fear pulsing in his.

'Say it, man. I want to know what she's been telling other men about me.'

'It's crude.'

'Don't make me laugh, reverend, with your jaundiced perception. I caught you shafting my wife, remember? Isn't that crude?'

'She said you were fabulous in bed. She said you made her come voluminously – every time. She said you made life fun, more interesting and variegated, more pleasurable to live.'

'That's puzzling, isn't it?' I say, glancing at Sophie's naked desirable traitorous body kneeling on the bed. 'If I made her come every time, if I made life more interesting and pleasurable to live, if I satisfied her so thoroughly, why did she want someone else?'

'She didn't say you satisfied her. She said you made her come unfailingly, gave her multiple orgasms.'

'Is this an example of casuistic hair-splitting, of church-talk, coming across as clever, erudite, but false? I made her come endlessly, I gave her orgasms, but I didn't satisfy her?'

'Manifestly not. She wanted a different, dare I say it, a superior sort of fulfilment. She clearly prefers sacred pleasure to the profane kind.'

'You came here for one reason only,' I remind him, 'To enjoy my wife, to touch her lovely tits and stroke her ass. You came here to get your kicks behind my back. You're a hypocrite, reverend. Did Sophie tell you how I get *my* kicks?'

He manages to say: 'No.'

'Have you guessed?'

'Guessed what?'

'How I assert my manhood.'

'No,' he replies with a wild eye. 'I'm not inquisitive. I don't poke my nose in other people's business.'

'Not your nose, no. You came here because you found my woman irresistibly desirable – despite your pie-in-the-sky teachings, your anti-flesh philosophy. Ain't that so?'

'I came to help her find peace. She turned out to be ravishing.'

'Ravishing, eh? I'm not a hasty man. I'm giving you a chance to say goodbye to Sophie.'

'What?'

'Say goodbye to the best pussy you ever had.'

Robert Paige turns his stricken face on the pillow. He tries to smile up at Sophie kneeling beside him. Sophie tries to smile back. They are both grimacing. The priest is visibly quaking.

I step round the bed, reach across the food-trolley to the sound system in the wood panelling and turn the volume up high. One of my tracks is playing; I recognise Coleman Hawkins blowing the rhapsodic notes of 'Body and soul' on tenor sax. I listen to that superb solo for a moment, the 64-bar masterpiece from 1939, magisterial, gruff, gloriously structured ad-libbing from my homeland, the founding improvisation of bebop, then go back to the bishop's side of the bed.

'Goodbye, Rob,' I say to him. 'I'm a man of my word.'

He turns his head again and looks up at me.

I smile down at him and squeeze the trigger.

'Shit!' I blurt as the blood leaps from his head and soils my scarf and tuxedo.

In a lucid aspect of the dream, where I *know* I'm dreaming, I wonder why I've been having such a destructive dream. What has come between Sophie and me for this shocking scenario to keep assailing my sleep? When we met by chance in a crowded hall on her Graduation Day almost exactly ten years ago, it was the dawning of a happiness I couldn't have imagined: fragrant expectation of going to bed at night, lying entwined with beauty, and seeing her beside me first thing in the morning. Fusion of flesh and fellowship, touch and thought, day in, day out: perennial bliss. What toxic particles have poisoned the air we breathe and polluted our rapport so foully? Exactly what is the trouble with Sophie Gresham?

Nausea quakes in my stomach when I realise that I've caught Sophie in bed with the enemy. I've caught her embracing, accepting all the way, a member of the tribe that is forever supercilious.

A surge of biliousness rises in me. I begin to retch and gag and can barely stop myself puking as the thought bears in on me that I still haven't won my woman over; I still haven't convinced her of the clean way ahead. I've tried reason and commonsense, so many times. I've been patient, painstaking, forbearing.

So the only recourse left to me is the one that involves ordnance, fire-power: the solid, emphatic, devastatingly American way.

Without my will or intention the pistol in my hand aims itself at Sophie's head. Without my desire or complicity the pistol steadies itself, getting ready to fire. I'm suddenly a bystander in the dream, looking on. Although the gun is in *my* grip, I'm not involved in what is about to happen.

'Don't, Charlie. Please, Charlie, don't,' Sophie cries out, *her* voice too sounding muffled as though coming from far away, one hand moving forward from her mouth in a gesture of protection.

Without any pressure from me, definitely without my wanting it to happen, the trigger draws itself back and the gun goes off with a dull report. The bullet, however, takes its time on the journey from the barrel to the middle of Sophie's brain. I see the bullet moving slowly, unwillingly, a delinquent dealer of death dawdling across the gap between myself and the woman it still pleases me enormously just to look at, as if to delay what is about to happen, slow the process down, dissociate itself from this unwanted deed. A morally conscious bullet, an ethically aware bullet, a bullet that thinks it would've been best not to have started the ballistic journey at all.

Then the piercing impact on Sophie's forehead penetrates her skull and hurls her off the edge of the bed. Her lovely breasts rise in slo-mo as her torso sails backwards, her thighs separating and revealing for the last time her patch of pubic hair, that place suddenly poignant with the pleasures of a different penetration.

There's a booming, echoing sound in my dream as

Sophie's body crashes against the wood panelling of the wall. The spray of blood from her head spatters on to the pillow as she slides to the floor.

She keeps sliding to the floor.

The woman I love, the love of my life, slides down the wall again and slumps to the floor, the blood pouring from the hole in her forehead lending her face the look of a red liqueous mask. I recognise her in the dream, but I don't recognise her because the booming as she keeps crashing against the wood panelling merges with the sonorous tenor saxophone and alters my vision, fusing sight and sound into a sensation of detached sorrow conjured from the bloody visage before me and the memory of an unblemished beauty who said time and again that she loved me, me alone, to the exclusion of all others.

3

I'd just had breakfast and was in the early stages of cooking moussaka for later in the day, forking a pound of extra-lean minced lamb into the pan where a large chopped onion and two cloves of crushed garlic had just turned gold in colour, when the phone rang. The moisture in the meat made a sizzling sound as it came into contact with the hot oil. I kept breaking down the lumps in the mince with the prongs of the fork and browning it, noticing the wisps of steam rising as I mixed the meat well and truly with the onion and garlic.

The phone kept ringing. It was a cream-coloured landline model, the receiver resting on the cradle, because there were no slim little mobiles, which we Americans call cellphones, in 1995, no texting or picture-messaging handsets we now call smartphones, certainly no BlackBerrys, or iPhones with their huge range of apps or the growing number of Samsungs with the Android operating system. The only cellphones available then were bulky things about the length of a Coke bottle which more than filled your hand; they had a clunky aerial sticking out of the top that reminded me of the gadget Dick Tracy used to lug around in his raincoat in the old comics I'd read at junior school.

I stepped to the other end of the narrow kitchen and picked up the receiver: 'Hello.'

'Happy birthday, Charlie.'

'Hi, Mom.'

'Many happy returns of the day. How are you, son?'

'I'm fine, Mom — it's great hearing your voice. Thanks

for calling. It must still be dark there in Boston cos it's just gone nine in the morning here.'

'What's the weather like there?'

I turned and looked out the window. 'It's a bright and sunny June day. The weather's been so changeable. I'm looking forward to going out.'

'I can't believe you're twenty-five. Doing anything special on your birthday?'

'I'm doing a moussaka right now. I've taken the day off – going to Queens' College a few minutes' walk away. It's not far from the lab in Trumpington Street either. Today is Graduation Day and I've been invited over for a drink by a lecturer acquaintance.'

I glanced at the slices of aubergine (eggplant in the States) on the chopping-board with the layer of salt I'd spread on them and at the six potatoes in the sink. The salt was doing its work: there were little runnels of liquid the colour of vinegar on each slice of aubergine, which meant that the bitterness was 'sweating out', as my mother used to say when I was a teenager and she encouraged me to see cooking as a kind of alchemy, a delicious form of chemistry. Cooking, she'd say, is a controlled transmutation of substances from one state to another, much more enjoyably edible, state. Because of my mother I began to enjoy preparing meals. I'm not a particularly good cook, certainly not up to professional standards, but I find that the chores involved in cobbling dishes together are a good way to relax.

My mother and father were both chemists working on industrial polymers. It was from my mother that I first heard the word *polymerase*, a biochemical term for an enzyme that brings about the formation of a substance with a particular molecular structure, including DNA and RNA.

I would soon be washing the salt off with water from the tap, before drying each slice of aubergine with kitchen paper and then frying it lightly. I'd be peeling and slicing the potatoes too and deep-frying them in another pan when the oil was so hot it let off a spiralling shimmer of blue.

Moussaka is one of the more time-consuming recipes, entailing lots of preparation of the layers that go into the pot one above the other like geological strata: first a layer of potato slices at the bottom followed by a sequence of layers of aubergine, slices of tomato, then potatoes again, each layer with a thick spread of the minced meat above and below it like a scrumptious mortar holding the structure together, until the final layer at the top, preferably potato, is covered completely with grated cheese and a sprinkling of paprika to seal everything in. Then I'll put the pot into the pre-heated oven at 190 degrees for 40 minutes.

It's a lot more work than stir-fried chicken on a wok or dry fish curry with coriander, cumin and ginger, say, but it's one of my favourite dishes and well worth the time and effort involved.

'So who's the moussaka for,' my mother asked, 'just yourself?'

'I hope not. I'm thinking of asking this lecturer woman over.'

'You think she'll come?'

'Who knows, Mom? I sure hope she does – I could do with some female company. She teaches physics. I met her in the Eagle pub last week and we started talking. She knows I'm not part of the university.'

'I miss you, Charlie.'

'I miss you too, Mom – lots.'

'You've been away eight months now.'

'That's right – been here since October. The work at the lab is going well, and so is my doctorate. ChimeroGene are keener than ever – they're investing more heavily in the project. They know transgenic faculties is the way ahead, that fixing damaged genes and harnessing genes from other species is the medical future. It won't be long before you see me again, Mom – possibly at Thanksgiving. I'm going to be flying back to the States to give personal reports about the project maybe once, maybe twice a year, depending on how things develop. Stateside say it's preferable to tele-conferencing.'

'That's excellent news. Your dad says to tell you he loves the reports you've been sending us. Please don't stop sending them, Charlie, even when you do start travelling back and forth. An overview once every few months is fine. We love to hear how the trans-species project is progressing – your work to enrich the human genome. It's so important. And the scientific gossip behind the scenes – what tidbits! Your father and I are both proud of you, Charlie, but he's asleep right now.'

'Don't wake him, Mom. Tell him I'll call. And thanks for the gifts – they arrived safely. I'll be in touch again in the next few days and will let you know how things panned out, whether anyone came and ate the moussaka with me.'

I had no idea when I said those words that my twenty-fifth birthday was going to be a major landmark in my life or that my sexual famine was about to come to an end, at long last. I was a migrant worker in England from a foreign land, the United States of America, and there weren't any unattached women at the institute where I spent the daylight hours. Nor had it occurred to my colleagues to introduce me to people outside, to locals, so I set about seeking women deliberately, something I'd never done before; I'm from a respectable family. I looked for women in bars, in department stores, on trains, in the foyers of theatres and cinemas. I would approach them on any pretext to get a conversation going.

'Isn't it a lovely day?' I'd say.

Or: 'Don't you wish it would stop raining?'

Or: 'What a cool jacket you're wearing.'

One morning in the corner shop where I used to buy

my fruit and veg a pale-faced woman with large brown eyes and braided hair was hesitating in front of a mound of cantaloupe melons. She couldn't make up her mind whether or not to take the melon she was holding. She was about nineteen or twenty years old and probably a student at one of the nearby colleges. She glanced at me and said: 'They aren't all the same, even though they look alike.'

'Some are larger and rounder than the others,' I pointed out.

'But which are the ripe ones?'

'There's a reliable way to find out,' I told her, taking the melon from her hands. 'Hold it like this,' I showed her, 'and press the ends with your thumbs. The more the melon yields, the riper it is.'

'Really?'

'Try it yourself,' I said, handing back the melon.

She did what I'd just done, made eye contact and said: 'This one's quite soft.'

'It must be ripe,' I replied, trying to think of a way to steer the brief exchange into a more romantic direction, but after flashing me a smile she turned with the melon to the shopkeeper and the moment was gone.

That's what frequently happened when I tried to get into conversation with a woman I didn't know. Although I did succeed in having a drink with two strangers on separate occasions in an otherwise desolate period, my reward was always an amiable smile at best, a polite exchange of words, and then a clear indication in body language that her interest in me had ceased entirely.

It beats me why scientists have such a bad press when it comes to human relations. How did the myth develop that scientists lack finer feelings? Whence came the notion that scientists are dull out of doors, that they have no existence away from their labs and apparatus, no cultural awareness, no social life or love life?

As for desire in scientists, sensuality, the consensus of public opinion still appears to be that there is no such thing. The man in the street, and the woman too for that matter, decided long ago that scientists are much too focused on their work, too engrossed in abstruse data, ever to want to take off their white coats, sag on to a bed and get a leg over now and then.

A lustful scientist longing for a lay, a researcher with a throbbing erection: that's a philosophical category without any members.

Whether it's because scientists have much the same anatomy, physiology and hormones as people in other walks of life, or for reasons that are more obscure, we too have sexual needs. We too have biological drives that must be satisfied despite the widespread image of us as cold unfeeling creatures who have no emotions, no inner life where desires, hopes and fears mingle and merge in a tumult that sometimes bursts through into bad dreams.

One would think that there've been no historical precedents of scientists with sex lives.

Marie Curie, née Maria Sklodowska from Poland, the first winner of two Nobel Prizes (for Physics in 1903 which she and her husband Pierre Curie shared with Henri Bequerel for their work in discovering radioactivity, and for Chemistry in 1911 for her discovery of the elements polonium and radium) – she had an affair in her prime with someone else's husband, the French physicist Paul Langevin, three years after her own husband died in 1906.

Charles Darwin married his cousin Emma Wedgwood in 1839 and had ten children. How did he find time to study the birds and the bees?

Albert Einstein, despite having flat feet and varicose veins, had two wives. His daughter Lieserl was born in 1902 before he and her mother, the brilliant Hungarian student Mileva Maric, were wed; they put the child up for adoption, married in 1903 and had two more children, both sons, one of whom is said to have been locked away in a mental institution for thirty years. Einstein divorced Mileva in 1919 and married his cousin Elsa Löwenthal.

J. Robert Oppenheimer, the American theoretical physicist who as director of the Los Alamos Laboratory was in charge of the Manhattan Project to develop the atom bomb, had a romantic relationship with Jean Tatlock, a psychiatry student, before marrying the biologist Katherine Harrison in 1940 with whom he had two children.

It is still imprinted on my brain: the tensions and agonising frustrations of life without sex, without emotional warmth and tenderness, for more than eight months. My libido was distraught, clamouring for relief. I was starving. I caught myself eyeing women as though they were food; I wanted to reach out, grab handfuls and start gobbling. Their lips and breasts and butts were like banquets walking by to which I hadn't been invited. It was anonymous, of course, all that passing flesh, but generically alluring, and my pangs of hunger often pushed me to the brink of despair.

I replaced the receiver on the phone's cradle and stepped back to the pan of minced lamb on the gas cooker. I opened a can of peeled tomatoes – when it comes to cooking, I'm not averse to taking shortcuts where possible – added half of them to the meat, plus all the liquid, and sprinkled in the smallest amount of sugar to counteract the tomatoes' natural acidity. I cut them to shreds, stirred them into the mixture, poured a mugful of boiling water on to a crumbled Oxo cube and tipped it in, to give the stuff more body.

When I shook in the dried mixed herbs and the oregano a little later, the bouquet that began to fill the kitchen was so appetising that I couldn't resist tasting a forkful even though the meat was still far from done. It needed more salt, so I sprinkled some in.

Thanks to my mother, I've been eating meat with garlic

ever since I was a young child. So much so that meat without garlic tastes off to me. Nor is the garlic just for flavour: it's one of the great gifts of nature to help people stay healthy. It keeps our veins and arteries clear, counteracts the furring and clogging effects of cholesterol and thereby prevents heart disease. *Viva* garlic! my mother used to exclaim with a smile on her face and a ladle in her hand. I see her face in my mind whenever I'm preparing a meal.

The blue-hot oil kept spitting as I slipped the potato slices in to fry and when I turned them over with the metal tongs. Feeling the texture of the fat tomatoes, red and juicy, made a nice change; they were cool to the touch and their runny innards leaking on to the chopping-board as I sliced them looked so thirst-quenching that I couldn't help savouring some of the stuff right away.

Why stint when it comes to tomatoes? They're a pleasant source of beta carotene, folate and potassium.

4

'You aren't a baby anymore, Bertha. It's time you learned to brush your teeth.'

'Why should I?'

'So you'll have clean, healthy teeth.'

'What's healthy?'

'Healthy means good and strong,' Flame said. She took the tube of toothpaste from the tumbler below the mirror, unscrewed it and squeezed a bit on to the brush in her other hand. 'Here,' she said, offering the brush to Bertha.

Bertha reached out, but instead of taking the brush she slapped it out of Flame's hand, spun around and scampered from the bathroom.

'You naughty girl!' Flame looked down at the brush sticking to one of the gleaming floor tiles, bent to pick it up, changed her mind and straightened up. She turned and dashed through the doorway into the corridor.

Bertha was already halfway to the staircase.

'Come back, Bertha!' Flame called out in a stern voice. 'Come back immediately!'

Her tone seemed to freeze Bertha in mid-motion. Bertha turned her head slowly and looked back over her shoulder.

'What's immedialy?'

'Immediately. It means right now. That's not the way to behave, knocking the brush out of my hand.'

'Outside. I want outside.'

'I'll take you outside. Of course I will. But first you learn to brush your teeth,' Flame said, beckoning with her hand. 'Come, Bertha. Be a good girl.'

Bertha turned around, lowered her head and came back towards the bathroom.

'That's a good girl,' Flame murmured in a gentle tone and squatted in front of Bertha. 'Don't you want to have healthy teeth like other people?'

'Yes.'

'Then come,' Flame said, rising, taking Bertha's hand and leading her back into the bathroom.

She picked up the toothbrush, tore a square of toilet paper from the roll and wiped off what was left of the toothpaste. She squeezed another bit from the tube and handed the brush to Bertha.

'You saw me brushing my teeth earlier this morning, didn't you?'

'Yes.'

'So you know how to do it, don't you?'

'Yes.'

'Come on, then,' Flame said in a mock-chiding voice. 'Get started. Open your lips and start brushing your teeth.'

The basin was low enough for Bertha to see herself in the mirror. Everything in the bathroom was low enough for her – the bowl of the toilet, the basin taps, the taps in the shower enclosure and the rack holding the shampoo. Bertha could easily reach the cord dangling from the ceiling to switch the light on or off. She stepped closer to her reflection in the mirror, no longer startled or astonished as she used to be by her image there, no longer turning her head and watching in bafflement or fascination as the reflected head moved in precisely the same way. She lifted the toothbrush, gazed at herself for a moment, then proceeded to brush, not her teeth, but her forehead.

Flame couldn't suppress the laugh that sprang from her throat. 'You silly little girl,' she said affectionately, then turned Bertha from the mirror, threw her arms around her and hugged her tight.

'What a darling you are. But this won't do,' Flame said into Bertha's ear.

'What won't do?'

'This messing about,' she replied, drawing away from Bertha to look into her face. 'You said you wanted to go outside. Do you?'

'Yes.'

'I'll take you outside. We'll walk along the river bank to the pub where the punts are moored. You'll see people there again, Bertha – standing on punts and pushing poles into the water. Would you like that?'

'Yes.'

'Yes what?'

'Yes, please.'

'Then wash the toothpaste off your forehead and brush your teeth. I'm beginning to lose patience with you.'

'What's patience?'

'Do as I say, Bertha. Wash your forehead, then brush your teeth, then I'll take you to the river.'

Bertha complied at last.

It was the system of rewards and punishments that worked best, Dr Flame McGovern knew, coupled with setting clear examples, clear and unambiguous, so they could be emulated confidently.

Flame watched with pride as her young charge brushed her teeth, watery toothpaste dribbling over her lower lip into the basin. Slow but sure, Flame thought. She was conscious every moment of every day what a pioneering project this was. There were no precedents to guide her. All she had to back up her professional training was her commonsense and her instincts. She knew that Dr Charlie Venn, the project's young American director, was also impressed with her accomplishments so far and keen for her to take Bertha's education to the next level. It would show people in every culture, throughout the human family, how unwise it was to remain aloof from transgenic faculties, from undamaged genes replacing the damaged ones inherited from one's parents with such dire consequences. People would begin to appreciate and value the hugely beneficial DNA of other species.

5

I had a shave, shower and a shampoo and got into a pair of off-white jeans and a pale-blue shirt. The red silk tie with blue dots my mother had mailed me as a birthday gift contrasted with the dark-blue linen jacket I'd bought in Boston before crossing the Atlantic. My father had sent chrome cufflinks in the shape of spirals of DNA. By the time I locked the door to the flat in Grange Road it was well gone eleven o'clock.

The sky had a bright sheen to it, the blazing sun reflecting off the paintwork of the cars parked at the kerb. I crossed the street and walked along Sidgwick Avenue, passing the entrance to Newnham College and pausing to look again at the architectural eccentricity of the Rare Books Library on the opposite side; with its barrel-like roof in the shape of an old jewel-box and brickwork in horizontal bands of red and blue it always looks to me like a building in a rugby jersey. There were vehicles parked bumper-to-bumper on both sides of the street. It was Graduation Day and people from all over the country, and from abroad too, had descended on Cambridge to be present at the ceremony in Senate House to witness with pride the academic achievement of their relations and friends.

I made my way across Queen's Road to Silver Street and the River Gate entrance to Queens' College opposite the Anchor pub. At the lodge there, one of the porters dressed in waistcoat and navy-blue tails and wearing a bowler hat approached me; he had a chubby face and smiled brightly. I smiled back and showed him my invitation card.

'It's that way, sir,' he said, giving me more directions and pointing to the arching wooden Mathematical Bridge spanning the River Cam from the Cripps Court 20th-century halls of residence on the near side to 16th-century Cloister Court on the far.

'Thank you,' I said, returning the invitation to my pocket.

I stepped from the porters' lodge towards the bridge, walked up the wooden slope and stopped midway across. It was a pleasant sensation being in the breeze in the sunshine watching students standing on punts with poles in their hands pushing their parents along the water towards Clare College and St Johns. I saw women holding their hats down on their heads and heard their voices and laughter as they glided away on the rippling surface of the river, then stepped down the slope of the bridge into the gap in the arch-windowed wall.

When I look back to that first time I crossed the Mathematical Bridge in 1995 and entered a place of learning that had been built more than five-hundred years previously, it seems to me with hindsight that I wasn't just moving from the present to enduring reminders of the past, but was also heading for the most important emotional encounter of my life.

Nor did I know, despite staying abreast of the literature, that a company known as the Beijing Genomics Institute with labs also in Hangzhou, Hong Kong, Boston, USA and Copenhagen, Denmark, would one day be sequencing the equivalent of 2,000 human genomes on a daily basis. By then it would be known as BGI, the world's largest genome-research organisation. They would also sequence the genomes of nine species of plant and twenty species of animal, including the South China tiger, Bengal tiger, African lion and a cloud leopard. Because of their diligence, those Chinese researchers would also ascertain the precise genetic makeup of two reciprocal hybrids, a tigon and a liger (tiger/lion blends). By that time America's Cancer Genome Atlas would be discerning the exact molecular makeup of thousands of tumours and healthy tissues from the same individuals in order to discover the causes of various inherited cancers.

The cost of DNA sequencing – determining the precise order of the nucleic acid bases in any given gene, i.e. the exact sequence of the adenine, thymine, guanine and cytosine molecules that marshal a stretch of DNA – has fallen steeply in recent years. In July 2007 it cost $8.9 million to sequence a human genome (the three billion bases in a full set of human chromosomes); by July 2011 the cost had collapsed to $10,500. In the coming period, the price of a person's genetic blueprint is set to fall below $1,000. People will be able to get their entire genetic makeup on a set of CDs for the price of a laptop computer, thanks to an Anglo-American machine about the size of a memory-stick. (One of the founders of BioCurious, a hacker space for biotech, thinks that by 2020 sequencing the human genome 'will be cheaper than flushing a toilet. That will affect everything from cancer treatments to longevity.'

Like other researchers at the molecular level, I had no notion that so much was going to happen quite so rapidly or with such extraordinary consequences for human nature. Who could have guessed that what used to be thought of as 'junk DNA' – DNA with no known purpose – would turn out to be genetic sequences capable of cutting out strips of damaged or wrongly copied DNA which code for diseases and inserting in their place genetic information that codes instead for proteins with healthy outcomes? Now known by the acronym CRISPR, this sequence was first discovered in bacteria by Japanese researchers in 1987. But it was only in 2011 that Professor Jennifer Doudna of the University of California at Berkeley and her colleague Professor

Emmanuelle Charpentier of Sweden's Umea University began to understand the tremendous transformational significance for human health and longevity of this amazing enzyme.

Snip out toxic bits of DNA and slot in flawless strips.

Nor did I have an inkling as I crossed the Mathematical Bridge that first time that I would one day be accused, quite seriously, of belittling God's work by helping to usher in a 'post-human' future.

I made my way from the bridge along porticoed walkways and shallow steps at the edge of the lawned courtyard. Students were chatting and gesticulating with glasses of wine in their hands as I went by, and moments later I came to the beamed and panelled Old Hall in medieval Old Court where Queens' College was founded in 1448. It was crowded; people seemed to be spilling out of the door. But when I finally managed to edge my way in I realised that the place wasn't that full. The bottleneck was caused by tables near the entrance where people were waiting their turn to choose a glass of red, white or bucks fizz before moving further into the hall.

Apart from the eye-catchingly ornate ceiling decoration – an arresting pattern of intricately carved wood – and the abundance of what looked like rosewood panelling on the walls, the dominant colour scheme was a shifting sea of black and white: black mortarboards on young heads, black academic gowns draped over young happy shoulders, and white blouses worn by the women and white shirts and white bow ties by the men who were no longer undergraduates but proud possessors of degrees from the supremely prestigious Cambridge University.

I wended my way with wine in hand through the hubbub of the conversations, looking for the woman who'd invited me over. Her name was Lorna Lambert and, if I remembered correctly, she had close-cropped brown hair and wore rimless glasses. I'm tall enough to see over some people's heads and shoulders, but I couldn't spot her anywhere in the chattering assembly. I should circulate, I thought; that way, if I didn't see her in due course, she would probably see me. I could then return the compliment and invite her to come and eat moussaka with me and enjoy anything else she might fancy.

But after circulating for about twenty minutes, I still hadn't bumped into her. Instead, as I stood near the wall on the far side from the wine tables, appreciating the carved panels and looking about me from time to time, a younger woman wearing a black academic gown over a white blouse and a mortarboard on her head approached me. With wavy hair down to her shoulders, lipstick on her mouth, a glass of red wine in one hand and her scrolled certificate tied with a little bow in the other, she came across as cerebral and sensual at the same time. She had obviously just come from the graduation ceremony at Senate House and had a happy expression on her face.

She stopped in front of me and looked at my eyes. 'You *do* have hazel-green eyes,' she said, and then, looking at the side of my face, 'and a jagged birthmark on your left cheek. Are you by any chance Charlie Venn?'

'Yes, I am,' I replied.

'I'm Sophie Gresham. Doctor Lambert stopped me in Cloister Court on my way here. She asked me to apologise to you on her behalf. She can't make it. She's in the President's office drinking tea with alumni from China and can't get away.'

'No wonder I couldn't find her. I was beginning to feel uncomfortable. I don't know anyone here. She invited me over for a drink.'

'You aren't a student here?'

'No. I'm doing postgraduate research at an institute in Trumpington Street.'

'Really? What sort of research?'

'Biochemistry – down among the molecules. We're

looking into chromosomes to see the ways in which human diseases have genetic causes.'

'That's looking very deeply, isn't it?'

'As deep as it's possible to look, I'd say.'

'To find some of the causes of human diseases? Sounds massively important.'

'In the long run, it probably is. Molecular biology has the potential to make a huge difference to people's health, in a preventative way. There might be ways one day to become immune to traditional diseases and slow down the ageing process.'

'How intriguing. So you graduated a few years ago?'

'That's right – in Cambridge, Massachusetts. Is that your degree certificate?' I asked, motioning with my head to the beribboned scroll in her hand.

'It is,' she beamed.

'Congratulations,' I said, raising my glass.

'Thank you. My parents are so proud. They've been taking endless photos of me on the Senate House lawn – me alone, me with my mother, me with my father, me with both of them thanks to passers-by. You'd think I'd become a film star,' she said with a self-mocking frown.

I couldn't see a couple nearby who might be her parents and asked where they were.

'Out in the sunshine,' she said with a chuckle, 'taking more photos – of Cloister Court from different angles, of the Mathematical Bridge, and of students standing on punts poling their friends along the water.'

'What have you been studying?' I asked.

'French and Arabic.'

'Are you fluent in those languages?'

'Fluent enough to get by,' she said with a smile.

'Did you go abroad as part of your studies?'

'I had to – it was compulsory. It's best to be among the people whose language you're learning. I spent six months in Paris, living in a flat in Cambronne, and six months in Avignon where the people were quite different, more approachable. I got permission to remain abroad the whole of the following year as well, and stayed half the time with an Arab paediatrician and her mother in the Shmeisani district of Amman. That was great. It was close to the Jabal al-Hussein market which was really busy – I got the chance to speak Arabic with loads of people. The rest of the time I stayed with an academic couple in the Cairo suburb of Heliopolis; their apartment was on the edge of the business district and handy for the Sphinx and pyramids at Giza.'

'You were away from college for two years straight, you mean? Didn't you lose touch with your studies?'

'Not really. I was studying the languages in the best places to do so. I also found time to write my first novel.'

'Wow. You *were* busy.'

She smiled. 'It was published earlier this year, in spring. It's an historical romance set in Canterbury and Cairo called *Kismet*.'

'Congratulations,' I said again, raising my glass of wine. 'What a year this has been for you – a book out and a Cambridge degree.'

'Thank you,' she said, keeping eye contact. 'Literature is my passion.'

I liked being with her. I liked the sound of her husky voice, her English intonation, and didn't want her to drift away to some other part of the hall, so I said: 'If you don't mind my asking, why did you choose to study Arabic?'

'Because it's a beautiful language with lovely poetry and a script that's simply gorgeous. That's the main reason, really. I also wanted to understand the ways in which the knowledge of ancient Greeks such as Galen and Hippocrates was saved from the Dark Ages and conveyed to Europe in Arabic translations. You know,' she smiled, 'texts such as Plato's *Republic* and Aristotle's *Categories* and *Physics*. Jordan

University's Museum of Archaeology wasn't far from where I was staying. Did you know that Europeans knew nothing about soap and the importance of washing regularly until we met the Muslims as a result of the First Crusade in 1096?'

'No, I didn't. Is that a fact?'

'It certainly is,' she nodded. 'Pope Urban the Second called for the first crusade in a speech at the Council of Clermont in November 1095, and the invasion of the Holy Land was launched the following year. The phrase in Arabic is *hurub al-salibiyya*, meaning "wars of the cross". Hundreds of Jews were casually slaughtered in the Rhineland by Christians on their way to Jerusalem. Did you know that our numerals also came from the Arabs?'

'Yes, I did,' I said. 'But I assumed our main inheritance was from the Romans.'

'In that case,' she challenged me with smile in the hubbub of the crowded hall, 'try to multiply five times eight, using Roman numerals.'

'Are you serious?'

'Yes, I am. Using Roman numerals, try to multiply five times eight.'

'Well, the answer's forty.'

'Of course it is. But how do you *arrive* at forty? By what logic do the Roman V and VIII yield XL? And how does X times X yield C?'

She gazed at me with her pale blue eyes, waiting for my response.

I shook my head, playing along, and said: 'There *is* no logic in it.'

'What about, say, subtracting one from a hundred – using the Roman numerals I and C? How on earth do you arrive at XCIX?'

I couldn't help grinning at her little experiment and said: 'It can't be done.'

'Which demonstrates just how dense and stymied the

Roman numerals were,' she replied. She glanced left and right at the other people wearing mortarboards around us, and I wondered whether she was looking for anyone in particular. Perhaps she thought her parents were now in the hall and she should be with them. Or perhaps she was trying to see her boyfriend. Then she turned back to me and added: 'Mathematics was sterile, blocked, until the Arabs opened it up as if releasing a genie from a bottle. If you stop to think about it, the Roman numerals are little more than labels, good only for use on the faces of clocks or on the prelim pages of books.'

'That's one way of putting it, I guess.'

'The thing is, the Romans had no concept of zero,' she said, shaking her head. 'It was Hindus in India who invented zero. The Arabs incorporated it into their number system and made it possible eventually for Einstein to express his revolutionary discoveries about time, space and matter in modern mathematics.' She paused, looked over my left shoulder, then over my right shoulder, her eyes darting about, searching, then she held my gaze again and said: 'It isn't over the top to suggest that without the Arabs, the world might never have come to know that $E=MC^2$.'

It wasn't exactly a revelation, but the truth bears repeating. The Roman numerals are dense; they contain no inner powers, no ability to add or subtract, let alone multiply or divide. Intellectually speaking, they're duds.

I kept smiling back at her, hoping she wouldn't say goodbye and walk away. She was too good-looking not to have a boyfriend. I wondered where he was in the hall. Perhaps he was circulating and would soon appear by her side, a mortarboard on his head too and a glass of wine in hand. With a girlfriend like her, he'd have a lot to celebrate.

6

Bertha kept tugging at Flame McGovern's hand as they strolled on the grass along the riverbank. The sun was bright and hot, but the breeze blowing across the water cooled them as it fanned their faces. What a lovely day to be out, Flame thought as she gripped Bertha's hand. Bertha kept pulling, tugging. She wanted to go running ahead to the pub at the river's edge where people were eating at tables on the terrace and where a dozen punts were moored and it was all Flame could do to restrain her.

'Punt!' Bertha cried out, pointing to where the shallow flat-bottomed boats were bobbing gently on the brown water and yanking Flame's arm.

'Control yourself,' Flame chided.

'What?'

'Stop pulling me so hard.'

'Punt! Let's go!'

'We'll be there in a minute. Calm down.'

'Calm?' Bertha turned her head and looked up at Flame. 'What's calm?'

'Slow down. Stop pulling me. You have to be patient. You can't have everything you want immediately.'

'Immediately. That's right now.'

'Yes, it is. Look at those swans, Bertha,' Flame said, pointing to the far side of the river.

'They not ducks?'

'No. Not ducks. See how elegant their long necks are, how gracefully they're gliding on the water.'

Bertha's arm went slack as her attention was seized.

She stared across the river at the group of swans floating in convoy past a clump of reeds. Flame let go of her hand and squatted beside her.

'See? They aren't in a hurry. They're calm and dignified.'

Bertha made eye contact with Flame, but didn't say anything. She looked at the swans again, then back to where the punts were moored up ahead.

'Punt,' she said again.

'What do you say if you want something?'

'Please. Please. We punt.'

'All right,' Flame said, remembering her earlier promise. 'But you must sit still in the punt. What must you do?'

'Sit still.'

'If you don't sit still, the punt will shake and you'll fall into the water. Do you want to fall into the water, Bertha?'

'No. No,' she said, not relishing the thought at all.

'What do you have to do then?'

'Sit still. Don't shake.'

Flame smiled. 'You're a clever girl, Bertha,' she said and stood up. 'Come, give me your hand.'

Bertha extended her arm and they walked hand in hand along the riverbank to the concrete steps leading up to the terrace where four individuals were eating their pub lunches at separate tables. There were about a dozen rusty metal rings fixed along the edge of the terrace; each of the punts, wobbling gently on the water parallel to one another and colliding softly, was secured with a rope to its metal ring. A large corpulent teenager in T-shirt, jeans and trainers watched Flame and Bertha as they approached.

'Hello,' he called out, waving a hand.

'Hello,' Flame replied. 'How long do you rent these punts out for nowadays?'

'Thirty minutes, or an hour – it's up to you.' He looked admiringly at Flame's head of thick ginger hair and her violet-blue eyes, longer than was strictly necessary. And with the sun behind her, he noticed the outline of her thighs through the fabric of the loose skirt she was wearing. He kept staring until Flame realised what he was up to; she smiled wryly at his popping eyes and held his gaze. He blushed, then turned his attention to Bertha. 'You both going?' he asked.

'Of course. I'm certainly not leaving her here.'

'Look after her,' he said.

'I do that all the time.'

'She's *your* responsibility, remember – not mine. You wouldn't want her to fall into the river, would you?'

Flame squatted in front of Bertha and asked in a solicitous tone of voice: 'You won't fall into the water, will you?'

'No. I sit still. Don't shake.'

The young man grinned and scratched his head; his fat cheeks quivered as he did so. Flame noticed the dimensions of his huge forearms and pudgy hands. 'Amazing,' he said.

Flame paid him for half an hour. She picked Bertha up, stepped carefully onto the first punt and felt it wobble as she put her down on the plank in the centre. Bertha grabbed hold of one side and held tight. She looked at the lapping water that was now much closer, noticed the ripples caused by the wind and saw bits of grass below the surface. She looked at Flame again, clearly nervous.

Flame smiled at her reassuringly. 'Remember to sit still,' she said. 'And don't shake.'

'I remember,' Bertha replied, but she didn't smile back as she watched Flame step on to the flat till at the stern of the punt.

'Here you are,' the young man said, passing the pole to Flame. 'Have a nice time.' He bent down and untied the knot in the rope.

The pole was as heavy as Flame remembered the poles of her university student days to have been. She and her friends used to punt upstream for much more than an hour through the tranquil countryside to the village of Grantchester.

They'd stop for lunch at the cosy Rupert Brooke pub with its huge thatched roof, chat over a pint of real ale, then head back to Cambridge, dropping the pole into the mud and pushing it to propel the punt along.

The river now reminded Flame of the river that flowed hard by the grounds of Balerno High School in the western suburbs of Edinburgh where she'd spent most of her teenage years. That river was called the Water of Leith and it flowed from its source in the Pentland Hills some thirty-five kilometres south, Flame recalled, passing through many old villages including Balerno, Currie, Juniper Green, and Colinton right in the heart of Edinburgh. It wasn't a mighty river. It wasn't intimidating. Its dimensions were nothing like those of the Mississippi, or the Nile, or the Ganges, but in its own way Flame had found it and its surrounding green spaces fascinating.

She and her high-school friends used to walk along the banks of the Water of Leith in summer. They'd listen to the birds in the trees, watch the mallards, the males with their dark green heads and white collars, trailing ripples behind them, count the different kinds of wild flowers as they moved along. She recalled that one hot day with sandwiches and fruit juice in their knapsacks, they walked from Dean Village which she later discovered in the school library used to be called the Village of the Water of Leith, then on to Stockbridge, then to Warriston and finally to the mouth of the river where it flowed into the Firth of Forth at Leith. The *habitats* through which she and her friends had strolled; the *relationships* of the birds and butterflies and foxes and bees to the plants around them, and of the animals to one another: it was on those summer walks along the banks of the Water of Leith that the teenage Flame McGovern's interest in zoology, and ecology in general, was originally sparked.

She had no way of knowing, of course, that the expertise she began to develop at that time would one day help her gain an undergraduate place in Cambridge University's Department of Zoology or that she would later deepen her knowledge by travelling far and wide, to the rainforests of West Africa, the jungles of Indonesia, the damp humidity of the Amazon Basin. Hers would become such a deep understanding of symbiotic relationships that Dr Charlie Venn, one of the project directors at the Institute of Molecular and Neural Genetics, would offer her a contract on the spot after her job interview, even though her studies had had nothing at all to do with genetics, with molecular medicine or with the judicious merging of different species.

7

Instead of walking away to join someone else in the crowded hall, Sophie Gresham took a sip of her wine and made eye contact again. She seemed in the mood to talk.

'It's amazing,' she said. 'While I was in the Middle East, I discovered that quite a few scientific terms also came from the Arabs. In chemistry, for example, the word *alkali* came from *al-qili*, and *arsenic* from *az-zarnikh*. In mathematics, words that derive from Arabic include *cipher*, *zero* and *algebra*. *Algebra* comes from the Arabic word *al-gebr* which connotes the putting together of pieces into a whole. And the term *algorithm*, believe it or not, came from the surname of the celebrated Muslim mathematician Muhammad ibn-Musa al-Khwarizmi who worked in Baghdad and lived from AD 780 to 850.'

'You're clearly fascinated by the subject,' I said.

'I suppose I am. I never dreamt when I started my course in Arabic that Europe owed the Middle East quite so much. I found that one can scarcely proceed in astronomy without coming across Arabic words, such as *zenith*, *nadir*, *azimuth*. The names of stars betray their Arabic etymology. For example, Betelgeuse, the second brightest star in the constellation Orion, is a corruption of the Arabic phrase *yad al-jawza* which means "hand of the central one". It was wrongly read as *bet al-jawza* and transliterated into Latin as *Bedalgeuse*, "armpit of the central one". It was from the realms of Islamic scholarship in natural history and medicine that we got the words *alcohol*, *elixir*, *sherbet*, *syrup* – even *candy* and *julep*. Most British naval terms came, via

French and Italian, from the Arabs who began to dominate the Mediterranean in the 8th century. I found it hard to believe at first,' Sophie said, shaking her head and grinning at me, 'the vocabulary we've inherited from them. The words *admiral*, *squadron*, *fleet*, *corvette*, *caravelle*, *sloop* all sprang from the Arabic language.'

It sticks in my mind how assertive and loquacious Sophie was during our very first exchange, how bold in expressing to a complete stranger her deepest interests. She came across as a cascade of precise information, drenching me with a sequence of data that took me by surprise.

And while I was absorbing her nuggets of knowledge, she made a sexual advance so unexpectedly and unmistakeably that I was mesmerised. Looking back on it now, perhaps she'd decided to celebrate her degree with a bout of sex to deepen the thrill of her achievement, to maintain the balance between her body and mind. In any case, her upfront behaviour forced me to reconsider once again the so-called 'standoffishness' of English people, their famous, or should one say notorious, 'reserve' which I'd heard about in Boston.

I had no idea what I was letting myself in for when I asked her why she'd chosen to study Arabic; it was just a ploy to prolong my conversation with her. I didn't know whether she was talkative, whether she liked to hold forth, or was simply charged up with her recent achievements and bubbling with an enthusiasm she couldn't contain, but a torrent of information spilled from her that day. I have since wondered whether I'd have noticed her wordiness if she'd been a man. As a woman, was she supposed to be rather more diffident, unforthcoming? Was she not supposed to be so knowledgeable?

At the time, however, this brand-new graduate with her mortarboard on her head appeared just a bit manic. She seemed to me to be talking nineteen to the dozen. And the stuff she was coming out with was news to me. I'd known very little about the Middle East as a source of our civilisation. She said the idea of an economic customs union, and even the word for it, *douane*, came from the Arabs. The book trade, commercial confectionery, the use in business agreements of contracts signed by witnesses – they were all Arab innovations.

We were in a place of higher education, Queens' College, Cambridge, so I guess I shouldn't have been surprised that she'd be so full of learning, especially as this was her Graduation Day. Was I in the presence of an encyclopaedic mind, I wondered as she disabused my ignorance.

'The person who laid the foundations of modern chemistry,' she told me, 'was Abubakr Muhammad ibn Zakariyya ar-Razi, known in the West as Rhazes. He lived from 865 to 925. His book *The Mystery of Mysteries – Secretum Secretorum* in Latin – is entirely free of legend, relying solely on laboratory techniques and scientific analysis. Among his other achievements, he wrote a ten-volume medical treatise which he named after his patron *Kitab at-Tib al-Mansuri – The Book of Mansuri on Medicine.* The title in Latin became *Liber Almansoris* when it was published in Milan in the latter part of the 15th century. But his main distinction was that he was the first person to give an accurate clinical description of smallpox and measles. His monograph on the subject was printed in London as late as 1848, in an English translation by W.A. Greenhill. That's partly why,' she added, nodding and keeping eye contact, 'there is in the chapel of Princeton University a stained-glass panel of a turbaned man holding a scroll inscribed with Arabic characters. It represents ar-Razi.'

Even though I couldn't take my eyes off her, and had to struggle not to keep glancing at her cleavage, and wondered whether she'd be just as manic in bed, it became abundantly clear during that first conversation that she wasn't just a beautiful face. I also noticed her long, elegant fingers.

She moved them so expressively when talking that I was surprised she wasn't spilling wine on to me or on to the floor or dropping her scrolled certificate.

'What did you say your name was?' I asked.

'Sophie Gresham. What's yours again?'

'Charlie Venn – Charles Hadley Venn,' I said, and told her more about my genetics work at the lab in Trumpington Street.

We'd only been chatting for ten minutes or so when she made her first reading suggestion. It turned out to be the beginning of a whole stream of texts she would urge me to get into. Perhaps she felt that as a scientist I was poorly read in history and the arts and consequently narrow-minded and uncouth. She was a treat to look at, compellingly attractive, so I wasn't focused on what she thought of my understanding. Little did I know then that a book would be my way into bed with her, that books would bring our bodies closer together and get them to merge rhapsodically. Books as an erotic catalyst: the concept hadn't occurred to me before. How glad I was to discover the joys of literacy.

'You should read Rudyard Kipling's short story about the Muslim invention of the microscope,' Sophie said. 'It's an eye-opener. I recommend that story, Charles. It's atmospheric, set in a 13th-century monastery and called "The Eye of Allah". Kipling shows why Mother Church believed the world wasn't ready for such a contrivance and saw fit to destroy it.'

'Is that the same Kipling who wrote *The Jungle Book* and the poem that starts "If you can keep your head when all about you are losing theirs and blaming it on you"?'

She grinned and said: 'Yes, it is. He was a champion of British imperialism whose poem "The White Man's Burden" glorified the conquest of other nations in openly racist language, but he wrote engrossing stories and he did know about other cultures.'

Sophie took a sip of wine from her glass, savoured it and swallowed.

'Kipling wouldn't have been as surprised as I was,' she said, 'when I discovered that the development of love poetry and of satire after Romans such as Juvenal and Apuleius, and the whole culture of chivalry and knights coming to the rescue on horseback, were products of Arab imaginations. I was amazed by what I found in *A Literary History of the Arabs* by Professor R.A. Nicholson. It demonstrates the immeasurable debt we all owe the Arab *zindiqs*.'

'What are *zindiqs*?' I enquired. I wanted to show my interest because I felt that the longer she spoke, the longer I'd be with her, and the longer I was with her, the closer to lunch time it would be and the more natural it would sound if I bit the bullet and asked her to come and eat some food with me. It wasn't the most sophisticated strategy to get to be alone with her, but I couldn't think of a better way to exploit this lucky opportunity.

'Freethinkers,' she said. '*Zindiqs* were intellectual mavericks who went their own way. They were reckless in their effrontery. They shattered taboos wherever they could. They loved wine and music, they simply adored poetry which they considered to be on a par with bravery, and they were devoted to science.'

And right there, holding her glass and her scrolled certificate and pausing momentarily to recall the words, Sophie recited from memory a few lines translated from what she said was the *Diwán* – collection of poems – of Abú Nuwás, composed around AD 810:

'Come, pour it out, ye gentle boys,
A vintage ten years old,
That seems as though 'twere in the cup
A lake of liquid gold.

And when the water mingles there,
To fancy's eye are set
Pearls over shining pearls close strung
As in a carcanet.'

'An Arab wrote that?' I asked.

She nodded. 'And other Arabs too were stunningly creative well over a thousand years ago, when Western literature had barely got started, when the Germanic folk epic *Beowulf* was still poignantly grunting its way towards meaning. Half a millennium before Shakespeare wrote his play about Romeo and Juliet, for example, Abú al-Sindi had written:

I dreamt of you as tawny spears
Between us shook,
With our twin bloods spilling
On the toasted sand.'

She seemed to know that I wanted her to keep talking. I'd only been in England eight months and was still enamoured of the English intonation. I loved the sounds of it, especially the sounds of women speaking. It didn't matter what they said; I just loved the cadences. But Sophie's voice that day wasn't only charming and enticing; it was charged also with an intriguing cargo.

'Hafiz of Shiraz,' she said, 'was a 14th-century poet whose extraordinary work is exemplified in this stanza translated by Gertrude Lowthian Bell in the late 19th century:

If the scent of her hair were to blow across my dust
When I had been dead a hundred years,
My mouldering bones would rise
And come dancing out of the tomb.'

Sophie then told me about the beautifully designed garden

alongside the Alhambra Palace at Granada in Spain, built by the Moorish kings in the 13th century.

'The soothing sound of water sprinkling from fountains and gurgling along channels with stones of different shapes and sizes – it complemented the serenity conjured from the arrangement of shade trees, shrubs and terracotta sculptures,' she said with yet another smile, 'the colour and fragrance of carefully chosen flowers a heady inhalation the while. There was nothing like it anywhere else in Europe at the time. It sticks in people's craw for some reason,' she added, shaking her head, 'and is hard for them to acknowledge: that we even got gardening as an aesthetic pursuit from the Arabs. Prince Charles is a famous fan of their horticultural style.'

'If they were as marvellous as you say they were,' I asked, wanting to stanch her pro-Arab gush, wanting to slow down her praise for people not exactly known today for peacefulness, 'if their culture was so fertile and full of radical intellects when Europe was still in the Dark Ages, why are they so backward, generally speaking? What happened? Why do they imprison women for fleeing abusive homes? Why do they jail women who've been raped? They torture their own people, their own children. Why the fall from such great heights?'

Sophie remained silent for a while. She pursed her lips. I could see the thoughtfulness in her eyes. Then she said: 'It's a longish answer. Sound-bites won't do. I'll tell you what happened, what went wrong, Charles, when I know you better.'

When she knew me better. So I was going to see her again? She wasn't going to disappear suddenly? I felt my heart thudding.

I turned twenty-five that day I first met Sophie. What a blissful birthday it was. I came away from the encounter feeling wooed by her literary talk, feeling a bit groggy, really, with excitement and erotic anticipation. The things she said that day did have something to do with her state of mind, I discovered later, with getting a double first at Cambridge and being a published novelist at the age of twenty-three.

I'd come to England the previous year after a research project at a lab in Baltimore where in a junior capacity I helped my American colleagues locate on chromosome 17 the cancer-tumour suppressor gene *p53*. When *p53* is missing for hereditary reasons, or is damaged in some way, the person concerned develops one or other of several types of cancer. Other colleagues of mine in the United States had discovered a defective gene on chromosome 5 whose mutations are responsible for the inherited neurological disorder hyperekplexia which triggers 'stiff baby syndrome' – spasms and muscular rigidity that cause many infants to die from a sudden cessation of breathing. And an international team of researchers had recently identified a gene on chromosome 2, called *MSH2*, which, due to a mutation, causes cancer of the colon, one of the most common inherited diseases in humans; it also increases the risk of cancer of the uterus.

Sophie was stunning, the sort of person you couldn't help noticing when she entered a room. There was an aura of freshness about her, a cool exterior containing passionate heat. When she smiles at you, it's like a balm; an extraordinary elation fills your heart. You feel enhanced when Sophie smiles at you; I do, anyway. When she turns her sultry, pale blue eyes on you there's a sense somehow that your moment has come.

Despite all the people around us and the drinks being carried on trays through the hum of the conversations; despite the professors and other faculty mingling with students with mortarboards on their heads and academic gowns draped over their shoulders, congratulating them on having graduated and wishing them well in their careers,

I found myself believing that Sophie had asked me to undress her quickly and make love right there in the midst of crowded academe.

I believed she had asked me to get stuck in there and then because of the way she'd flicked her fingers at my flies, repeatedly. Her expressive fingers had touched my dick, deliberately, roused it from its torpor in a pretty blatant way, making the most overt sexual advance possible while she gazed at me with her cool, clear eyes and talked about the comprehensive Arab influence on the West.

I was disturbed by the discovery that there was in my heritage a pervasive Arab presence that had been systematically suppressed. Mathematics, experimental science, love poetry, satire, medicine among other intellectual pursuits: their early templates had been set by Arab scholars half-a-millennium before the Renaissance even began, much in the way that, as Sophie pointed out, all the thoroughbred horses in racing today are descended from the three Arab stallions brought from Syria in 1704 by the British consul Thomas Darley to his father's estate near York – the Byerley Turk, the Darley Arabian and the Godolphin Arabian.

It was a lot to take in while also sensing the vibrations pulsing at me from this desirable woman who smiled so frequently. I tried to respond in kind to the calmness of her beautiful countenance by gazing back in the most nonchalant way I could manage, remembering all the while the call of her beckoning fingers and the kind of encounter they had surely promised.

I was in a bind. I was roused, excited, yet constrained by the context. I ended up feeling that mounting this gorgeous creature would be the right thing, the chivalrous thing, to do, even in that crowded academic scene, as long as I didn't dent her mortarboard.

'I've just cooked a pot of moussaka,' I told her. 'Do you like moussaka?'

'You cooked it yourself?'

'Yes,' I said, nodding vigorously. 'With these hands,' lifting them.

'Fantastic,' she said, keeping eye contact. 'I love moussaka.'

'It's my twenty-fifth birthday today,' I blurted. 'Where are you having lunch? Why not have lunch with me, Sophie?'

'I'm supposed to be joining my parents and all the others at the formal meal with the President of Queens' College.' She looked at her watch, then looked into my eyes again. 'They drove over from Bristol, my mum and dad.'

'In that case, forgive me – I wasn't suggesting that you stand them up.'

'Does moussaka keep well?' she asked. 'Does it have to be eaten right away?'

'It does keep well,' I said. 'The flavours are seeping into one another right now. The mixed herbs, the oregano in the minced lamb and tomato, plus the garlic and onions, will simply marinate more thoroughly.'

'Sounds delicious, Charles.'

'Most people call me Charlie.'

She smiled again. 'Could we have it for supper, Charlie, instead of lunch?'

'We certainly could. I'll open a bottle of red to breathe before you come.'

'No. Let *me* bring the wine. Where exactly should I come? What's the address?'

'Just a few minutes' walk from here. D'you know where Grange Road is?'

'Yes, of course – it's beyond Newnham College.'

I told her the number in the block of flats, that it was behind a hedge at the end of a gravelled drive, wondering if she really would come and not drive home to Bristol with her parents after the formal lunch. 'Is six o'clock too early for you? All I'll have to do is switch the oven on for a while to heat up the food.'

She smiled and I noticed again her gleaming white teeth between those very kissable lips. 'Six o'clock is fine,' she said. 'Happy birthday, Charlie. I'll be there on time.'

I couldn't believe my luck. 'Really?'

'Here,' she said, handing me the scrolled certificate tied with a little bow, 'look after this for me for a few hours. Now I must go and find my parents.'

8

Bertha was staring through the locked window of her room on the second floor, her attention held by a group of people on the river below; they were on three punts and were talking and laughing in the sunshine. Bertha recalled Flame taking her downstream on a punt after they'd seen some swans moving along in convoy. She'd gripped the side of the punt, held it tight, as instructed. Nor did she shake the punt either – not once. She hadn't fancied the idea of falling into the water and being thoroughly soaked. Bertha did wonder, though, whether she'd be able to do the punting herself one day. It seemed quite easy, the way Flame had done it. Bertha was sure that when *she* had a go she wouldn't move about unnecessarily. She'd just hold the pole tight and drop it in the mud, the way Flame kept doing when they passed under two bridges on the way to Clare College and then back.

'Come on, Bertha,' Flame said now. 'You can't stare out of the window all day. It's drawing time.'

'What?'

'Drawing time. Look, I've put a sheet of drawing paper on your desk. And the crayons are ready. Come, Bertha. See the rainbow in this book.'

Bertha came over to her desk and sat down. There was a large poster on the wall, a CD player on the floor below it and several CDs strewn about. She looked at the crayons; there were about eight of them. Flame held the book open and showed Bertha the diagram of a rainbow: a set of perfectly semi-circular bands, each a different colour.

'Pretty, isn't it?'

'Yes. Pretty.'

'Look at the picture carefully, Bertha, then try to draw your own rainbow. Do you think you can draw a rainbow?'

Bertha lifted the book with both hands, brought the page closer and looked at the printed multi-coloured rainbow for a long moment. Then she dropped the book on the floor, picked up a crayon at random and proceeded to draw what she intended to be an arc. It wasn't very arc-like. She put the crayon down, picked up another one and had another go at drawing an arc. It too turned out to be a wobbly squiggle. Then Bertha took a third crayon and began rubbing it across the sheet of paper, left to right, left to right, repeatedly, smearing the colour pretty much at random.

Flame watched her closely. Bertha's control of the crayon wasn't sophisticated at all, she saw. Instead of holding it between her thumb and index-finger, she was gripping it in her fist as though it were a dagger. Not that Bertha had ever handled a dagger or seen anyone do so. She was born in this large old house, in this very room with its high ceiling and large windows, and had never been anywhere on her own. She was too young and far too much expertise and money had been invested in her to risk allowing her anywhere on her own. It would take time, Flame thought, much more time.

'Let me show you,' she said.

She took the crayon from Bertha's hand and held it between her thumb and index-finger. 'Look. See how I'm holding it?' She dropped the crayon onto the desk and moved the thumb and index-finger of her right hand apart. She moved those digits apart several times. 'See?'

'Yes.'

Flame picked up the crayon from the desk. 'Then I move it like this,' she said, placing the tip of the crayon on the sheet of paper, 'up, up, over to the right, then down, down. Try to do it like that.'

She offered the crayon back, but Bertha picked up another one from those on the desk in front of her. She looked at the crayon in her right hand, looked at her left hand, took the crayon from her right hand with her left hand and tried to separate the thumb and index-finger of her right hand. She managed it, but somehow it looked different from when Flame had done it. She looked up at Flame, stymied.

Flame lifted her hand so Bertha could see again and closed the gap between her thumb and index-finger several times. Bertha looked at her own right hand and tried to copy her. Again, it didn't quite work.

'Never mind,' Flame said, 'It doesn't really matter how you hold the crayon. Just make sure you hold it tight enough. See?'

After a few attempts, in a little fit of exasperation Bertha settled for holding the crayon vertically between her index-finger and third finger and began drawing what were very, very approximate arcs of colour on the sheet of paper.

'You clever girl!' Flame exclaimed with a big smile. 'That's very good.'

It would be unrealistic to expect her to master the skills involved, even in the simplest drawing, in one go, Flame thought, to say nothing of the coordination of hand and eye. Fortunately, Dr Venn understood that. He wasn't pushy. He wasn't in any sort of hurry. He wanted Bertha's education to be based on the soundest possible foundations, on her innate abilities and potential which still had to be discovered, rather than have her go through the motions of particular tasks without understanding what she was doing simply so that the institute might be able to make a short-lived impression in the scientific community.

Although Dr Venn's area of expertise was quite different from hers, Flame McGovern knew they were qualified to the same high level; both of them had published many peer-reviewed papers in learned journals and made presentations at international conferences. Flame felt no sense of professional competition between herself and Dr Venn. There weren't any negative vibes between them, not the slightest tension. Although she was two years older and originally from Edinburgh where people had a stereotypical reputation – quite false, she felt – for being dour, mirthless, she and the American project director had developed a rapport whose entire purpose was the kind of scientific breakthrough few individuals anywhere were expecting.

When she and Dr Venn and the rest of the team finally showed their hand, Flame believed, people's understanding of interpersonal relationships would be utterly transformed and the world would never be the same again as far as the reach of empathy was concerned. It would extend beyond mankind. Mankind would no longer be 'an island entire of itself' in John Donne's phrase, but would, Flame felt sure, have an extended family spreading throughout the flora and fauna of planet Earth. Another Rubicon, very much wider than the river Julius Caesar's army crossed in 49BC in his insurrection against the Roman republic, would have been crossed. But this time the crossing would be at the level of molecules in human and animal genomes.

One more restraining status quo would have been shattered.

9

Like other people I know, I didn't get to choose my parents. No one asked me before I was born what sort of mother and what sort of father I would like to have. No one asked me whether I wanted to be fit or frail, handsome or hideous, mentally bright or slow off the mark. I had no say whatever in the most important details of my identity. Nobody consulted me in the womb, by ultrasound scan or any other technique, about the type of personality I fancied being when I grew up, about the timbre, pitch and range of my voice, or whether I preferred to be born in a rich neighbourhood or in the squalor of a slum.

No one asked me what sort of person I wanted to be for the simple reason, probably, that they wouldn't have been able to do anything about my request.

Until recently, people generally had no clue that there was a realm of infinitesimal molecules in the nucleus of every one of our many trillion cells, a place where people's physical features and psychological abilities are orchestrated by precise sequences of adenine, thymine, guanine and cytosine.

They never dreamt that strings of amino acids fold over into proteins with peculiar three-dimensional structures which serve particular purposes in the body and brain. They couldn't guess that molecules many thousands of times thinner than a human hair would one day be reached by switched-off viruses, that enzymes would be used to dissect strands of DNA, that gels would tease their constituent pieces apart, or that other enzymes would slot in and glue together replacement strips.

It was beyond the public's imagination that damaged sequences which code for fatal diseases such as breast cancer or Fanconi anaemia would one day be replaced with undamaged sequences, or that a person's eyesight, bone structure, height and quality of memory would all become susceptible to rearrangement with the most extraordinary precision.

People had no faith – that was the problem. They didn't believe passionately enough in reason's penetrating power or in the scientific method's endlessly sustainable knack of delivering the goods.

That being so, I guess the actual outcome in *my* case could have been worse. I could, when I was born, have been a throwback to Quasimodo, the bell-ringing hunchback of Notre Dame within whose bulk there burned an unquenchable flame, a longing to be hugged, comforted and reassured by the beautiful Esmeralda.

I might have been born with a degenerative disease. I might have entered the world female in a place such as Nahr e Saraj or Musa Qala or Sangin, that blood-spattered terrain of improvised explosive devices in Afghanistan's Helmand province. Pitiless zealots are in control there, keen on destroying girls' schools and expert at repeating passages of religion like uncomprehending parrots. I might have been married off to a bearded goat and given birth to eight children in eight years, two of them still-born, never enough food to eat or clean water to drink, reduced to gobbling grass and locusts, no doctors around, no medicine, two of my children's feet blown off by Russian landmines, one son's hand amputated for pinching a piece of bread for his starving sisters, my children falling down from faintness and dying one after the other, my husband away fighting with some warlord or dead in a distant ravine, not allowed to leave the house on my own, not allowed schooling, not allowed to work for a living, reduced to begging, no say at all in public affairs, forced to be faceless, forced to wear a suffocating tent-like *burka* and run the gauntlet of being hit with a stout stick every day and everywhere by the ubiquitous *muttawa* – religious police for the promotion of virtue and the prevention of vice.

I would have been born into hell on Earth with no need to die first and wait for the Day of Resurrection, the Day of Judgement, Islam's famous *Yoam mid'deen*. I'd have been proof then of the Christian concept of 'original sin', my total corruption from the moment I was born, even before I'd done anything at all, and got my just deserts. Perhaps I should thank the Lord fervently for not making me female, as devout Jewish males do first thing every morning.

As chance would have it, the identity that *was* foisted on me without my agreement, without the least consultation, has stood me in fairly good stead. It's been pure luck, though. Who I am, Charles Hadley Venn, only child of Oscar and Ida Venn, the colour of my hazel-green eyes, my mop of fairish hair, have had little to do with good judgement on my part. It's kind of a fluke that I've remained intact, physically robust and sound in the head. Perhaps that is why it has never occurred to me to sue my mother for getting pregnant without my permission. I've never thought of condemning her in public for the jagged birthmark on my left cheek that looks as though I was burned with a branding-iron, or for the unsightly patch on the outside of my left bicep which becomes visible when I wear a T-shirt.

I don't complain because I know from other people I've seen that things could have been very much worse.

Although no one checked with me beforehand to find out what I thought of it, I was born and raised in Boston. My parents owned a brownstone house on Boylston Street in the area known as Back Bay, not far from the Newbury Street shopping district and within easy walking distance of the Charles River Basin. Boylston Street runs parallel with Commonwealth Avenue, the area's main thoroughfare, and is just as busy as Washington Street downtown.

To raise money when the time came for me to study molecular biology at university, my parents moved to a smaller place on the North Slope of Beacon Hill, not far from Old North Church and Paul Revere's House. I made new friends in the bustling Hanover Street neighbourhood where the many Italian families organised feasts and filled the streets in the summer months in celebration of their patron saints.

The house of my childhood on Boylston Street was spacious with lots of light on three floors and a basement that was out of bounds to visitors because my mother and father, both chemists specialising in polymers, had transformed it into a laboratory. They did their stuff there in their spare time, setting up apparatus and doing experiments to verify or refute some hypothesis or other. Much in the way that the great Marie Curie and her husband Pierre had wrestled with intellectual problems together, probing the guises of reality which they suspected concealed deeper levels of truth, so too were my parents a team, never so happy as when, in their long white coats, they were trying to figure out one of nature's conundra. They pursued their hunches, their ideas that were sometimes outlandish, in the lab in the basement, working long after other researchers had called it a day and headed home.

When I was small my parents used to take me around Boston. I'd walk between them, each holding one of my hands as we stepped along Commonwealth Avenue and crossed Arlington Street, heading for the public gardens and Boston Common beyond. They took me to the 19th-century Quincy Market on the waterfront, and to Faneuil Hall which, they explained, was called 'the cradle of liberty' because it was the building where meetings and discussions were held that led to noisy protests against various British colonial practices.

My parents took me to the Old Corner Bookstore where Henry Longfellow, Nathaniel Hawthorne, Ralph Waldo Emerson and other 19th-century writers used to meet. I also went with them to Dorchester Heights in the south of the city where the fortifications built by the early Americans forced the British to evacuate Boston in what turned out to be the first major victory won by the newly appointed Commander-in-Chief, George Washington.

One day my mom and dad took me a few miles up the North Shore to the town of Salem and the Peabody Museum, the oldest museum in the United States, and to the Salem Witch Museum. They wanted me to see the cameos that illustrate the misery and brutality which hysterical ignorance used to bring down on people in the past.

On a regular basis when I was small, my mother and father used to take me to the Little Angel Theatre that was housed in an old fire-station building located near the corner of Charles and Beacon Streets.

The Little Angel Theatre is long gone, and the fire-station too, but it used to put on puppet shows. I remember those puppets as being real people. They were alive and vibrant, full of strong emotions, always laughing or crying or quarrelling at the tops of their voices. When the storyline took a sad turn and everyone was down in the dumps, one of the puppets would start singing a song, thinking aloud in melody about the better times that lay ahead. The other puppets would join in the singing one by one and pretty soon the stage would be lit up again with dancing happiness. The music was like medicine. It dispelled the sadness and lifted my spirits in the darkness of the auditorium. The problems the puppets had to contend with, their difficulties and misunderstandings, were infectious. It was impossible not to empathise with them. We kids would call out to them from our rows of seats, warn them about approaching danger, sigh in relief when they avoided harm, and squeal with laughter at the way their bodies bounced about the floor in a rough-and-tumble fight.

When the show ended and we filed out of the theatre with all the other parents and young children, I would ask when we'd be coming to see the puppet people again. Soon, my mother and father would say, soon. That would placate me and we'd walk back home along the sidewalks with me in the middle again, all three of us licking the ice-creams they'd bought and talking about the puppet characters and why they'd said and done the things they had. We used to go to the puppets twice a year. They remain more real to me, those figures made of cloth and paper, than many of the characters I subsequently came across in the reading books that were handed out at school.

My parents took me along one day when they went to look at the paintings by Rembrandt, Raphael and Matisse at the Isabella Stewart Gardner Museum. That museum, housed in a well preserved Venetian-style palazzo on the Fenway, I found attractive in its own right, as a building, and went back to look at it several times when I was old enough to go there on my own.

Some kind of breakthrough took place in my young mind when my parents showed me around the exhibits at the Science Museum in the Science Park on the Charles River Dam. They were just so intriguing. They raised far more questions than the paintings of morose middle-aged men, full-bodied women and the colourful canvases I had seen earlier at the other place. Anthropology, medicine, and early electronics and computers made one realise suddenly how complex the world was, that there were numberless systems at work whose existence one had had no inkling of. The Hayden Planetarium with its changing programmes was a humdinger, a real eye-opener. Even my seven-year-old mind grasped a larger context there, a perspective that placed people, and the human condition, in a light that wasn't particularly ennobling.

And in the John Fitzgerald Kennedy Library at Columbia Point on Dorchester Bay I saw for the first time in my young life some of the proofs of human brutality and violence. I saw exhibits, photographs and film depicting the life and the sudden bloody death of one of the finest sons of Massachusetts, shot dead in an open car whilst seated next to his wife in a motorcade moving along a street in Dallas, Texas on 22 November 1963.

I wondered even then, albeit it in the opaque, emotional manner of a sad and angry child, whether there was a way to stop people being so violent, so unkind, without putting them in jail, without punishing them or being violent to them in turn.

And then I learned about the equally cruel murder in June 1968 of Bobby Kennedy, US Senator from New York at the time and brother of the slain president, in the kitchen of the Ambassador hotel in downtown Los Angeles where a conference was being held. My parents used to talk about that murder too when I was young. And about the murder of Martin Luther King, Jr who had a dream that all men could live together in peace regardless of their skin colour but whose Nobel Prize for Peace in 1964 was unable to shield him from an assassin's bullet at the Lorraine Motel in Memphis, Tennessee in the evening of April 4, 1968 when he was 39; and about the earlier murder of Malcolm Little, alias 'Detroit Red', later known as Malcolm X, later still as Haj Malik El Shabaaz after he visited Mecca and stopped seeing the Caucasian oppressors of black people as white devils but as misguided members of humanity – *he* was gunned down in a hail of bullets by two black hitmen in February 1965, also at the age of 39, whilst making a speech in the Audubon Ballroom on Harlem's West 166th Street.

Those memorable murders kept cropping up in my parents' conversations over the years. They made me know in my heart that the problem of human vengefulness wasn't a temporary one. When good men with good intentions regardless of their faults are killed at such a prodigal rate, and not only in America, then, it occurred to me, something in the human psyche must be out of kilter. Some fault in ourselves, some deeply infelicitous aspect of our brains, out of synch with our sympathies and our tendency to empathise with those experiencing misfortune, a left-over from our snarling, primal past of fangs and claws dripping blood, perhaps, is reserving a place for violence in the human condition.

It's a condition crying bitterly for a cure.

And the thought began to grow in my mind that the best way to effect a cure before the disease had a chance to overwhelm people's behaviour and become an entrenched habit might be to scotch it at source. Rid people of this malicious malady *before* it took hold. And do so by manipulating particular bits of the human genome, that is to say, by means of genetic enhancement. That was when I tuned into synthetic biology. And that was the reason why, after focusing for several years on particular chromosomes in search of the causes of inherited diseases and of the ageing process, I came to England. I crossed the Atlantic Ocean to work as a project leader at the Institute of Molecular and Neural Genetics in Cambridge. The institute was – still is – funded by ChimeroGene, a consortium of US venture capitalists convinced that improved genes and genes from other species was the way ahead for molecular medicine and that there were astronomical sums of money to be made by companies that got in early.

A delightful consequence of my arrival in Cambridge was that I met, quite by chance whilst looking for someone else, an extraordinary woman called Sophie Gresham. I'm a research scientist. I tended up to that point not to mix socially with many people in the arts. I had no idea I was going to fall in love with anyone, let alone with a linguist, an Englishwoman who'd read books I hadn't even heard of and spoke languages beyond my ken.

Nor did I have a clue that we'd become such a happy item. How could I have guessed that our life together would turn out to be mutually fulfilling and sexually satisfying, the deepest, most vivifying relationship? (The sex was pressingly important to me because, by the time I met Sophie, I hadn't been intimate with any woman anywhere for eight months and five days and was dying for close companionship.)

And then, imperceptibly at first, the tone of my days and nights with Sophie Gresham changed. Things between us became awkward and, gradually, frustrating. This happened, I think, because of her unexpected attitude to what my colleagues and I were doing at the institute. She used the phrase 'towering arrogance' several times and intimated that she'd heard people saying we were 'reaching too high', that we were 'playing God' by trying to make improvements to what was simply unimprovable. Mankind, Sophie had heard church people say, was made in the image of God and since God was omniscient, almighty and merciful, His handiwork – men, women, children, animals – was already perfect. There was 'no room at all' for improvement.

It is plain cruelty to have to choose between the love of your life, the person who has filled you with joy and made it a pleasure simply to wake up in the morning, and the lab work with your colleagues that is on the brink of bringing about nothing less than a paradigm shift in human nature. Women free of the deadly curse of breast cancer; children born without Down syndrome, without muscular dystrophy, without cystic fibrosis or sickle-cell anaemia: why are such objectives considered to be 'reaching too high'?

Sophie Gresham let loose in me a sensation of euphoria, an elation that made me feel vivid. Sometimes I felt for months on end that I was ablaze. And it was through Sophie also I discovered that disgruntlement, frustration, corrosive jealousy can lie concealed in the very heart of one's happiness, gnawing away silently.

Is it inevitable, I find myself wondering, that people in the arts will in some way be at loggerheads with those pursuing scientific projects? Even couples in love – will they too be held apart by this schism? Is it really the case that artists and scientists are by definition diametrically opposed in their values? Doesn't our common humanity transcend such points of conflict?

I've been making notes and compiling this memoir in England. That's why the spelling and most of the usages are British – to convey a sense of the older, much-loved version of our language still in use on these shores.

As for the story's climax, I know what it is because, like Walt Whitman, 'I am the man, I suffered, I was there'. It's a tableau of distraught, weeping people aching for shortcuts to healthy longevity. Who doesn't hate the encroachments of old age, the accumulation of ailments, the loss of vigour and optimism? The sad gathering at a house in Chesterton where this story ends is a traditional, very common but distinctly weird way of trying to escape the clutches of decrepitude.

10

It was early morning and Flame McGovern could see that Bertha was fresh, alert. They'd had breakfast together and been out for a stroll through the mist along the riverbank. They'd breathed in the crisp air and raced each other back to the grand old house.

They were now in Flame's spacious office on the second floor adjacent to Bertha's room. The wooden floorboards were stained dark gold, there were about a dozen photos on the walls which Flame had taken of habitats in the remotest regions, and the window was open; they could hear pigeons cooing outside. The couch they were relaxing on was old-fashioned, comfortable, covered in a floral-patterned fabric. Flame's large, leather-topped desk and swivel-chair were on the other side of the room and, within arm's length of the desk, the steel filing-cabinet containing her notebooks and print-offs of her journal articles.

'I'm going to teach you to read,' Flame told Bertha with a warm smile. 'You're a clever girl and I'm sure you'll become a good reader.' She had a deck of white cards in her hand, about the size of playing cards, each of which had a short word she'd written on it in very clear lower-case letters with a black felt-tip pen. 'Each time I show you a card I'll say what's written on it. You must look at the card carefully and say what I say. All right?'

'Yes,' Bertha said. She sat up and turned slightly toward Flame.

Flame peeled off a card from the deck in her left hand, looked at the word on it, held it in her right hand so that

Bertha could see the word, and enunciated clearly: 'punt.'

Bertha kept her eyes on the card and repeated the word: 'punt'.

'That's very good, Bertha,' Flame said. She turned the card down for a moment, then flashed it up again.

Bertha looked at it and said again: 'punt'.

'What a clever girl you are.' Flame peeled off the next card, looked at the word on it, held it up to Bertha and said: 'pole.'

Bertha looked at the word and said: 'pole.' A smile crept into her face, and in her eyes Flame thought she saw a flicker of recognition.

Flame beamed at her. 'Good girl, Bertha,' and flashed up the previous card again.

Bertha looked at it, glanced at Flame, and said: 'punt.'

The next card had *swans* on it and the following one *ducks*, and Bertha repeated each time what Flame said. And when Flame flashed up the four cards, slowly, in random order, Bertha uttered each word correctly without hesitation.

Flame sighed in satisfaction and sagged back on the couch. She decided not to show Bertha the next word in the set of cards: *water*. It might be too many words for an introductory session. The realisation should settle in Bertha's mind that written words referred to things in the real world that were part of Bertha's own previous experience. Bertha's correct responses reminded Flame in a rush of nostalgia of how her mother had taught *her* to read with flash cards at their home in Edinburgh when she was three years old. Her parents still lived in that house in Glendevon Avenue on the edge of the Carrick Knowe Golf Course.

If done properly, Flame knew, the flash-card method was very effective. The idea, right from the beginning, was to associate reading with praise and reward in the child's mind, link reading with pleasure and esteem in a very direct way. Flame had gone on to read dozens of little picture books by the time she was four, and had such a head start when she entered primary school which her mother encouraged her to build on that she eventually won a scholarship to Cambridge University where she graduated with straight As. Her brother had also been taught to read with flash cards, two years earlier; he eventually went on to study medicine and was now a consultant immunologist at Edinburgh's Royal Infirmary.

Flame knew there had been other factors involved in their reading success, not just the cards. Nutritious food for them to eat regularly was crucial, a good roof over their heads, a quiet room where they could read their books undisturbed, and enough time to do so. Nevertheless, the fact remained: her mother had taught them to read when they were three years old and kept encouraging the habit.

Whether Bertha would link pleasure so closely with reading remained to be seen; it wasn't yet possible to say whether she would have the kind of tenacity Flame had had. But there was no harm at all in getting her started, getting her accustomed to written words and phrases. Who could say what the capacity of her brain was going to be, Flame wondered. The best she could do at this stage was get Bertha to associate reading with positive vibes, with smiles, and the meanings of the words she read with enhanced self-esteem.

'That's enough for today,' Flame said.

'Enough reading.'

'That's right. Come, Bertha, put your arms around me and give me a hug.'

Bertha turned and hugged her teacher. 'Punt, pole, swans, ducks,' she said.

'What a clever girl you are. We'll do more reading tomorrow. You'll remember the man who gave us the pole. You'll remember you had to hold tight, not fall into the water. Will you like to do more reading, Bertha?'

'Yes. I will.'

'Good. Let's go down to the kitchen. There's some chocolate ice-cream in the fridge. You like ice-cream, don't you?

'I do. Ice-cream is nice.'

11

Sophie's a treat to look at.

With her mass of long wavy hair, pale blue eyes, full kissable lips and gleaming white teeth, she is magnetically beautiful. She's far more attractive and alluring than any animal, of course, but her steady desire for sex, her almost constant longing to couple, reminds me of the female spotted hyena whose clitoris is fully as large as the male hyena's penis, and frequently erect as well, clearly visible outside her body as she prowls the African savannah protecting her young and sending signals to the adult males in the pack.

It's vivid. It's memorable. The female is almost indistinguishable from the male in the genital area. It's the outcome of evolutionary development, a genetic mechanism of survival. The female of the species must have found that sex was far too important for her ever to pretend to be coy, so she lets her longing literally stick out; it's a thin, fleshy sensitivity emerging from the lips of her vulva, pink and moist and shiny, man enough to take on any male who wants to have a go.

It's easy to see how a possessive male could be made jealous by such unabashed signalling to all the other males in the vicinity.

I know how a possessive male hyena must feel.

I know what it's like to feel jealous.

I know how it sears your heart, how it mangles and weighs down your state of mind and leaves you lacerated and diminished.

I'd say jealousy is an inevitable experience when you live

with a woman like Sophie. You become privy to aspects of personal beauty, private loveliness, which you can't conceive as belonging to the public domain, as having to be shared with anyone else. When you undress with her in the same room for months and years on end and frequently see how she removes her blouse, the movements her arms make behind her back when she unclips her bra and her breasts quiver as the garment comes away and reveals the full extent of her cleavage; the sensual wriggle of her hips as she pulls down her skirt and the narrowness of her waist surges in front of your eyes into the earthy curves of her arse; and her soggy hair when she stands under the shower not quite matching the colour of her pubic hair, a thick patch in the shape of a triangle protecting the entrance to the best place in your life: these rhapsodies, ravishments of flesh, induce a possessiveness in the fortunate onlooker, a kind of egoism born, not of avarice, but of a feeling that one has been chosen by fate to dwell in the presence of human splendour.

The joy of it all sometimes makes you feel weak.

And vulnerable.

I am still amazed that Sophie was a virgin the first time we slept together. She gave me her cherry in the evening of the day we met, after reading me the Rudyard Kipling short story she'd told me about at Queens' College on her Graduation Day. What an improbable meeting that was. It happened also to be my twenty-fifth birthday. I was still living in a small flat in Grange Road in Cambridge, nearly ten years ago. I used to cook for myself in those days. I didn't have an especially large repertoire of dishes, nor was my palate particularly discerning, but preparing my own meals had a strategic importance: it made me more self-sufficient. And I still had the time in those days to spend in a kitchen.

After we'd tucked into the moussaka I had cooked earlier that day, and we'd drunk some of the red wine Sophie had brought, she asked if she could kiss me Happy Birthday.

We rose from the table, embraced and my lips touched hers for the first time. What an extraordinary sensation it was, that lingering, exploratory first kiss. Feeling her body pressed warm against mine whilst inhaling her pastel perfume transported me to a place I'd never inhabited before. She squeezed my butt as we kissed, and rummaged her hand between my legs, letting me know beyond a shadow of a doubt what was on her mind. Then she asked me point blank if I'd like to undress her and take her to bed.

I was ablaze with desire by then, in a state of fever, scarcely able to believe my good fortune or contain my lust, my roaring erection leaking lubrication the while. I hadn't even been alone just talking with a woman anywhere in thirteen weeks, let alone a gorgeous, lightly tanned, randy one asking to be stripped.

I peeled off Sophie's clothes while trying to control my shaking hands. Then I lifted her in my arms, placed her naked on the narrow bachelor bed and lay down beside her.

'You are so beautiful, Sophie,' I said into her ear, 'so very lovely.'

I hadn't been in a romantic situation for such a long time that I had to remind myself what I was supposed to do. When I remembered, I began to prime her with my fingers, and with my lips and tongue, slowly, steadily, until she was heaving, her breath coming in little bursts which suggested I was probably on the right track. Her breasts rose and fell, her nipples, dark pink and firm, pointing; they rose and fell, slowly at first, then more and more rapidly.

'I think you should lift your knees and spread them,' I suggested politely.

'Why?' she asked, holding my gaze, puzzled.

'It will make access easier,' I explained.

She gave me such a measuring look that I knew instantly she hadn't lifted her thighs like that for anyone before, but she was keen, she was moist, fully aroused, and complied readily.

'Oh Charlie, Charlie, Charlie,' she cried out a while later with her eyes shut, binding my name to her blissful abandon as she held me close. *I* had to hold *her* close too, with my arms and palms, to save myself from falling off the narrow bed in pleasure. The bed was just about wide enough for the two of us and I didn't fancy banging my head on the floor if I fell off it, so I clung happily to her flesh.

'Bloody hell, Charlie,' she said afterwards, using a phrase I hadn't heard her utter before in her very English accent. 'Such pleasure! Such ecstasy! I'd read that sex could be nice, even very nice, but not *so* encompassingly joyful.'

There was an awe-struck look of discovery in her eyes. They were sparkling too with tears. We lay in silence for a long while, on our sides, face to face, but in separate cocoons of consciousness. Then she touched the back of my head, kissed me on the lips, and said: 'Charlie, would you mind doing it again?'

I was of course more than happy to oblige; the ecstatic sensations were mutual. After a particularly orgasmic session when grunting sounds again rose from her throat and her head thrashed from side to side and her tongue kept darting out of her mouth to wet her parched lips, Sophie got off the bed, went to the bathroom and brought back one of the cotton face-cloths she'd found folded over the towels.

'Would you mind if I used this?' she asked, standing in the doorway and holding the cloth out in her hand.

I smiled and said: 'Be my guest.'

She spread her legs, bent forward and wiped herself dry with the cloth, then dabbed her inner thighs. Then she knelt at the side of the bed and wiped me dry too. That must have been when she got the idea to keep a cloth in her handbag wherever we went. She called it 'our love rag' and said: 'You never know when we might need it.'

Sophie got into the routine of placing our love rag on a small plastic sheet, rolling it into the shape of a rather long and thick tampon, and placing it at the bottom of her handbag, ready to be used whenever our love-making created the need for post-coital wipes.

Her orgasms are voluminous; they cascade forth. Her vagina drools its pleasure.

In the house we moved to in Granchester a year after we met, Sophie sees to it that there's a freshly washed absorbent love rag under every pillow. We sleep each night in a different one of our four bedrooms to vary the setting of our sex life – except of course when guests are staying overnight after a garrulous party which Sophie throws for her literary friends twice a year. There's always a lot of delicious food, all kinds of drink and a hot band belting out the music.

The guests tend to lie in late the following morning; they're hung over, some of them. They turn up bleary-eyed and dishevelled for breakfast prepared by Margot Lane, our very able cook/housekeeper. They grin sheepishly and don't know where to look when told about the wine they spilled, the glasses they broke, their spicy language, and about their canoodling escapades.

Sophie's parties gradually become noisy and reckless, with much laughter and dancing. Otherwise, she protects her time jealously. She's highly focused on her fiction and the historical research informing it.

I don't know whether it's because she's a novelist for whom every experience is grist to the mill and has to be put into words, but Sophie speaks from time to time of that evening she gave me her virginity.

'I thought it was a different kind of period the way the stuff poured out of me as I came and came,' she says. 'I felt so dazzlingly beautiful I thought I was going to die of pleasure and become an angel. God must surely love me. I'll never forget that night, Charlie – ever. It was my Graduation Day and I moved into a whole new sensibility.'

A few days after our first night together she asked me

over the phone whether I was able to take a week of my annual holiday so we could go away together. I said yes, I could leave the lab for up to a fortnight at a time. It turned out Sophie had already booked a hotel room with a balcony view of the lovely Parc Monceau across the Boulevard de Courcelles in the 17th *arrondissement* of Paris. That was the first I heard of it. What a pleasant surprise; I'd not been to France before, or anywhere else in Europe .

'We'll get to know each other, Charlie,' Sophie said when we met at Heathrow Airport.

'I'd like nothing better.'

'D'you speak any French?'

'None whatever.'

'It doesn't matter. I'll do the talking and be your guide.'

'What a treat. How long are we going for?'

'A week. Five days and five nights,' she said, keeping eye contact. 'You'll learn French words.'

'Five nights alone together – in the same room?' She was the only tri-lingual woman I'd slept with, a speaker of French and Arabic as well as English, a 23-year-old virgin, according to the blood that had seeped from her and smudged my bedsheet.

'In the same bed,' she said, answering my real question and waving the airline tickets, 'without interruptions. I'm so glad I waited until I graduated. What joy! What a cornucopia to look forward to.'

I was amazed by her appetite during that first holiday together. It was a kind of gluttony. Was she making up for lost time? She wanted sex morning, noon and night, all over the place – in our hotel room, in the empty bath, in the shower cubicle, out on the balcony as she leaned forward on her arms on the low wall, pushed out her shapely butt so I could enter her from behind and get a rhythm going while my hands gripped her waist and she gazed across the Boulevard de Courcelles at the ornate gold-tipped black railings of Parc Monceau and the trees beyond, a view which *I* saw over her shoulder through a prism of the most erotic sensations.

And we enjoyed each other *in* that park too. We stood against a tree lit up by lamps in the shrubs around us; an owl was hooting among the branches and we could hear the midnight sounds of Paris subdued in the distance.

Sophie wanted me inside her even after her period started the last night of our holiday. I realised what was what when I withdrew from her and saw that the stickiness on my cock wasn't only from the semen of orgasms; there were also soggy streaks of blood. I felt kind of grisly for a moment, like a butcher on vacation. I thought at first she was still a bit of a virgin: that's why she was bleeding. Perhaps her hymen hadn't been pierced properly when we first fucked. But how could that be? She'd been wanting me inside her day and night. There was this desirous, imploring look in her eyes each time she was in the mood, and a shy smile each time she touched my groin or stroked my chest. That tactile talk told me about her appetite, her craving pussy, or, to put it more formally, her voracious vagina.

It was the height of summer and only started getting dark around 10pm. There was a *boulangerie* near our hotel where I said '*Bon jour*' every day to the couple in white aprons behind the counter when Sophie bought fresh pastries from the *patisserie* section. We ate them in the park before setting off on our sight-seeing jaunts in the Latin Quarter, Pigalle, Montparnasse, Bois de Boulogne.

We went walking every day, strolling, looking, pointing, Sophie bare-legged in a loose summer frock and green-and-white tennis shoes, me in jeans, short-sleeved shirt and sneakers. We slept with the window open at night and every morning could smell the *baguettes* baking in the *boulangerie*, a truly appetising way to start the day.

We've been to Paris three times since then, but my more

recent memories of that metropolis are steeped in the images of my first visit, seasoned for ever with the flavours of the food we ate then, and imbued with the kind of vivifying happiness I hadn't known existed until Sophie took me to the City of Light along the Seine.

Sophie is in the arts and I'm a research scientist, yet our rapport seemed to have no limits, no demarcating lines. She seemed to be asserting ownership, the way she kept gripping my erection in her fist and squeezing it. After a week of seemingly non-stop kissing, fondling, stroking, legs spread wide on the rug with cushions under her butt; she straddling me on the bed; her calves enclosing my midriff; the smell of ejaculated semen filling the room as we lay side by side, foreheads touching, our exertions interspersed with room service, food on a trolley, wine bottle and glasses on a tray, and hot showers and fresh clothes – after five days and five nights going at it hammer and tongs as though we were on honeymoon, Sophie asked me on the plane back to England if I would marry her.

She thanked me for Paris on that flight. It was *her* idea. *She* had paid for the tickets and taken me on my first journey anywhere in Europe. Yet she thanked me for what she said had been the most blissful week of her life.

12

'I haven't played table tennis in ages,' Flame McGovern said, looking across the net at Peter Lynn, the burly porter with aquiline nose and forward-sloping chin. He usually manned the reception desk in the entrance hall with its large black-and-white marble floor tiles and the oak banister leading up to the mezzanine level, but it was part of his job to cooperate, to help whenever he could with Bertha's training. He was standing poised with his bat at the opposite edge of the table, which was lower than usual, resting on two specially made short trestles, waiting for Flame to serve the ball.

'Don't make excuses,' he said, grinning at her. He glanced at Bertha standing on a chair against the wall, the better to see what was going on. 'Watch closely, Bertha,' he said. 'Flame is going to serve the ball to me, over the net, and I am going to try to hit the ball back, over the net.'

'Here goes,' Flame said. She tossed the ball up, hit it with her bat as it came down and watched it bounce from the table over the net. Peter leaned forward and hit it downwards so that it bounced back over the net; it rose towards Flame who had all the time she needed to return it with a backhand stroke. They played a slow game on the low table, deliberately slow, ping pong, ping pong, rather than a fast sophisticated match with spinning serves and smashing shots, so that Bertha could see clearly what was involved.

Bertha was intrigued. She'd never seen table tennis before. She watched raptly as the ball was knocked from one side to the other until Peter unintentionally hit it back so hard that it bounced from his side of the table over the net and on to the floor.

'Gone,' Bertha exclaimed. She jumped from the chair and dashed round to the opposite side of the table to retrieve the ball. She picked it up from the spotlessly clean floor, turned and offered it to Flame.

'Thank you, Bertha. You're a kind girl,' Flame told her. 'Go back to the chair and keep watching.'

Bertha complied; but she managed to restrain herself for less than a minute before she began hopping up and down on the chair.

'Let me, let me,' she cried out.

'You want to play table tennis?' Peter asked her.

'Yes,' she replied.

'Yes, what?' Flame interjected.

'Yes please.'

'All right. Who do you want to play with? Peter or me?'

'Play you.'

'Lucky you,' Peter said and grinned at Flame. He loved looking at her; she was easy on the eye, he thought, with her thick ginger hair and violet-blue eyes, and he found the remains of her Scottish accent charming. But she was way above him in professional knowledge and experience. He felt that in certain ways he'd be out of his depth with her, so he never made a pass at her, chatty though she was and much though he would have liked their relationship to be a bit more intimate. He stepped to the side of the table and offered his bat to Bertha. 'Do you know how to hold the bat?' he asked.

Bertha looked at him, then at Flame, then said: 'No.'

'I'll show you. Open your hand,' Peter said and when Bertha did, he put the handle of the bat on her palm, folded her fingers around it and said: 'Hold it tight when you hit the ball.'

Bertha certainly knew how to hit the ball. The trouble

was, she hit it much too hard when Flame served it to her, and with little sense of direction. It was a different aspect of the same problem, Flame thought: her lack of restraint. Holding back didn't come naturally to Bertha. But that was precisely the object of the training programme which Flame had drawn up and embarked on with Dr Venn's encouragement. It was just a matter of time, she felt. Slow but sure was the best way to proceed. Sooner or later, the examples she set would sink in and gradually become part of Bertha's repertoire of abilities. Flame knew that what they were involved in was nothing less than building an individual's character. It was a noble enterprise, she was convinced, and her spirit of adventure, of probing the unknown, bringing into being an extraordinary personality, would be amply rewarded in due course.

She smiled at Bertha, and when Peter picked up the ball and handed it to her, Flame said:

'You were at the meeting when Dr Venn mentioned another baby, weren't you?'

'I was. The thought of another child here seemed to invigorate him.'

'Can you remember when it was due – the new child?'

'I think he said next spring, in April or May,' Peter said, 'so we'd have enough time to make the necessary preparations.'

'I think it's a very good idea. Bertha could do with a companion closer to her own age.'

'I agree. Having a real friend, as opposed to friendly teachers, friendly mentors, will help her relax. She won't have the feeling that she's in school all the time, that she has to be on her best behaviour non-stop. But the new child, when it arrives – I'm sure Doctor Venn said he hoped it would be a boy.'

'Yes, that's what he said,' Flame replied. 'It's going to be another challenge. I can't wait for the day.'

13

I married Sophie because she asked me to, on a plane on the way back from our first holiday together, in Paris. *She* proposed to *me*, not the other way round. We were above a blanket of cloud and could hear the drone of the jet engines and smell the aroma of coffee wafting from our cups. With her in the window seat and our fingers touching on the armrest, our hand-luggage in an overhead compartment, and a uniformed flight attendant with shiny make-up pulling a drinks cabinet along the aisle, Sophie thanked me for Paris. *She* had taken me there; I'd never been anywhere in Europe before. The trip was *her* idea. *She* had bought the tickets, yet she thanked me for what she said was the most blissful week of her life. Would I marry her?

I grinned, said I certainly would and we kissed in that crowded plane heading back to London. Agreeing to throw in my lot with Sophie has been the easiest thing I've ever done: she was beautiful, irresistibly erotic, and clever. I thought I'd won a rare jackpot; I couldn't believe my luck. The fact that I was a research scientist from the States and she an Englishwoman in the arts didn't seem to be an obstacle at the time. Nor did her dreamy sensibility strike me as odd in any way; on the contrary, I found it charming, thought it was part of her artistic temperament. Despite everything that's happened due to our 'clash of cultures', the bad vibes that gradually strained our relationship, I still love her. Food still tastes better when I'm eating it with Sophie.

It never occurred to me that her cuddles would one day confuse me, that her embrace would become ambiguous.

For months after the wedding I'd be sexually aroused just thinking about approaching night. I'd get a hard-on every time we went up to our bedroom, my mind and my body amazed at my good fortune, at the joy that lay in store, the pleasure of turning my head on the pillow and seeing a certain lovely face looking at *me*, desirable lips that would kiss me awake in the morning and make the daylight hours resonate with happiness and my problems at work shrink to chores easily encompassed.

Love altered the orientation of my world. I seemed to tilt to a new vertical. I felt, curiously, more complete.

This woman took her clothes off in front of me. Every night.

Cool beyond words.

She would turn around slowly to show me her gorgeous body, her waist curving out into the spheres of her smooth *derrière*, the cleavage of her fulsome breasts, her slender thighs and mat of pubic hair. As I gaped at her goods, she would quote Katherine Mansfield to me: 'How idiotic civilisation is. Why be given a body if you have to keep it shut up in a case like a rare, rare fiddle?'

She'd look at me steadily and tell me in that husky voice of hers: 'I love you to the exclusion of all others. I'm yours, Charlie Venn. Take me whenever you want to, wherever you like. Love me with all your heart. That is how I shall love you.'

Then she'd undo my belt, pull down my zip and rummage her hand in my boxer shorts. She'd touch me up, stroke me to the fullest extent of my dimensions. She wanted me just as much as I wanted her.

'Winning the jackpot' isn't the right phrase at all – that's usually a one-off event. This desirable woman crawled on to me every night. She smothered me with kisses and smiled the most ravishing smile while making passionate love.

I was so happy. Our passion made me deliriously happy.

I felt in my heart that if there was a heaven anywhere in the universe, this must be it. I still feel that way, nearly ten years later, despite everything. It will be our tenth anniversary in a few days' time.

It's a heaven quite unlike the biblical heaven where flesh and blood have no entry, where sex is a vile sin and the only folks who make it through the Pearly Gates are those who checked in their dicks and desire down on Earth along with their pride and worldly possessions in order to dwell in a realm devoid of all sensuousness. Thenceforth for all eternity they'll speak to one another and taste food without having tongues. They'll hear without ears, smell without nostrils, see without eyes, and feel the pressure of things without any sense of touch in a kind of divine autism promoted by clerics on Earth as the apotheosis of existence.

Even though as an undergraduate she'd been surrounded for four years by horny students away from home for the first time with ample opportunity to satisfy the lust throbbing in their loins, and despite having travelled abroad where she moved unchaperoned among all manner of men while practising her spoken French and then her Arabic, Sophie Gresham was a virgin when we first made love.

She *had* kissed a few boys, she told me. She would push her tongue into their mouths, perhaps, but that was all. She never went any farther until she and I met quite by chance in a crowded hall where I was looking for someone else; she wouldn't even let them touch her breasts. She didn't want to be distracted from her studies, she said, and promised herself that if she got a double first in her finals she would then surrender her virginity, 'lose' it; she would embark on her sex life as a reward for achieving her academic objective.

Why she approached *me* on her Graduation Day is a puzzle. No one has ever described me as handsome. *I* don't think I'm particularly handsome. Why she zeroed in on *me* and asked me that same evening to undress her and take her to bed I still haven't figured out. I guess the wise thing to do is be thankful for the cultural chemistry between a scientific researcher from America and a budding English novelist that got things developing between us with such a special *frisson*. Perhaps it was one of those cases where ignorance is bliss.

Sophie was a virgin then. I saw the blood on my bedsheet afterwards. In a moment of delirious insight those red smudges looked like a message in code intended only for someone in a state of rapture. Like a tribal doctor concentrating hard, I deciphered the stains and concluded that an essence of Sophie had seeped into my life as a marker of her commitment. A virgin at the age of twenty-three is rare enough in the world – and Sophie says she still hasn't been to bed with anyone else, nearly ten years later.

She says she hasn't had sex with anyone else. I try to believe her. There was a time when I simply didn't believe her. Virginity, after all, doesn't have the same commodity value it used to have when women were possessions, when they were owned, first by their fathers, then by their husbands and traded as though they were objects whose worth depended on their being 'untouched', 'unspoilt', not second-hand goods like an old mattress or worn-out tyre.

For the first two years or so after I lifted Sophie's veil and she turned her lovely lips to mine in the church in Bristol she'd insisted on despite my protests, and I affirmed to a fresh-faced fellow in fancy dress that I would love, cherish and protect her, in sickness and in health, for better and for worse, till death do us part, and kissed her in front of her twin brothers, our parents and the other witnesses who were all stunned by how quickly things had happened – for about two years after the wedding and our honeymoon in Singapore where we first ate chicken satay with its peanut-flavoured sauce, went to the wonderful walk-in Jurong Bird Park and saw the curious sculptural cameos in the Tiger Balm Garden, I couldn't believe Sophie was being faithful to me. Those pale-blue eyes of hers, so coquettish, her body, so firm and handfullish, had me believing otherwise.

Sophie's erotic charms are magnetic. They pull without any intention on her part. I've often wondered how much time she spends fending off fellows who come on to her; it makes me grind my teeth on the brink of apoplexy. How could other men fail to see what I've seen in her eyes – the smouldering come-hither invitation, the extraordinarily brazen suggestiveness, the here-I-am, take-me availability, like a naked woman with nice tits stepping into the steam of a shower-room where randy men are stripped to the skin?

I learned something about myself during those tortured months. I got an insight into the dynamics of jealousy which have plagued me periodically ever since, and jealousy's debilitating effects. Feelings of insecurity, of not measuring up, fear that she'd make a monkey of me behind my back, were the kind of seizures that had me running scared and behaving in ways I would previously not have thought possible.

Magnanimity went out the window. I shrank as a person. I became petty. I accused Sophie of making eyes at other men, of leading them on, of arranging secret trysts. I followed her car in my car to see who she was going to meet. I watched the clock when she went out and waited fretfully for her to return. I had bad dreams of Sophie leaving me for someone else, dreams that varied slightly but always explored the same theme. During my waking hours I set traps for her.

Sophie never fell into the traps. She didn't even stumble. She didn't do a single thing to vindicate my frantic vigilance. And the reason why I was fretting pointlessly, according to Sophie, was that, as she kept saying, she had no intention of two-timing me.

'You're the one I love, Charlie – to the exclusion of all others. How many times do I have to tell you?' she said one afternoon with tears in her eyes. 'You satisfy me, Charlie.

My cup runneth over – I'm in my glory. That's why we have the love rags. I don't need one of those gadgets implanted above my bum with electrodes into my spine to get an orgasm,' she smiled wanly. 'And why should I risk sexually transmitted diseases like chlamydia and HIV when I have a generous lover in my own house? I'm not stupid or shallow. Don't be like that, Charlie. Don't be suspicious. Jealousy spoils everything, darling. And it's completely uncalled for.'

Jealousy does spoil everything.

It certainly spoils my sleep.

It visits dark dreams on me, dreams of Sophie leaving me, different versions of how our relationship ends. Sometimes there's more detail in the dream; sometimes the details change a bit. In one dream that recurs with minor differences, Sophie is in the front of a car with some guy at the wheel, the two of them laughing happily, carefree. The whole point of the dream I know from its nauseous sensation and lurid colour is that the guy at the wheel *isn't me*. It's another man. He is reaching parts of Sophie I have obviously not been able to get to. He's putting her at ease at the deepest level of her being.

I never get to see the face of my competition. He's always just beyond recognition, so I wouldn't know him if I met him during the day. How I'd love to see this guy's face, know my nemesis.

Even when the setting of the dream changes, to Sophie and this guy sipping cocktails in a bar as they gaze into each other's eyes; holding hands as they stroll between the newly opened pavilions of the futuristic Centre for Mathematical Sciences off Clarkson Road; trying on hats at a Market Hill stall in the centre of Cambridge; looking at great works of 20th-century art at Kettle's Yard on Castle Street; standing on the elegant Garret Hostel footbridge over the River Cam and admiring the architecture of Trinity Hall's Jerwood Library, its panels of wood conjuring up a modern version of an Elizabethan structure known to the locals as 'the ship on the Cam' – all the things Sophie and I have done together, except that in the dreams it's always some other guy she's with, someone whose mere presence keeps her beaming endlessly. Regardless of the details of time and place, the message of the dream is the same, and so is my misery.

Despite Sophie's reassurances during my waking hours, despite her kisses and cuddles when I emerge from the dream in a fevered sweat, and the soothing way she hums a melody into my ear to calm me down and send me into peaceful slumber, a contradictory signal periodically fills me with dread. An intuition rises from my perceptions into bad meanings in my mind. Sophie loves to make love, and yet somehow she's making a fool of me: that's the vibe I get as I lie in bed beside her, gazing at her sleeping face, her hair spread across the pillow, and feeling the gentle rise and fall of her flesh as she dreams the kind of dreams that allow her to remain so tranquil.

I gaze at my lovely wife as she sleeps. I look at the heart-shaped ring on my wedding-finger; Sophie was a teenager when her grandmother gave her this ring on a farm at Wormelow near the border with Wales. I face the ceiling in the dead of night and hope that, despite everything, I'll manage to keep the promise I made her grandmother a week before our wedding: that I would always love and be kind to her dear darling Sophie.

14

To show that her proposal of marriage on the plane back from Paris was serious in this age of uncommitted living together, something which at the time I thought that I too preferred, bondless co-habitation, no engagement or wedding rings, no signatures on any document, Sophie drove me in her white convertible Jaguar across the country to her parents' home outside Bristol.

Their place was on a wooded knoll overlooking the Clifton Suspension Bridge across the River Avon. I was surprised to discover what a rich family they were. Theirs is a large, airy, tastefully appointed Victorian house in the midst of landscaped gardens. It turned out that they own grand properties in Cheltenham and Bath too, and rows of business premises in Birmingham and Hereford. The only hint I'd had of their wealth was when I asked Sophie how long she'd had her Jaguar car; it was a gleaming white coupé with white leather upholstery that smelled new. We were speeding on the M5 motorway beyond Gloucester and heading south. 'One week,' she replied. 'My parents gave it to me as a graduation present.'

'Mummy, this is Doctor Charles Hadley Venn,' Sophie said immediately we entered the drawing-room with its heritage-red and green walls and picture-frames picked out in gold. That was the setting in which I first saw her mother, a woman of charismatic elegance and superb scented beauty from whom Sophie had obviously inherited a great deal of her charm and loveliness.

'Charlie's a molecular biologist from America, a gene-transfer specialist working here at a lab in Cambridge,' Sophie told her mother. 'He's the man I'm going to marry.'

'Does he have any say in the matter?'

'Only if he says yes.'

'Is that what you're likely to say?' her mother asked me, the amused expression on the fine features of her face not quite concealing the once-over she was giving me. She was dressed in a cashmere slash-neck lace top with multi-coloured hem, her pleated trousers chiming in with gold sandals showing toe-nails painted a sensuous red.

'I've already said yes, Missus Gresham. I can't express how fortunate I feel to be meeting you in these circumstances. I wouldn't want to make the mistake of losing the most alluring woman I have ever met.'

'In that case, you should both pause, to be doubly sure. Take your time. Take her out, Charlie. But don't commit yourself until you're quite sure you want to take Sophie into your heart.'

Take it or leave it: those were my options.

Sophie's mother led us to an elegant chaise-longue covered in cream damask facing a flower-bed in the garden ablaze with crimson and orange dahlias. She bade us sit down and disappeared for a while. I took the opportunity to look at the oil paintings on the walls. When she reappeared, it was with a silver tray of tea-things which she put on a side-table. I sat down next to Sophie. Her mother drew a wing-chair closer and sat facing me.

'Please explain, Charlie,' she said as she lifted the tea-pot and began to pour, 'what exactly your work involves. What do molecular biologists actually *do*?'

'Well,' I replied, smiling at her and glancing at Sophie, 'it's such a vast field, there are so many lines of research being pursued, that I don't know where to start.'

'Keep it basic, whatever you do. I was a lecturer in English literature at Bristol University before I married, and for six years after our honeymoon. But when Sophie and then her twin brothers were born, I focused on them full-time. I've never studied science, so I won't understand if you come over all technical.'

I reached out and took the cup and saucer she proffered. She poured some for Sophie who was seated by my side, and then for herself.

I took a sip of the tea and thought about how to explain the work I do. My fear was that I would come across as boring, that their attention would drift away. I suddenly recalled what my father had told me more than once: that it was a common delusion among people in the arts, though perhaps not all of them, that everyday language is subtle and nuanced enough to explain the complexities in which scientists delve. That was why, my father used to say, literary people tend to be impatient with what they insist on calling *jargon*. Their eyes enable them to see only surface things; they believe that if they can't understand something then it isn't worth paying attention to. So I was presented with a dilemma: I had to speak as plainly as possible to be understood by lay people, using no *jargon* at all, but I also had to be faithful to the core truths of my work. It wasn't going to be easy.

'As a mother,' I began, 'you know of course that when a child is born it inherits genes from each parent.'

'That much I do know – yes. Some of us in England call it breeding.'

'And that if the child inherits the genes that code for the proteins which determine, say, hair colour, from her mother,' I looked from the lovely head of hair beside mine to the one in front of me, 'she will grow up to have the same colour of hair as her mother.'

'Likewise the colour of her eyes.'

'Likewise,' I smiled, 'although it's not that straightforward. It *is* possible for two blue-eyed parents to produce brown-eyed children. This is because a person's eye colour depends on the distribution of melanocyte cells which produce the melanin pigment that appears more commonly in brown eyes. Blue eyes in fact result from a light-scattering effect of the melanin. Sometimes, however, in the process of cell division in the womb, a gene is wrongly copied, or is damaged, and the child is then born with a disability – for example, the fatal blood disorder thalassaemia beta which disrupts formation of the protein haemoglobin which carries oxygen in the blood, or cystic fibrosis, which makes it agonisingly difficult to breathe because of a layer of mucus covering the lungs.'

'Cystic fibrosis is dreadful,' Sophie's mother said. 'The children concerned don't live very long, do they?'

'Not long, no. Some don't even survive beyond the age of twenty. The point to remember is that we humans have around thirty-thousand genes, any of which could be damaged and which then code for the wrong sort of proteins, resulting in disease – various forms of cancer, heart problems, you name it.'

'Is that where you geneticists come in?'

'Yes,' I replied, not sure how interested she was, how much she'd want to hear. 'We try to locate along the length of the chromosome concerned the genetic mutation – the wrongly copied or damaged gene – so that we can remove it and insert in its place a gene that's in perfect condition. Researchers used to think that most of the DNA along human chromosomes had no coding function and referred to it as "junk DNA". But evidence is emerging that the purpose of non-coding DNA is to *regulate* minutely the working of our organs – kidneys, heart, whatever.'

Sophie's mother sipped some tea, put the cup back on the saucer, then said: 'You mentioned the word chromosome. What do *you* understand by chromosome?'

'It's best to think of a chromosome as a very long

strand of DNA, with particular genes comprising particular stretches of that DNA. Think of a very long pearl necklace. The whole necklace is the chromosome, and each pearl a particular gene, except – and this is crucially important – except that genes aren't single entities like a pearl, they aren't monolithic.'

'What are they, then?'

'They're complex, Missus Gresham. They're made up of very many molecules of four acid bases called adenine, thymine, guanine and cytosine.'

'Sounds like the names of four pretty little girls.'

'They're pretty important, that's for sure. These four acid bases always occur in pairs. Adenine always pairs with thymine; guanine always pairs with cytosine. And the *sequences* in which these four bases occur are crucial, because it is the sequences that make up the code of life.'

'The code of life,' Sophie's mother murmurs. 'I've heard that phrase before. What exactly d'you mean by it?'

'I mean,' I say, glancing at Sophie and hoping I'm making myself clear, 'that the *order* in which the bases occur along the chromosome is of the greatest importance. Each set of three bases is called a *codon*, and each is a code which specifies the precise order in which the body's twenty amino acids have to be assembled in the cells to produce a particular protein that folds into its own peculiar three-dimensional structure. For example, *guanine thymine adenine* codes for the amino acid hystidine; but *guanine adenine cytosine* codes for the amino acid leucine. The codes that result in skin, hair, bone, nerves – they're made up of different sequences of the bases.'

'Fascinating,' Sophie's mother says. 'There seems to be an intelligence at work in our cells.'

'A very subtle and delicate intelligence,' I confirm, 'that has evolved over four billion years. Most human genes are between ten-thousand and a hundred-thousand base pairs in length, although some are very much longer. The Duchenne gene on the X chromosome, for example, is about a hundred and fifty-five *million* base pairs long. It is bases missing from this gene that causes muscular dystrophy in the person concerned, with its attendant suffering and family grief. The gene that codes for spastic paraplegia is also on the tip of the X chromosome. In fact, the X chromosome alone contains genes that are involved in something like three-hundred inherited diseases, including haemophilia, mental backwardness, autism, cleft palate, infertility, deafness, leukaemia and epilepsy.'

'I had no idea things were quite so complex in our cells,' the elder Gresham says with a pensive smile. 'If I thought about them at all, I took our cells to be discrete items interlocking with one another, like thousands of tiny sultanas packed together.'

'It's not only *our* cells that are so complex. The same complexity applies to all living things.'

'To plants as well?' she asks.

'To plants as well. To grass, flowers, apples, and to worms, fish, spiders, birds and horses. The nucleic acid bases adenine, thymine, guanine and cytosine combine in different sequences to code for the proteins that comprise every form of life on Earth.' I look into her lovely blue eyes and hold her gaze as I tell her: 'We are related to oak trees and chihuahuas, Missus Gresham, as surely as we are related to shrubs and pythons in the jungle, and to the sea urchins of the Antarctic.'

'Are you saying that plants too have chromosomes?'

'Yes I am. Our human cells have forty-six chromosomes, except for the sex cells which have twenty-three chromo-somes. Tomatoes have twenty-four chromosomes, mice have forty, the fruit-fly four, potatoes forty-eight. Without chromosomes comprising genes, how would a potato know what size to grow to, what shape to become, how thick its skin should be?'

Mrs Gresham glances at Sophie who raises her eyebrows to acknowledge the abstruse information.

'You probably know that peaches and nectarines belong to the same species, *Prunus persica.* But it's because the nectarine has a recessive gene that it's skin doesn't become fuzzy like a peach's skin. The world is changing much more profoundly than people realise, Missus Gresham. Scientists at the Rubber Research Institute in Kuala Lumpur inserted the gene for albumin into a rubber tree's DNA sequence which then began producing albumin, the protein in human blood conveyed in transfusions. Rubber trees are now being tapped, not only for latex sap, but also for vast quantities of this urgently needed protein to drip into the veins of people injured in accidents or undergoing surgery.'

'Tapping human blood protein from rubber trees?' Mrs Gresham is perplexed. She looks at Sophie, then back at me. 'You aren't pulling my leg, are you, Charlie?'

'I wouldn't kid about anything so important.'

'It just sounds fantastical.'

'I know – like pie in the sky. But it's true. It's another secret of the laws of nature we've brought to light. As I said, we humans are related to plants, animals, birds and fish in the sea. Just how *helpfully* we're related is now becoming clearer. We're earning new truths by hard work.'

'Human blood protein from rubber trees,' Sophie's mother murmurs again, trying to take in the significance of this particular breakthrough. 'I honestly think that is more creative, Charlie, truly creative, than anything the art world has produced.'

'What a pity the art world is too small-hearted to acknowledge it. By similar gene-transfer techniques, banana DNA has been modified to begin yielding human vaccines, and strawberries to produce anti-decay toothpaste.'

I sense from the expressions on their faces that mother and daughter are somewhat in awe of the discoveries molecular biologists have made, of nature's mysterious processes that are being understood and redeployed so fruitfully.

For my part, I begin to feel uncomfortable. I feel I'm on the brink of alienating these two lovely women by seeming to flaunt my knowledge of esoteric things. The last thing I want is to be thought of as blinding people with science, mesmerising them with deep mysteries. As far as I'm concerned, science *unlocks* the mysterious and lays bare its workings. Science sheds light on areas of darkness. It is the polar opposite of religious mysticism. Its practitioners are deadly opponents of the sort of individuals who'd prefer all learning still to be in Latin which very few people can read and which would enable the Church, even today, to lord it over what it considers to be 'mere mortals' who should be burned at the stake in public for disagreeing with doddery old men wearing long dresses and ludicrously pompous headgear.

Far from being alienated, however, Mrs Gresham expresses further interest.

'You say diseases are caused when genes have some of the bases missing – when adenine, thy—?'

'Thymine, guanine and cytosine.'

'When some of those bits are missing?'

'Yes, or damaged. The codes are then incorrect and the resulting proteins fold into the wrong shapes. Faulty folding is implicated in Alzheimer's disease and in "mad-cow" disease, for example. A useful analogy is the way a word's *meaning* changes when its spelling is changed by just one letter. For example, the three letters R A T in that order is code for a word that connotes a well-known rodent. But changing just one of those three letters, say the last letter, from T to G, changes the meaning of the word entirely. Or reversing the sequence of the letters, from R A T to T A R, again changes the meaning profoundly. Each little change has a tremendous impact on the meaning conveyed. Likewise at the level of molecules. The gene that codes for retinoblastoma – childhood cancer of the eye – is on chromosome 13. The gene for manic depression we think is on the tip of one arm of chromosome 11. Researchers at Ehime University in Japan have found that men who suffer panic attacks for no obvious reason have in a gene called *white* on chromosome 21 an adenine base where there should be a guanine base. The "spelling" is wrong. Inherited disease is all about wrong spelling.'

'Japanese researchers discovered that?'

'Yes. They reported it in *Molecular Psychiatry* journal. The precise sequence of the one-point-four million bases that code for the bacterium which causes syphilis – *Treponema pallidum* – was published by a team of researchers from the University of Texas and the Institute of Genomic Research in Maryland. Scientists at the National Cancer Research Institute here in Britain have found that the likelihood of breast cancer is increased by numerous natural variations in a number of genes which are, individually, insignificant in their impact. More than forty-one thousand cases of breast cancer are diagnosed every year in the UK, and around twelve thousand women die from it annually. The genes *BRCA1* and *BRCA2* increase the risk of breast cancer markedly if they mutate. The exact molecular make-up of the proteins which cause tuberculosis and stomach ulcers have also been discerned. Scientists in Seattle are discovering what part the neurotransmitter acetylcholine plays in mental alertness and memory. Two years ago separate teams of researchers in France and the United States discovered the gene for progeria, a condition in which children age very rapidly and look and feel like adults in their seventies before they are ten years old.'

'Before they are ten?' Sophie's mother repeats with a frown.

I nod. 'Such children tend to die when they're about thirteen. The researchers found that progeria was caused by one of the acid bases in the gene called *LMNA* being in the wrong position. Investigating *LMNA* more thoroughly promises to yield insights into the mechanics of the ageing process and how it might be slowed down. Extended youthfulness could well be the result.

'Meanwhile, researchers at Emory University in Atlanta, Georgia have pinpointed a neurotransmitter, called vasopressin, whose effect is to curb polygamous sexual tendencies in animals such as mice and make them content with just one sexual partner. It's a remarkable achievement. Those scientists write in the journal *Nature* that vasopressin could well have a similar effect on certain sorts of human – you know, the oversexed kind, high-powered libidos whose urges always threaten to break through the bounds of decorum.'

'How deep you and your colleagues are delving,' Mrs Gresham says, 'down to the very core of what we are, it seems.'

15

As Sophie and I sit on the elegant chaise-longue facing her mother, I'm not sure whether there's admonition in Mrs Gresham's tone of voice or admiration. Searching the expression on her face doesn't help, so I continue telling her about work in genetics labs worldwide.

'The genes associated with cancer of the prostate gland include *HPC*-1 on chromosome 1 and *E2F3* whose over-expression indicates how aggressive the cancer might be. This cancer affects about thirty-thousand men every year in the UK alone and kills ten-thousand of them annually. The prostate gland normally produces an alkaline fluid which is released during ejaculation to help the sperm on their way, but when cancerous it has disastrous effects.'

Sophie, I notice, is blushing. She'd rather I hadn't used the word *ejaculation* in front of her mother. Her mother, however, isn't fazed at all.

'What sort of effects?' she asks.

'If prostate cancer isn't noticed in time and dealt with by non-surgical treatment, then removal of the walnut-shaped gland located below the bladder becomes necessary. Otherwise it causes humiliating incontinence, progressive impotence and one of the most hideous deaths of all cancers: the person's bones are rotted away by tumours.'

'You said it affects thousands of men every year – all over the world?'

'All over the world,' I nod. 'Nelson Mandela was saved from its ravages by timely surgery while still in prison in the Cape. Archbishop Desmond Tutu was diagnosed with prostate cancer in the late 1990s and was successfully treated in the United States. Individuals it has killed in recent times include the rock star Frank Zappa, the bald-headed TV and movie actor Telly Savalas of *Kojak* fame, and the Iranian religious heavy Ayatollah Khomeini.'

'Is that right?' Sophie chips in. 'Ayatollah Khomeini too?'

'Him too.'

'So his belief in God didn't protect him from the cancer in his own cells.'

'Evidently not. Human genes code for many diseases that are passed on from generation to generation. Research teams at Oxford University and Cardiff University have found genes that are involved in dyslexia. Their discoveries explain why some pupils have reading ability well below what it should be for their age and intelligence. Our bodies harbour so many causes of premature death and so many sources of pain and suffering that robust good health is one of history's great improbabilities.'

'You seem to be saying,' Mrs Gresham replies, 'that we are the sources of our own diseases. Is that what you're saying?'

'In a sense, yes, I am. We inherit some diseases from our parents. A high-profile example is Queen Victoria. She adored her German husband Prince Albert – their passion for each other gave them nine children.'

Mrs Gresham smiles. 'That's right,' she says, 'five daughters and four sons. She loved him so much that she commissioned the Albert Memorial in Kensington Gardens in his memory when he died in 1861.'

'What the queen didn't know at the time,' I add, 'was that she had passed on to two of her daughters, Princess Alice and Princess Beatrice, a mutant gene for haemophilia which *they* then, through marriage, passed on to various royal families across Europe.'

'One of those families were the Romanovs in Russia, weren't they?' Sophie says, turning to her mother, then looking at me. 'They were the czars in power when the Bolshevik revolution broke out.'

'They were,' I nod. 'Queen Victoria had passed down to them the Haemophilia B form of the disease. Since then, researchers have discovered that fragile X syndrome, an inherited form of mental retardation that attacks mainly human males, is caused by bits of unstable DNA called trinucleotide DNA. This kind of DNA disables people very seriously and eventually kills them. It's involved in Huntington's disease and in myotonic dystrophy and is an important factor in genetic diseases generally.'

'I've never had a conversation with a scientist before,' Mrs Gresham says, 'and I can't remember when last I learned so much so quickly. I'm glad Sophie brought you here, Charlie. Your comments remind me of what Shakespeare said.'

'Shakespeare?' Sophie exclaims.

Her mother nods: 'In *Julius Caesar*.' She leans forward, puts her cup and saucer on the table and sits back in her chair. She shuts her eyes for a moment as she recalls the words, then looks at me and quotes:

'Men at some time are masters of their fates:
The fault, dear Brutus, is not in our stars
But in ourselves, that we are underlings.'

'If that's what Shakespeare said,' I reply, 'then he was brilliant, spot on. The only way we humans can stop being underlings is by reinventing ourselves, by doing something about our frailties, adjusting our genetic makeup so that we evolve out of disease and out of early ageing and the vindictiveness and tendency to violence that have kept us morally stunted.'

'That's not all the Bard says about the secular nature of human beings,' Sophie's mother adds. 'His plays are sprinkled with evidence that he didn't believe in the supernatural. For example, he has Helena say in *All's Well That Ends Well:*

Our remedies oft in ourselves do lie,
Which we ascribe to heaven.

And in *Othello, The Moor of Venice*, Iago says to Roderigo:

'Tis in ourselves that we are thus or thus.'

'Clearly,' I respond, 'the man was a genius, extraordinarily prescient. If, as some people insist, we are made "in God's image", then God is not only grossly incompetent and disease-ridden, but also unforgivably guileful. He says he loves us, yet leaves us with loathsome time-bombs ticking in our bodies. God's embrace is so ambiguous it is plain treacherous.'

'You don't sound as though you have great faith in God,' Mrs Gresham says. 'I thought Americans were religious people, devout.'

'Many of us are,' I reply. 'At any one time there are hundreds of workshops, discussion groups, thinktanks across America devoted to religion and the existence of God.'

'It's part of popular culture there.'

'It sure is. America has long been a fertile land for new cults and sects. Silver-tongued saviours who promise spiritual enlightenment and salvation in exchange for donations belong to a well established tradition. So much so that individuals who proclaim themselves to be prophets of God pointing the way to heaven are held in awe and sometimes attain the status of national heroes.'

'That's the sort of thing Sinclair Lewis's novel *Elmer Gantry* was all about,' Sophie says.

I nod and reply: 'Religious hustling still goes on in the States.'

'That isn't surprising, is it?' Mrs Gresham says. 'It's a land of free speech.'

'Not as free as you might think.'

'What d'you mean, Charlie?' she asks and glances at Sophie.

'Not when it comes to disagreeing about God. People are afraid of being persecuted, of losing their jobs, losing funding for their projects if they let it be known that they don't believe in God. Politicians won't be elected if they say they don't believe in God – that's for sure. Some truths still aren't politically acceptable. But the internet is full of blogs showing that growing numbers of Americans *don't* believe that there really *was* a Garden of Eden, or that there were dinosaurs in the Garden of Eden,' I say, smiling at Sophie, 'and only six thousand years ago. People who do accept that story wilfully ignore all the carbon-dating evidence of Earth's tremendous age – the archean eon, the proterzoic eon, the more recent phanerozoic eon five-hundred million years ago, the triassic age about two-hundred-and-forty million years ago when small dinosaurs and mammals began to appear. They're my fellow Americans, my compatriots, but they're wallowing in tides of kitsch.They were well characterised by Maureen Dowd, the Pulitzer Prize-winning columnist of *The New York Times*, when she wrote: "Truthiness is a good story, one that feels right, but doesn't correspond to reality. Truthiness is what you *want* to be true."

'But not all Americans are like that. As I said, growing numbers are freethinkers who don't believe in a supernatural source of the universe. More and more people are coming out of the closet, saying things like: "the Bible is the best tool we have to convert people to rationalism". They belong to organisations in nearly every state of the Union that are affiliated to the Secular Coalition for America.'

'Organisations such as?' Sophie asks.

'Such as,' I pause to think and sag back on the chaise-longue, glancing around the room. In doing so I notice how closely the colours in one of the paintings on my left, a non-figurative work of art, resemble the crimson and orange dahlias blooming in the bed beyond the garden door. 'The American Humanist Association, the American Ethical Union, the Council for Secular Humanism, the Military Association for Atheists and Freethinkers,' I tell Sophie. 'There's also the Secular Student Alliance, and a Society for Humanistic Judaism. These organisations stand up for the view that a truly democratic and open society can only exist when all citizens are able to express their thoughts honestly, without fear of persecution or hostility.' I smile at Mrs Gresham and add: 'Just as Henry Ford said you can have any colour car you like as long as it's black, so there is freedom of belief in America as long as you believe in God. If you have doubts about the supernatural, or if you only accept naturalistic explanations, evidence-based arguments, you are considered unpatriotic by the noisy zealots. They've been transforming politics in America into a game for morons.'

'It's that bad, is it?' Sophie asks.

I nod. 'It's very narrow-minded, and quite recent. Anyone who listens carefully to evangelists holding forth in front of their audiences will come away convinced that much of religion in America is emotional masturbation. So many so-called patriots have become traitors. They've betrayed America's legendary open-mindedness. They are betraying the principle which the Founding Fathers emphasised repeatedly: that the United States would be a fastidiously secular nation. George Washington hardly ever referred to Jesus. He never took communion, he didn't ask for a Christian minister to be present at his deathbed. Thomas Jefferson was known for his hatred of priests; it was he who argued for a "wall of separation" between church and state. James Madison, fourth

President of the United States and author of the country's Bill of Rights, always championed freedom of conscience. *Those* are the principles that made America so inventive and new, so exciting and powerful – not decrepit dogma which even old oppressive Europe is abandoning.'

'Charlie doesn't have faith in dogma,' Sophie tells her mother. 'He says faith blinds people, it prevents them from thinking clearly. It stops them being self-reliant, keeps them infantile.'

'I was once a fervent believer,' her mother says. 'Now I'm barely lukewarm. I don't see how a merciful, all-powerful God can countenance so much suffering in the world. All the people killed and maimed by earthquakes and hurricanes; all the millions of babies born with the Aids virus, all their pain and suffering as they grow into childhood – is all this part of some divine plan?'

'It's a simple matter of fact,' I say, 'that there is no evidence whatever that we are made "in the image of God". We have no inkling what God "looks like". That God should look like *us* is proof instead that God is made in *our* image. I think it's vain in the extreme, a political sleight of hand foisted on the world long ago, the ultimate chauvinism, to pretend that divine perfection resides in the perishable goods which men and women manifestly comprise, who age and become decrepit, then die and rot and fertilise the fields as Earth continues to turn on its axis and the planets keep moving along their gravitational paths on the margins of our swirling galaxy.'

'I'm inclined to agree, though I hate to admit it. In the larger scheme of things we hardly matter at all,' Mrs Gresham says.

'Shakespeare would've got on well with Darwin,' I suggest, 'if they'd managed to meet across the centuries. Two magnificent Englishmen – what a chat they'd've had, how the ideas would've popped!'

'What makes you say that?' Mrs Gresham asks.

'Darwin's vision. He wrote in one of his notebooks, "Man is a frontier instance" by which he meant that we humans as a species were always arriving at a new horizon, we were always longing to transcend the status quo. Darwin believed it was in our nature to want to move beyond settled traditions into new realities.

'Fundamentally, we are not a conservative species, he believed. We want to go forward, not stay put. We want a better life, better health, better relationships. That's why we no longer hang, draw and quarter prisoners, or force children to work down the mines, or enslave black people, or pogromise Jews in the name of God for two thousand years, or believe in witchcraft.

'That's why people throughout history have migrated to other lands in search of better opportunities. They came in huge numbers to the United States, the land *par excellence* of immigrants, I am proud to say. That's why we have so many research institutes and pour so many billions into projects aimed at changing conditions in every realm we inhabit. Now we're in process of improving our human nature itself.'

'What's in all this knowledge for you personally, Charlie?' Mrs Gresham asks. 'What sort of livelihood does molecular biology afford?'

I smile sweetly at her. She's wondering whether I can afford her daughter's lifestyle. I love being with her daughter. I want to be with her all the time. But the truth is I'm not sure how Sophie and I will actually get on. She and her mother are arts people, whereas I'm a scientist. I have a premonition that love alone might not be enough to bring fulfilment. One's interests, the work one does, can't be left out if the relationship is to be truly satisfying. It astonishes me how shallow many people think the human spirit is, how one-dimensional.

'My colleagues and I at the Institute of Molecular and

Neural Genetics in Cambridge have long ago computerised the sequencing of base pairs,' I explain to Mrs Gresham. 'In the digital representation of a genome, each of the bases appears on screen as a differently coloured rectangular strip. The first draft of the entire human genome is in the public domain, thanks to the staunch public spiritedness of the Sanger Centre led by John Sulston who made their findings available to everyone as soon as they emerged. But *we* are doing fine-tuning work. We're filling in gaps, discerning the precise and complex order in which the millions of molecules of adenine, thymine, guanine and cytosine appear in any particular stretch of DNA.

'So far, we've stored on silicon chips about a quarter of the three-billion base pairs of which the human genome consists; and we're adding many more each month. With any luck, faster sequencing methods will become available to speed up our work. We're convinced that digital disks will in due course hold people's entire genetic blueprint. People can then acquire their genetic profiles in a matter of minutes by providing saliva from a mouth swab or a small piece of skin or a single hair taken from any part of their body. We already screen for mutations and problem genes for hospitals and insurance firms, and carry out forensic DNA analysis for the police.

'The new field of medicine called pharmacogenomics will soon be tailoring treatment to individual patients. The medicine used will depend on individuals' own precise DNA makeup, with no negative side-effects. Likewise nutritional genomics: we're beginning to understand how food interacts with genes, why some people get fat on certain diets while others don't, for example. And how drugs such as crack, cocaine, heroin and alcohol interact with genes – why some users get hooked more quickly than others.

'The money involved, the extent of the global market, hasn't yet been computed, but we're talking massive billions, Missus Gresham, not mere millions.'

Mrs Gresham now smiles sweetly at *me*.

We sit together for another hour in that tastefully furnished room, and the rest of our conversation covers everything but science.

Not wanting to bore them by going too deeply into the complexities of my work, I don't mention the DNA microarrays that enable us to study dozens and even hundreds of genes simultaneously. I don't refer to the subtle ways in which groups of genes work together, faulty ones combining to produce breast cancer, for example. I don't tell them that colleagues in labs around the world have so far sequenced the complete genetic makeup of 600 viruses, 37 bacteria, one fungus, a worm, a fruitfly, a honeybee, a bonobo ape, as well as the human genome which I did mention to them. Agriculture too is going to be transformed. Researchers have laid bare the 116 million base pairs that comprise *Arabidopsis thalia*, popularly known as thalecress, which, though a weed, is closely related to edible cabbage.

I don't trouble Sophie and her mother with details of the ribosomes, the machinery within each of our cells that takes each strip of DNA code and assembles the chains of amino acids which fold into proteins with peculiar three-dimensional structures, including testosterone and oestrogen; ribosomes 'read' the DNA code of life and turn it into life itself: it might be too complicated for them to grasp all of it in one afternoon. I don't touch on the role of messenger RNA, or the mitochondria inherited only from the mother, or mitochondrial DNA's function of turning sugars into energy. Nor do I mention that our understanding of the mechanisms of inheritance has been transformed. Research colleagues have found that the gene *daf-2* controls the *rate* of ageing throughout the organism and they are manipulating the way it works in order to understand and slow down the ageing process.

Telomeres are the protective caps at the ends of chromosomes, and scientists at Spain's National Cancer Research Centre have found that biological ageing corrodes people's telomeres, shortening them. A point comes when the shortening initiates cell death; the stem cells of people's tissues stop regenerating and the process of ageing starts. This indicates that ageing is actually a disease and that telomere re-activation has the potential to *reverse* the ageing process. Teams of researchers are pursuing that line of inquiry.

Meanwhile, work at the University of California, Los Angeles has shown that the transcription gene FOXP2, though generally the same in humans and chimpanzees, has in humans two different amino acids which make for differences in the structure of brain tissue and the neural circuitry involved in our ability to speak. The amino-acid composition of the FOXP2 gene in humans changed approximately at the same time that spoken language began to appear in evolutionary history.

Our project at the institute in Cambridge has been to isolate this gene and insert it into the genome of bonobo chimpanzees to see if that would enable them to speak too, by way of developing our transgenic skills for medical purposes. Our objective is *not* to change chimpanzees into ventriloquists for the amusement of shallow humans – we aren't running a circus. Our purpose is to zero in on the molecular sources of inherited diseases and to slow down the ageing process. To do *that*, however, we have to hone our transgenic skills. We have to swap genes as a matter of routine. Results so far of speech in a chimpanzee have been encouraging; they demonstrate that our ability to manipulate genes precisely is growing steadily.

Synthetic biologists are on the brink of transcending some of the ancient legacies of disease and disability. We are getting closer to alleviating the pain and suffering that have assaulted human dignity so pitilessly ever since our evolutionary ancestors, *Homo erectus*, the planet's original hunter-gatherers, left the forests nearly two million years ago and began walking upright. They walked approximately eight miles a day across the grasslands in search of food.

16

I'd already said I *would* marry Sophie – said it wholeheartedly in a state close to euphoria on that plane bringing us back from Paris. Even so, the truth is that I did begin to wonder how well Sophie's work interests and mine would gel. She was in the arts, after all. Might our different occupations come into conflict one day in some unforeseen way and spoil our rapport? *Should* I marry this gorgeous woman? Such were the hesitations and doubts assailing me as she showed me around Bristol in her car. What would her father have said had he been there when Sophie introduced me to her mother? He was away someplace on business; I only saw his thick, greying eyebrows a few weeks later.

Like a sober, clear-headed scientist I thought again about the snags there might be in marrying Sophie as she told me about Bristol's history, about its role in the slave trade in the 18th century. She took me in her convertible Jaguar to streets reminiscent of those times called Whiteladies Road and Blackboy Hill, and to the statue of Edward Colston in Colston Street in memory of 'one of the most virtuous and wise men of the city'. Sophie told me that Colston's company transported 100,000 slaves from west Africa to the West Indies and America. She said the slaves included women and children as young as six years old, each of them branded on their chest with the company's initials, RAC. The ships were crammed full of slaves for maximum profit, with no space to move or air to breathe. Those thousands of slaves who died in the atrocious conditions during the crossing of the Atlantic Ocean were thrown overbroard by the ship's crew.

Sophie then drove me from Colston Street partway up Park Street to Great George Street to visit Georgian House, the opulent one-time home of John Pinney who'd made his fortune from sugar plantations on the island of Nevis in the Caribbean.

The house was now a museum. Its spacious kitchen had a high ceiling and large windows; a big black kettle was hanging over the fireplace, and brass ladles, bowls and basins were in their dedicated places. The cabinet where the china, cutlery and tableware used to be kept was imposing, as were the dining room's gleaming mahogany table and chairs. The rich textiles and pillowcases in the bedrooms were pristine. In the rooms on the upper floors there were paintings and drawings with text of various aspects of the slave trade. Framed placards lined the walls: *Slave labour; Slavery through John Pinney's eyes; Buying slaves; John Pinney plantation owner; John Pinney moves to Bristol*, and other visual insights.

Pinney had no qualms about the source of his wealth, saying, according to one of the displays: 'It's as impossible for a man to make sugar without slaves, without the assistance of Negroes, as to make bricks without straw.'

We then drove up to Brandon Hill Park near the university with its tall monument on a knoll called Cabot Tower, erected in memory of the Venetian sailors John and Sebastian Cabot who, in ships fitted out by Bristol merchants, set sail in 1497 and came upon Newfoundland and, in the following year, what came to be called Hudson Bay.

I knew before the day was over what my decision was going to be, despite my professional work being so different from Sophie's. Her beauty was compelling, her erotic vibes irresistible. I didn't fully realise, however, not at that stage anyway, that ours *would* be a mixed marriage, that we'd be reaching out to each other across a major cultural divide – the arts versus the sciences – and that we would remain protective of the backgrounds from which we'd come, even though each of us might have surrendered some sovereignty to make a go of it.

Nor did I know then that I would become disgruntled by Sophie's refusal to come to the lab in Trumpington Street to see the huge transgenic breakthrough my colleagues and I had achieved, or that the resulting tension between Sophie and me would become a jarring, draining dissonance that threatened to destroy our relationship. I couldn't see into the future. I never guessed that lovely Sophie would put me under tremendous stress just by being herself, that in some way I would fall prey to the tyranny of good looks. Perhaps the pleasures of being in her company, hearing the modulations of her voice, inhaling her fragrance, blinded me to the signs that she would remain fiercely loyal to her background, as would I to mine, that we would turn out to be fiercely partisan to our old affinities.

My parents flew over from Boston for the wedding. After meeting Sophie and her family my mother took me to one side, kissed and hugged me and whispered in my ear: 'Look after her, Charlie. Cherish her. She's a treasure. You're a lucky boy – and she's a lucky a girl.' I was twenty-five years old, Sophie twenty-three.

My mother and father took the opportunity after the wedding to go and see the Georgian terraces and the remains of the Roman spa in the city of Bath, and drove to the charming town of Bradford-on-Avon not far away in Wiltshire with its small 11th-century Anglo-Saxon church of St Laurence and medieval tithe barn, and the grand houses built by wool merchants of yore. It wasn't their first visit to England. They'd come a couple of decades before, and brought me with them – I was eight years old at the time – to see the land which our ancestors had worked as tenant farmers before they migrated to America in the 1700s.

Sophie isn't particularly keen on the rigid, military-like hierarchy of the Church whose organisation she considers much too steeped in medieval cruelty and mysticism to appeal to modern men and women. So it never occurred to me that her allegiance to a higher power, to a god untrammelled by the pomp and circumstance of earthly office, would one day make her find fault with my work in molecular biology and refuse to come to the lab in Trumpington Street.

I didn't know when I agreed to marry her nearly ten years ago – it will be our tenth anniversary quite soon: we were married during an Indian summer less than a year after I arrived in England – that Sophie would lose her imagination for a while and forget what my colleagues and I were striving for. Or that she'd hold back from me something I valued greatly: her esteem and encouragement.

Nor did I have an inkling that a blond boy bleeding in a road accident which I'd witnessed and who was taken to hospital after I called an ambulance was going to strengthen the bonds between my lovely darling and me – or so it seemed.

It became clear soon after our wedding that Sophie was intent on 'opening your mind', as she put it. She found a way to firm me up with her fingers and flesh out the pleasures awaiting anyone willing to enter the world of literature without preconceptions – even a biologist steeped in molecules and more accustomed to manipulating nucleic acid bases than browsing through what my wife insisted were among the best books ever written.

Sophie the budding novelist guided me through those books.

She gave me private tuition that couldn't possibly have been more private. She went out of her way to 'broaden your reading', as she put it, to acquaint me with what she called the 'key works of literature' which I as a scientist was unlikely to have come across. Her assumption when she set out to 'cultivate' my mind was that as a research scientist uncovering the secrets of chromosomes I was bound to be ill-read, if indeed I had read anything of value at all. Soon after we met, Sophie started putting books in front of me, novels she recommended I read, short stories, poetry.

She continued her 'civilising' mission even on our honeymoon in Singapore.

She told me in our hotel suite about the legend of Oedipus and before I knew it I was reading how he killed his father in a quarrel without recognising him and then married his own mother Jocasta, not knowing who she was, and giving her four children. When the truth emerged Jocasta hanged herself, Oedipus blinded himself and spent his life as an exiled wanderer led by his daughter Antigone.

In the same way, by rousing my interest with a fascinating titbit about how the carpenter's wife cuckolded her gullible husband, Sophie had me devouring Nevill Coghill's translation of Chaucer's *Canterbury Tales* as fast as I could turn the pages. She thought it hilarious when Alison the lecherous wife in 'The Miller's Tale' stuck her naked bum out of the window at night so that Absalon, the love-sick church clerk waiting in the dark alley, could kiss what he thought were her lovely lips. Sophie read those lines to me as we lay together in the light of the bedside lamps:

'She flung the window open then in haste
And said, "Have done, come on, no time to waste,
The neighbours here are always on the spy."
Absalon started wiping his mouth dry.
Dark was the night as pitch, as black as coal,
And at the window out she put her hole,
And Absalon, so fortune framed the farce,
Put up his mouth and kissed her naked arse
Most savourously before he knew of this.
And back he started. Something was amiss;
He knew quite well a woman has no beard,

Yet something rough and hairy had appeared.

"What have I done?" he said. "Can that be you?"

"Teehee!" she cried and clapped the window to.'

Sophie's laughter in bed rises from her body like billowing waves of brown sugar.

'That was written more than six-hundred years ago,' she told me, shutting the book and placing it on my bare chest. 'Its vigour and earthiness was a breakthrough of the human spirit. It presented people as they actually were in flesh and blood, in all walks of life – not as the insipid, ethereal fakes they were supposed to model themselves on. It liberated feelings from suffocating dogma and freed people's inner selves in a way that no technology has ever managed to do.'

'You sound quite sure of that.'

'Unless of course,' Sophie added, turning her head to face me on the pillow, 'unless we think of poetry as a technology of words, a precise deployment of meanings and music that makes people more sensitive to feelings they only vaguely perceived before – then poetry and technology, poetry and science, are seen to be doing the same kind of work and aren't in conflict at all: raising consciousness, opening doors of perception in different parts of our minds.'

Sophie would talk to me in bed about what I'd read, and stroke my skin while she talked, and kiss it, making my appreciation expand and my interest rise up, so that I soon came to associate novels and poetry with soothing sensations and physical pleasure. I became a keen reader of the way-out stuff she put my way. I looked forward to our sexy seminars. My teacher never left me frustrated. She rewarded me fully for familiarising myself with the text she'd recommended.

A few of Shakespeare's plays and sonnets, Milton's *Paradise Lost*, Cervantes' *Don Quixote* whose incorrigibly romantic imagination impels him to see ordinary things as frightening adversaries everywhere; at one point, mounted on his knackered horse Rocinante, he tilts at windmills with a lance, taking them for giants: I read them all, at Sophie's sensuous behest.

Little booklists began to be compiled in our pillow-talk, as a result of which I found myself reading the charming stories within stories ending in cliff-hangers which the beautiful Scheherazade told King Shahryar in his bedroom to keep him from beheading her for *A Thousand and One Nights.*

My mind was then opened to the poetry in translation of someone I hadn't even heard of, the 13th-century founder of the Whirling Dervishes mystic order, Jalal ad-Din Rumi, whose thoughts, Sophie said, go to the heart of every religion, to the core of humanity's quest for meaning:

> Who makes these changes?
> I shoot an arrow right.
> It lands left.
> I ride after a deer and find myself
> Chased by a hog.
> I plot to get what I want
> And end up in prison.
> I dig pits to trap others
> And fall in.
> I should be suspicious
> Of what I want.

Sophie then introduced me to Wordsworth's 'Tintern Abbey', 'Lyrical Ballads' and the 'Lucy Poems'. Thereafter I registered the imagery in Coleridge's opium vision called 'Kubla Khan' and the 'Rime of the Ancient Mariner'. Then Byron and Keats were put my way, and Robert Browning – 'What became of soul, I wonder, / When the kissing had to stop?'

I was in two minds about Keats. On the one hand he struck me as primitive and self-deluded, exclaiming, ironically perhaps, in a letter to Benjamin Bailey in 1817: 'O for a life of sensations rather than of thoughts'; but on the other, he came across as sharp-eyed in a letter to Fanny Brawne in 1819: 'I have met with women whom I really think would like to be married to a poem and to be given away by a novel'.

Invisible bonds tied my heart closer to Sophie's when she handed me some writings of Ralph Waldo Emerson who was born in my native city of Boston in 1803 and whose works we kids had studied at school. Emerson was a founding father of the American attitude to life. In his essay on 'Self-Reliance' he says: 'whoso would be a man, must be a non-conformist'. He urged people always to strive for originality. He was surrounded in his youth by unusually brilliant and well educated women, one of whom, his poverty-stricken aunt, Mary Moody Emerson, taught him: 'Always do what you are afraid to do.'

Emerson had been a Unitarian minister at Boston's Second Church, but when his young wife Ellen died when he was twenty-seven he rejected the central tenet of Christianity, i.e. that humanity's redemption after the original sin of Adam and Eve was through Christ's sacrifice on the cross. He quit the ministry in 1832 and wrote: 'I will not live out of me/I will not see with others' eyes/My good is good, my evil ill/I would be free.'

Emerson's object was to turn the American mentality away from European models, away from uncritical copying of the past and toward its own fresh exuberance. 'We have not to lay the foundations of our houses on the ashes of a former civilisation,' he wrote. Nor was he particularly impressed by the past: 'What is history but a fable agreed upon?'

Among the novels I've read on Sophie's recommendation in the ten years I've known her are Balzac's *Lost Illusions*, Flaubert's *Madame Bovary*, Jane Austen's *Pride and Prejudice*, Emily Brontë's *Wuthering Heights*, *Middlemarch* by George

Eliot, and works by Dickens, Hardy, Tolstoy and Thomas Mann. And among the scenes that linger in my mind is the one from Dostoevski's *Crime and Punishment* in which Raskolnikov's beautiful sister Dunya is lured to Svidrigailov's room where he turns the key in the door and locks her in with him, intending to seduce her, by force if necessary, i.e. rape her. To his amazement, however, she draws a gun from her bag and aims it at his heart. As a scientist, I was convinced and satisfied by that scene. I like the way that a seemingly hopeless situation is changed by technology, in this case by the power of her gun.

Some people refer to Henry James, another anglophile American, as 'the master' and there are many reasons for doing so, not least his subtle analysis of relationships between individuals, his extraordinarily delicate monitoring of the way people's moods shift in the changing seasons of their hearts. His writing is like an ultra-sensitive thermometer registering even the slightest change in temperature in the feelings of couples romantically involved or intimate in other ways. I am no literary critic and have no such pretensions, but perhaps it is this disappearingly fine subtlety that eventually struck me as, if not effete, then specious. A point came when I found it difficult to finish another book by him which Sophie had handed me. Increasingly, he seemed to want to say everything in the same breath, in the same sentence that became ever more involved and convoluted, laden with endless subordinate clauses. I wasn't surprised to hear from Sophie that Henry James had told a friend in a letter that his books had become 'insurmountably unsaleable'. Poor aesthete: his clusters of sinuous subtlety made him unreadable in the end.

Having died in 1916, Henry James didn't live long enough to read the professor's advice to Lucy Nelson in Philip Roth's 1967 novel *When She Was Good*: 'please don't stuff your sentences so'.

Sophie assured me that James's sentences, with their

accumulating parentheses well on the way to being sclerotic, were nowhere near as dense as the endless digressions full of microscopic details which comprise Marcel Proust's 'vapid sludge' known in the English-speaking world as *Remembrance of Things Past*. More than three-thousand pages of high-society gossip and condescension in seven volumes, endlessly minute detailing of the quality of the air in a room, or the effect of a fleeting glance, or the flutter of a falling petal in an otherwise soundless garden, *A la recherché du temps perdu* is, Sophie said, a French classic in which a handful of priceless gems are deeply buried. I had to take her word for it; I only read one volume of Proust.

At one point as I read these books, I began to hear my wife's voice in my head. I began to hear *her* reading the lines which *I* was reading. It was as though I was being *read to* by her, read to the way a child is read to, spoonfed the 'great' literary works of Western culture. I knew for sure then that Sophie, who loves me, was trying to make up for what she considers my great moral loss: she was attempting to make good the 'intellectual emptiness' that became 'inevitable' once I decided to make my career in science.

What strikes me, despite Sophie's wide-eyed adoration, is that, with the passage of time, many of the books she put my way have become passé: filigree museum-pieces of the mind. They are exhibits under glass to mull over for a moment, scratch one's nose and say 'Mmm' about and then move on to the next embalmed relic.

Those books are the cultural analogues of dinosaurs and dodos. Each is a museum of antique fossils, and we as readers are unavoidably palaeontologists studying extinct forms of life. We are immeasurably more informed nowadays. We are more knowledgeable of structure and inner workings, more aggressively protective of our freedom – our modern spirit energetically keen as the 21st century proceeds to manipulate genes and compile improved versions of ourselves that have yet to live and make their mark on the history of our species.

We are locked into what is truly new.

We are at a brand-new beginning.

Transgenic faculties are the foundations of our future.

We have the wherewithal to transform human nature by looking beyond what Proust called 'the rusted gaze of old men', and we genetic explorers are getting on with the transformation work, enthusiastically.

The past, we now see with clear eyes, has served its purpose. The past is a placenta, a messy after-birth no longer needed and most hygienically dealt with by being flushed away down the lavatory bowl.

17

Whenever I ask Sophie why she won't come to the Institute in Trumpington Street, she waffles, she prevaricates. She never gives me what I consider to be a straight answer. She becomes defensive. She trivialises science, quite uncharacteristically, as if she's mentally confused. She comes out with stuff about how science is making the world more and more artificial, more and more false, how it's leaving society with less and less spontaneity, decreasing amounts of freedom.

One is expected to believe that the convertible Jaguar which Sophie loves so much is a natural, spontaneous phenomenon; the vehicle she drives every day grows in a garden and gets bigger naturally every time it rains. And the airliners we fly in each time we travel to the States, the quartz watch Sophie wears on her wrist, the cellphone in her handbag and the television we watch to see the latest news: all these products of science and technology are such integral parts of Sophie's life that she subconsciously considers them to be natural.

Everything is supposed to be *natural*. Only *natural* things are good, a logic which for some people seems to imply that bad eyesight is good because it's *natural*. And deafness is good because it occurs *naturally*, and cancer and memory loss and the ageing process.

And people who go to doctors to alleviate their conditions and lessen their pain must all be bad people, or at least false people, because everything the doctors do is *unnatural*. Taking X-rays is unnatural. Removing ulcers is unnatural. Performing hernia operations is unnatural. Putting fillings into teeth is unnatural – fillings don't occur spontaneously in nature. Nor do dentures, bandages, eye tests, blood tests or plaster casts after bones are broken.

There are people all over the world with metal strips in their heads, pacemakers in their hearts, artificial hips, prosthetic, that is to say, *artificial* limbs and artificial fingers, intraocular lens implants after cataract operations: they're alive and well and productive, enjoying their remaining years thanks to a whole array of astonishingly effective *unnatural* aids.

To say nothing of the increasingly popular 'natural' procedures involved in cosmetic surgery for which people all over the world have been paying willingly: facelifts, eye-bag removal, skin peeling, Botox injections, liposuction. We owe Mother Nature so much for these spontaneous, unplanned transformations.

From the look Sophie sometimes gives me – a look of embarrassment, of a longing for me to understand her plight – I get the impression that, despite what she says, my woman does want to break out of her inner prison, but can't do so without help because she hasn't figured out a sufficiently decorous way to unburden herself of outdated loyalties. She hasn't yet figured out how to be seemly as well as brave.

Sophie still suspects that there is in some undefined way something wrong, something scandalous, about animals being a bit more like people. Her attitude is strange, given the many way in which people show their love for animals. They kiss and cuddle them. They talk to them. They put garments on them – little jackets, caps, scarves, motorbike goggles. They send them greeting cards on their birthdays and keep an entire pet-foods industry in profits with the cash they regularly spend on food and other products for their animals.

An article in the business section of *The New York Times*

reported that companies traditionally known for human products, such as Gucci, Harley-Davidson, Ikea, Ralph Lauren, had begun selling products for pets, from shampoos to nail polish to gold-plated bowls, in the hope that their familiar brand names would appeal to America's 76 million owners of dogs and cats. Spending on pets had doubled in the last decade, the article said, to $34.3 billion, propelling it ahead of the toy industry, $20.7 billion, and the candy industry, $25.8 billion – and the amount spent on pets looked set to increase.

Pets in the United States are increasingly undergoing cosmetic surgery. They are having their ears pinned back or cropped, and being subjected to liposuction and Botox injections: being humanised still further.

The advertisement of one pet-foods manufacturer declares: '91% of cats like to be fed differently'. How does he know? How can he be so precise? Did he hand out to a representative sample of cats a questionnaire about their culinary preferences, along with pencils to tick the boxes?

It is all so anthropomorphic, so person-chauvinistic.

People train their animals to stand up on their hind legs in imitation of human beings. They train them to bring in the newspaper from the porch, to go and find game-birds that have been shot and retrieve them from the undergrowth, to take brandy to individuals who lie injured in the snow. They train tigers to jump through flaming hoops, seals to balance balls on their noses, chimps to walk on a tight-rope whilst clutching an open umbrella and a walking-stick and not be put off by the noise when the human spectators cheer and clap and whistle their acclaim.

All the evidence indicates that people want their animals to be more like themselves. This extends to the realm of psychology. Dogs, they say, are 'man's best friend'; cats are 'perfidious'; elephants 'never forget'. It is this anthropomorphic mentality that makes Walt Disney movies such as *Jungle Book* and *The Lion King* so very popular with adults as well as children all over the world: the films project on to the animal kingdom the moral concerns and perspectives of human beings.

So why the superstitious resistance to an animal that actually *is* a bit more like human beings thanks to genetic manipulation? Why the keenness to recoil from an animal that has inherited a human faculty which enables it to utter words and make its feelings known less ambiguously?

Our genetically enhanced bonobo has been learning to draw, learning to read simple words, learning to play some of the games humans play. A member of our team has developed an invaluable one-to-one rapport with her; she has taught the bonobo a few of the multiplication tables, taught her to memorise them by steady repetition, the way human children do. Ask this bonobo to point on a map of the world to where the USA is, or India, or South Africa, and she remembers precisely what we've taught her: she uses the pointer accurately. It is possible that her grasp of basic geography is better than that of some neglected children.

What the hell does it matter that her knuckles sometimes touch the floor as she moves around the institute, or that, instead of having skin like ordinary people, she's covered in dark-brown fur?

Why are people so jealous of their status as human beings?

Why are they so supercilious about it, so uptight?

Throughout history humans have been the prime species on the planet with malice in their hearts, the only creatures who deliberately and systematically lynch, shoot, bomb and terrorise their fellow creatures in batches of hundreds and thousands, with, they often say, the blessing of some god or other. A god who proves to be incorrigibly vindictive.

Humans are the only species who enslave entire communities and ship them across the ocean in chains, work them to death for profit, plan and carry out devastating missile and rocket attacks with calm precision, rape their slaves, rape their servants, rape elderly women and baby girls, beat wives and partners black and blue, throw acid in the faces of their brides because, *yaar*, the dowry is too small, bulldoze people's houses to make them homeless, chop their hands off in public places and conduct beheadings with curved swords in front of spectators *pour encourager les autres*, stab, poison and gas their fellow human beings without compunction, with organised zeal, in brutally ingenious ways.

Arbeit macht frei was the motto in the black metal gate at Dachau, a suburb of Munich where the ways and means of death camps were first tried out; and it became the welcome sign at the entrance to Auschwitz.

'The white race is the cancer of human history,' the celebrated American essayist, playwright and novelist Susan Sontag, herself white, declared in *Partisan Review*. She based her assertion on the cruel, grasping and contemptuous ways in which white people had treated other nations for centuries.

So why does everyone still think that being a person is such a big deal?

Why do they think that human identity is the bee's knees, is perfection, as if evolution has ended and there's no room for improvement?

Sophie doesn't care to respond to these queries; they aren't her cup of tea. She makes out she can't grasp why I'm so keen on slipping free of the past. She keeps blanking out the future when I refer to it. She blocks off that realm where renegades dwell, individuals who follow a star few others see as they try to escape the straightjacket of convention to become acquainted with scary, dangerous, exciting edges of the unknown.

Sophie's attitude is strange, a conundrum. She writes fiction, after all; she invents realities of her own. She's a novelist, and very successful. Her name is well known among a certain worldwide readership: Sophie Gresham. There's a spate of feature articles about her in newspapers and magazines every two years or so which dwell on her talent and keep going on about how creative she was from a very early age. She was creative when she was seven years old. She used to scribble her stories with a pencil and illustrate them herself with drawings of her characters made with crayons. She used to grip the crayons so hard, with such intense creativity, her teeth clamping her tongue sticking out of her mouth, that the heat of her little hand and its pressure would crush and melt the crayon and make a sticky mess on the page, on her palm and on the bodice of her dress when she wiped the stuff on it irritatedly.

Sophie is interviewed on television too. She is lionised there each time a new novel of hers is published or when she brings out a collection of short stories. I'm not sure the viewers hear everything that's said in those interviews because one tends to concentrate on Sophie's beautiful face, her wavy hair down to her shoulders, her lovely tits which she knows how to dress to best effect and then pretend she's forgotten about when she's responding to the interviewer's queries.

I admit, I can't take my eyes off her when she's on the telly. Sophie is the visual equivalent of what journalists call 'good copy'; you can't stop 'reading' her. Her father mentions female movie icons and says proudly that Sophie's sex appeal outstrips them all; her husky voice, he says, corroborates the erotic signals her body can't help sending.

I make sure the colour and contrast of the television are perfectly adjusted and the volume high enough. I wouldn't want the DVDs I make of the interviews to be spoiled in any way; their sentimental value in the future is going to be priceless. The children Sophie and I plan to have will be knocked out when they are born and see the sort of impact their mother used to make when she was younger.

It's like a party at our house when Sophie is on TV. Her mother and father come from Bristol for the occasion. Her mother's mature beauty is elegantly turned out as usual and lends our home a certain established style, a taste and distinction vitalised by a sensuality that is still seductive. Sophie's mother always reminds me of how gracefully Sophie is likely to age; seeing her from time to time reminds me that I have to look after my health if I hope to keep up with Sophie as the years go by. Sophie's father too is well preserved; his grey eyebrows and moustache give his happy face an authority that is neither heavy nor unduly staid. He is affable and suave, smart in blazer, chinos and shiny brogue shoes. My guess is that, as well as a successful property business, he's had a long and satisfying sex life.

I invite a couple of friends along as well for the TV gig and lay out on low tables salmon-and-cucumber sandwiches to eat as we watch the screen. I uncork bottles of our best wine. I, too, feel proud. I know how lucky I am to be plugged in to a woman with such pulling power. There on the screen I see the source of all my sexual pleasure, the source of my happiness, the source, I have to say for the sake of completeness, of some of my disappointment.

I'm in a tricky position. If I say out loud what I truly feel, people will say I'm jealous. They'll say I *envy* my woman. And because I periodically do find myself in the grip of *sexual* jealousy, my protestations would sound false. The subtleties of what I feel would come out garbled. Embarrassed at having to explain what I mean, I'd find it hard to specify the difference between *sexual* jealousy and being jealous of my wife's literary work. I am most definitely *not* jealous of her work. Her work leaves a lot to be desired, the way I see it. But I might not be able to convince people of this. After all, as they say, I'm only a scientist. I don't have the gift of the gab.

The conventional wisdom is that I'm not a creative

person; I don't bring new things into the world. All my publications have been peer-reviewed papers in journals such as *Cell, Nature Genetics, Molecular Neuroscience, Proceedings of the National Academy of Sciences, Evolutionary Anthropology*, so who am I to speak?

People are poised to misconstrue. They don't read as well as they think they do. If I make a comment about Sophie's books, about the contents of her stories, they'll say it's just sour grapes on my part. They'll make out I'm finding fault with a lovely woman because I'm bitter in some way, because I'm a small-hearted shit.

Sophie's novels have won prizes. The sanitised, prettied-up past is constantly honoured by colluding sensibilities. The past need not be historically authentic, apparently; distortions, half-truths, evasions and disingenuousness are all acceptable. Sophie has been acclaimed for describing how glorious it was to be alive when Elizabeth I was on the throne; for tales about the marauding French buccaneers who ravaged the hill town of Rye in the 14th and 15th centuries when the sea still came right up to its walls and Huguenots fleeing religious persecution in their own country transferred their weaving skills to England; about life in the small Sussex town of Hawkhurst when it was an iron-founding centre in the 17th century and William Penn, later the founder of Pennsylvania in the United States, owned most of the smelting furnaces.

The Haunted Moat was reviewed in every paper and literary magazine when it appeared; a number of critics said it showed a different side of Sophie's talent, a sense of humour subtle and mischievous as well as droll. It was Sophie's re-working of the 18th-century legend of a revenue man from Kent who drowned in the moat of Scotney Castle and whose ghost used to rise from the waters and go knocking on the drawbridge, trying again and again to finish in death what he'd failed to accomplish in life: collect a sum of tax-money owing to the Exchequer.

'Why don't you write about the present,' I ask Sophie from time to time, 'about the world we live in today?'

'Why should I?' she replies.

'Because the present is much more interesting than the past.'

'Oh yeah? In what way?'

'A ghost knocking on a drawbridge – whatever next?'

'The ghost-story genre is entirely respectable – it goes back at least to Dickens' *A Christmas Carol*. In *The Turn of the Screw* by Henry James, the narrator/governess cares for two children haunted by dead servants. Edith Wharton, Ruth Rendell, A.S. Byatt, Penelope Lively have all written ghost stories. Supernatural tales can be fun – don't take them so seriously.'

'Ghosts are so clichéd, so kitschy. They can do things we can't do. They can rise up from the waters of a moat – real handy that ability will be in the 21st century.'

'It isn't just ghosts, though, is it?' she says. 'It's the past as such that you don't like, being American. You Americans hate the past.'

'The past is grossly over-rated, let's face it. We learned from the people who lived there, gained invaluable knowledge and insights from the likes of Newton, Boyle, Benjamin Franklin. But we've gone way beyond them. They had short days and dark nights. They had no electric light, no telephones, no movies or public libraries, no cars, trains or planes, no fountain-pens or typewriters, let alone computers, just quills which you couldn't grip properly, and gunky ink. Their medicine was primitive, Sophie. Disease forced families to funerals almost every month, no matter how long or hard they prayed.'

I remind Sophie that people in the past had no recorded music – only the rich could be present when music was made. But *we* can enjoy CDs of Haydn symphonies or Maria Callas singing Puccini arias. We can marvel at Ella

Fitzgerald's scat-singing with Louis Armstrong on trumpet whenever we like. Available to us any time is the fiery voice of Aretha Franklin from Memphis, Tennessee, Ike and Tina Turner's hurricane of emotion called 'River deep, mountain high', and Queen's enduring performance of 'Bohemian rhapsody'. We can appreciate with no hassle Bob Marley, Radiohead, Franz Ferdinand, the Kaiser Chiefs, Courtney Pine. We have so much choice thanks to technology that in our tastes we are now all eclectic.

'Even Voltaire and George Washington had no running water. People in the past used to stink — that's why the rich splashed themselves with perfume. There was no sanitation. People used to shit and piss in the fields, just like the horses and dogs.'

Sophie smiles when I make those sorts of points. 'I know,' she says. 'Their standards were much lower than ours.'

'Well then. Why don't you write about *our* times? Things are more complicated now, much more challenging. In the midst of supermarkets with great mounds of food there are anorexic women who look like sticks and think they're fat. And in the same neighbourhoods hugely obese people waddle and roll around their lives with the most enormous arms, bellies and backsides. In conditions of unparalleled convenience and comfort more people than ever are clinically depressed. Something new in the annals of human history: teenagers, even pre-teens, who commit suicide. An interdependent world full of anger exploding with violence. You have the brains, Sophie. Let go of the ghosts and turn your mind to more urgent matters.'

'I might do so, one day,' she says, dead serious, keeping eye contact. 'Who knows? I'd like to, Charlie — write a modern novel. If only I can find a way into an engrossing modern theme.'

Sophie always gazes at me after these exchanges. The look in her eyes seems to indicate that I've struck a chord, that I've reached something. It doesn't last long, though. Her expression soon changes, back to her customary way of seeing things, back to her belief that she's on safer ground when she's delving in the past.

That's the trouble with Sophie: she keeps playing safe, even though she sometimes says she definitely will write about our own times if she can think of a sufficiently interesting theme, something emblematic.

Her parents, a couple of our friends and I settle down in a semi-circle in front of the huge flat television on the wall. We eat the salmon-and-cucumber sandwiches, sip the wine, and pay close attention as the interview begins.

'One of the ideas of your novel,' the interviewer says, 'possibly the central idea, is that love between individuals, no matter how intimate, is always in the public domain. When did you get that idea?'

'Certainly not the day before I started writing,' Sophie replies with a friendly smile. 'You get the germ of an idea, who knows where from, and it gradually grows in your mind and bounces about there as you get on with your life. It's often weeks, perhaps months, before the idea is sufficiently developed, sufficiently rooted in a social context. And until it *is* rooted in a context, all you'll have is abstract ideas floating in your head, third-rate philosophy. You won't have the beginnings of fiction.'

'You mean there's an analogy between individuals who are in love always being in a public domain, and ideas for a novel always being in a social context?'

'I've never put it that way, but yes, I think you're right. Individuals only have resonance in relation to the rest of society. No matter how individualistic or self-centred they are, they depend on society for their jobs, their incomes, petrol, tap water, electricity, other things to spend their money on – the architecture surrounding them, what their life chances are. When they fall ill, they depend on the knowledge and skills of doctors who've been trained at some expense in reputable institutions. People don't live in the Garden of Eden where everything is laid on free of charge,' Sophie says with a charming smile. 'They tend to live in a rat race, forced to consume, to display the rewards of their success – no matter how meagre their success might be. That is the context in which God wants people to cope. It is God's will that love be a challenge, not a boring scenario of couples nodding off.'

'And yet your novels and stories aren't about the rat race, and never have been.'

'That's true.'

'Surely that's inconsistent.'

'How d'you mean?'

'You say most people live under pressure, in a situation that tends to create stress, yet you've never written about stress. All your work is set in the calmer atmosphere of the past.'

This interviewer isn't as dull as his grey suit suggested. He has zeroed in on the main criticism I myself have of Sophie's work – the contradiction between what she *says* and what she *writes*.

He keeps smiling at Sophie in an embarrassed sort of way, however. He keeps lifting his arm and running his fingers through his hair. He's nervous, twitchy. It's his eyes that are giving him problems; he can't take them off Sophie's tits. He can't stop staring at her cleavage. He's obviously not used to women in the flesh. Maybe he went to one of those all-boys private schools the Brits call public schools. His professional demeanour is being undermined by the sex appeal pulsing from the person in front of him. The way he fidgets about, crossing and uncrossing his legs, suggests he might have a hard-on; his dick might be adding to his disarray. He's talking fiction, but his heart is focused on the facts of the female in front of him. If he doesn't get his act together, he's going to be feeling a dampness down in the region of his dick.

'The past may have been calmer, more ordered,' Sophie says, 'but it wasn't a paradise. Tremendous social upheavals were taking place. Families were being driven off the land as farming became mechanised. People in Oklahoma who were caught in the dreadful Dustbowl preferred to head west to pick fruit and vegetables in California where they earned a pittance that was preferable to being utterly destitute, as shown so graphically in John Steinbeck's great novel *The Grapes of Wrath*. Don't think that modern times have a monopoly on anguish. They don't. People used to be transported to Australia for stealing a loaf of bread. They used to be hung, drawn and quartered for crimes we wouldn't consider capital offences at all. The attitude of the wealthy was nothing less than shocking. That's why people felt there was no justice in the world.'

'The past is a hard place, a cruel place,' the interviewer declares.

'It manifestly is,' Sophie replies. 'As Margaret Atwood reminds us: "Nostalgia is the past without the pain." The gaps between the rich and the poor were much wider, disease and disability were more prevalent, and very few people had the benefits of an education.'

'But Sophie – sorry, I mean Mizz Gresham – although what you're saying is true, it's not there on the pages you write. There is no stress in your books, no suffering. Your books are full of beating hearts and flushed cheeks, clandestine assignations, fan-flapping, and concern about how many acres will be inherited along with the house on the hill.'

'And what is wrong with that, may I ask?' Sophie replies. The passion of her response makes her lean towards him, makes him see her cleavage from a different angle. A nervous smile flickers across his face. His hand shoots up to his head like a proxy dick roused and bewildered. 'What is wrong with writing stories about love that sell well,' Sophie asks him, 'that keep readers clamouring for more?'

'I'm not saying it's *wrong*,' he blurts.

'Then what the hell *are* you saying?'

I'll say it again: Sophie my woman is feisty enough to take on any male who wants to have a go.

In spite of her undoubted imagination, however, which is celebrated in the media every two or three years, she can't seem to grasp *my* point of view. She can't, or won't, see things from *my* professional angle. As folks in my native America put it, she doesn't dig where I'm coming from. It sometimes seems that we speak a different language, or at least radically different dialects of the tongue which Shakespeare, Marvell and Pepys are also said to have spoken. We smile and kiss and cuddle quite a lot, Sophie and I, but on one intellectual plane our minds seldom meet.

And it is there, in the gap between our perceptions, that a worrying tension has been getting worse.

Divorce is as rampant here in the UK as it is in the US. Divorce, the breakdown of relationships and marriages no matter how happy they once were, grows from small seeds. It grows because of negligence and carelessness, because of immaturity and/or shallowness. There might be old angers inside individuals that have congealed into protective shields, angers that have stopped them seeing things clearly or hearing unambiguously what other people say.

I don't want Sophie and me to split up, ever. I love her too much. So I have to be on guard. I have to tend the garden of our marriage and plan for the future. I have to find a way to change Sophie's mind and get her to come to the institute of her own free will. She'll see then that in this age of stem-cell research, molecular cloning, in-vivo imaging of protein interactions, tissue-engineered bones, regenerative medicine and keyhole surgery it is simply weak-minded to believe that human inventiveness has come to an end. Instead, Sophie will see for herself that we're in the midst of a quantum leap into a new biological dispensation.

We've begun to close the gap between other denizens of Earth and ourselves and to share immunities to diseases that lie in particular spirals of DNA.

Borrowing resistance to human maladies which our primate cousins have enjoyed since the year dot – *that* is now the name of the game: *chimerics*.

As for the public's response, it will probably be a matter of getting over the yuk factor. There's likely to be a period of shuddering at the thought of such sharing of immunities, a deep kind of heebie-jeebies revulsion. The root of this reaction will of course be people's supercilious attitude to other forms of life on Earth, based on their ignorance of the many molecules which we have for aeons shared not only with animals but with insects as well.

The gains in health, however, are definitely going to be ours.

That is what's in the offing: built-in protections from diseases through rearrangements of molecules in our cells, the fending off of ageing in a *natural* way and the resulting extension of intellectual and physical vigour of a kind our ancestors could not even have dreamt of.

18

His blond hair had a sheen to it, his chin was pointed and he was pedalling a bicycle in the on-coming lane. Crouched forward as he gripped the handlebars, he was swaying slightly from side to side. I saw him clearly through the windscreen of my stationary car as I waited in a line of vehicles for the traffic lights to change. He was about twelve years old and wearing a T-shirt and short pants; I noticed the paleness of his knees and shins rising and falling on the pedals. There was a wickerwork basket fixed to the front of the handlebars.

He hadn't quite come abreast of my car when the removals van behind him surged forward suddenly under a burst of acceleration and struck the back wheel of his bike. I heard a sound of metal crumpling as the fender, what English people call the mudguard, was crushed into the rim of the wheel, bending it out of shape, and saw the shock in the boy's face as the impact of the large vehicle flung the bike sideways and propelled him upwards. He went hurtling over the handlebars like an ungainly four-limbed missile on to the sidewalk, his head taking the brunt when he landed on the paving stone.

I opened the door of my car, waited for a gap in the traffic, and dashed across the street. Blood was flowing from his nose. Under the side of his head, flat on the ground, was a circular seepage of gore like a red corona which made me think he was bleeding also from his left ear or from a badly lacerated left cheek. The blood was thick and dark, shining like lacquer. He was dead still. His torso was on the sidewalk but his feet in white sneakers were on the tarmac, in danger from the vehicles passing by. The removals van hadn't stopped.

I took hold of his thin legs just above his socks and moved them on to the sidewalk, turning his body some ninety degrees in the process. I thought it best not to touch his head; it might be fractured. I checked his pulse – he was definitely alive – and registered the time; it was 19:07 and beginning to get dark. I pulled my phone from my jacket pocket, keyed 999 and asked for the ambulance service.

'A boy was knocked off his bike about two minutes ago by a removals van that didn't stop,' I said. 'He's lying unconscious and is bleeding from his nose and head. He needs medical attention as soon as possible.'

'Where exactly is he?'

'In Silver Street, around the corner from Trumpington Street, opposite the Anchor pub, near the River Gate entrance to Queens' College. I can see the wooden Mathematical Bridge across the River Cam from here. D'you know where I mean?'

'I know Cambridge, sir,' the woman replied. 'You're on the bridge at Mill Pond.'

'Exactly right. How long will you be?'

'Not long. Depending on the traffic, about fifteen minutes. Hold on a moment, please.'

I held on for about thirty seconds.

'An ambulance is on its way to you,' she announced.

'The sooner it gets here, the better.'

'Can you stay with the boy until the ambulance arrives?'

'I guess I could, but my car is blocking a row of other cars. Can you hear the impatient honking?' I asked, moving the phone from my ear and pushing it towards the sound of the blaring horns.

'It would be best if you stayed with the boy,' the woman's voice came back. 'If it's possible, drive your car on to the pavement so the traffic behind it can move away and then wait with him until the ambulance gets there. But meanwhile, what's your name, please?'

I wondered why my name was necessary, but, not wanting to be the cause of a delay, I said: 'Charlie Venn. Doctor Charles Hadley Venn, but I'm not a medical doctor.'

'Do you spell that with two Ns?'

'Yes, two Ns. I was on my way home from work at the Institute of Molecular and Neural Genetics in Trumpington Street when I saw the accident happen. It was a green removals van that knocked him off his bike, but I didn't see the number-plate or the company's name.'

'A green van? Sounds like it might be a local firm. Do you know the boy's name by any chance?'

'No, I don't. I don't know him at all,' I replied and switched my phone off.

I looked down, noticed the blood seeping from the boy's nostrils and blood spreading also from under his head. And I saw two paperback books which must have fallen from the basket when the bike tilted and crashed to the ground. I stooped and picked them up; one was a book of Sudoku puzzles, the title of the other was *CHESS: The Art of Deep Strategy*. I put them in the basket and dragged the bike with its bent back wheel across the sidewalk and left it against the wall.

I waited again for a gap in the traffic, hurried across the street and drove my car on to the opposite sidewalk. The cars I'd been blocking roared away immediately. Then I came back to the blond boy with the pointed chin and saw that his blood was still spreading; the red pattern around his head was bigger than before.

Four or five pedestrians who looked as though they might be heading home from work stopped briefly and stared at the boy lying motionless, and at his twisted bike against the wall.

'The poor child,' a middle-aged woman wearing a beret

and glasses said to me. 'You'd've thought he would have stopped, the driver of that van.'

'Did you see his number-plate?'

'I only caught the last part – 6JGN, I think – or perhaps 8JGN.'

'That might be enough, plus the fact it was a green removals van. I called the ambulance. Will *you* tell the police? It's a case of hit and run.'

'Yes,' she said, 'right away.' She opened her handbag, brought out her mobile, thumbed in the digits and put the phone to her ear. Looking down at the boy, she said again: 'The poor child. I hope he's going to be all right.'

I hoped so too, and as I stood guard over his maimed body in the breeze of that September evening, watching the lights of the cars passing by and the silhouettes of their drivers and seeing people going into the pub directly opposite, I had no idea that he was going to enter my life again, vicariously. I couldn't know he was going to change my relationship with Sophie greatly for the better by ending the disagreement between her and me that was putting the skids under our life together, poisoning our happiness.

I had no idea that a boy we didn't know at all was going to achieve in one afternoon what all my cajoling, sweet-talk and exhortations had failed to do for well over thirty months. It was the furthest thing from my mind: that a complete stranger was going to melt Sophie's obduracy in a few days' time, change her mind at last and, despite her shuddering distaste, make her come to the institute of her own free will and see for herself the transformation we'd accomplished.

I got my phone out again and sent Sophie a text message about the accident. I said I was OK and that I'd probably be home in about a half-hour. On an impulse I took a photo with the phone of the bleeding boy and sent it to Sophie as well.

As I waited for the ambulance in the gathering gloom

and kept an eye on the damaged bike, I thought again about Sophie's stubborn refusal to come to the lab and meet my colleagues. She'd been refusing point blank for more than three years to come to my place of work, a research institute internationally renowned for its investigations into genes on particular chromosomes. I couldn't understand why. It wasn't as though I'd been asking her to help me commit murder or some other heinous crime. I'd been wanting her to come and see our landmark achievement and understand its implications for human health, that was all.

What was so wrong with scotching inherited diseases at source and extending youthfulness? Who would find fault with 100 vigorous years as the standard life-span? Why was it unacceptable to prevent breast cancer before the women concerned were born, or childhood diseases before the infant emerged from the womb, such as inherited cancer of the eye, known as retinoblastoma?

Can sexual pleasure never be pure? Must there always be some bitterness sabotaging the bliss?

It struck me as sneaky, treacherous, how disgruntlement lies concealed in the very heart of one's happiness, how it eats away quietly, corrosively, at one's sense of contentment.

Just as my project at work was coming to fruition after nearly ten years of painstaking concentration, steady slog, and we were planning to fly Bertha to New York to show the world what we'd achieved and take our bows in the blaze of publicity; just when it was time to start congratulating my colleagues and preparing ourselves for the backlash from traditionalists around the world – poor deluded traditionalists: their beliefs were about to implode again under the pressures of reality – the atmosphere at home turned negative.

In the last three years particularly, when the early signs of success began to appear and I found it difficult to contain my excitement, the vibes in my private life started to jangle.

My enthusiasm left Sophie cold. She refused to share it. Each time I invited her to the institute to come and see for herself what a huge breakthrough we'd achieved, she shook her head and said No. She was adamant. She made derogatory comments about my work, something she'd never done before; Sophie had always been well disposed to learning, to new knowledge. She said my colleagues and I were reaching too high. Who did we think we were, she wondered with uncharacteristic anti-science hauteur, trying to distort human nature like this, trying to play God. I'd never heard her talking like that before. Who'd been polluting her brain?

Our life together, which had been full of sex, lots of conversation, laughter in bed, long walks hand-in-hand ever since we'd met by chance on her Graduation Day – our relationship began three years ago to have something heavy in it, an invisible quality that made it sag, drag our spirits down, despite our happiness in every other respect.

I wondered as I stood on the sidewalk waiting for the ambulance how someone else, another man in my place, would proceed. If *he* had a desirable woman with a big sexual appetite who kept demonstrating in all sorts of ways that she loved *him* and no one else – meals in intimate restaurants, gifts of ties, shoes, tickets to concerts and the theatre, trips to Paris, Florence, Prague – what would *he* have done when she turned around and told him she had serious reservations about his tampering with human nature, 'diluting its sacredness', as she put it, with baser animal nature, and in the process siphoning off what was divine in people and replacing it with profane stuff bound to be crude and ignoble?

Sophie was convinced my colleagues and I were involved in a stupid bargain; we were trying to swap in our lab the divine spark in human beings for something that couldn't but be dull and deficient.

How would another guy in my place have responded when this unfailing source of sexual bliss, this intelligent woman with a double first in modern languages who'd become a prize-winning novelist described his project as 'scientific arrogance' and refused adamantly to come to the institute to meet his colleagues and see for herself what he was up to?

Why do I still believe there *is* a way to change Sophie's mind and make her come to the lab of her own free will?

Sophie is bright. She's well educated, a graduate of Cambridge University where she studied French and Arabic. She isn't in-grown. She isn't parochial. She doesn't believe hers is the only country in the world or that there's only one point of view on all the continents. She's travelled abroad, talked with locals in their own languages, read foreign books and ancient texts. She's come to America with me about eight times over the past ten years when I've gone to give progress reports on the project – even though Sophie has always done her own thing while in the States. She's visited the Frick Museum to see Holbein's portraits of Thomas More and Thomas Cromwell. She's been to the Metropolitan Museum of Art on Fifth Avenue at 82nd Street to appreciate more than a hundred of Van Gogh's drawings from the late 1880s, including, she said, 'The Courtyard of the Hospital in Arles', 'Olive Trees' and 'Cottage Garden', and she has gone to check out the 9th-century Lindau Gospels and the 1455 Gutenberg Bible at the Pierpont Morgan Library on East 36th Street.

Sophie has never accompanied me to my genetics meetings.

Airports with their check-in routines, armed security guards, identity scans, passport controls and baggage reclaim remind Sophie and me regularly of the huge Atlantic Ocean between our two countries which airliners carry us across as we sit tilted back in our seats, talking, sleeping, watching the in-flight films with earphones on our heads.

If only I can find a way to dispel the misconceptions

clouding Sophie's otherwise clear judgement, we'll be more deeply in touch with each other, more attuned to each other's inner life, and move to a higher plane of happiness.

Except when we're doing our own thing, following our different professions – Sophie writing fiction in her spacious study overlooking a garden on two sides at our Georgian house in Grantchester, me at the institute in Cambridge just over a mile away manipulating nucleotides, the molecules which in their hundreds of thousands and sometimes millions comprise genes along the chromosomes – we go everywhere together. We swim in a college pool. We play squash twice a week.

It's impossible not to notice as I dart about the court with my racket, rushing to return the ball as it keeps thudding at speed from between the red parallel lines, how sexy Sophie looks in her hotpants patterned with sweat and her T-shirt sticking to her tits as she feints and falsefoots me, making me think she's going to backhand the ball diagonally across the court and then, at the very last moment, when I've already started to react accordingly, sending the ball instead straight down her own side, leaving me completely out of position, running the wrong way, thoroughly gulled and foxed.

Sophie is in control of her body, marvellously so. She speeds up suddenly, bounding backwards and forwards, twisting at the waist as she swings her racket, turning in anticipation of the returning ball's trajectory, bending low and stretching to lift the ball into a deceptive lob, and then, seconds later, whacking it in a way you wouldn't expect from a completely different angle, her hair tied in a ponytail swinging about, the sweatband on her forehead a narrow strap of blue, her feet moving in a blur of white socks and trainer shoes.

Sophie beats me at squash as frequently as I beat her. Her answer to the power of some of my shots is a cunning strategy: she doesn't try to power back but goes instead for awkward angles, dead balls near the bottom line, forcing me to move move move if I want to stay in the game. When she misses a shot that should've been easy to hit, her laughter rings out across the court. And when our bodies collide occasionally as we zigzag about, she gives me a quick kiss on the mouth before spinning away to reach the ball. We both know that the best way to keep fit and keep the game interesting is to play to win. Even so, she has the loveliest ways of reminding me that it is nevertheless only a game which we play principally for pleasure.

We're out of breath, heaving and oozing sweat when we step out of the court after the best part of an hour. Unfortunately, we can't shower together after the game; that's not allowed in a public place. I'd love to peel off my woman's T-shirt and suck her hot tits, then pull down her pants and shampoo her pubic hair under the jets of water, as I do at home every day. Instead, we have to part for a while and go separate ways down the tiled corridor adjacent to the swimming pool. Public showers don't accommodate erotic passion. Washing your woman in a place designed specifically for washing is considered too lascivious.

I have to control myself and wait until we get home.

'Don't be long in there,' I tell her as she heads for the women's showers.

'I won't be long,' she says, looking over her shoulder and smiling.

'I want to get home as soon as possible.'

'So do I.'

'I can't bear these separations. They leave me feeling bereft.'

'I love you, Charlie Venn,' she says, turning to me and swinging her racket in a downward arc, 'even though you're a sucker for a dead ball near the bottom line.'

Sophie and I make love incessantly, all over the place. She calls me to soap her back as she sits in the bath water and the next thing I know there are wet tit-marks on my shirt, the waist of my jeans and pants are on my shoes and suds are sliding down my stiffness into my pubic hair.

She sometimes parks her Jaguar in a quiet country lane around Grantchester Meadows near the village where we live, adjusts my reclining seat to horizontal and then climbs astride me, knowing that I know she has no knickers on.

Sophie isn't a tease. She doesn't work me up just to leave me frustrated with an unassuaged erection. She isn't like that. She always goes the whole hog. She always wants the full performance, preferably with a grand finale that has her heaving and panting and dripping her viscous joy down on to me. She likes being on top. She likes to make the running, to set the pace. It probably comes from the way she was raised, with nannies in uniform and summer trips to Seville and Venice, the indoor swimming pool they had at home where she and her twin brothers became excellent swimmers – it had sliding glass-doors to the terrace where jugs of fruit juice stood ready on the table; the private school she went to at Clifton in Bristol, and the knowledge that she was going to inherit a fortune and had better get used to having her way.

She looks into my eyes and says: 'Come on, Charlie. I'm yours for the taking. Don't keep me waiting.'

Afterwards, when we've both used the love rag, she drives me to the scented tranquillity of the Orchard Tea Garden behind a sagging country wall where we restore our strength with honeyed scones and a pot of tea at a table under the apple trees.

'The poet Rupert Brooke and the novelists Virginia Woolf and E.M. Forster used to take tea here between 1909 and 1914,' Sophie tells me between sips of tea, 'along with their philosopher friends Bertrand Russell and Wittgenstein.'

'They used to come here – to this place?'

'Yes, quite regularly, and two other friends of theirs, the

economist John Maynard Keynes and the painter Augustus John.'

For some reason I'm impressed. 'They used to come and drink tea here?'

Sophie nods. 'They'd come and relax here from the pressures of their work. You wouldn't guess, would you, from this unpretentious little garden serving tea that famous personalities used to be regulars here while they were at Cambridge. Jawaharlal Nehru, who later became the first prime minister of independent India; the students who went on to be pro-Soviet spies fighting fascism, Burgess, Maclean, Philby and Blunt; and Francis Crick and James Watson who got the credit for discovering the structure of DNA in 1953 – they'd get here by punting up the placid waters of the Granta river, or by pedalling bicycles along the path that crosses Grantchester Meadows.'

The first time Sophie took *me* for a stroll along a bank of the river it was a three-mile saunter on a hot cloudless day in summer. The sun was sparkling on the water, ducks and ducklings were gliding by in convoys trailing little ripples behind them, and the occasional crow came swooping from the trees for a nibble on the path in front of us.

Sophie had lived in the countryside as a young girl. Now in a wispy dress of white gossamer, a straw hat on her head, her feet in sandals, she pointed out and named for me some of the wild plants indigenous to England as we strolled along. The spindly, pale cluster-patterns of cow parsley; the chunkier, sticky weed called sweetheart; patiently waiting stinging nettles, Sophie said with a smile; the large, low-lying leaves of wild rhubarb; the tiny pink petals of campion; the delicate pointed yellows of celandine; and may, the other name for the hawthorn's blossom at the heart, as Sophie told me, of the piece of folk-wisdom about seasonal clothes: 'Cast ne'er a clout, till may be out'.

The last reminded her, she said, of other country rhymes

from her childhood: 'Red sky at night, shepherd's delight. Red sky in the morning, shepherd's warning'.

By the time the ambulance with its headlights blazing and blue light pulsing swung into Silver Street and pulled up at the kerb where the blond boy lay in his sticky blood, I had managed to control my disgruntlement and place it in perspective. Even before two paramedics opened the back doors and stooped and lifted the boy on to a bed with fold-away wheels, I had counted my blessings and realised again how fortunate I was to have a woman like Sophie.

And when I stepped to the damaged bicycle leaning against the wall and dragged it to the ambulance to ensure that it and the two books in the basket went with the boy, I didn't know that a few days later Sophie's refusal to come to the lab would have dissolved completely.

I had no clue that an unconscious kid on his way to hospital whose T-shirt was soaked with blood was going to enter my life again and deepen my relationship with Sophie in a single afternoon.

Genetic enhancement; undamaged genes replacing damaged ones that code for proteins which fold into the wrong shapes and cause diseases; genes from other species upgrading people's health and extending their youthfulness: Sophie would at last come and see for herself what my colleagues and I are embarked on: inherited cancers scotched at source and a whole range of killer maladies consigned to history.

As an American working in England, I often think of the early 20th-century dictum pronounced by US Supreme Court Justice Oliver Wendell Holmes, Jr: 'A man's mind, stretched by a new idea, never goes back to its original dimensions.'

19

Sophie hates being disturbed when her writing is in full spate: it blocks the flow of her thoughts, she says, it loses time and puts her in a foul mood, especially when she's working to a publisher's deadline. And as I'm usually away at the institute during working hours, it's our cook/housekeeper Margot Lane who normally answers the door when someone rings the bell. But on this fateful occasion Margot has the day off. She's had her hair cut into a sleek bob, applied lipstick to her mouth and gone to Wisbech to visit her sister, a ruddy, outdoors type with a woolly hat on her head and mud on her boots who trains greyhounds for racing.

So Sophie and I have arranged to dine out in Cambridge tonight. We've played an invigorating game of squash, freshened ourselves under separate showers, and Sophie has gone to University Library to continue researching aspects of life in medieval times for a collection of stories she's contracted to deliver. If the parking spaces at the library are all taken, Sophie leaves her car in front of one of the houses in Grange Road or near the gates of Newnham College in Sidgwick Avenue. Opposite is the Rare Books Library, one of the odder structures in Cambridge; its barrel-like roof gives it the appearance of an old-style jewel-box which I can't help staring at, while the brickwork in alternate horizontal bands of red and blue makes it look, to me anyway, like a building in a rugby jersey.

It's a short walk from there and Sophie stays at the library as long as necessary. Once she passes through the doors of the reading room she becomes immersed in long-gone realities and has to be jogged by a librarian when it's closing time. Sophie has been staying well into the night for the past week, poring over texts in the pool of light from a table-lamp. She's often up in the stacks, standing on one of the ladders to reach the dust-covered tomes from which a mustiness rises when she opens them and turns the yellowed pages. Sophie is endlessly diligent in her research, fastidious even about minute details.

So I'm at home alone on that red-letter day, drinking coffee in the kitchen, when the doorbell rings.

I can't think who it might be pulling into our drive and coming to see us in the middle of the afternoon. At this hour I'm usually at the institute in Cambridge, which is just over a mile from our house in the village of Grantchester.

Monday 12 September: I remember that day vividly. It marked the beginning of Sophie's change of attitude to my gene-transfer project. It marked what began to be a deepening of our love, thanks to the intervention of an unknown and unexpected visitor who came and rang our doorbell out of the blue. It was the day Sophie's adamant refusal dissolved and she decided at last to come to the institute, happily, of her own free will, to meet Bertha and see for herself what exactly our work entailed. Sophie told me she was going to switch genres; she was going to ditch historical romance and write a cutting-edge novel. She'd discovered her modern theme at last, she said.

That day was so important to me that I couldn't help registering three other unusual events which also took place then. (1) It was the day England regained the Ashes from Australia for the first time since 1987 under captain Michael Vaughan. After hours of nail-bitingly tense cricket at the Oval in London there was much passionate singing by the euphoric crowds in Trafalgar Square of Blake's stirring anthem 'Jerusalem'. I don't really understand cricket. As an American, I have no clue what 'silly mid on' or 'long off' signify, or 'gully' or 'square leg', but I couldn't help noticing the rapturous celebrations all over the country shown on television. (2) It was the day on which *the guardian* newspaper, founded in 1821, first appeared in its smaller, Berliner format with a fresh font for the headlines and colour on many more pages; and (3) it was the day on which President George W.Bush finally arrived in the centre of New Orleans fourteen days after Hurricane Katrina had struck; TV pictures showed him standing next to Mayor Ray Nagin on the back of a flatbed military vehicle moving along the flooded streets.

Those three events formed the public context of a very private development: an emotional breakthrough in my relationship with Sophie. It was the beginning of the disappearance of the single disagreement between us that had prevented our erotic joy from attaining perfection – and the harmonious start, or so it seemed anyway, of closer, tension-free times ahead.

When the doorbell rings, however, I'm at a loss as to who has come to see us at this hour. Thinking that it might be a letter or parcel arriving by special delivery, I don't bother to put down my mug of coffee when I go to open the front door.

Standing between the stone flowerpots at the top of the steps leading up from our drive with his back to his car at the edge of the circular lawn is a man of medium height. His grey hair is thick, neatly combed with a side parting. His eyes are bright blue, his jaw square and clean-shaven, and he is conservatively dressed in dark suit and tie. There's a faint whiff of soap about him. His bearing is upright and youthful. His face, dominated by the promontory of his nose and his high cheekbones, would be young too were it not for the blotchy, florid tones one tends to associate with heavy consumption of liquor or with the habit of being dyspeptic with rage, shouting angrily at every opportunity, vocationally livid. Such, at any rate, are my first impressions.

'Doctor Venn?' he checks, looking me straight in the eye. 'Doctor Charles Hadley Venn?'

'Yes?'

'The research scientist married to the novelist Sophie Gresham?'

His voice is crisp, distinct, nothing alcoholic about it at all. 'Yes?'

'I'm Jem Baldock, Doctor Venn. I wonder if you'd be good enough to spare me a few minutes of your time.'

'What's it about?'

'It's about the boy who was knocked off his bike in Cambridge last week.'

'How does that concern me?'

'I understand you were in the immediate vicinity when the accident happened and that you phoned for the ambulance.'

I cast my mind back. 'D'you mean the collision in Silver Street?'

'Yes.'

'At the River Gate entrance to Queens' College?' He nods. 'The boy was unconscious and bleeding from his nose and head. I waited with him until the ambulance came and made sure his bike went with him.'

'I've come to tell you, sadly, that he died.'

'Really? He died?'

'He did, I'm afraid.'

'I'm real sorry to hear that.' The news is so unexpected I don't know what else to say; I just stare at the man's face for a long moment. 'I was driving along on the other side,' I tell him. 'I'd just passed the Anchor pub and had to stop on the bridge at Mill Pond – you can see the wooden Mathematical Bridge from there. There's a high hedge that runs in front of the Fisher Building, and traffic lights at the pedestrian crossing to the benches on the other side.'

'I understand you might have witnessed the actual collision.'

'That's right, I did. I had to stop because the cars in front of me were waiting for the lights to change. The boy was pedalling along in the on-coming lane and I saw him tilt to one side and go flying over the handlebars when the removals van struck his back wheel. His head hit the sidewalk when he landed. I noticed his hair – it was shiny blond, and he had a pointed chin. A few pedestrians gathered round him for a while, and one of them, a woman wearing glasses, called the police.'

'As you say, his head hit the pavement. He was unconscious when the ambulance took him and his damaged bike to Addenbrooke's Hospital, but he regained consciousness the next day for about an hour. Although he was weak and pale, he managed to speak. He said the last thing he remembered was that he was pedalling along Silver Street towards the right-hand bend into Trumpington Street, something he'd done many times before. He wondered how he'd got to the hospital. When we told him *you* had phoned the ambulance and waited with him until it arrived, he asked us to thank you for your kindness. He wished you good health and a long happy life. His skull was fractured when his head hit the pavement, the surgeon said. Fragments of bone pierced the blood vessels around his brain. The operation to remove the fragments and relieve the pressure on his brain failed. He was certified dead two days ago. A member of the ambulance service gave us your name.'

'What did you say *your* name was?'

'Baldock. Jem Baldock.'

'What dreadful news, Mister Baldock, especially for the boy's family. Such an unexpected death.'

'Have you been along Silver Street since then?'

'No. I usually drive down Trumpington Street – it's the more direct way home. Why d'you ask?'

'The pavement where the boy fell from his bike is covered with flowers. His parents and other people have been placing bouquets on the ground where the fatal accident happened.'

'What a poignant sight it must be.'

'It *is* poignant. May I come in, Doctor Venn?'

'Yes, of course – please do.'

20

I open the door wider and stand back to let him in. He glances at the pictures on the wall, at the umbrella stand in the corner and at himself in the mirror above the old-phone table.

'I've just poured myself a coffee,' I say, lifting the mug. 'Would you like some?'

'If it's not too much trouble.'

'It's no trouble at all.'

I lead him from the hall through the house and in the kitchen motion to the chairs around the table. He smiles wanly and pulls out a chair; it makes a scraping noise on the flagstone floor and makes him look at me and pull a face in apology. He sits down, resting his forearms on the table. I get another mug from the Welsh dresser and take it across to the coffee bubbling in the percolator.

'Do you take milk, sugar?'

'Neither. Black is fine.'

I fill the mug with coffee, hand it to him and sit down in the chair opposite his. 'Are you with the police, Mister Baldock?'

'No, I've nothing to do with the police, nothing to do with earthly laws. I'm here on a much more important errand.'

He lifts the mug and takes a sip. The coffee is steaming hot. He blows on it and I notice how well defined his lips are; their pale colouring contrasts with the purply red complexion of the rest of his face. There are tufts of hair sticking out of his nostrils. He takes another sip and puts the mug down and I see grey hairs on the back of his hand jutting from the cuff of his white shirt.

'The police have traced the driver of the removals van that knocked the boy down,' he says. 'I understand the driver is going to be prosecuted for manslaughter. But it isn't only the boy's parents who are upset and sad. God isn't happy either when a young person dies. It upsets God when young lives are wasted.'

He looks at me directly, keeping eye contact.

I have no idea how he expects me to respond.

'Life is sacred,' he says, 'and we should do everything we can to save it.'

'It's too late, though, isn't it?' I reply. 'You said the boy was dead. You said that although he regained consciousness briefly, he was certified dead two days ago.'

'He's only twelve years old. He has his whole life in front of him. That's why we shouldn't give up easily.'

Baldock's eyes are bright blue, but there's nothing manic in them, nothing eerie. Nor is his voice unduly intense. On the contrary, it is relaxed, matter of fact. He sounds as though he knows exactly what he's talking about.

'What was his name?' I ask.

'Daniel Mullins, but his family and friends call him Danny. They all want him back. He has so much to live for, so much promise to fulfil.'

'I don't mean to be rude, Mister Baldock, but I'd better come clean. I'm a research scientist and—'

'I know you're a research scientist.'

'A molecular biologist.'

'Yes, I know. You work at the Institute of Molecular and Neural Genetics in Trumpington Street, in the Audley Hall mansion between Peterhouse College and the Fitzwilliam Museum. You're American, from Boston, and the institute is funded by a consortium of American venture capitalists called ChimeroGene.'

'You're well informed for someone who doesn't know me. You said you weren't with the police, so why've you been checking up on me?'

'We haven't been checking up on you,' he says and takes another sip of coffee. 'We've just been finding out, Doctor Venn.'

'Finding out what?'

'What you do, the kind of person you are. You're one of the institute's project directors. You've been flying to the States once or twice a year. Your wife Sophie Gresham the novelist is English – from Bristol. She graduated in French and Arabic from Queens' College, Cambridge and lived in France and in two Arab countries while she was a student – Egypt and Jordan.'

'You *have* been finding out, haven't you? But what have my wife's experiences to do with Danny Mullins or his death?'

'They give us an idea of the kind of person she is and, by association, a glimpse into *your* inner being.'

A stranger talking about my wife's experiences and my inner being. It occurs to me that if I smile it might seem as though I'm being rude, so I stop myself smiling by faking a cough and covering my mouth with the back of my hand.

'My wife doesn't even know you exist. And my inner being, as you put it, rests on foundations that are wholly secular. I'm sorry to hear that Danny Mullins died from that accident. I called the ambulance and waited for it to arrive because that's what any morally conscious person would've done. And if I knew them I would offer my condolences to his family, but I don't know them.'

'Ask and it will be given to you.'

'Excuse me?'

'That's what Jesus teaches us. Ask and it will be given to you. I've come to ask you to help us bring Danny back.'

'Bring him back? Where from – the hospital?'

'From death back to life.'

'Are you pulling my leg, Mister Baldock?'

'I'm serious, Doctor Venn.'

'You can't be serious. You said he was dead. He died two days ago and a certificate was made out to that effect.'

'O ye of little faith,' Baldock replies with a smile that is *so* patronising. 'The committee sounded out the members, a vote was taken and I was chosen as the emissary to come and appeal to your higher instincts.'

'What committee would that be?'

'The outreach committee.'

'And what is that?'

'It's the committee of our church which—'

'Your *church*? Look, Mister Baldock, I don't see how your church has anything to do with me.'

'I was coming to that.'

'Do you mean the Baptist church?'

He shakes his head: 'No.'

'What then? The Episcopal church? Pentacostal?' I try to think of another denomination. 'Catholic?' He shakes his head and it occurs to me that the death of Danny Mullins was just a pretext, a ploy to gain entry to our house. 'Tell me straight, Baldock – are you selling something? What are you peddling?'

He smiles at me, not exactly condescendingly, but with a degree of amusement in his eyes that is hard to miss.

'To each his own,' he says. 'If people are misguided enough to cling to institutions that have deserted them and left them stranded in the modern world, then that is down to them. If they want to go on bowing their heads to bureaucrats who don't give a damn about their difficulties and suffering, who break God's laws behind closed doors and think their cassocks and vestments conceal their guilt, then that is *their* choice. Priests who get their parishioners pregnant and then deny responsibility when the baby is born; bishops who rape under-age boys, bugger them in the locked vestry for years and years – there've been so many cases reported in the papers and on TV – here, in America, Australia, Ireland, Poland, you name it. Wherever there are Catholic priests there seems to be betrayal, rape, sexual violation. Is it any wonder that people have had enough of the hypocrites? Jesus warns us for good reason. Beware of false prophets, he says; they come to you in sheep's clothing, but inwardly they are ravening wolves – Matthew chapter seven, verse fifteen. So many of these sanctimonious clerics have been abusing little boys, seducing helpless women. Is it any wonder that they are being taken to court in droves, that their church, at last seen for what it is, is dying the death, losing trust, losing massive money in fines – more than a billion dollars so far?'

'And your church isn't dying?'

'On the contrary, our church is growing by leaps and bounds. We have twice as many members as we had last year. We are born again stronger each day. Do you know why this is, Doctor Venn?' he asks calmly, holding my gaze with his bright blue eyes.

'I can't say I do. And to be perfectly honest, I'm not really interested. As you just said, to each his own.'

'Yes indeed. To each his own.'

'If you aren't with the police and you haven't come to convert me to your religion, then why are you here?' I look at my watch. 'I have things to do.'

'I'm here to appeal to your higher instincts.'

'What exactly are they – my higher instincts?'

'Your sense of the value of a human life. Your sense that a man does not live on bread alone, but on every word that comes from the mouth of God. Don't you value human life highly, Doctor Venn?'

'Of course I do. That's why I went to Danny's aid – because of my solidarity with human beings. That's what molecular medicine is all about – solidarity with people, rooting out the genetic causes of disease, disability and ageing. It's the chemistry of love, as I've been trying to explain to my wife, the chemistry of being hale and hearty.'

'If you could save the life of Danny Mullins, would you do so?'

'You said he was dead.'

'Would you save his life,' Baldock insists, 'if it was in your power to do so?'

'If it was in my power – of course I would.'

'Well it *is* in your power. We in the alliance believe—'

'The alliance? What alliance?'

'God's Alliance – our church. We allies believe that everybody who knew Danny, who ever saw him alive, has appropriated an element of his vital force. And if all the people who knew or ever saw him are gathered together in prayer, the elements of his vital force which they perceived separately can be concentrated together and, with God's blessing, the spark of his life can be re-ignited by a collective effort of belief. Such is God's power to resuscitate and resurrect. Jesus said to Martha, the sister of Lazarus: "I am the resurrection, and the life: he that believeth in me, though he were dead, yet shall he live: and whosoever liveth and believeth in me shall never die," Book of John, chapter eleven, verses twenty-five and twenty-six. Jesus rose from the dead, Doctor Venn, and so can we if we have enough faith in his supernatural powers. You saw Danny at a crucial moment in his life – just before his head hit the pavement. Probably no one else witnessed that exact moment, so you have a unique contribution to make. Will you join us in prayer and play your crucial part in resurrecting Danny Mullins?'

'Look, this conversation is going downhill. I'm a scientist. I analyse reality objectively. My work is reviewed by my peers, checked, replicated. I don't pray, Mister Baldock. There's no one listening in the sky. The only collective efforts I'm keen on are the ones that deepen human solidarity. Professionally, I've been keen on the Human Genome Project. Do you know what that is – the Human Genome Project?'

'I've heard of it but can't say I do. Another smarmy army, sounds like.'

'It's the worldwide project whose purpose is to locate and analyse every single gene inside every cell in our bodies. It is based on the understanding we have of life as DNA triggering RNA triggering Protein. It's on the way to conquering diseases at source. A team of Scottish scientists at Ninewells Medical School in Dundee have identified a gene which codes for creation of the *glutathione S-transferase* enzyme which prevents the development of cancer in the first place. It's a breakthrough that heralds the transcendence of cancer in due course. My colleagues and I are deploying synthetic biology to achieve long, healthy, vibrant life for whoever wants it. You have *your* allies in heaven, Mister Baldock, but *our* allies are right here on Earth – the creative powers of secular knowledge, human insight and high-precision skills. Our passion and persistence are based on empirical evidence, not on the kind of zeal that keeps being translated into gobbledegook.'

21

Baldock doesn't react. He just keeps eye contact across the kitchen table. He seems so sure of himself. He lifts the mug and drinks more coffee, slurping audibly. I wonder how much longer I have to put up with him. He appears to be one of those people who are convinced that you have to be religious to have moral principles. He isn't exactly my cup of tea. I'd rather be with Sophie and I'm looking forward to dining with her in Cambridge tonight.

Eating with Sophie is doubly nutritious: drinking in her loveliness while swallowing the food vitalises all parts of me. We agreed to meet at the Eagle pub in Benet Street, have a drink there, then stroll across to the Greek taverna a few metres away in the paved alley alongside St Bene't's Church called Free School Lane. Sophie loves the *dolmades* they serve there in the Athens style: minced beef, herbs and rice wrapped in succulent vine leaves; and the *sousoukákia*, spicy meatballs cooked with aromatic herbs, tomatoes and wine, topped, according to taste, with a cheese and cream sauce. We'll probably share a bottle of *retsina*, preceded most likely by *taramasalata* and followed by *baklava* dripping with honey. Sophie loves her food.

But food isn't the only treat in that part of Cambridge. I love that little area of the city for a mixture of historical reasons as well. St Bene't's Church directly opposite the Eagle pub has a Saxon tower that was built during the Dark Ages, in 1025, and is probably the oldest surviving building in the city, its small yard enclosed by black metal railings.

No more than eight paces away, just across the narrow

street, is the drinking hole I cherish most in all of England. I've been working at the Institute of Molecular and Neural Genetics in Trumpington Street since October 1994 and have been popping two or three times a week into the Eagle pub, which I first heard about whilst still at Harvard. I go there, not so much for the Greene King beer for which I've cultivated a taste, or because of the modernised old-world ambience of beamed ceilings, wooden casks and pewter tankards, or because the food can be eaten either indoors or at one of the tables in the cobbled courtyard under a balcony adorned with hanging baskets of flowers and foliage, but because it was in that pub in 1953 that the helical structure of DNA was drawn on the back of a beer mat by two brilliant researchers: that famous expatriate American, as he then was, James Watson, and his older English colleague Francis Crick. They had based their initial drawing on DNA theory and a visionary hunch that soon proved to be wrong.

Beyond the Greek taverna in Free School Lane is the Whipple Museum of the History of Science housed in a hall of the Free School that was built in 1624. A few metres further along on the left-hand side is the honey-coloured stone façade of the Cavendish Laboratory where the Nobel Laureate Ernest Rutherford became director in 1919 after splitting the atom at Manchester University in 1917 in a nuclear reaction between nitrogen and alpha particles in which he discovered, and named, the proton. The laboratory was named after Henry Cavendish, the gifted English physicist who discovered hydrogen which he called 'inflammable air' in 1766; he also discovered the composition of water, the composition of nitric acid and, among many other breakthroughs, anticipated Ohm's Law and the principles of electrical conductivity. The first Cavendish Professor, the Scotsman James Clerk Maxwell, headed the department of physics where he contributed to knowledge of gases, optics, colour sensations, electricity and magnetism. His theoretical work in magnetism opened the way for wireless telegraphy and telephony.

It was in this city of extraordinary scientific fruitfulness which has changed the world out of all recognition that Watson and Crick came to prominence. But when they invited the X-ray crystallographer Rosalind Franklin who shared a lab with their friendly rival Maurice Wilkins at King's College London to come and visit them in Cambridge, Franklin knew their triple-helix model of DNA couldn't be correct. She had in 1951 directed a beam of X-rays through a crystal and allowed the scattered beam to hit a photographic plate. The picture that emerged showed that the structure of DNA was a *double* helix.

When the Cambridge team saw that priceless picture, without Franklin's knowledge, they were able to deduce that the component nucleotides – adenine and thymine, guanine and cytosine – were arranged in a particular order: adenine always paired with thymine, guanine always with cytosine. This in turn showed how chromosomes are duplicated during cell division and how copies are made, influencing the genetic makeup of the next generation.

It then took another thirteen years, from 1953 to 1966, for them properly to understand the genetic code. Unfortunately, Rosalind Franklin, whose profoundly important contribution to genetic science was downplayed and sidelined in a research community still male chauvinist in tenor, died before the Nobel Prize was awarded for that transformation of our understanding of human nature.

Since those distant days, however, DNA has shown itself to be much more complex than researchers initially thought. Bacteria have been found that have *circular* DNA. Z-DNA has a *zigzag* helical structure. And *parallel-stranded* DNA, and DNA with a *triple* helix, have been reported in the literature. As for DNA's durability over time, under appropriate conditions it tends to remain intact in teeth and bones for tens of thousands of years, even though it has been known to dissolve in water and to crumble under the impact of sunlight; sometimes it falls prey to particular enzymes in the cells.

The lab where Watson and Crick worked and built their model of DNA's structure was close to where those earlier scientific breakthroughs took place, in just one narrow street only marginally longer than King's College Chapel, which is around the corner in King's Parade, some fifty paces from the Eagle pub. King Henry VI cleared away a quarter of the town as it then was to make space for what he intended should be 'the loveliest Chapel in England', and laid the foundation stone in 1446; it turned out to be the most splendid Gothic church in Europe and one of the world's best-known buildings. It's a stone's throw from the beamed and panelled Old Hall in medieval Old Court where Queens' College – so punctuated because it had *two* royal patrons – was founded in 1448 and where I first laid eyes on the woman who became my bride on 18 September 1995.

Even if I tried to, I couldn't overstate the importance to me of Cambridge. Apart from the charming atmosphere conjured up by the architecture of this unique city, it is where I met the love of my life and where my colleagues and I find ourselves on the brink of transforming human nature. We've been figuring our way towards modes of post-humanity – human beings shorn of their debilitating dross, their inherited diseases and frailties – by means of human-animal chimeric combinations.

My colleagues and I refer to the Sphinx near the pyramids at Giza in Egypt: the statue of a creature resting on a plinth, its body that of a lion, but its face that of a human being. It is a *chimera* of the ancient world, a metaphorical fusing of two different species: the intellect and imagination of a human being with the strength and speed of a lion. *Our* post-humans, however, will have fused with other animals,

185

not merely metaphorically, i.e. *yearningly*, but actually, at the molecular level, incorporating within our genomes the immunities to particular diseases and rapid ageing which we know certain animals enjoy.

We are turning to beasts supposedly below us on the evolutionary scale in order to rise to an altogether higher plane of life.

Baldock is still here in the kitchen, gazing at me across the table. He is full of a crumbled, sterile wisdom in his buttoned-down shirt collar, dark suit and tie.

'Have you been inside a molecular biology lab?' I ask him.

'No,' he says. 'Never.'

'You should visit one some time.'

'Why should I do that?'

'Hel-lo. Welcome to the new millennium. Because that's where the secrets of life are being laid bare. That's where the code of life is being redeployed. There are no graven images in our labs, no icons on walls, nothing to induce people to debase themselves in front of idols – just Petrie dishes, gels, centrifuges, pipettes, electrophoresis apparatus, time-lapse microscopes, gene-sequencing machines, vats of liquid nitrogen. You'll see things which most people in the history of the world never knew existed because they were grossly ignorant.'

'What things?'

'Things so tiny they are measured in millionths of a metre – blood cells, bone cells, chains of amino acids we call polypeptides. You'll see some of the hundred thousand different kinds of protein of which we humans are constituted and which our genes code for. And things infinitely smaller still, the *membranes* of cells whose dimensions we measure in nanometres – *billionths* of a metre. You'll see that genes don't exist in magical isolation, but depend crucially on their cellular environment, on the cytoplasmic fluid in which they are immersed, and on the catalysing enzymes with which they interact. Cells are tremendously busy places, Mister Baldock – they're chemical factories where the structures of our bodies and brains are made, repaired, bits killed off as necessary. Don't you think that your god can be known through human intellect, that Providence, if it exists at all, achieves its ends through human means? Has it ever occurred to you that our minds can, step by step, discover the infinitesimal foundations of personhood and perhaps recognise thereby traces of our own transcendence?'

Baldock doesn't reply. He just looks at me. It is *he* who has invaded my privacy, not I his, so I keep eye contact and tell him straight: 'Researchers in labs like ours have no time for quacks who know next to nothing about the nature of life.'

'That's not life – that's science. That's got nothing to do with life as God created it. It's the work of mad scientists running amok.'

'In that case, I'm glad to be mad. Did your god give us brains, Baldock?'

'Of course God gave us brains,' he says, looking askance at me. 'He made us the highest form of life in his creation.'

'Shouldn't we use the brains we have – to improve our lives, to improve our conditions, as people have always done – even if some say it's mad to do so?'

'Of course we should, but that's quite different from doing the Devil's work, trying to play God, changing human nature, cobbling monsters together in those temples of arrogance.'

I don't respond. It seems pointless to do so, so there's a long pause in our conversation during which we keep gazing at each other. The purpose of his visit puts me in mind of the automobile manufacturer Henry Ford who, in 1913, when Lenin and his comrades in Russia were eulogising the workers of the world, ushered in a more enduring revolution in Detroit. Henry Ford used the time-and-motion studies of the 1890s to introduce the moving conveyer-belt assembly-line which boosted worker efficiency enormously and made industrial production soar.

Henry Ford famously said that history was a load of bunk.

History, after all, was when disease and ignorance reigned supreme despite entire populations praying to a plethora of supposedly powerful gods: god of fire, god of the sea, goddess of wisdom, god of war – you name it, there was a god for it.

Who but the incorrigibly dense today believe in a god of storms and winds? Or in a messenger god, whether it's called Hermes or Mercury? Or in a god of pain that has to be bribed with sacrifices to make the agony in stomach ulcers subside and go away? Probably, disease and ignorance held sway *because* people bowed their heads to gods instead of getting on with the job of being self-reliant, discovering the true causes of things, and improving their conditions.

It occurs to me during the pause in the conversation with Baldock that those impotent gods have merged over the centuries into a divine essence that makes extraordinary promises, which is why it is adored by so many millions of devotees on both sides of the Atlantic.

On the one hand, it promises to lift whole swathes of my fellow Americans, including officials at the highest levels of government, bodily right out of their clothes and, despite the laws of gravity and the principles of aerodynamics, let alone the total lack of oxygen and the high-energy cosmic rays that are lethal beyond Earth's magnetic field, waft them in a process called 'the Rapture' up to a piece of real estate in the sky known as 'heaven for born-agains'. This is to be their reward for resolutely despising homosexuals whom they regard as 'abominations', for opposing or, better still, bombing, abortion clinics, for undermining the Constitution by forcing Bible discussion in schools, repealing habeas corpus in a de facto way which the *Boston Globe* described as 'part of a larger slide toward tyranny', suppressing dissenting opinions, tapping the phone-calls of American citizens, monitoring the books that people read as happens in a police state, and for brain-washing women to refrain from sex no matter how old they are until their union with one particular man – until death do them part – has been ritually sanctified in a place of self-abasement.

Such are the criteria for being 'saved'. Such behaviour is what 'goodness' connotes. This is the route to the Pearly Gates. In that exclusive place in the sky they shall dwell in unchanging bliss forever more, bliss characterised by their ability to continue eating, thanks to their unperished bodies, pizzas and burgers and freedom fries and huge tubs of popcorn and sugared water in endless supplies.

And as a consequence of this patriotic diet, it will be their honour, not only to use celestial lavatories where their celestial shit is flushed away down a celestial sanitation system (where *to*? back on Earth?), but also to waddle through eternity as they congratulate themselves on being part of the select cohort chosen for immortality.

On the other hand, this divine essence that goes by various names promises bearded men in the Middle East and their spiritual kin elsewhere on the planet sole sexual use in paradise of seventy-two virgins if they become martyrs and die while killing as many infidels as possible. Hence the attractions of suicide trucks laden with explosives. Hence the appeal of bombing commuter trains taking workers to their jobs and blowing up people on holiday eating in restaurants. Hence the fervour with which airliners full of shrieking passengers are crashed into skyscrapers.

It's all for religion. It's all for credit piled up in a ledger beyond the clouds, for the glorification of a demonic obsession.

The pull of religion's death-wish is so powerful that it instils zealots with a peculiar inventiveness: they come up again and again with ingenious ways to overcome apparently impregnable fortifications, though they aren't averse to bombing soft targets.

Their reward for departing this mortal coil in such grisly fashion – body parts blown on to roofs across the road, brains splattered on shards of shattered glass, blood and splintered bone everywhere – and for persecuting women at every turn, frustrating them and smothering their potential, and for vilifying gays and lesbians to the nth degree just as their counterpart Taliban brandishing Bibles in America do – their reward includes, not only doe-eyed *houris* whom no man or *jinn* has ever touched before and whose luscious breasts and pubic hair can be seen from afar through their diaphanous garments, and who never say no to your erection in that blessèd milieu, but also couches to recline on lined with silk brocade and green cushions on the finest carpets, and fruit trees near to hand, and date-palms and pomegranates, and a fountain sprinkling water until the cows come home no matter where in that circumcised Valhalla you happen to be located.

Wishful thinking: a kaleidoscope of comely outcomes for the terminally deluded. The rewards in paradise for *female* suicide bombers aren't specified, according to my wife Sophie who studied French and Arabic and lived for a while in France, Jordan and Egypt. Perhaps women jihadis don't warrant rewards in a Bedouin, Wahhabi heaven, Sophie says, no matter how good they were on Earth, no matter how many bombs they planted. No handsome well-built studs, then, who can keep their cocks erect for all eternity.

Or are there rewards only for *non-Arab non-Wahhabi* Muslim women, Sophie wonders, whose understandings of the Qur'an and Sunnah are by way of gentler interpretations, not so red in tooth and claw?

The credulity of so many of my fellow Americans and so many other people in every hemisphere puts me in mind of a sentence written 150 years ago by another American Henry, Henry David Thoreau, in his enduring book about self-reliance called *Walden*: 'Shams and delusions are esteemed for soundest truths, while reality is fabulous.'

22

The aroma of coffee wafting between Baldock and me doesn't quite mask his soapy aura. I lift my mug and take a sip, then tell him across the table:

'I welcomed you, a complete stranger, into my house. I've been hospitable to you, so please answer my question.'

'What question?'

'Do you enjoy going to the dentist?'

'What?' He is taken aback by the change of subject.

'The dentist. Do you like going there?'

'I go because I have to, like everyone else,' he says, looking puzzled. 'Twice a year, usually for fillings. But I hate it, the way I have to keep my head tilted back and my mouth wide open. I can't reply properly when the dentist asks me a question and I hear myself going "Ga ga ghhn gaa". The hum of the drill keeps me tense and worried that his hand might slip and drill a hole in my tongue.' Baldock frowns in thought. 'While he's drilling into a tooth, my mouth always sounds and feels like a building site; the rubble is washed away by water spraying in from the tube resting on my lip. It isn't very dignified.'

'And the pain?'

'It can be unbearable. Sharp, piercing pain whenever a nerve is exposed. I don't go to the dentist because I enjoy it, that's for sure.'

'I have good news for you, Baldock,' I tell him across the table. 'The time is coming when people won't have go to the dentist at all.'

His eyes hold mine. 'Why d'you say that?'

'Because science has again come to the rescue. A researcher at one of the Florida universities has devised a simple way to prevent cavities forming in teeth in the first place.'

'How has he managed that?'

'By means of gene therapy. He's a molecular biologist too. *Streptococcus mutans* is a bacterium that has been dwelling in our mouths since time immemorial,' I explain. 'It lives on whatever traces of sugar it can find in our saliva and produces lactic acid – and it's the lactic acid that corrodes tooth enamel and keeps making the cavities that need filling. By removing from the *streptococcus* DNA the gene that codes for lactic acid, the professor has rendered the bacterium harmless. Tests on rats, which also get cavities in their teeth from lactic acid, have shown that the new strain of bacterium dominates the original, harmful strain. It thrives on the sugar in saliva – the more sugar, the better – but reduces almost to nil the lactic acid that causes the cavities. Is that creative or what, Mister Baldock?'

I pause, wait for his reply. He doesn't answer.

'People can eat as much chocolate and candy as they like,' I continue. 'It won't harm their teeth. Simply gargling with a solution of the new harmless bacterium will put an end forever to the need for fillings. I can't wait to buy a bottle of it.'

Baldock's eyes are incredulous, his face half-frown, half-grin. 'You really believe it's going happen?'

'I do, when all the necessary research has been done. Then it'll just be the patenting and marketing that have to be sorted. Dentists aren't going to like it. They might start putting out anti-gene-therapy propaganda to save their livelihoods. That's how things improve in science – incrementally. We have no magic wand like you religious lot. Solutions to problems often create new problems, however. That's what cultural developments are all about, and why employment patterns change. It's my guess that dentists will soon only have people's gums to be experts on. But for how much longer? As a profession, they might even become extinct. Remember what I'm saying: you'll be hearing about many more genetic breakthroughs in the coming period. Medicine is in the process of transforming itself, and people too along the way. But tell me, Baldock: what work do *you* do?'

'I was a printer for a long time,' he says, pushing his arms forward on the table and threading his fingers together; there are fine grey hairs on the knuckles and around his wrists. 'My printshop did work for all sorts of professional associations – annual reports, the proceedings of conferences, academic papers, brochures, business cards, letterheads, you name it. Then we went into receivership because our clients had a habit of keeping me waiting for payment – they never paid up as agreed. It was a cashflow problem we couldn't solve. The time came when I couldn't pay the rent for the premises or meet the bills from suppliers – for paper, electricity, toner and so on because our income was so erratic. It was maddening. When my firm folded, I ran a pub. I pulled pints, organised meals in the kitchen and was chatty with the customers. But there wasn't enough trade. The pub scene is dying, dominated by the chains. People nowadays buy cans of beer from supermarkets and stay at home to watch DVDs or play games on consoles. We had to cut our losses and close down. The sense of community is disappearing. People are becoming isolated atoms in the midst of one another, and so many of them are stressed out.'

'What d'you do now?'

'I'm a steeplejack and, thank God, I found Jesus five years ago. Jesus gives me the strength to go on.'

'That's an unusual job, isn't it – being a steeplejack? What does it involve?'

'Climbing ladders to reach the tops of buildings or industrial chimneys. Some of them are about three-hundred metres high. I restore the masonry up there or replace worn firebrick linings. I've always been good with my hands,' he says, turning his palms up and glancing at them. 'Sometimes we demolish old chimneys. Now and then we get a contract to repair church roofs and spires. We also repoint domestic chimneys and roofs and replace worn tiles.'

'You need a head for heights, don't you?'

'You certainly do.'

'Did your god create the first long ladder, or was it invented by human beings?'

Baldock raises an open palm to stop me dead. His hands are chunky, his fingers thick as sausages.

'Don't try that stuff on me,' he says.

'What stuff?'

'Fancy arguments about logic and reason aimed to make me lose my faith in God. God doesn't leave you in the lurch. Jesus isn't a fickle friend. Don't even *try* to question my faith – it's a waste of time.'

'You can say that again.' I look at my watch.

'Are you saying you don't care if Danny Mullins dies?' Baldock asks, the possibility suddenly dawning on him.

'I'm not saying that at all.'

'Then why won't you come to his parents' house? It's in the Chesterton part of Cambridge, less than two miles from here.'

Baldock's eyes are pleading. His blue eyes are full of a compassion trying to connect with my feelings, trying to reach something primal in me that might take precedence over what he probably sees as the cold aloofness of logic.

Something in his pleading eyes reminds me suddenly of the way I've been begging Sophie to come and meet Bertha, and of the way Sophie has been refusing to oblige, refusing point blank to grant my heartfelt wish. Sophie has been refusing to come to the lab because she believes that what I've been doing there is, as she calls it crudely, 'monkey

195

business'. You'd think I'd been asking her to do something crazy, something criminal. I just haven't been able to get through to her.

I suddenly twig how Baldock must be feeling, blocked off from something he wants badly: that I comply with his outlandish request.

He's a born-again evangelical Christian fortified by a set of certainties to ward off the uncertainties and unhappiness of the modern world. He won't allow anyone to question his certainties, whereas I'm convinced that questioning is the only way our minds can relate fruitfully with reality. Questioning is the only way to further our understanding of the universe and transform it to humanity's benefit.

Which is what our human-animal gene-swapping project is all about.

Yet I recognise something in Baldock's longing. It's akin to my longing to get through to Sophie, to win her credence and esteem and escape the frustration of her ambiguous embrace, of being enclosed lovingly in her arms but not fully enjoying her trust.

I see something of myself in Baldock, even though my face isn't blotchy and there aren't any tufts of hair sticking out of my nostrils or thatching my arms

Am I a sucker to notice parallels between us?

Am I heading for a fall by paying attention to this man's blather?

After all, it was *his* forebears, his ideological mentors, who humiliated Galileo and threatened him with dire punishments for daring to assert that the Earth goes around the Sun and not the Sun around the Earth. Galileo was the first to show how counter-intuitive scientific truths are. 'Nature does not accommodate itself to the comprehension of man,' he said. He had developed an astronomical telescope and was the first person to see sunspots, the first to see Jupiter's four main satellites, mountains and craters on the surface of the moon, and the changing appearance of Venus as it orbited the Sun. He was the first to understand that the universe above the moon was intimately related to reality on Earth, that mathematics and physics would in due course join forces and help to integrate all the realms of perception. 'The Book of Nature,' Galileo asserted, 'is written in mathematical characters.'

He was accused of heresy and blasphemous utterances for teachings that contradicted Scripture. In his defence he warned that it would be 'a terrible detriment for the souls of people if they found themselves convinced by proof of something that it was then made a sin to believe'.

Galileo saw clearly how rooted in ignorance the power of the Church was, and why ignorance had to be vindicated if the Church was to continue enjoying its palaces and enormous wealth. On pain of torture and threat of death he was made to recant in public by Pope Urban VIII in 1633; he had to acknowledge that ignorance was truth and that truth was the work of insidious devils.

Baldock's doctrinal forebears were also ruthless and systematically cruel in defence of their earthly privileges. They showed no mercy when they burned the freethinking scholar Giordano Bruno in Rome in February 1600 for questioning and then rejecting the authority of the Church. Their psychotic jealousy impelled them to kill everyone who disagreed with their beliefs: homicidal hauteur on a mass scale.

Am I a patsy setting myself up for a shakedown?

Is it cool, a viable entity: a research scientist who takes cognisance of his feelings and allows them significant sway?

Am I mad to be listening to this nonsense?

23

'You want me to accompany you to Chesterton where Danny Mullins is lying dead – because I *saw* him before the accident?'

'Yes,' Baldock says, 'for no other reason.'

'I'm supposed to have a touch of his life because I *saw* him? For about twenty minutes as his blood spread on the sidewalk? That's why you've come to my house – to make this outlandish request?'

'That's the only reason, Doctor Venn. You registered his being, that crucial moment of his life – you are a priceless witness.'

'I'm also a sceptical scientist. Won't that spoil the gig?'

'You saw Danny – he didn't know you from Adam. You could've been a Sikh with a turban on your head, a Buddhist sitting under a tree, a Hindu with a red spot on your forehead, or a pagan fire worshipper – it would've made no difference. You saw Danny. You witnessed the moments before his life spiralled to its end, something no one else we know saw. You have something of him which I'm begging you to bring to his parents' house on Sunday. Heal the sick, cleanse the lepers, raise the dead, Jesus instructs us – Matthew chapter ten, verse eight. We take that instruction very seriously. It's the teaching that defines us. Just come to the house, Doctor Venn. You don't have to pray if it rubs you up the wrong way. No one will force you. You can think about physics and chemistry if you want to, while looking at Danny's face.'

Baldock must think he has me going, has me wavering, because he puts a hand into the inside pocket of his jacket and brings out a sheet of newspaper folded over several times. He unfolds the tabloid-size page and flattens the creases on the kitchen table with his hand. Then he turns the page around so I can read it and pushes it across to me.

Under the banner headline 'Danny does it again' is a colour photo of a blond young boy holding a trophy flanked by a man in a suit and tie and an attractive woman wearing an elegant hat. The boy is beaming. One tooth near the front of his mouth is missing; it adds to the mischievous, impish look created by his button nose and pointed chin. His hair is close-cropped high above his ears, but there's a clump covering the left side of his forehead.

'That's Danny with his mum and dad,' Baldock tells me.

'What's the trophy for?'

'A chess championship. He's very good at chess. He keeps beating players old enough to be his parents – even professional chess players.'

That reminds me of the chess book I put back into the basket of Danny's bike after the collision, along with the book of Sudoku puzzles.

The caption under the picture says: 'Deploying rook and knight, Danny again gets it right'.

The accompanying article gives a rundown of the competition that has succumbed to Danny Mullins's prowess at the chessboard and the ways in which his string of victories have come to seem inevitable. He started playing chess when he was five years old. When his parents found there was no way they could beat him, they began buying him books about the game so he could study it seriously. Opening gambits, moves made famous by national champions and grandmasters, the psychology of deep strategy which they explained to him – the newspaper article tells how Danny soaked it all up. He was playing against a dozen grown-ups in community centres and town halls around East Anglia when he was nine years old, moving from table to table in his T-shirt and short pants, glancing quickly at the pieces and making his moves – and beating all his opponents more or less at the same time.

'It says here he'd begun to teach himself Russian,' I say, glancing up at Baldock.

'He had. He was learning Russian from a phrasebook. He used to practise on me. *Privet* – Hello. *Kak u vas dela?* – How are you? *Kak semya?* – How's your family? *Do svidaniya* – Goodbye. Danny wanted to go to Russia to play chess against Russians. He wanted to meet the world chess champion Vladimir Kramnik and get his autograph. I honestly think Danny was on the way to becoming a chess grandmaster himself. He was twelve when that van knocked him off his bike.'

'It says here,' I say tapping the sheet of newspaper, 'that he's restless at school. He gets into trouble for being disruptive.'

'School isn't challenging enough for him, that's why. All the tests, all the exams, they make kids numb. The chores at school don't engage Danny's imagination. He plays chess against the computer in his bedroom, instead of doing his homework.'

The article goes on to explain the mixed feelings of Danny's parents, how proud they are of their son's ability on the one hand, of the honour he's brought them, but how upset they are on the other hand by his apparent inability to pay attention at school and his regular run-ins with the teachers for distracting the other pupils in his class and getting them to become boisterous and unruly too.

The article ends with a quote from the school's headteacher. 'Danny has a great future,' she says. 'He'll go from strength to strength and put East Anglia on the world chess map, but only if he succeeds in controlling his impulses and disciplining his wilder instincts.'

When I look up at Baldock and push the page back

to him across the table, he points with a finger to the date above the article.

'That was printed just a week ago,' he says. He folds the page carefully along the creases and puts it back into his jacket pocket. 'I'm talking about a person who was well known and well loved in these parts. His parents are shattered. Danny died so suddenly.'

'The point is that he died and there's nothing I can do about it.'

'But there *is* something you can do, Doctor Venn. I assure you there is. You are the only person we know who saw Danny when the accident actually happened and you therefore have something in your power that is priceless. I wouldn't be here if I didn't know that to be God's truth.'

Baldock stares hard at me again, as though trying to change my mind by sheer force of will. The blotchy complexion of his face and the paleness of his well-defined lips give his countenance the aspect of an exotic mask. His face suddenly reminds me of one of those masks from the interior of Africa which inspired Picasso in the early years of the 20th century, especially the revolutionary painting called *Les demoiselles d'Avignon* and the one known as *Nu dans une foret*.

Baldock and I look at each other across the table for a long while, neither of us saying a word. Something in his blue eyes makes me feel he's giving me a moral once-over. I get the impression that he's assessing the depth of my feelings, the quality of my compassion.

After a long silence, he puts his hand into the inside pocket of his jacket again. Instead of a newspaper article, however, he brings out this time a leather card-holder. He flips it open, pulls out a business card and reaches it across the table to me between his thick fingers.

I take the card and read it.

GOD'S ALLIANCE it says in bold italic lettering and,

in smaller type below, *Rejoice in Jesus*. It gives the address of the regional headquarters in East Anglia, along with telephone number and a website and email address.

'So your god is now hi-tech,' I say, glancing at Baldock. 'Your god has email. He doesn't mind using the products of science and technology.'

'No, God doesn't mind. We are creatures of our time. We have religious chatrooms online and we send prayers by email. New angel sites are cropping up on the web all the time.'

'So are new knowledge sites. There are endless scientific sites on the web publicising projects and lines of inquiry.'

'We email home churches across the USA,' Baldock tells me, ignoring what I've just said as if I hadn't said it. 'Religious politicians in Alabama and other states have succeeded in getting a printed message pasted in the front of biology textbooks warning students that Darwin's theory of evolution is an unproven theory and that, as sensible people know, human beings are descended from Adam and Eve who were made by God in the Garden of Eden, not from monkeys in the jungle.'

'You believe that bull? Eighty years after the so-called Monkey Trial in Tennessee when the schoolteacher John Scopes was prosecuted by William Jennings Bryan and fined a hundred dollars for teaching the theory of evolution? As an American I still feel ashamed of that. You still believe *politicians* are qualified to decide on the validity of scientific knowledge?'

'What I believe is not the point of what I'm saying. I'm saying we email people all over the world. Rodney Howard-Browne filled the venue at Olympia in London with a Toronto Blessing meeting.'

'You're losing me, Baldock. Who's Rodney Brown? What's a Toronto blessing?'

'Howard-Browne – he's a fundamentalist leader from

South Africa. A Toronto Blessing is when the whole congregation explodes with religious laughter and everyone sighs and screams and thrashes about. They bark like dogs and bitches and fall to the floor of the auditorium when the preacher slays them in the spirit, their old unbelieving selves killed stone dead. Then, born again, they rise as true believers in the supernatural powers of Jesus. As Jesus told Nicodemus the Pharisee: "Except a man be born again, he cannot see the Kingdom of God" – the Gospel According to St John, chapter three, verse three. The number of people in South Africa who are members of churches like ours has shot up, black and white together, racially integrated. We're forging ahead in South America too. People everywhere are marching for Jesus, Doctor Venn. They know that entry to God's heaven with all its wonders can be theirs if they just have faith in the Lord's supernatural powers. You should read the Bible, especially the Book of Revelation – it's entirely inerrant. Every statement in it is fundamentally true.'

'Is that why you call yourselves fundamentalists?'

'That's right. Everything in the Bible is fundamental, unchanging truth.' He pauses and takes another sip of coffee; it must be cold by now, like mine. Then he points to the card I'm holding and says in a lower tone of voice: 'Look on the other side.'

I turn the card over. Handwritten in ink are the names *John and Ceri Mullins* and an address in the Chesterton district of Cambridge. There's also a sketch of local streets with their names neatly penned in, and arrows pointing the way.

'That's where Danny's mum and dad live,' Baldock says. 'That map will get you there. Just come, Doctor Venn. They're good allies, fine people. They care about what happens to their neighbours.'

'Is this where Danny grew up and learned to play chess?'

'Yes, and it's where his family and all his friends are going to congregate when we bring his body from the mortuary.'

'His body should be left at the mortuary – until the funeral.'

'There isn't going to *be* a funeral.'

'But Danny died two days ago – you said he was certified dead.'

'I also said we're going to resurrect him. We're going to meet in strength at his house this coming Sunday, September the eighteenth, and raise our hands in prayer. We're going to pray with all the power in our hearts. God knows our wishes are pure and Jesus will intercede – that's what the passion of Jesus is all about. He'll help us do his work, help us raise Danny from the dead. It's going to be a glorious occasion.'

Baldock's idea of a glorious occasion is obviously different from mine and Sophie's. His religious zeal on the other side of the kitchen table sets up a barrier whose unrelenting obduracy finally undermines my concentration. As he chunters on I catch myself not paying full attention and taking refuge in musings about Sophie's lovely body, so warm and welcoming, so different from her attitude to my work at the lab. I'd much rather be with Sophie than with this evangelist who has wangled his way into our house with pie-in-the-sky talk about reviving a dead chess player.

Sophie and I are more down to Earth. Until I met her I'd only travelled once outside the United States, to England. Now she takes me to distant places. She likes climbing coconut trees in the Seychelles which, I discover, is a nation of scattered islands off the east coast of Africa. Sophie's toes and fingers grip the bark fast and a short length of rope looped round her ankles helps her climb. Her shapely butt sticks out as she inches higher and higher up the curving tree, her flimsy skirt flapping in the breeze. Sophie is brave, that's for sure: those trees on Praslin Island are very tall. Like a koala bear, only much more sleek and beautiful, she claws her way to the very top, vivid in the sunshine against the blue sky. She reaches her hands up while pressing her thighs to the bark, and tugs a coconut free.

'Stand clear!' she cries out, waves an arm, then tosses the coconut away. I watch in admiration and fear for her safety as it falls in an arc on to the patch of thick green grass. When she comes down the tree, slowly, carefully, hugging it close, I notice the scratches from the bark on her calves and inner thighs. I go down on my knees and kiss them away, happy to have her back safe and sound.

We take the coconut to our hotel, have it slit open at a table on the terrace overlooking the Indian Ocean and drink the cool milk straight from the fibrous husk. Sophie then guides me to one of the Coco de Mer nuts growing in the forested part of the island. It turns out to be a memorable sight. Closely resembling a woman's clean-shaven vulva, but larger, it is the most sexually suggestive fruit I have ever laid eyes on. No wonder it's sometimes called the 'love nut'. Its colour is toffee, like the complexion of many a Creole woman, I guess. I keep looking, staring. Devoid of nature's natural hairy protection, it is almost pornographic in its overtness, alluring in a shiny, slightly mesmeric way.

'This island was once a British possession,' Sophie tells me, 'and General Gordon believed it was the site in ancient times of the Garden of Eden.'

We then fly twenty minutes north to Bird Island to see Esmeralda, reputed to be the world's oldest giant tortoise. 'They say she was born in 1771 and weighs nearly nine-hundred pounds,' Sophie says as we watch the creature tilt from side to side as it moves forward on the beach, its leathery neck protruding from under its huge dome-like shell, its eyes and mouth as old as history, its feet white with grains of the powdery sand.

Sophie also likes exploring, as do I, the red, yellow and amber rock villages of Cappadocia in Turkey. We spend a week after that unusual experience in Istanbul, the only city, Sophie tells me, that is located on two continents. We find that the view from our hotel room is magnificent, across the waters of the Bosphorus from the Europe side of Istanbul to the Asia side. It's a busy stretch of water that links the Black Sea with the Sea of Marmara and the Golden Horn; ferries, oil tankers, military craft with gun turrets and radar, cabin cruisers and gleaming white yachts are continually crisscrossing that maritime highway.

Each night of our stay, after exploring the old part of the city, Aya Sophia (Church of the Divine Wisdom) which dates from the 4th century AD; and Sultanahmet Mosque, also known as the Blue Mosque because of its tiles, the only one outside Mecca, Sophie tells me, with six minarets; and Topkapi Palace, situated in a spectacular setting at the very tip of a finger of land surrounded by the Golden Horn and the Sea of Marmara, from where the Ottoman Empire was run; and Çapali Çarşi, the Grand Bazaar, reputedly the largest covered market in the world and ancient forerunner of the modern shopping mall – each night after exploring this intriguing city we see from our hotel room the opposite, Asia, coastline, lit up with a thousand twinkling lights reflected in the dark lapping water.

Sophie has also taken me, a previously untravelled American, to Vienna where we roamed around the house in the sloping street called Berggasse where Sigmund Freud used to live and do his psychoanalysis work before he had to flee the Nazis who arrived in Vienna in March 1938. Then, about an hour's drive from there, we went to Bratislava in the Slovak Republic where we saw a performance of the charming ballet by Delibes called *Coppélia* in an ornate theatre close to a bend of the Danube river. 'The communists might have been short of food, money and freedom,' Sophie said, 'but they enjoyed loads of culture inexpensively.'

We've been to Rio de Janeiro as well. Sophie loves strolling in a flimsy dental-floss bikini on the soft sands of

Copacabana Beach. She has the figure for it, she has the shape, though not the sensational colour tattoos of birds, flowers and fruit which Brazilian beauties flaunt on their naked backsides as they promenade along the shore.

Sophie is forever buying tickets to concerts and drama performances. She's always taking me to some cultural event or other. It's to broaden my horizons, she says, to give me, a scientist, insights into what the arts are about and thereby to civilise me.

The assumptions of arts people about the mentality of scientists are so derogatory and belittling, an on-going scandal.

One show Sophie took me to – 'a surprise outing' she called it before we left the house – was the triennial Cambridge Greek Play at the Corn Exchange on Wheeler Street. It was a lively, bawdy interpretation by Dictynna Hood of Aristophanes' satirical comedy called *Birds*.

Performed almost entirely in classical Greek by students who were from Germany, India, Turkey as well as the UK, *Birds* was sprinkled with obscenities in English for extra impact and showed conspicuous amounts of bare flesh and cleavage. About ambition, utopian dreams and betrayal against the background of Athens in a disastrous war with Sparta, the play was a joy to behold. It presented an idyllic society populated by birds high above planet Earth in a country called Cloudcuckooland, away from all disease and fighting, away from political corruption and a legal system where everyone is suing everyone else – a nation of feathered friends where no one ever pays a fine or gets into debt. The choreography, the feathery costumes, the music, colour and speech-making fused seamlessly into superb entertainment.

I was feeling relaxed and reassured when Sophie and I left the theatre. And the image of Procne was fixed firmly in my mind. Procne was the nightingale-wife of Tereus who used to be a man but was now a hoopoe bird that flew above human cities and saw all the trouble and strife there; he had metamorphosed from one form of life into another. A dark-eyed fetching beauty with a large red feather rising from her head, black gossamer gloves up to her elbows, cooing sounds coming from her throat, her torso tilted forwards, arms extended backwards, fingers spread and vibrating in a semblance of ruffled feathers as she paced to and fro, the birdlike rubbery movements of her head stabilised by her shapely stern and her bare feet on the floor, Procne the nightingale was a dual ideal: the sort of bird every person with ornithological yearnings would choose to be, and the kind of person every sensible bird – whether raven, eagle, starling or hawk – would wish to emulate if a human form were called for.

Procne, and likewise the dozen or so birds who flew and fluttered and twittered and screeched and hopped about the stage of Aristophanes' imagination, was a wonderful example of cross-dressing across the species barrier. It was an ancient, pre-Christian longing to change over and live in a different genetic realm. How delighted I was to discover, thanks to Sophie's ticket-buying mania and with her seated by my side, that transgenic faculties were a favoured fantasy, a dream of better things to come, even as far back as the 5th century BC.

How gratifying it was to learn that we geneticists have a pedigree that goes so far back it is identifiable even in the world's earliest literature; that literary snobs who look down on molecular biologists don't realise the extent to which they are exposing their ignorance.

I found that I loved the Corn Exchange on Wheeler Street.

I loved the way the stage was at floor level halfway down the auditorium, with the rows of seats in two banks facing each other, the cast coming and going down the central aisle and in and out of the door at one side of the 'stage'.

Under the arched ceiling against one of the walls was a metal cage in which a female bird sat throughout the duration of the play. There were feathers in her tophat. Her bodice made of down was heaving slowly like a pigeon's. Her thighs were sheathed in stockings the same colour as the iron bars of her cage. She warbled and cawed every now and then, her head jerking forwards and backwards from time to time, conjuring up a sense of the bird world into which we humans had been admitted on sufferance.

I felt indebted to Sophie, despite the surges of sexual jealousy that had been assailing me and the dark dreams I'd been having of her leaving me for someone else.

I felt indebted to her for taking me to what she'd called 'a surprise outing' to see students acting in an ancient Greek play. I hadn't had the slightest inkling that it was going to dovetail with DNA. I saw before my eyes a yearning for metamorphosis at the dawn of history, a dream of transformations of identity which my colleagues and I at the Institute of Molecular and Neural Genetics in Trumpington Street, two-and-a-half thousand years later, were at last on the brink of fulfilling.

24

'Please, Doctor Venn,' Baldock is saying across the kitchen table, 'it would do so much good if you came to Danny's house. Jesus urges us to raise the dead. We do what God asks because God is all-knowing and almighty, supremely good and merciful. God loves us. He loves you too, Doctor Venn, even though you're deluded. He is our maker and our saviour. Everything that happens is by his will.'

'There's something I'd like to ask you, Baldock.'

'What is it?'

'You're in my house, so I don't mean to be offensive or crude, but there's a question that's been bothering me for some time.'

'Ask away.'

'If as you say God is almighty, good and merciful, and everything that happens is by his will, why does he kill so many of us so indiscriminately so often? Why does he unleash earthquakes that destroy entire communities who pray to him fervently and regularly? Why does he kill children and crush the limbs of other children with boulders and leave them bereft, orphans without food or clothes against the bitter winter weather? Why does he smash churches and mosques to bits as if they were of no significance to him?'

Baldock just stares at me.

'Please answer me,' I prompt him.

He remains silent.

'It's bizarre, to say the least, that people describe as loving and merciful a god who destroys their houses, schools, hospitals and livelihoods with huge tsunami waves and hurricanes that make no distinction between believers and non-believers, tall people and short people, male and female, fat and thin. Don't you think it's bizarre?'

Baldock's eyes are on mine, but they are motionless; his body too is absolutely still, his forearms on the table.

'It's a phenomenon noteworthy for its ubiquity. On every continent there are people who insist that their god is merciful even after he destroys without warning everything they've worked for all their lives. If their parents behaved like that, they'd be taken to court and severely dealt with by the authorities. If CEOs of companies behaved like that, they'd be given short shrift, not worshipped. If politicians in a democracy adopted such a vengeful attitude and pushed through policies so harmful and destructive, they'd be removed from office in a flash. It's as if people can't *see* clearly. Or perhaps they can't *think* clearly, or think at all. That's why some medical experts consider religious belief to be a form of psychosis, a psychiatric condition. Psychiatric wards are full of patients who hear voices from what they say is God. Some of them say they are themselves Jesus. Some say they are Napoleon, some say Admiral Nelson. One notices that they never say they are the milkman, or the postman, or the person at the cinema complex who tears your tickets and tells you which way to go. They never say they are tramps or asylum seekers. Their psychotic identities are never delusions of ordinariness or delusions of insignificance. They are always delusions of grandeur. Perhaps it's the result of a long unthinking habit – praying, praying, praying to what they say is the highest power; saying the same words over and over again, persistent mantras of self-hypnosis. "Our father, who art in heaven"; "Dear Lord"; "Please God"; "Dear Mary, Mother of God", "*Bismillah*" which my wife Sophie says is classical Arabic for "in the name of God". And "*Adonai YHWH*", the phrase that occurs hundreds of times, Sophie says, in the Hebrew scriptures – "our Lord Yahveh. Great is our Lord and full of power; his wisdom is beyond reckoning." Again and again, endlessly, people kneel in prayer, bow their heads, prostrate themselves, uttering those same words, and again and again, endlessly, their god wipes out thousands of them at a time, sometimes many more, smashes their lives, traumatises survivors with cyclones, tornados and raging forest fires. He visits droughts on them, and famines, and still they say he loves them, even when he hurls entire towns down the sides of collapsing mountains – massive killer earthquakes in Armenia, Greece, Turkey, Iran, Japan, Pakistan, Kashmir, and droughts and fires in Australia and deadly hurricanes again and again in the Gulf states of my own country, the United States. Their beliefs are clearly insane.'

Baldock doesn't even blink. Our conversation seems to be moving into monologue mode, but I feel I have to put to him in an unambiguous way the question about God's ambiguous embrace.

'If, as you say, God is omniscient, good and merciful, if everything that happens is due to his will, where was he and his host of angels on the thirteenth of March 1996 when sixteen five- and six-year-old children and their teacher were shot dead by a gunman in Dunblane Primary School?'

Baldock's face is dead still, like a mask. I wait, but he doesn't reply.

'Where was God when all those innocent children and their lovely teacher were massacred and twelve other kids seriously maimed?'

Baldock seems to have no answer. He swallows hard; I notice the way his Adam's apple moves up and down his throat.

'Where was God and his host of angels when Thomas Hamilton, with mass murder in his heart, was hiring a white Ford van in Stirling to drive to the school the next day? Where was omniscient God when Hamilton was buying seventeen-hundred of the nine-millimetre rounds he used to slaughter the kids and their teacher in the school's gymnasium?'

Baldock's blotchy face looks as if it has frozen. His eyes are immobile. His tongue too remains immobile.

'You've been holding forth all afternoon, so tell me,' I persist. 'Why did God do nothing when Hamilton loaded his four guns? God who sees everything and understands everything and is merciful – why didn't he intervene when Hamilton parked the Ford van near a telephone pole in front of the school and proceeded to cut the phone wires so no one would be able to call for help?'

Baldock remains tongue-tied. His countenance has shrunk, his purplish-pink complexion drained almost to a pasty hue. He takes refuge in the coffee, swigging the dregs from the mug. He wipes his lips with the back of his hand. He looks at his hand. He purses his lips. When at last he speaks, his voice is hoarse, little more than a whisper.

'God works in a mysterious way,' he says, looking straight at me. 'Human beings are much too shallow to understand.'

'It isn't a very humane way, is it? – leaving the school and the families and the whole nation in such deep shock. One of the ambulance men said the gym where the massacre took place was like a scene from a medieval torture chamber – bodies piled up everywhere, blood on the walls and floor and huge holes in the kids' heads. The consequences of the Dunblane massacre are still being felt by many people. Where was God when that carnage was being carried out and the place was reeking of cordite?'

I wait for an answer, a long pause, but Baldock says nothing. The look in his eyes is now a mixture of pain and disbelief. He cannot understand why I am treating him like this, subjecting him to the torture of a simple question. I try again.

'Where was all-knowing, all-merciful God in October 2002 when holidaymakers and locals in restaurants on the Indonesian island of Bali were bombed by Muslim terrorists?

Where was God when Muslim bombs killed innocent people on trains in Madrid in March 2004, and when Londoners were suicide-bombed on tube trains and a number 30 bus in Tavistock Square during the morning rush hour on the seventh of July this year? Fifty-two unarmed, innocent people were murdered and about seven-hundred injured in the London bombings. It happened the day after Londoners celebrated the euphoric news that their city had won the right to stage the 2012 Olympic Games. Then at the Egyptian holiday resort at Sharm el-Sheikh another despicable atrocity, then in Istanbul. Why did all-powerful, all-merciful God allow those obscenities to happen?'

Still no response.

'In April 1999 when those teenage classmates Dylan Klebold and Eric Harris opened fire and murdered twelve of their fellow students and one of their teachers at Columbine High School near Denver, Colorado – what held God back then from preventing *that* massacre?'

It's as if Baldock isn't there, only an effigy of him seated at the table, for all the feedback I get.

'Tell me,' I prompt him. 'Many of my fellow Americans are famous for having a personal god – there must be at least a hundred-million personal gods in the USA. So where were all these gods when Klebold and Harris were loading their two shotguns, their semi-automatic rifle and their rapid-fire pistol? Why do these gods always withhold their protection, even from the most vulnerable people in the world? Don't all these marvellous gods have any power over the god of the Gun Lobby? Or is it simply that there *are* no gods – which is why they can never help anyone? They are simply emperor's clothes.'

Baldock's gaze gives away nothing. His eyes are incommunicado. I wait for him to reply. I give him time to formulate a response, to answer my questions, but he doesn't oblige.

'Whenever people are murdered in a mass shooting in America by gunmen on the rampage,' I tell him, 'there's always an outburst of irrationality. Good, honest individuals take leave of their senses. In a knee-jerk way they say about the victims "May God bless them. May God protect them" when it is perfectly obvious that God did *not* protect them from the gunmen. They are suddenly dead, meaninglessly, but the authorities, the police, families and friends seem unable to think clearly and lapse unfailingly into a religious cliché. Very few individuals mention the elephant in the room, the two-hundred million guns in private hands in America. I speak as an American who loves his country when I say that it seems to be unpatriotic to criticise guns, anti-American, even. The Gun Lobby has got the public mind well and truly stitched up. It's a kind of warped nationalism, the right to bear arms, a twisted patriotic pride. Who needs al-Qaida when we have our homegrown, apple-pie, well armed American terrorists to slaughter thirty-thousand of us every year – *every year* thirty-thousand – regular as clockwork?'

Baldock still doesn't respond. He keeps gazing at me. I wonder whether he's asleep with his eyes open. I wonder about the Holocaust as well, but something tells me I'd be wasting my breath to ask him why God let it happen. The conference in January 1942 where the Final Solution, the genocide of the Jewish people, was planned – why did compassionate God let it happen? The concentration camps and death camps, the gas chambers where unsuspecting people thought they were going to have a shower and were killed with carbon monoxide. The well organised rounding up of Jews in cities, towns and villages all over Europe, packed into cattle-cars and shipped by train to systematically prepared places of mass murder at Dachau, Sachsenhausen, Auschwitz-Birkenau, Chelmo, Treblinka and many others. Why did merciful God let it happen, I wonder silently.

Doctors, lawyers, bankers, scientists, teachers, men, women, children, the blind, the ill, rich people, poor people – they were all killed, willy-nilly and pell mell. The Germans murdered musicians too. They murdered cabaret singers, composers. My parents told me when I was younger that the Nazis didn't care which walk of life their victims belonged to. Card-sharps, hustlers, hookers, art collectors, carpenters, tailors, cantors in synagogues – they were all the same in being Jewish or part-Jewish. They were herded together, worked to death dressed in filthy rags, starved to death, shot dead in the woods.

And Gypsies were murdered too, and communists, so-cialists, democrats and homosexuals: 'undesirables' according to Nazi criteria.

And the governments of supposedly anti-fascist Europe and America all looked the other way. They pretended they didn't know what was happening despite their networks of spies and informers. Hence their remorse today, much too late, and their histrionic contrition which is being preyed upon and systematically milked as they force their guilt on to another defenceless people who were worlds away from the Christian places of genocide but are now being cynically reduced to destitution in their own historic land. Cruel, unjust, unrelenting revenge on the wrong people, the catastrophic Palestinian *nakba*.

'Why did God let that monstrous outrage go on and on?' I ask Baldock aloud.

'What monstrous outrage?' he replies.

'The *Shoah* – what do you think? The Holocaust and its nasty, hideous aftermath. Is it because he's *meshugenah*, perhaps?'

Baldock eyes me blankly. He doesn't answer. He clearly hasn't heard the Yiddish word for *crazy* before. I wonder if he's met any Ashkenazim. Perhaps he hasn't been to New York.

His god is a fantasy like every other god. I'm sitting in

my own kitchen, looking forward to having supper with Sophie in town this evening, yet I find myself beginning to fume. What the hell am I doing chinwagging with a cement-brain fundamentalist?

Across the table from me Baldock opens his mouth. I wait for his words. I wait and wait, but no sound comes out. He passes his tongue across his pale, well-defined lips, wetting them, first the upper one, then the lower. It makes me think he's getting ready to speak, to come forth at last with more of his religious wisdom, with a statement that might give me pause, something to ponder, but it's all mouth and no trousers, as English women say. He says nothing.

I become conscious of the thick silence in the kitchen and of the distance between us across the table that is now a huge chasm.

25

'As an American living and working in England, I ask you one last time, Baldock. Please answer. Where was God on that day of infamy, September eleventh, two-thousand and one, when terrorists murdered nearly three-thousand of my fellow Americans in New York and Washington by crashing hijacked planes into the towers of the World Trade Center and into the Pentagon? So many innocent people from dozens of countries killed and maimed so cruelly – why did your god let it happen? There were dozens of Muslims in the World Trade Center when it was attacked, mainly menial workers – janitors, messengers, kitchen assistants – and there was a mosque on one of the floors. Why did God in his guise as Allah murder those humble people? Why did he aid and abet their destruction by looking the other way, even as they were praying to him? Why did he make more than two-hundred people jump to their deaths to escape being burned alive and let three-hundred and forty-three selfless firefighters die? Why did God abandon so many children without a breadwinner?'

I pause, give him a chance to answer. He doesn't say anything.

'And United Airlines Flight 93,' I add, 'why did merciful God let it crash into a field in Pennsylvania south of Pittsburg when some of the passengers tried to regain control of the plane from the hijackers?'

'Please be kind, Doctor Venn,' Baldock says at last in a dry, weak voice, ignoring my questions entirely. He ignores what I've been saying as if I haven't said a thing. It's as though my voice doesn't exist and there are no problems at all where he's coming from. Such is the psychosis. Such is the reality he inhabits, made up almost entirely of blindspots. 'It would do so much good,' he says. 'Because you saw Danny Mullins just before his head hit the pavement your presence on Sunday will make a major contribution to our effort. You are very important to us.' His eyes are focused on mine again with a soft pleading look. 'Are you going to be there, Doctor Venn?'

'It's our tenth wedding anniversary on Sunday. My wife and I are going to celebrate it at a jazz club in London the night before.'

'Congratulations. It's always a pleasure to hear about marriages that endure. Marriage is what makes the flesh of a man and a woman one flesh – that's what Jesus told the Pharisees on the other side of the Jordan. A man shall cleave to his wife, and they twain shall be one flesh, no longer two – Matthew chapter nineteen, verses five to six.'

'Are *you* married, Baldock?'

'Yes,' he nods emphatically with a deep smile. 'Been married thirty-two years to the same woman. We have a grown-up daughter who runs a pet shop with her husband in Norwich, and a son who's an electrician. They have their own families. My wife is like my other self. I can't enjoy anything if she's not there to share it with me. It's a marvellous coincidence too, which must have a hidden meaning.'

'What is?'

'That Danny's resurrection ceremony is fixed for the same Sunday, the afternoon of your wedding anniversary.'

'It's just a coincidence, Baldock – pure chance.'

'Nothing happens by chance, Doctor Venn. Everything is pre-ordained. You obviously love your wife if you're looking forward to celebrating your anniversary with her. I'm now more convinced that meeting you today was meant to be. We'd love you to bring your wife Sophie Gresham to Danny's resurrection ceremony because family solidarity goes down well with God. Family solidarity is a reflection of the Holy Family – there is no bigger plus. When families hold together societies thrive and flourish. That's true all over the world. Can I tell Danny's mum and dad that you and your wife care enough to come and save his life?'

'I can't speak for my wife. She has her own mind, her own priorities. She may or may not come to the house in Chesterton. She believes in a god, a supreme deity, but has never thought much of organised religion or its agents strutting about in fancy dress. The college of cardinals in the Vatican with their crimson skullcaps, crimson cloaks over their ankle-length white dresses – Sophie says they're all cross-dressers, transvestites, every last one of them, whether they're from Europe, Africa, Asia or the Americas. As for myself, I don't care what people wear or which fabrics they get their sexual kicks from. What I'd like to know, however, is whether you believe in health and well-being here on Earth and not just in that place you call heaven.'

'Of course I do. That's precisely our work – to build God's kingdom on Earth.'

'In that case, I'll make a deal with you.'

'What sort of deal?'

'A simple, fair-exchange deal. If you come with me to the Institute of Molecular and Neural Genetics in Trumpington Street tomorrow or the day after to meet Bertha—'

'Who's Bertha?'

'She's our genetically enhanced bonobo chimpanzee. We took the human gene FOXP2 which controls the structure of brain tissue involved in speech, and another gene, *ProtocadherinXY*, and spliced them into her parents, and Bertha was born with some of the faculty of speech.'

A pained expression contorts Baldock's face. His eyes take on a stricken look, a kind of fascinated horror.

'A chimp that can speak?' he says hoarsely. 'It's an abomination.'

'No it isn't. It's a chimeric experiment, profoundly important to the future well-being of humanity. Chimerics is the surest way to improve a species prone to fatal diseases like the human species. The idea is to import into the human genome the immunities to our diseases which other species enjoy – once we've mastered the gene-swapping skills. There's still much to learn, swapping genes in both directions.'

'Humans and animals aren't supposed to mix. It's not what God intended.'

'How d'you know what God intends? Are you a meta-physical mind-reader as well? Why is it always *your* prejudices that God intends?'

'A chimp that can speak,' he murmurs, his eyes out of focus.

'Her utterances are clear,' I tell him. 'We've made a point of talking to her every day – slowly, clearly. We point things out to Bertha and name them. She's been listening to the lab staff, to me, mainly to Doctor Flame McGovern our primatologist, and her vocabulary is growing by the week. Slowly but surely, little Bertha has been getting used to expressing her thoughts in words.'

'Her thoughts? She's a monkey and she has thoughts?'

'She's not a monkey. She's a bonobo, sometimes known as a pygmy chimpanzee.'

'What's the difference?' Baldock sneers.

'The difference is that unlike monkeys and other chimpanzees bonobos are calm, placid. They aren't violent. They're an intelligent species with a communication system of their own. We've simply enhanced it with a particular complement of human genes and Bertha has inherited the ability to speak. Okay, so the tone of her voice is odd – it's a kind of high-pitched grating with bits of baritone. But that's because of the position of the bonobo larynx, which affects the structure of the vocal cords.'

'It's not right. Only humans are born to speak.'

'Only humans? Have you ever heard a parrot speak?'

Baldock glances at me sharply, as if brought up short. 'Why d'you ask?'

'*Have* you?' I press. 'Have you ever heard a parrot speak?'

'Many times, as a matter of fact. Our daughter has an African Grey in a large cage in her living room. It's mainly grey in colour, but there's a bit of white around the eyes, and the tail's red. It's quite a big bird, more than thirty centimetres. Doris – that's our daughter – Doris says Amazon parrots are much bigger still, more than a metre in length. They live quite long too, did you know?'

'How long?'

'Between fifty and sixty-five years.'

'Really? I didn't know that.'

'That's what Doris says. She and her husband have booklets about the animals they sell in their pet shop.'

'What's her parrot's name?'

'Gabby,' Baldock smiles wanly. 'You know, talkative. Parrots have a talent for imitating human speech, the things they hear people say.'

'What have *you* actually heard Gabby say?'

'Every time the phone rings, Gabby says loud and clear in her cage: "It's for you".'

'Really?'

'And when someone turns on the telly, she says: "Beam me up, Scottie". When Dan, my son-in-law, comes home and goes into the living room, Gabby says: "I'm starving. I'm starving." Doris is convinced that parrot understands what it's saying because it always says things in the right context. When someone says "Goodbye", Gabby says "See you soon".' Baldock rubs his chin in thought. 'I know the proper name, the Latin name,' he says. 'Yeah, that's it,' he wags a finger absently. '*Psittacus erithacus*. That's the right name of the African Grey Parrot, according to the booklet.'

'They don't have big brains, do they?'

'Parrots, you mean?'

'Yeah, and birds generally.'

'I suppose not.'

'And yet parrots can say words and phrases which are perfectly enunciated and sensible. Bonobos are much more complex, their brains are very much bigger – much more like *our* brains.'

'This bonobo of yours – what's her name did you say?'

'Bertha.'

'Bertha speaks…English?'

'Yes. Grammatically correct English sentences. We've given her lots of opportunities to hear how spoken words in our language are strung together – that's how human children learn to speak. And when Bertha was a baby, colleagues at the institute took it in turns to sing to her soothingly before tucking her into bed.'

'She sleeps in a bed?'

'Yes, and she has her own table, chair and hi-fi system. Her ability to speak, to express preferences in words, although it's poor and still developing, is further proof that bonobos are so close to us humans on the evolutionary scale that they can actually become more like us with a bit of genetic manipulation. I don't suppose you've heard of Nim Chimpsky.'

'Nim who?'

'Chimpsky. He was the chimpanzee at the centre of an experiment at Columbia University under Professor Herbert Terrace in the nineteen seventies. Nim was brought up in the same way as human children and taught to use sign language. The researchers wanted to show that Noam Chomsky, professor of linguistics at the Massachusetts Institute of Technology, was wrong when he argued that only humans can speak, can utter "an infinite hierarchy of expressions". Chomsky believed this – that people speak in sentences – because they have, among other things, a specific set of genes that enable them to do so. Nim the chimp was dressed in human children's clothes, he was even breastfed by a human mother for a while, and had intense relationships with several human beings over many months.'

'But why?' Baldock asks, an expression of distaste on his face. 'Why pretend he was a human child when he plainly wasn't?'

'To try to show that speech was simply a matter of copying the behaviour of the humans around him. It didn't work, of course. The experiment was a dismal failure, and was bound to be.'

'There you are,' Baldock smirks, waving a hand dismissively. 'What's so different about *your* chimpanzee that she can speak?'

'I told you. Because of the human genes we spliced into her parents, Bertha was born with the right brain tissue for speech. She has the appropriate genetic endowment, which Professor Chomsky stated clearly was a fundamental condition for speech. The ground beneath the world has shifted seismically, thanks to new knowledge. We are living in a paradigm shift. The only way to adjust healthily to the new dispensation is by abandoning the false assumptions we've all accepted about human nature. So what d'you say, Baldock? I'll come to Danny's resurrection ceremony in Chesterton if you first come to the institute to meet Bertha.'

'You'll bring your wife Sophie Gresham?'

'I'll convey your invitation to her and bring her if she agrees to come. I can't say more than that. She's been refusing point blank to come to the institute and meet Bertha. Very derogatory, her attitude – so at odds with her sensible self.'

The turmoil in Baldock's heart is visible in the tortured expressions that chase one another across his face. He obviously can't think far ahead. He's like the ancients who thought their horsemen carrying messages were the ultimate in communications technology. He thinks the future must be the same as the past. The shades of purple and pink of his face seem to blend and coagulate in an unsettled confusion. He looks to the right, then to the left, notices the empty coffee mug in front of him and pushes it away. Presently he rises from his chair and steps from one end of the floor to the other.

He paces the length of the kitchen twice, deep in thought, his shoulders hunched forward, his chunky hands clasped behind his back. Then he stops at the Welsh dresser and turns to me.

'To do what Jesus urges us, for no other reason – for the sake only of Danny's resurrection – I'll do it. I'll come to your institute. I'll walk into the Devil's lair to do God's work.'

'Can you be here tomorrow morning at nine sharp?'

'Yes, I can. But why don't I meet you at the institute? I live in Cambridge – that would be more convenient for me.'

'For security reasons. We have entry and exit protocols. People aren't allowed access without careful vetting. There are competitors in this line of chimeric research who'd love us to mess up and lose the lead we have on other labs.'

'You trust me enough to take me there?'

'You aren't into molecular biology, are you?'

'Of course I'm not.'

'Well then. I'll inform security in advance. You won't get in otherwise. Make sure you're here, alone, tomorrow morning at nine.'

'I'll be here tomorrow morning at nine – you have my word. All I ask in return is that you do your best to bring your wife to the Mullins house in Chesterton this coming Sunday afternoon.'

'I'll do what I can, Baldock. My wife and I are dining in

Cambridge tonight – I'll convey your invitation then. But it's up to her whether or not she comes. She's been refusing steadfastly to come to my place of work, so what she'll think about *your* gig I have no idea.'

'Just read the Book of Revelation,' he urges me as I lead him from the kitchen through the house to the front door. 'See for yourself, Doctor Venn. Open your heart – for your own good.'

'I'll read it,' I nod with a smile and clasp his proffered hand. 'And thanks for coming all this way to tell me about Danny Mullins.'

'He needs your help, urgently. It's important that you convey my invitation to your wife. It would be best if you turned up together.'

'I'll tell her – rest assured,' I reply, keeping eye contact. 'But it's up to her, really, whether she comes or not.'

'So much good would result if you came as a couple, as two who have become one,' he makes the point again before stepping out of the house. 'It's only in Chesterton, Doctor Venn, just north of Jesus College and Midsummer Common in Cambridge,' he turns and adds, 'less than two miles from here.'

26

I'm a research scientist, a molecular biologist. New knowledge is my stock in trade. I keep an open mind. So after I see Baldock to the door and watch his car pull round the circular lawn and out of our drive, I take his advice. I go into the library and find our three editions of the Bible on the shelf where we keep our philosophy books: the *King James Bible* of 1611, the *Common English Version of the American Bible Union* published in 1864, and the *American Standard Version of the Holy Bible* of 1901 which is known as the 'Rock of Biblical Honesty'.

I sit down at the leather-topped table, switch on one of the lamps and proceed to read the twenty-two chapters of the Book of Revelation. It's the closing book of the New Testament and was written, Sophie tells me later, in Greek by the apostle John while he was on the island of Patmos; he'd been banished there by the emperor Domitian in about AD 64. I turn from edition to edition as I read, comparing the verses and the chapters, and can't help noticing that the translations differ, in syntax, idiom and cadence. For want of other insights, I conclude that these differences result from the varying usages of English in the historical periods concerned, the King James version being written in Jacobean English, the other two in more recent dialects but still based closely on the 'authorised' version.

Sophie and I are dining out tonight, but there are a few hours left before I'm due to meet her in Cambridge.

I read with an open mind: 'The revelation of Jesus Christ, which God gave him to show his servants what must soon take place. He made it known by sending his angel to his servant John, who testifies to everything he saw...'

I read: '"I am the Alpha and the Omega," says the Lord, "who is, who was, and who is to come, the Almighty."'

I'm about to read on when I feel my phone vibrating with a buzz in a pocket of my jeans. I get the phone out and see that there's a text message from Sophie: *Hi Charlie. See you at the taverna at 8. Love you.* I have plenty of time. I definitely won't be late. I never keep Sophie waiting.

I continue reading: 'After this I looked, and there before me was a door standing open in heaven. And the voice I had heard first speaking to me like a trumpet said, "Come up here, and I will show you what must take place after this." At once I was in the Spirit, and there before me was a throne in heaven with someone sitting on it. And the one who sat there had the appearance of jasper and carnelian. A rainbow resembling an emerald encircled the throne. Surrounding the throne were twenty-four other thrones, and seated on them were twenty-four elders. They were dressed in white and had crowns of gold on their heads. From the throne came flashes of lightning, rumblings and peals of thunder.'

I persevere and keep reading, page after page, continually switching between the three versions: 'Each of the four living creatures had six wings and was covered with eyes all around, even under his wings. Day and night they never stop saying:

Holy, holy, holy
is the Lord God Almighty,
who was, and is, and is to come.'

And I read about scrolls and lambs who open seals on the scrolls, about a black horse and a rider holding a pair of scales, about a great multitude wearing white robes which they've washed in lamb's blood and holding palm branches in their hands, all of them crying out that salvation belongs to their God who sits on the throne, and to the lamb.

Then I come to chapter eight which tells how 'a third of the sun was struck, a third of the moon, and a third of the stars, so that a third of them turned dark. A third of the day was without light, and also a third of the night.'

The poetry allows us to acknowledge 'a woman clothed with the sun' who has 'the moon under her feet and a crown of twelve stars on her head'; she is confronted by 'an enormous red dragon' which has seven heads and ten horns and seven crowns on its heads. The tail of this dragon sweeps a third of the stars out of the sky and flings them to Earth. The laws of physics must have been set aside to accommodate these events; stars have always been suns which simply cannot be 'flung to earth'.

Meanwhile, the woman clothed in the sun is pregnant and about to give birth, and the dragon hopes to devour her child as soon as it is born. But the dragon is foiled. The woman gives birth to a 'male son' who is snatched up to God and his throne. And the male son is scheduled to 'rule all the nations with an iron sceptre'.

The imagery is vivid. In chapter fourteen, for example, there is a white cloud and seated on the cloud is one 'like a son of man' with a golden crown on his head and a sharp sickle in his hand. He swings the sickle over the Earth 'and the earth was harvested'.

There are also seven plagues, seven bowls of God's wrath, and a woman dressed in purple and scarlet sitting on a scarlet beast, holding in her hand a golden cup 'filled with abominable things and the filth of her adulteries' – the archetype of all prostitutes, prototype of the hooker. The depth of the misogyny and the unmitigated rancour it rouses is unashamed and upfront: etched into the forehead of the woman in purple and scarlet for all to see is the text:

MYSTERY
BABYLON THE GREAT
THE MOTHER OF PROSTITUTES
AND OF THE ABOMINATIONS
OF THE EARTH.

Then an angel explains that the woman is 'the great city that rules over the kings of the earth'; she will be brought to ruin when God accomplishes his purpose. The beast and the ten horns will destroy her and leave her naked; 'they will eat her flesh and burn her with fire'.

And a great multitude raise their voices in heaven and shout: 'Hallelujah! The smoke from her goes up for ever and ever.' And the twenty-four elders and the four living creatures fall down and worship God, who is seated on the throne – and they cry out: 'Amen. Hallelujah.'

Then the Holy City, the new Jerusalem, comes down out of heaven from God, 'prepared as a bride adorned for her husband. And I heard a great voice out of heaven saying, Behold, the tabernacle of God is with men, and he will dwell with them, and they shall be his people, and God himself shall be with them, and be their God. And God shall wipe away all tears from their eyes; and there shall be no more death, neither sorrow, nor crying, neither shall there be any more pain: for the former things are passed away.'

And the being on the throne then says: 'Behold, I make all things new.' And he said unto me, Write: for these words are true and faithful.'

There will be no more death or mourning or crying or pain, he said, and since then there has not been a single conflict in the world, no wars, crusades or jihads, no military invasions for land or oil, no bombardment of unarmed civilians who pose no threat, no tit-for-tat boomerangs of violence when the victims strike back, no slaughter of innocents or untimely deaths, let alone miserable ways of dying such as bubonic plague, Lassa fever or malaria.

There have not been any beheadings since that voice boomed out its good news, no drawings-and-quartering, no burnings alive, no hanging or use of the electric chair, no legally administered lethal injections under the gaze of municipal witnesses. Neither has there been any tar-and-feathering or strange fruit hanging from a poplar tree with members of the master race laughing and pointing at the twisting corpse.

The crushing frustrations of institutional racism have never been experienced by anyone anywhere ever, and slavery and chained bodies stacked in piles in the holds of ships crossing the Atlantic are merely figments of someone's fevered imagination, as are the hallucinations known as the Holocaust, concentration camps, apartheid, ethnic cleansing, starvation wages, and villages where young girls and boys are sold to paedophile tourists with lots of money in their pockets.

What a powerful god is the Abrahamic god. Wow!

Since his voice filled the sky with that message of peace, there hasn't been any unhappiness in any country, no tears of grief, no bereaved families wailing or tugging their hair in bewildered sorrow, no Semites with their claws on one another's throats as they jerk about in a ghoulish dance to the sounds of houses being blown up, schoolchildren shot dead, buses, restaurants and nightclubs suicide-bombed and women giving birth to babies in the rubble of a place called 'the Holy Land'.

What a superb accomplishment; just what the doctor ordered. No women raped, beaten or brutalised anywhere; no mothers abandoned in squalor to care for their children on a pittance; no debilitating diseases, no Aids pandemic, no homeless cripples begging for crumbs, no one in prison for stealing food, no homophobia or gay-bashing or gay-killing, no unwanted infants left on doorsteps, no floods carrying towns away on tides of mud or famines reducing whole populations to dust-covered skeletons so alluring to parasitic flies.

There have been no earthquakes or tsunamis that devastate coastal communities, no hurricanes that drown dozens, no inundating floods.

Truly marvellous: not a single source in creation of pain, suffering or depravity anywhere in the world.

We should bow our heads to the almighty Abrahamic god.

Thanks to him there has been nothing but joy, prosperity and the spirit of carnival for over two thousand years. Enough food for everyone, lumps of meat even for the dogs who lie bloated on their backs in the warmth of the sun, and crates of beer bottles everywhere.

No doubt about it: every word is true; every word is, as Baldock said, 'inerrant'. Check it out: 'I am making everything new! There will be no more death or mourning or crying or pain.'

Such is the ambiguous embrace of the almighty who loves the creatures he has conjured into being, loves them unreservedly, people and animals, children and adults alike, yet slaughters them regularly, the frail as well as the fit, rich and poor, black and white. On a whim he crushes them under collapsing mountains. He destroys their property and livelihoods and leaves them destitute, exposed to the freezing winds, the blazing sun, without food, without succour, their churches and mosques smashed to smithereens like so much garbage.

I close the three Bibles with their different linguistic effects and take them back to their places on the shelf. As I do so, my mind turns to a statement my fellow American, the stand-up comic George Carlin, once made: 'When it comes to bullshit, big-time major league bullshit, you have to stand in awe of the all-time champion of false promises and exaggerated claims, religion. Religion has the greatest bullshit story ever told.'

George Carlin recorded eighteen comedy albums, four of them gold, and performed eleven solo HBO comedy specials. His 1997 book *Brain Droppings* spent 40 weeks in *The New York Times* bestseller list. He once said: 'First thing they do is tell you there's an invisible man in the sky who's going to march you down to a burning place if he doesn't like you. If they can get you to believe that, it's all over… There's no real education. It's an indoctrination…' He also said: 'It's called the American Dream because you have to be asleep to believe it.'

I have time to shower and get dressed for dinner with Sophie in Cambridge. I have time to think about what I've just read. It occurs to me that George Carlin's sentiments might have come across less intemperately, and more poetically, perhaps, if he'd described religion's outpourings by using a phrase which Angela Carter deployed in a different context in her novel *The Passion of New Eve:* 'arabesques of kitsch and hyperbole'.

I'm not at all sure how Sophie is going to react when I tell her we've been invited to a resurrection ceremony at Chesterton this coming Sunday afternoon, the day of our tenth wedding anniversary. I'm not even sure why I responded to such an outlandish request the way I did: 'Please come with your wife, Doctor Venn'. Shouldn't I have sent Baldock packing as soon as he started talking about everlasting happiness in a place unsullied by things profane?

As I stand under the jets of water in the shower room, shampooing my hair and washing my body with a fragrant gel which Sophie bought for us, I see in my mind's eye the bleeding boy who'd been knocked off his bicycle by a removals van in Silver Street. His name was Daniel Mullins, Baldock said; he thanked me for calling the ambulance and wished me a long and happy life.

I wish he hadn't died. At the time of the accident it didn't occur to me that his injuries would prove fatal. He was so young, only twelve years old. He was a very good chess player with lots of potential, keen to meet the Russian champion of the world, so keen that he started teaching himself Russian from a phrase-book. I feel sad as the jets of water hit my head and the suds slide down my shoulders and torso. The poor boy. I suddenly wish I knew him. I wish I'd had the chance to play a game of chess with him, hear the sounds of his voice, find out his likes and dislikes as he destroyed me with one of the moves in his brilliant young mind.

It is so sad, so cruel, when a child dies, when a life that might have grown into vibrant adulthood is suddenly snuffed out meaninglessly.

I wonder how Sophie's going to respond when I tell her that Danny Mullins, the blond boy with the pointed chin whose photo I took with my phone and sent her as he lay bleeding a few days ago, is dead, and that we've been invited to his resurrection ceremony.

27

'I saw those flowers on the pavement on my way here,' Sophie says.

'At the River Gate entrance to Queens' College?'

'Yes, opposite the Anchor pub. There were so many bouquets I had to step around them. Lovely flowers, many of them wrapped in cellophane tied with ribbons. They looked sad on the cold stone.'

'Where'd you leave your car?'

'In Sidgwick Avenue. I walked by the Fisher Building and there they were, all over the pavement. We really should go, Charlie. If Baldock said he'd prefer us to come as a married couple, as a reflection of the Holy Family, then why shouldn't we go together? You're my husband and I'm your wife. We were married in church – it's perfect. We really must go.'

'Didn't you hear what I said? It's a resurrection ceremony he was wanting us to attend – in the presence possibly of angels.'

'I heard you.'

'A resurrection, Sophie. An attempt to bring a dead boy back to life.'

'I know – with the power of prayer and the presence of as many people as possible who knew or saw Danny Mullins when he was alive.'

'Am I hearing you right? You sound keen to go.'

'I am keen, Charlie – very.'

Sophie slices one of the *dolmades* on her plate into sections, stabs a piece with her fork and puts it into her mouth. She chews it, shuts her eyes and savours the flavours of herbs and minced beef wrapped in vine leaf.

'Mmm,' she smiles, 'delicious.'

The sauce smudges her lips and trickles down the side of her mouth. She dabs it away with her napkin and tucks into the food, smiling at me from time to time. Presently she reaches for the bottle of *retsina* between us on the white tablecloth, tops up my glass and refills hers.

We're in a cosy nook on the lower floor of the taverna, a grotto-like alcove of unplastered stone just large enough for a table for two. We're hidden from most of the other diners, a few of them students in jeans with college scarves round their necks, and from the waiters balancing trays as they glide to and fro, each with a cloth folded over a sleeve of his white shirt. The food is good, but Sophie likes this place also because of its unpretentious ambience. The plain-coloured walls and Greek motifs remind her of a taverna in the countryside south of Athens where we stopped to have a meal when driving along the coast road to see the Temple of Poseidon at Cape Sunion on the way back from our honeymoon in Singapore.

'It's a rare opportunity, too good miss,' Sophie says, lifting her glass and taking a sip.

'An opportunity for what?'

'To see fundamentalists in their element. It's like a natural experiment, Charlie – organised by someone else for us to observe without any sense of being peeping toms or gate-crashers.'

'It isn't a party, Sophie. It's an event they take very seriously.'

'Of course it is. That's why I want to be there. We aren't invited to this sort of function every day.' Sophie puts down her knife and fork, opens her handbag and brings out her phone. She flicks it open, presses a key and looks at the screen. 'We've been invited thanks to him,' she says, turning the phone so I can see the photo on the screen: it's the shot of injured Danny in Silver Street which I sent her a few days ago when it simply hadn't occurred to me that he would soon be dead.

'I can't help feeling that Danny's mother and father are in for another shock,' I say when Sophie returns the phone to her bag. 'They've lost their son and they're bound to feel they've lost him again when the prayers and the collective presence don't work. Their understanding of resurrection is too literal. There's no way Danny's ever going to come back and play chess again. Nor will he ever get to Russia, no matter how many Russian words and phrases he'd learnt before he died.'

'Somehow I don't think they're as sceptical as you, Charlie.'

'Sceptical? What d'you mean *sceptical*? There's no *room* for scepticism. The boy has been certified clinically dead – period. He should remain in a mortuary, not in a bed in a suburban house that's going to be milling with people chanting prayers and doing their damndest to pretend the laws of chemistry don't apply to members of their sect.'

'But that's what they *believe*. Rising from the dead is the central tenet of their faith. It's what Jesus urges them to do, as you told me Baldock said, quoting the Bible, Matthew chapter ten, verse eight.'

'It's the central tenet of other faiths too, Sophie, but that doesn't make it true. Rising from the dead, whether to live again on Earth or to go to a place called Heaven – that idea goes a long way back. It goes back at least nine-thousand years to the time when agriculture started in Anatolia in what is now called Turkey. Human beings realised at that time that if you planted seeds and rain fell on the soil they would grow into crops. It was then that people stopped being hunter-gatherers. They stopped following the food, stopped moving across the land picking fruit and berries

237

from the trees and bushes and trapping wild animals. They settled down beside their cultivated fields, and that was the beginning of civilisation.'

'People then built more permanent dwellings with streets between them, the hypothesis goes, and had time for handicrafts and other occupations.'

'It isn't just hypothesis, Sophie. There's archaeological evidence to support it. It wasn't necessary any more for everyone to be out foraging for food. Food ceased to command the attention of every man, woman and child twenty-four seven. That's when some individuals started worshipping the gods full time – they were the first priests. They started making offerings to the gods whom they believed controlled the weather and thus the supply of food from their fields. They noticed that although the crops died down and disappeared in winter, they rose to life again in spring and summer.'

'They noticed the changing seasons, you mean?'

'Yeah, and that's where they got the idea of resurrection from – the crops in their fields. They began to think that people too came back to life after death. Isn't it strange,' I say to Sophie across the table as we eat our food and drink our wine, 'that the superstition of human resurrection came from the life-and-death cycle of the agricultural seasons.'

Sophie chews her food, clears her teeth with her tongue and takes a sip of wine. 'I discovered at the library,' she says, 'that people in West Africa believed the god Pemba sacrificed himself regularly. He kept living again as a tree so that human souls could be created from the bark of the tree.'

'So the Christian resurrection story of Easter is a version of an older theme, you're saying? It's a pagan idea that pre-dates Jesus by many centuries?'

Sophie nods. 'It would seem so,' she says, reaching out with her knife and fork and helping herself to two more *dolmades*. 'According to the novelist Chinua Achebe in *Things*

238

Fall Apart, there was among the Ibo people of Nigeria even a god of yams called Ifejioku, and an earth goddess called Ani who was the source of all fertility and the ultimate judge of morality and conduct.'

A god of yams, I think, watching Sophie chewing her food, and an ideological hierarchy of fruit and vegetables tries to form in my mind: saintly pumpkins, holy carrots and venerable bunches of radish, but the concept is too way out to develop any farther.

'People have always wanted to know where they came from, what their origins were,' Sophie says. 'They've always wanted someone else to take responsibility for their well-being. Muslims too believe in resurrection – that their souls will go to *jannah*, heaven, after what they call *Yoam mid'deen*, the Day of Judgement, literally the Day of Religion. They believe they'll go to heaven if, on balance, they were good in this life, or they'll go to hell, *jahannam*, if they were bad. I discovered this while I was living in Cairo. The more emotional among them believe the Prophet Muhammad rose from the dead when he died in 632 and ascended to heaven on the back of a white Arab stallion called Buraq. That event is known to Muslims as the *miraj* – "the night journey". He ascended from Jerusalem, which Muslims call al-Quds – that's one reason why Jerusalem is so important to them. But many Muslim scholars don't accept the story of the horse. They say it's a legend, a myth created by devout people tempted to project super-human qualities on to the Prophet Muhammad. There was no horse, they say. The Prophet was a human being like all other humans; he never made any claims to being a deity of any kind. That's why it's always been a gross misrepresentation of their religion to call it Mohammadenism. Muslims believe in God, not in Muhammad. They believe the Prophet was the last messenger of God to humanity. A white Arab stallion with flowing mane taking him bare-back across the star-studded night skies to paradise – stunning though that image is, it is pure romance.' Sophie reaches out and lifts the bottle. 'Some more wine?'

'Please,' I nod, and she refills my glass.

'I've been going to University Library for the past week,' she says, 'researching social life in the Middle Ages, making endless notes. People were so superstitious then, so unbelievably ignorant. Pope Innocent the Eighth issued a document in 1486 called *Malleus Maleficarum* – hammer of the witches – to guide the witch hunts. Because burning supposedly drove out the demons from a person's body, those thought to be witches had to be burned *alive*,' Sophie stresses. 'If a woman had a mind of her own, if she was independent in any way, she was thought to be possessed by demons which had to be exorcised. It was the duty of her neighbours to report her to the Church authorities. A woman wasn't supposed to have opinions of her own – she wasn't supposed to contradict her husband or the men in the community. It was God's word she was contradicting if she contradicted the men she knew.'

'God's word? How come it was God's word she was contradicting?'

'Every word in the Bible was believed to be literally true. As Paul's second letter to Timothy points out: "All Scripture is God-breathed and is used for teaching, rebuking, correcting and training in righteousness." And the Bible teaches that women should shut up and bow to men.'

'Have you been reading the Bible too'

'Yes – to cross-check the historical documents.'

'Where does it say women should bow to men?'

'In several places. It's the general tone of gender relations, and also in Paul's first letter to Timothy, chapter two, verses eleven to fifteen.'

'You sound like Baldock, Sophie – he has the Bible at his fingertips.'

'I have the Bible as a reference document. The verses

concerned say that a woman should learn in quietness and full submission. "Let the woman learn in silence with all subjection," are the exact words. "I suffer not a woman to teach, nor to usurp authority over the man, but to be in silence." A woman is not permitted to teach or to have authority over a man. She must be silent. Those are the exact words: *she must be silent*. This is because Adam was formed first, then Eve. That is supposed to be a reason. And it wasn't Adam who was deceived by the Devil. It was Eve, the woman, who was deceived and became a sinner.'

'So if a woman argued with men and contradicted them, she was under the influence of Satan?'

'Yes, no doubt about it.'

'That implies that Mrs Thatcher, a mover and shaker if ever there was one, was in Satan's control for at least eleven years.'

'She wasn't called the Iron Lady for nothing,' Sophie replies.

'I know. We used to hear about her in the States – all the men in her cabinet quaking in her presence. Satan obviously has an eye for extraordinary women.'

'It would seem so,' Sophie smiles. 'The Bible at that point goes on to say that nevertheless women will be kept safe through childbirth. By giving birth to babies, women's souls will be safe.'

'What about women who didn't *want* to have children?'

'They had no choice – it was their main purpose in life.'

'What if they *couldn't* give birth, couldn't get pregnant?'

'Then that was proof that they were witches and had to be burned alive. When the Church had power, the last thing its priests wanted to do was talk and behave like social workers, counsellors, environmental activists, as they do all the time today, trying to be useful in secular ways. Priests and bishops kept baying for blood when they had power, and there were fires burning in towns and villages all over Europe.'

'And in Salem, Massachusetts too,' I add. 'People were condemned as witches there as well. Arthur Miller shows in his play *The Crucible* a witch trial in the late 17th century. But the method of execution changed from burning to hanging. And those who refused to enter a plea, who tried to remain aloof from the proceedings by pleading neither "innocent" nor "guilty", were presumed to be guilty and sentenced to "pressing" – rocks were piled on their chests, abdomen and limbs until they were crushed to death. Baldock told me that the members of his church – God's Alliance – also have Jesus in their hearts and believe that every word in the Bible is, as he put it, *inerrant*.'

'They do,' Sophie says. 'They aren't allowed to doubt. People who doubt the Bible are called doubting Thomases. Doubt is a sign that the Devil's seduction is working, whilst certainty is a sign of righteousness. The amazing thing is that even as late as Shakespeare's time the witch craze in England and Europe hadn't yet reached its peak. Who knows how that man stayed so calm and clear-eyed in those terrible times and distilled such everlasting poetry. All around him the old world of aristocratic dominance was crumbling, undermined by the modern energies of an emerging mercantile class. He completed five of his tragedies between 1605 and 1608 – *King Lear, Macbeth, Timon of Athens, Antony and Cleopatra* and *Coriolanus*. Talk about productivity!' Sophie grins. 'It was a time of tremendous changes in ethos and conduct. Shakespeare's was a border-age between the medieval past when people were taught, and believed, that they were steeped in sin, that they were evil and corrupt from the word go, even as babies, and a future no longer completely sold on superstition but still unsure of the way ahead.'

28

Sophie pauses and a pensive look comes into her eyes. For a long moment her mind is elsewhere, far away. When she focuses on me again, there's a curious expression on her face.

'I've done a helluva lot of research lately,' she says, 'and by a process of serendipity I came across something intriguing. It could be an example of the sort of superstition that still grips some people's minds today, but I'm not so sure. I think there might be more to it than that.'

'What's it about?'

'It's about William Shakespeare's genius.'

'What about it?'

'Its origins, where it came from. Shakespeare wasn't an aristocrat – he went to the same free school in Stratford-on-Avon as other common boys. His mother Mary Arden was of yeoman farming stock. His father John was illiterate; he couldn't sign his name on documents so he drew the symbol of his trade, a pair of glove-makers' compasses. Even though John Shakespeare rose to become an important man in Stratford's politics, and became wealthy from trading illegally in wool, his son William never had a posh education. In fact he had to leave school at the age of fourteen when his father's illegal wool trading was discovered by the authorities. It isn't the sort of background one associates with poetic sensitivity, let alone psychological genius. So what accounts for the supreme, enduring quality of William Shakespeare's work?'

'Are you asking me, Sophie – or are you going to tell me?'

'It's the question of the origins of Shakespeare's genius which gave rise to the number explanation.'

'The *what* explanation?'

'The number explanation, the number twenty-three. I came across it in University Library quite by chance,' Sophie says, the smile on her face not cancelling the fascination in her eyes. 'It goes something like this. Shakespeare was born on the twenty-third of April and he died on the twenty-third of April. He'd written all his work within twenty-three years. His first play, *Titus Andronicus*, was published when he was twenty-three. The first Folio of his works appeared in 1623. If you add the dates of his birth and death, twenty-three and twenty-three, you get forty-six. Go to Psalm forty-six in the Bible and you'll find, as I did, that the forty-sixth word from the beginning is "Shake" and the forty-sixth word from the end is "Spear".'

'Are you kidding, Sophie?'

'No,' she replies, shaking her head. 'I'm dead serious.'

'My first reaction is to say that it must be a series of coincidences.'

'But?'

'But...well, it's a bit glib, isn't it? – simply to say it's no more than coincidence.'

'That's what *I* thought, Charlie. And then I started reading about the magical properties of numbers which people in the past were so plugged into. Why is it the *Bible* that the two parts of his name appear in? Why not some other book, an anthology of poetry, say, or the script of a famous play?'

I can't think of an answer. I simply return Sophie's gaze. The charges of witchcraft that used to be brought against people were very often based on chance events or coincidences, such as a woman talking in her sleep who'd be accused of communing with the Devil, or a man whose fields gave him a better yield of crops for several years in a row than his neighbours got from *their* fields. The results of intelligence and hard work were sometimes construed as proof of Satan's presence.

It occurs to me as I glance at the couple eating at the table visible from our alcove how easy it would be for those days of ignorant cruelty to return. Baldock said that politicians in Alabama and other states had succeeded in getting a warning pasted in biology textbooks that Darwin's theory of evolution is nothing more than an unproven theory (demonstrating their scientific illiteracy: theories are never *proven*; at best, a theory is *verified* by all the available evidence, *supported* by the relevant data, never *contradicted* by any material facts of reality). Their unashamed purpose all along has been to strengthen the case of creationism – that humanity came direct from God via Adam and Eve, and not, as those of like mind tend to put it, from monkeys in the jungle. The fact that we molecular biologists possess irrefutable DNA evidence that humans have shared the same biological heritage with plants, insects and animals for millions of years obviously counts for nothing. The ignorant are again sitting in judgement on those who have arduously wrested new knowledge from nature. The ignorant still base their assertions on manifest falsehoods. They derive sustenance from a book brimful of nastiness and exhortations to cruelty and slaughter that was written when all their mentors believed the world was flat and that intelligent women were incorrigible agents of the Devil. Empirical evidence is worthless to them. The gullible cohorts believe blind faith is all that matters.

But what's to stop God's Alliance from becoming literal in other ways? What's to stop them saying that those who disagree with them are possessed by demons, that free speech is evil, free speech is unpatriotic? Or that all women should return to the path of God and stop arguing with men, stop demanding equal rights, stop striving for senior positions in society, such as headteacher, chief executive, prime minister, president or secretary of state? They'll get a lot of support, no doubt, and lots of petro-dollars too, from regimes in the Middle East, Asia and the American Bible Belt where medieval customs are alive and kicking. Not far down that road one can see piles of firewood and long wooden planks ordered from timber merchants – preparations being made to resume the hallowed tradition of tying people to the stake and burning them alive in public, smirking and gloating when the unfortunates shriek in pain as their skin begins to blister, blacken and dissolve, the way onlookers are still invited to smirk and gloat at public beheadings with curved swords in a certain part of the world.

Once enough minds have been closed by the righteous clamour, and kept closed by the stifling effects of political correctness; once large enough numbers of disaffected and economically pauperised individuals have been recruited into God's Alliance by means of advertising campaigns, evangelical television programmes, mass rallies in football stadiums and pamphlets whose appeal lies in their simplistic messages – enough minds to win local elections by the democratic process – then very little stands in the way of the school system being controlled by bigots, as it already is in parts of America and as it's beginning to be in England where Christian entrepreneurs who have two million pounds to spare can buy influence and authority from the government. The sprouting of 'faith schools' is another symptom of the backward slide. The use of taxpayers' money to finance classrooms where various brands of superstition are propagated and reinforced is entirely unjust: non-believers, secularists, humanists, agnostics find themselves financing against their will slightly varying versions of obscurantism in these schools.

Biology and other 'anti-religious' subjects could one day be banned from every school curriculum and college syllabus. We would bear witness again and again to instances of *auto-da-fé*, people being burned as an act of faith by the pious, by agents of the Inquisition for being 'heretics', or, in today's parlance, for being 'dissidents', 'politically incorrect', 'unpatriotic'. Laboratories, libraries and lecture rooms might well be put to the torch and burned to the ground – by 'adults' throwing tantrums and insisting that things are the way they want them to be, never changing, stagnant from epoch to epoch, and not the way things actually are – subject constantly to change, ever in a state of metamorphosis.

There are excellent historical reasons for one's fears.

'Watch out for false prophets,' Baldock quoted from the Bible when he was having coffee with me in the kitchen. 'They come to you in sheep's clothing, but inwardly they are ravening wolves.'

I feel Sophie's hand touching mine on the tablecloth. She smiles and motions with her head to the waiter standing by our table with a bowl in his hands.

'More *dolmades*, sir?' he asks.

I glance up at him and shake my head. 'No, thanks.'

The waiter looks at Sophie; she too shakes her head. 'Bring the *sousoukákia*, please,' she tells him.

He gathers up our plates and cutlery, turns on his heels and darts away.

'So you think we really should go to Danny's resurrection ceremony.'

'Yes,' Sophie says, 'I do. It'll be instructive.'

'You're looking at it as a writer, aren't you?'

'Why not? I'm a writer – it's all grist to the mill. You said Baldock said that most born-again fundamentalists suffered a traumatic experience of one kind or another and that their conversion had a therapeutic effect, making them in many cases bark like dogs and writhe on the floor in front of hundreds of other people, with no embarrassment or sense of losing their dignity. It sounds as if this born-again religion

247

is interchangeable with psychiatric treatment, that godliness has become a mental stabiliser in the face of unbearable stress – from fear of unemployment, loss of status, loss of savings or partner, whatever. If we went to Danny's house and met his parents, I could talk to people there, find out what they think, when exactly they joined the alliance and why. This could be an excellent opportunity to change my genre.'

'From historical romance to modern fiction?'

'Yes. I've been wanting to give it a go for a long time, but haven't figured out how to make the switch. An engrossing theme – I just couldn't think of one. To tell you the truth, Charlie, I've been afraid to change. I've got so used to being successful, being well reviewed, that I've not wanted to risk a new departure. But I know in my heart I'll start repeating myself and become boring if I don't gird my loins and make the move while I still have the energy. The time has come for courage,' she adds, smiling, pursing her lips and nodding. 'Perhaps when I do manage the switch, you'll take what I write more seriously.'

I can see she's serious, but I've had no idea she put so much store by my opinion of her work. I've always assumed that being successful at selling yarns was the end of her writing ambition, despite my periodic suggestions that she focus on the problems of the present. Her longing to switch to modern themes comes as a revelation – even though we've been together nearly ten full years.

'Are you serious, Sophie – or just kidding?'

'I'm not kidding, Charlie.'

'Why haven't you told me before? I've been suggesting for years that you switch over – really use your brains.'

'Because I felt you'd think I was just saying it to please you. I thought it would be best to surprise you one day with a different kind of novel, something that isn't quite so distant from the work *you* do. I first have to complete my present project, though – the collection of historical tales

I'm contracted to deliver. But I can feel it in my guts already – the rigours are going to be different. There'll be no going back once I make the change – unless of course I produce my work as separate personas.'

'Using a pseudonym? Two separate identities?'

'Possibly.'

'Why not? This is wonderful news, Sophie. You have so much to offer. I'm sure you'll thrive there and grow – in a genre with a sharper edge. Your work will be more incisive and rewarding than so much fiction today – all good-looking gums and soporific pap.'

She grins, her lovely lips revealing perfect white teeth plastered with bits of vine leaf. Looking at her mouth, I remember again how much I love her, how much pleasure her presence has given me over the years.

'It's our tenth anniversary on Sunday the eighteenth of September, darling. Are you still keen on going to that jazz club in London the night before?'

'Very much so,' she replies. 'I booked a table ages ago. We take a taxi from our hotel in London to that gig, spend the night at the hotel, have lunch there next day, then drive back to Cambridge. I'll take the M25 to junction twenty-seven and up the M11 past the Duxford Aircraft Museum to junction twelve. We go straight to the Mullins house in Chesterton. It's just beyond Wesley House and Jesus College, on the other side of the Cam. What d'you say, Charlie?'

'Okay, if that's what you want. I like that club. The atmosphere there reminds me of one or two clubs in Boston.' I keep eye contact and try to keep my voice even, try not to spoil the mood. 'There's something I have to tell you, Sophie, something I feel you should know – even if you think I'm being small-hearted or silly.'

'What is it, Charlie?'

'It's – how shall I put it? It's…how easily and quickly you've chosen Baldock over me.'

There's a pause before she replies: 'What on Earth do you mean? I don't understand.'

'I tell you that a stranger called Jem Baldock came to our house today and wants us to help him bring a dead boy back to life, he wants us to mingle with born-again evangelicals who believe, on the basis of nothing sensible whatever, that prayer can put life back into a corpse – and you can't get to that house fast enough. Yet I've been asking you for endless months, for at least three years now, to come to the institute to meet Bertha who's been the subject of a highly sophisticated transfer of genes based on the most advanced scientific knowledge in the world – and you've consistently refused to come. Why are you novelists so keen on entertaining primitive bullshit, but shy away from rationality, from lucid vision? You've been refusing me the only thing I've ever asked for, but you grant a total stranger the most outlandish request – just like that,' I say, snapping a finger against my thumb.

Sophie blushes. She goes red in the face. The redness spreads down her throat and fills the part of her bosom revealed by her silk shirtdress. Her lovely body in that moment becomes suffused with the embarrassment seeping from her mind. I find out again in the most authentic way that her feelings for me are fresh and vivid; her love for me isn't jaded at all.

'The irony is too bitter to swallow, Sophie. What a weird anniversary present you're giving me – a bag of gall.'

'Oh Charlie,' she cries out as tears well up in her eyes. 'Charlie, it's not like that. I love *you*, Charlie, to the exclusion of all others. What an idiot I've been.'

There's a long pause as she struggles to gain control of her emotions. I hear the murmur of conversations at the other tables and the sounds of knives and forks on plates.

Then Sophie leans forward and reaches her hand across the table, beckoning mine. The look in those blue eyes of hers, so often alluring and coquettish, is stricken, contrite. A tear rolls down her cheek and makes me wonder with a pang whether I've done the right thing; how can upsetting her improve matters in any way? I move my hand across the table; she grasps and squeezes it.

'I'm sorry, Charlie. Please forgive me, darling. Please. I'll make it up to you, Charlie – you'll see. I'll come along tomorrow morning when you take Baldock to the institute to meet Bertha.'

'Will you, Sophie? Really?'

'Yes,' she nods, keeping eye contact and smiling, 'I will.'

'You aren't kidding? You'll meet Bertha and talk with her?'

'I will, Charlie. It's the least I can do. You mean far more to me than this Baldock whom I haven't even met. There's no way I'd choose him over you, darling – it's out of the question.'

'You'll come to the lab tomorrow morning, whole-heartedly?'

'I promise.'

'To join in the passion of our times, make a voyage of discovery deeper into the 21st century?'

'I will,' she says. She squeezes my hand again and the come-hither look reappears in her eyes. 'You'll see,' she says, 'it's not a bag of gall you're going to get from me on our anniversary. I'm going to make sure it's the best anniversary we've ever had. So eat well from now on – you're going to need all your strength.'

The waiter brings clean plates and cutlery and them out in front of us. Then he brings a bowl of the spicy meatballs done in wine with herbs and tomatoes. He lays out a bed of rice on each of our plates, dishes on to it a big helping of the *sousoukákia*, and covers the steaming flavours with a layer of cheese and cream sauce.

He stands back, pleased with his work, smiles at Sophie

and me in turn and urges us to 'Enjoy'.

We obey him immediately.

We concentrate on eating and there's a long break in our conversation. I can see the trail on Sophie's cheek left by the tear as it rolled from her eye. The mixture of spices and herbs and the wine in the food and the *retsina* in our glasses creates a special tang on the tongue; and as we eat, an inner warmth begins to glow, a succulent sensation that increases the more we satisfy our appetites. What a pleasure it is to dine with the person you love, sharing sustenance and secrets with her and anticipating the other joys lying in store.

And it's such good news that Sophie is going to change her genre, switch to writing with a sharper edge, prose that isn't her usual romantic guff. As we eat the food and drink the wine, I can't help smiling, can't help being amazed by how things have changed since Baldock rang our doorbell earlier today. He came to tell me that the boy in the road accident I'd witnessed had died. A boy I didn't know at all; a boy who wished me good health and a long happy life, has transformed my relationship with Sophie through his death. Without even meeting her, Danny has made Sophie change her mind and agree to come to the lab with me of her own free will. He has achieved something I failed to do for a full three years.

I can almost feel the disgruntlement dissolving in me, the tension seeping away, the unspoken resentment that had been growing like a tumour heavy in my heart.

29

When Jem Baldock rings our bell at precisely nine o'clock the following morning and I open the door, he is cradling in his arm a large leather-bound book.

'Good morning,' he says.

'Good morning,' I reply. 'Please come in. My wife will be accompanying us to the institute and she'll be along in a bit.'

He steps into the hall and glances at himself in the mirror above the telephone table. He is conservatively dressed again in a dark suit and tie. The side-parting of his neatly combed greying hair is perfectly straight. His bright blue eyes are shining in his clean-shaven face and there is about him again a noticeably soapy aura.

'You said your lab was security conscious. Will they mind my bringing this?' he asks, raising the large book in the crook of his arm.

'What is it?'

'It's the Bible, the Holy Bible.'

'Why've you brought it?'

'For comfort and protection.'

'Protection from what?'

'From whatever spirits dwell in the temple of arrogance you're taking me to.'

'You don't have to come, Baldock – no one's forcing you,' I tell him, keeping eye contact and noticing again the pattern in his purply-red complexion. The paler tone of his well defined lips is hard to miss, as are the tufts of hair sticking out of his nostrils. 'You shouldn't come if you feel it's going to be an ordeal. I'm not a sadist,' I say, smiling in a friendly way. 'It's not my purpose to make you suffer.'

'We made a deal,' he says, 'and I'm a man of my word. I'm here because you promised that in return you'd help with Danny Mullins's resurrection – that you'd ask Sophie Gresham to be there too as your lawful wedded wife.'

'You've nothing to worry about on that score. I conveyed your invitation to her and she gladly accepts.'

'She'll be in Chesterton with you this coming Sunday afternoon?'

'Definitely. She's keen to come. We're going to drive straight there from London after celebrating our tenth anniversary.'

Baldock's face breaks into a grin, revealing his rows of large square teeth.

'Thank you, thank you very much,' he says 'from myself and on behalf of Danny's parents, John and Ceri Mullins.'

'Let's have some coffee while we wait for my wife.'

'Yes, let's do that.'

I lead him through the house into the kitchen.

Margot Lane, our cook/housekeeper, is back from the visit to her sister in Wisbech. She'd had her hair cut into a bob and, with lipstick on her mouth, looks much younger than her fifty years. She's reaching up for mugs on the Welsh dresser as we come through the door.

'Margot,' I say with a wave of my hand, 'this is Mister Jem Baldock I was telling you about. Jem Baldock, this is Margot Lane, our housekeeper.'

'Hello,' Margot says, turning to face us, a mug in each hand.

'Hello,' Baldock replies with a slight nod of his head.

'Mister Baldock will be having coffee too,' I tell Margot. 'Black without sugar, if I remember correctly.'

'That's right,' he says.

'Would you like a croissant, or some toast perhaps?' Margot asks.

'No, thanks. I've had a full English breakfast.'

'Do sit down, Baldock,' I say, motioning to the chairs around the table.

'I'd prefer it if you called me Jem. I'm not used to being called Baldock.'

'In that case, please sit down, Jem.'

He places the Bible on the table and pulls out one of the chairs. It makes a loud scraping noise on the flagstone floor, as it did when he came to see me yesterday, and he frowns again by way of apology. Then he sits down and rests his elbows on the table.

'I think I should give you some information about Bertha, our experimental bonobo chimpanzee, so you have some conception of the creature you'll be meeting shortly.'

'You want to give me monkey information?'

'I want to give you relevant information, so you can appreciate the baseline from which Bertha's development has taken place. That way you'll—'

'Good morning. You must be Jem Baldock,' Sophie calls out, smiling brightly as she enters the kitchen and extending her hand. She's wearing a white jersey printed jacket over a white silk sweater and black tapering trousers, her wavy hair falling to her shoulders.

'Good morning, Mizz Gresham,' Baldock replies, rising from his chair and clasping her hand. 'I'm glad to meet you and very glad you've agreed to come to the resurrection of Danny Mullins.'

'I'm looking forward to it.'

'You are?'

'Very much so. I've never been to a resurrection cere-mony before.'

'Are you a believer, Mizz Gresham?'

'I believe there is a God, if that's what you mean.'

'That's what I mean,' he says, shaking her hand again. 'God doesn't demand much of us – only that we do the right

255

thing,' pointing to the Bible on the table.

'Heal the sick, cleanse the lepers, raise the dead and cast out devils, d'you mean? – as Jesus instructs us in Matthew chapter ten, verse eight.'

'Now you're talking,' Baldock beams.

'What were you chatting about when I interrupted?' Sophie asks me.

'I was telling Jem that he'd appreciate Bertha's linguistic development more fully if I gave him some background information about the species she's descended from.'

'Good idea,' Sophie says. 'I'll pay attention too this time.'

She steps to the table on the side opposite from where I'm seated and pulls out the chair next to Baldock's. He glances at her, smiles and then looks up at Margot and takes the mug of coffee she hands him. Margot gives Sophie a mugful, passes one to me, and the bob of her hair bounces as she turns and leaves the kitchen.

'Bertha is a bonobo chimpanzee,' I begin my explanation, glancing in turn at my born-again visitor, whose thick fingers are tapping the top of his leather-bound Bible, tapping out silently for all I know a religious tattoo to fend off any curse that might be wafting his way on the wings of my words, then at my legal wedded wife sitting fresh and lovely alongside him, sitting on *his* side of the table, not on mine. 'Bonobos are the highest species of animal on the evolutionary scale barring only ourselves, *Homo sapiens*. Their DNA is more than ninety-eight per cent homologous with ours, which means that they differ from us in less than two per cent of DNA. That's what accounts for their relatively high intelligence. It's what our genes *do* that matters, not how many we have. Their natural habitat is the rainforest of the Ivory Coast and the forested part of the Congo – that's where we acquired Bertha's parents. We paid cash for two bonobos, a male and a female, to villagers who are known to enjoy bonobo and monkey meat in their cuisine, especially fried primate brains.'

'D'you mean Bertha's parents would've been eaten if you hadn't bought them?' Sophie asks.

'It's distinctly possible – and the other bonobos we've bought since then. Humans are carnivores in that part of the world too – they've been eating our fellow primates since who knows when.'

'It's disgusting,' Baldock says.

'Why d'you say that?' I ask.

'Why d'you think? It's so uncivilised.'

'The Chinese eat cat meat and snake and stir-fried dog done with soy sauce—'

'That's uncivilised too.'

'—and say they've been civilised much longer than we in the West have been. Do you eat the meat of cows, Jem?'

'You mean beef?'

'Yeah.'

'Course I do. I'm English, and eating roast beef and Yorkshire pudding is part of what it is to be English.'

'Despite the risk of mad-cow disease caused by genetic mutations in the animals' brains and spinal cords, and variant Creuzfeldt-Jacob disease? And mutton and lamb?'

'Of course – and pork, ham and bacon too. There's nothing as tasty as a bit of crackling, nothing as appetising as the sound of bacon sizzling in a pan.'

'Despite all the foot-and-mouth disease? But not monkey meat, or fillet of chimpanzee? What about sheep's brains, which Arabs and other people enjoy, and frogs' legs, which the French favour, and the snails in garlic sauce they call *l'escargots*?'

'It's so close to cannibalism,' Sophie says.

'What is?'

'Eating creatures whose DNA is, as you say, less than two per cent different from ours.'

'Bertha's community do the same.'

'Really?'

'They hunt species of monkey, make traps for them and ambush them – to kill and eat. Just as humans do. Bonobos aren't squeamish. They were born with a taste for meat and go for it with gusto. Bonobos are definitely not vegetarians, and they don't feel bad about it. They have a sophisticated communication system, with particular vocalisations for particular messages, and an obvious ethical sense. When one of their kind has died, they commiserate with the dead spouse, cuddling him or her, stroking them tenderly, and uttering the most poignant sounds. And they don't leave the dead body until there's no doubt that it's not coming back to life.'

'Do they bury their dead?' Sophie asks.

'Sort of. They don't dig a hole for the corpse, but they do cover it up completely with branches, twigs and leaves. That's a pretty human act, when you remember what people in Persia used to do.'

'People in Persia?' Sophie says with a frown.

'Yeah. The ancient Persians whose religion was Zoroastrianism. It was founded by the prophet Zarathustra and its theology was the first to posit the concepts that have characterised Judaism, Christianity and Islam. Zoroastrianism originated the idea of a single god who was in permanent battle with the essence of evil, i.e. Satan. There was going to be a final showdown at the end of time between good and evil – that was where the idea of Armageddon originated. Zarathustra posited two destinations for the souls of the dead – heaven or hell. He referred to a saviour who would come and save humanity's souls, and promised resurrection depending on the outcome of a final judgement by the all-powerful creator of everything, Ahura Mazda.'

'What's that got to do with bonobos burying their dead under branches and twigs?' Sophie asks.

'I was coming to that,' I reply. 'Jem here brandishing his Bible like a shield against bad vibes in this house,' I say, hoping I'm managing to keep the annoyance out of my voice, 'I wanted to disabuse him quickly. I wanted to let him know who he should thank for his beliefs. The ancient Persians, ancestors of today's Iranians, used to leave their dead exposed to the elements, sometimes on mountain ledges, where the corpse would be pecked by flesh-eating birds or shrivelled by the sun. So bonobos covering the corpses of their dead with branches and twigs demonstrates that they have a sense of the dignity of death. Bonobos are very important medically. Something in their genetic makeup renders them resistant to quite a few diseases that strike and kill us humans, such as malaria, Aids, Alzheimer's disease and a whole range of cancers. They have immunities that are priceless.'

I must be getting through to Sophie, at long last, judging by the expression on her face. The look in her eyes is akin to the way she looks at me in bed when I've withdrawn from her and she's stopped kissing my lips and cheek and chest. She's looking at me across the table, not exactly as though she's undressing me in public with her eyes, but as if she's thanking me for a different kind of pleasure, the sort that comes with fresh understanding.

'Unlike gorillas and urang-utans in the wild, bonobos share the kill with their relatives and friends. They share their food. They have a sense of loyalty. They feel themselves to be part of a larger whole, members, one is tempted to say, of a society where the ethos is reminiscent of that among D'Artagnan and Alexandre Dumas' three musketeers: "One for all and all for one".'

'Don't get carried away,' Baldock says with a smirk. 'You're talking about a bunch of monkeys in the jungle. Don't get poetic. You can't con intelligent people with a load of flannel. You can't con *me*, anyway. Fancy words don't make things less far-fetched.'

I glance at Sophie. She rolls her eyes, pulls a face and shakes her head.

'Apart from monkey flesh, what else do bonobos eat?' she asks.

'All sorts of food – honey, fruit, fungus. They're also keen on nuts. Our primatologist Flame McGovern says they make use of up to nineteen different tools in various aspects of their lives. They consider a problem and figure out what sort of implement will help them solve it. For cracking open nuts they have a specially shaped stone with a flat side for pounding the nut, and a side with a ledge that's easy to grip. They place the nut in a suitably shaped niche or furrow in a rock from which it can't roll away when struck. When they want to catch termites or ants to eat, they look around and find a long thin stick, break off any protruding twigs, lick the stick until it's wet and then insert it into one of the holes where the termites or ants live. When they reckon enough of the insects have become stuck to the stick, they withdraw it from the hole and proceed to enjoy the delicacies.'

'They plan ahead, you're saying,' Sophie says.

'No doubt about it. And what does that imply?'

'That they're intelligent enough to plan ahead.'

'Yes, but what else? – something more fundamental, more profound.'

I look at Baldock for an answer. The earlier expression of distaste on his face has deepened to a kind of revulsion. He doesn't respond. He's doing the bare minimum. He's keeping his side of the bargain, but in a spirit almost entirely of contempt.

'So come on, Charlie,' Sophie prompts, 'what else does it imply?'

'It implies the best thing on Earth, the best thing in the universe – that bonobos not only *can* think, but *do* think. They *think* all the time, every day, about their world and how to survive in it – unlike many humans who seem to prefer not to think for themselves.' I look at Baldock and tell him: 'Sophie knows that every time we go to America I visit the

Primate Research Center at Ellensburg in Washington State where apes who've been taught human sign language have been studied to see how exactly the use of language affects behaviour and relationships.'

'That's right,' Sophie says. 'We've been flying across the Atlantic, sometimes twice a year. I met Charlie's parents there again, at Thanksgiving again. They'd come to our wedding in Bristol.'

'Have *you* been visiting these research places too?' Baldock asks her.

'No, I haven't. I've taken the opportunities to visit the Frick museum in Manhattan and other art galleries and various theatres. But from now on I'm going everywhere Charlie goes,' she smiles at me.

'The point I'm making,' I say to Baldock, 'is that unlike apes in the wild who never look at one another when they communicate, those who've lived among humans for a period of time tend to make eye contact when exchanging information with each other. They also hold the gaze of humans when conversing with them in the sign language. In the Department of Biology and Language Research Center at Georgia State University, Atlanta where I also go for baseline data against which to compare Bertha's development, there are a dozen chimpanzees, urang-utans, gorillas and bonobos who've been taught to use sign language. They now do so as a matter of course when conversing with one another and with their human trainers. These animals don't merely imitate signs. They use their new language creatively. Not knowing the sign for "slice of watermelon", one bonobo referred to it as a "candy fruit drink". Another described snow falling outdoors as "broken TV". They have a sign-language vocabulary of well over a thousand words. So when it comes to thinking, they're pretty much like us in that respect: Bonobo *sapiens*.'

30

'Bonobo *sapiens*? Never heard of it,' Baldock says, looking me straight in the eye. 'There's no such term – you're making things up as you go along.'

'No, he isn't,' Sophie says. 'He's telling a deeper truth than you or I have heard before.'

'He's telling tall tales, that's what he's doing. You're his wife, so I understand your loyalty to him. But this is going too far, much too far. It's like a woman who tells lies in court to protect her husband whom she knows to be a killer – admirable in a lesser way, but conniving at evil in a greater way. You can't lie to God. God knows what's in our hearts. He knows what's behind us and in front of us. He knows what's above us and below us. He knows what is all around us. Even the thoughts we haven't had yet, God reads them like writing on a wall.'

'Now *you're* getting poetic, Jem,' I say. '"The moving finger writes, and, having writ, moves on—"'

'"Nor all your piety nor wit shall lure it back to cancel half a line,/Nor all your tears wash out a word of it,"' Sophie finishes the stanza from *The Rubaiyyat of Omar Khayyam*, the 11th-century Persian mathematician/astronomer whose hobby was writing superb poetry. Sophie read me this particular poem soon after we were married; I take it now to be a way of showing solidarity with me, of distancing herself from Baldock's position, as she promised last night in the restaurant she would. She said Baldock meant nothing at all to her, that there was no way she'd choose him over me. And now she's showing it. Her words at any rate are the right sort.

'What about bonobo family life?' she asks. 'What have you learnt about that?'

'They go everywhere together in family groups,' I tell her with a smile. 'They move through the tree-tops as well as on the ground. They have favourite sleeping trees and will travel great distances to return to a tree they particularly like, to make their nests for the night's sleep. They bend the branches into shape to make comfortable cots. And when it rains, they make personal shelters with the leafy branches – umbrella-like coverings. They don't enjoy being drenched any more than we do. Females are dominant in bonobo society. The leader of the group is nearly always female. Females have the first choice of whatever food is available, but they usually share their food with their children and friends. They're a tolerant community in which there's rarely any violence. The young ones watch closely everything the adults do; theirs is quite a slow maturation process. They only start using the nut-cracking tool when they're about five years old and they remain dependent on their elders until they're about fifteen – a pretty similar age to human children in cultures all over the world. They tend to live for at least thirty-five years, and usually much longer.'

'What sort of sex life do they have?' Sophie asks with a straight face.

'Hectic – that's the best way to describe bonobo sex life. Once they get started in their teens, they're at it all the time. They fuck anywhere and everywhere and don't have the slightest notion of monogamy. Sex for them is also a way of defusing tension. Everyone does it with everyone else – males with females, females with females, males with males, the young with the old. Bonobos on the move through the forest will stop to screw in the grass, or up in the trees on a suitably thick branch, or on a rock in the sun. They sometimes have sex in the face-to-face position, like humans, which no other creatures in the wild do. The mature females get pregnant and give birth after a gestation period of approximately two-hundred and twenty-seven days. They give birth at five-yearly intervals, but like humans they can give birth at any time of the year. It may be this relative freedom from the burden of multiple babies that accounts for their free-for-all sexuality. They don't need condoms or the rhythm method. As far as they're concerned, there's nothing to be embarrassed about a quick bang and then goodbye.'

'Admit it, Charlie,' Sophie says. 'You wish *you* were a bonobo, don't you?'

'No way. I'd be too jealous. I'd hate the other males touching up my female and making free with her – especially if she was anything like you. I'd have bonobo bad dreams and would probably die in my sleep from the crushing bonobo sadness.'

'It's disgusting, and far more immoral than I realised,' Baldock interjects. 'But I suppose that's the level people sink to when they behave like animals.'

'People *are* animals,' I tell Baldock.

'People have to eat, drink, sleep and have sex like other biological creatures,' Sophie follows up, looking sideways at Baldock. 'They have digestive systems and have to defecate like dogs and horses, and the male members are designed to slot into their females. Why d'you still deny these basic facts?'

'They're biological facts,' Baldock says, 'and biology is what low life is about. The body succumbs. It ages and breaks down, and always dies. It isn't spiritual and can never enter the kingdom of heaven.'

'You remind me of Pope Innocent the Third's list of detestable human traits,' Sophie tells him. She counts them off on her fingers as she says them. 'Impure conception, loathsome feeding in the mother's womb, wretchedness of physical substance, vile stench, discharge of spittle, urine and faeces. Those were *his* words, more or less. He simply hated human nature, even though he believed we were created in God's image – a typical contradiction.'

'I'm not surprised,' Baldock counters. 'Human nature is not what the kingdom of heaven is about.'

'You're getting poetic again, Jem,' I chip in. 'The kingdom of heaven is a rhetorical construct. It's a place that exists only in people's imagination.'

'And in their hearts,' Sophie adds, glancing again at Baldock in a way that makes me wonder whether she's reinforcing *my* point or assuaging the pain my words might have caused *him*. 'The kingdom of heaven sounds like a place,' she says, 'a supremely idyllic location, but it's something even more wonderful. It's the yearning for transcendence which people throughout history and all over the world have felt. In ancient Egypt, before the Pharaoh died he made careful arrangements for the journey to the after-life. He laid in stocks of food and drink and images of his favourite servants to sustain him until he reached that longed-for destination. The kingdom of heaven is the apotheosis of the human mind. It's a product of consciousness, of a longing for perfection so deeply rooted that it elevates and bathes in glory the perishable brain from whose crevices it began to rise at some point in evolution.'

Baldock and I just gape at her.

His torso is twisted sideways on his chair so he can see her face properly. The expression on his own face is caught between heaven and hell; it would have been blissfully sublime but for the purply red blotches of his skin and the contrasting paleness of his clearly defined lips which give his countenance a tribal look and remind me again of those African masks that inspired Picasso's revolutionary painting called *Les demoiselles d'Avignon*.

'You *do* believe in God,' Baldock breathes, his eyes locked on Sophie's.

'In a supreme being with no terrestrial interests or loyalties – of course I do.'

'That's why you're coming to Danny's resurrection on Sunday.'

'That's right. I want to bear witness.'

'You want to do *what*?' I ask from my side of the table.

'Bear witness,' she repeats. 'See for myself, with my own eyes, how deep people's longing is for everlasting life.'

'That's what you *will* see, have no fear, Mizz Gresham.'

'I have no fear on that score. What I do have at the moment,' Sophie says, turning her head from him and looking at me, 'is another question, Charlie, about the bonobos you've been studying.'

'What's the question?'

'You said they call out to one another. They have special sounds for special messages. What do they sound like when they utter their cries?'

'They don't sound like us, that's for sure. And their facial expressions are quite static when they communicate; they don't have the large number of facial muscles we humans have which reinforce the meanings of our statements. Their voices are higher pitched too. That's because of the position of the bonobo larynx in relation to the rest of the respiratory tract. The larynx of humans – sometimes called the "voice box" or "vocal cords" – is lower in the throat and further away from the soft palate than in other primates. This lower position caused a sort of cylindrical, resonating cavity in which sounds have a markedly lower pitch. The lower position of the larynx in its turn resulted from humanity's development over time of erect posture and the enlargement of our braincases. The larynx moved lower down as the *foramen magnum* – the hole in the skull for the spinal cord – moved forwards and as the lower jaw became smaller.'

'So although Bertha can utter words that are intelligible—'

'Not just words – whole sentences, which she makes up according to the conversation, as you're about to witness.'

'Okay, whole sentences. But in a higher pitch?'

'Yeah. It's an extraordinary sound – a kind of grating but with baritone patches here and there, brought, it seems, by the vowels and consonants being uttered.'

'Brought by arrogant individuals who think they can improve on God's handiwork, more likely,' Baldock says. He looks at me with a mixture in his eyes of defiance and distaste. 'Bad things are going to come of this – mark my words. You scientists are trying to play God. Your presumption is appalling – your punishment will be fittingly harsh. You are trying to reach too high.'

'"A man's reach should exceed his grasp – or what's a heaven for?" Sophie says. 'That's what the poet Robert Browning wrote in the 19th century – and *he* knew the Bible very well.'

'He must've been a ditherer,' Baldock replies sarcastically. 'I'm not surprised to hear the rot set in more than a century ago.'

'It's time we drove to the institute,' I say, looking at my watch. 'The porters are expecting us in a little while.'

'Shall we go in my car?' Sophie asks me.

'Why not?' I reply and, glancing at Baldock: 'I didn't notice your car when I opened the door for you.'

'My wife gave me a lift here,' he says, reaching for his leather-bound Bible. 'I'm meeting her in town afterwards.'

'D'you want me to turn left at the Rupert Brooke pub and go via the rugby grounds,' Sophie asks me, 'or go up Trumpington Road to Trumpington Street?'

'Go up Trumpington – it's more direct. When we get to the institute, pull up in front of the gates. I have to identify myself through the intercom, or we won't get in.'

31

The weather has been warm and bright lately even though we're well into September and the evenings have been drawing in. The early morning mist has cleared away and the sun is out again in the gaps between the clouds. Sophie steers her convertible Jaguar round the lawn in the middle of our drive towards the gateway. Although there's a light breeze, it's muggy enough, she decides, to leave the hood down. A car is pulling out of the drive of the house on the other side of the street from us as we inch across the sidewalk. The woman driver is wearing a pink scarf; she smiles and waves at Sophie as she passes by and Sophie waves back.

I can't remember when last I felt quite so happy. Sophie coming to the institute with me of her own free will: I've been longing for this to happen for more than three years. I've been longing for her to meet my colleagues and see for herself what sane, upstanding people they are. I've been aching for her to have a chat with Bertha and perhaps hold in her arms one of the infant bonobos that are still being bottle-fed and having objects pointed out to them and named aloud. I'm sure Sophie is going to be captivated, caught up in the passion of our times. And when she is, the fly in the ointment will finally have been removed; there'll be nothing spoiling our happiness and nothing mangling the two sides of my self. The love of my life will no longer be at loggerheads with my life's work. Perhaps as a result the bad dreams that have been ruining my sleep will stop recurring too.

As we drive by the entrance to the Orchard Tea Gardens

in Grantchester, passing barns with thatched roofs and farm-yards where people in Wellington boots are at work, and garden walls sagging with age at the edge of the winding country lane, I take a deep breath of the bracing air; it fills my lungs with a fresh exuberance.

'I love you, I love you, England,' I cry out.

Sophie turns her head and smiles at me.

'Thank you, darling,' I say to her. 'Thanks for everything.'

'There's nothing to thank *me* for,' she replies, her hair blowing in the wind, her hands clutching the steering-wheel. 'Perhaps both of us should thank Baldock for making this happen.'

I can't thank Danny Mullins whose accident in Silver Street is what started this process of reconciliation between Sophie and me. Danny is dead. He wished me good health and a long happy life, and I feel in my heart that things are already changing for the better. So I turn in my seat to thank Baldock instead, the emissary from the road-accident boy, but Baldock on the backseat is bent over his Bible, reading with great intensity, reading as if his life depends on it.

'So we say with confidence,' I hear him reading, 'the Lord is my helper; I will not be afraid. What can man do to me?'

He glances up at me, then looks down again and continues reciting aloud, as though he knows the words by heart but finds comfort in holding the Bible in his hands.

'Do not be carried away by all kinds of strange teachings. It is good for our hearts to be strengthened by grace.' He turns a page and carries on: 'See to it, brothers, that none of you has a sinful, unbelieving heart that turns away from the living God. But encourage one another daily, as long as it is called Today, so that none of you may be hardened by sin's deceitfulness. We have come to share in Christ if we hold firmly till the end the confidence we had at first.'

I don't dislike Baldock. As Sophie says, it is thanks to him that she and I have been brought closer together, that our feelings for each other have deepened. I don't mind him reading the Bible either, except that the sounds of the words seem to seal him off from us. The words cling together in a cadence that is kind of mesmeric. The verses he is chanting are filling his ears with a fervour that fends off everything considered to be profane, so that he's enclosed in a kind of sacred stupor in Sophie's convertible car, unable to acknowledge the language that really *is* alive all around him and rooted in the secular intellect.

I prefer the Baldock who told me about his printing business going bust. I prefer the fighting spirit that led him to run a pub, oversee meals being prepared in the kitchen and be chatty with the customers. I prefer the courage that enabled him to become a steeplejack; that's what made me respect his chunky hands. I respect the man who spoke English to me, not the lingo that is familiar on the surface but, like Latin, static underneath.

Sophie slows the car down and comes to a halt at the junction with the A10. She waits for a gap in the traffic, then turns left and heads north towards Cambridge, passing through Trumpington village with its little post office and big bright filling-station. We pass the grounds of the Perse School on the right-hand side where, according to Sophie, the literary critic F.R. Leavis, an early champion of the poets T.S. Eliot and Ezra Pound, went as a boy. We then move past the University Botanic Garden. The traffic gets heavier as we approach the Fen Causeway and the Royal Cambridge Hotel, the point at which Trumpington Road becomes Trumpington Street.

We're crawling along in a stream of vehicles, behind a yellow newspaper van with a headline of yesterday's events in large letters fixed to each of its back doors. The one on the left says: *'Ashes regained. Pietersen maiden Test century soars to 158*'; the one on the right: '*President Bush in flooded New Orleans 14 days after Hurricane Katrina*'. Soon we're moving by the pillared facade of Brown's restaurant on the right and, alongside it on the site where Addenbrooke's Hospital used to be until it moved to larger premises, the Judge Institute of Management, Cambridge University's business school. Sophie slows down and flicks on her left indicator.

'Here we are,' she says as we pass the neo-classical columns and pediment of the Fitzwilliam Museum on the left-hand side. Suspended between two of the columns is a long bright poster announcing a photographic exhibition inside of *New York, New York 1880s–1990*. Sophie pulls in to the lay-by and stops the car in front of the institute's black metal gates, diagonally opposite the façade of Pembroke College.

I turn to tell Baldock on the backseat that we've arrived, but he's still reading assiduously.

'The Lord said to me: My grace is sufficient for you, for my power is made perfect in weakness. Therefore I will boast all the more gladly about my weaknesses, so that Christ's power may rest on me. That is why, for Christ's sake, I delight in weaknesses, in insults, in hardships, in persecutions, in difficulties. For when I am weak, then I am strong.'

'Jem,' I interject when he pauses for breath, 'we're here – at the Institute of Molecular and Neural Genetics.'

He looks up from the Bible at the high gates fixed into their massive concrete piers. 'So we are,' he murmurs.

He seems to have lost a bit of colour; the red blotches of his complexion are now merely pink. He swallows hard and I notice his Adam's apple moving in his throat. He shuts the Bible and presses it to his breast.

'I won't be a sec,' I tell him. 'Just going to get the gates opened for us.'

I get out of the car and step to the concrete pier on

the left-hand side where the metal buttons and grille of the intercom are located beside the smaller pedestrian gate. I key in my personal ID number and my project code number and wait for the vocal response.

'Your date of birth, please,' a voice requests.

'It's me, Peter – Charlie Venn.'

'You know the drill. Your date of birth, please.'

I tell him, moving my mouth closer to the grille.

'You have two guests – is that correct?'

'Yes.'

'Their names, please.'

'I gave them to you yesterday.'

'Their names, please.'

'Sophie Gresham , my wife—'

'So I see. She's condescended to come at last.'

'She's come, that's the main thing. And Jem Baldock.'

'Jem the steeplejack.'

'That's correct.'

There's a pause, then I hear a humming electric sound as the gates move away and separate in the middle. The two halves swing open inwards a full ninety degrees, making enough space for a couple of vehicles to pass through side by side.

I step back to the car and get in.

'Drive right down to the mansion,' I tell Sophie. 'There's a semi-circular car park opposite the front door.'

Sophie nods, changes down to first gear and pulls through the gateway. I see in the wing-mirror the black gates swing shut again behind us. The leaves of the trees leading to the edge of the River Cam are on the turn. The long, high hedge on the left marks the perimeter dividing the institute's site from that of the Fitzwilliam Museum. A gardener in dungarees with a cap on his head is kneeling near one of the flowerbeds; he is pruning a rosebush with a pair of secateurs. Even though it's mid-September, the place is still alive with colour: creamy yellow magnolias contrast with the lilac flowers and grey leaves of buddleia, and as we drive along we see pink belladonna lilies standing out against the stately silver plumes of pampas grass. Another gardener is pushing a wheelbarrow of cuttings across the lawn towards a huge plastic container on wheels.

'Shall I turn right here?' Sophie asks as we approach the junction with an unpaved driveway that leads to the parking area and the main entrance to Audley Hall. There's a bench on the lawn near the junction, and an elegant street-light with three lamps designed to look like tulips.

'Yes. Park wherever you like.'

'It's a beautiful house, Charlie – grander than I expected,' Sophie says. She looks up at the rows of windows picked out in white paint and at the two stone cherubs above the arch of the main door; the cherubs are holding a shield carved with the motto of the ornithologist and zoologist Sir William Audley who built this mansion in 1798: *Scientiae alis surgimus* – We rise on the wings of knowledge.

'I've been telling you about this house for years, Sophie, but you always made out you weren't interested. It's in the Palladian style and was built to the highest standards without regard to cost. And it's been well cared for. You'll see, the floor of the entrance hall is black-and-white marble, and the banister of the staircase to the mezzanine gallery is made of solid oak. The rooms were converted long ago for use as labs, libraries, lecture theatres and accommodation for our bonobos and for the staff who stay overnight. It's a pleasure working in this house.'

'Does Bertha live in this house too?'

'Of course she does. She's the apple of our collective eye. She represents a multi-million dollar investment in synthetic biology that promises to transform human health.'

'And make you famous and very rich.'

'Possibly – when we put our products on the market.'

'Who else are you going to introduce me to?'

'Whoever is free to talk – Flame McGovern, probably.'

'Flame, did you say?'

'Yeah. Doctor Flame McGovern. She's the expert in primatology I've tried to tell you about. She's known Bertha ever since our bonobo was born in a room on the second floor.'

'What's she like?'

'Bertha?'

'No – Flame McGovern.'

'You'll see for yourself in a minute. She's famous in her field of work, been publishing books and scientific papers for twelve, fifteen years. She spends a good part of each year in the forests of west Africa – in the Congo, Senegal, Guinea-Bissau – and in Sumatra, Sarawak and Borneo. She lies concealed in a series of hides whilst observing and comparing the behaviour of various species of gorilla, orangutan, chimpanzee and bonobo. Flame says the habitats of all these creatures are being destroyed by logging companies, by road-building projects, forest fires and the spread of the Ebola virus. She says Ebola is one of the most deadly infectious diseases. Ebola-infected animal tissues are dangerous to hunters of bushmeat and anyone else who might touch the carcases of infected animals. Doctor McGovern was one of the seventy-five primatologists and other experts who met in Brazzaville, Congo Republic, earlier this year to draft an action plan to save some of humanity's closest relations from extinction. She brings back from her field trips valuable videos. She's really tough – sleeps in the bush at night in all weathers, alone, eating what sound like military rations.'

I turn and look at Baldock on the backseat.

'Are you all right?' I ask.

He nods, but remains silent.

'As I said before, Jem – nobody's forcing you to come into the house. I won't be aggrieved if you feel you aren't up to meeting a bonobo ape with some of the faculty of speech. I don't want you to feel that I'm pressuring you. You can leave now if you like.'

'I gave you my word,' he says in a voice that's dry and barely audible. 'And I'm a man of my word. And you gave me *your* word that you and your wife would be at the resurrection of Danny Mullins.'

'That's right. I gave you my word and you can depend on it. Sophie and I will be at the Mullins house in Chesterton on Sunday. Now come on,' I smile at him, 'this is an historic moment. You are the first person in the entire history of your family who's about to have a conversation with an animal from a non-human species.'

Baldock tries to smile back but doesn't really succeed. He gets out of the car and walks between Sophie and me up the stone steps, through the doorway and into the reception hall.

I guess that if I knew what was about to happen I, too, would have been finding it hard to smile.

32

'This is Sophie Gresham, my wife,' I tell Peter Lynn, the burly porter with aquiline nose and forward-sloping chin manning the reception desk, 'and this is Jem Baldock. They've come to meet Bertha.'

Lynn gives each of them a long, slightly unnerving look with his deep brown eyes, turns the heavy ledger around, picks up one of the ballpoint pens and says: 'This is the visitors' book. Please write your name in block letters, then your signature and time of arrival, which is,' he adds, glancing at his wrist-watch, 'nine thirty-eight.'

Sophie takes the pen and while she's writing her name Lynn points to the leather-bound book Baldock is cradling in his arm.

'What's that you have there?' he asks.

'My Bible,' Baldock replies.

'Your Bible? Why've you brought a Bible?'

'D'you have any objections to it?'

'This is a scientific research institute,' Lynn says suspiciously. 'May I have a look at it, please?'

Baldock steps closer and hands over the Bible. Lynn takes it, opens it, lifts a wad of the pages then lets them cascade from his thumb, watching closely to see if there's anything concealed inside.

'What are you looking for?' Baldock asks.

'Just checking.'

'Checking for what?'

'How would *I* know why anyone would want to bring the Bible into a molecular biology lab?'

'There's nothing in it but God's word.'

'I suppose you're right,' Lynn says, nodding and pursing his lips. 'It looks harmless enough.'

He flicks the front cover down, hands the book back to Baldock and strokes his sharp chin. His tone of voice is just within the bounds of politeness, like a policeman whose job it is to regard everyone as a suspect, not excluding gangsters and conmen who play the piety card, who dress up as priests or nuns to make their get-away and expect special treatment.

'It's your go,' Sophie says to Baldock, motioning to the ledger where she's left the pen. She looks up at the high ceiling again with all its sculpted animal figures.

'I'm already regretting I came,' Baldock says. 'It's not the warmest welcome, is it?'

'It's security procedures, Jem,' I tell him, 'nothing else.'

He bends over the book, writes his name and signature, tosses the pen onto the page and pushes the ledger back towards Lynn.

'You don't have to sign your name to enter a church,' he says. 'You can go in whenever you like.'

'I know you can,' Lynn says, keeping eye contact. 'That's why churches are open to all and sundry, because anything goes – money laundering, child rape, intimidation, you name it.'

'I'm taking them up to Bertha's room,' I tell Lynn, 'and then to see Doctor McGovern.'

He nods and waves his arm to the wooden banister curving up the staircase.

I lead Sophie and Baldock beyond the noticeboard where messages, memos, details of seminars and other communications are pinned. We pass the huge rubber plant in its brightly coloured tub of soil and the rack of journals and scientific papers. They step beside me across the black-and-white marble floor to the wide staircase and up to the mezzanine gallery. I can smell the wood polish; the banister is gleaming. We all look as we go at the portraits in gilt frames of William Audley and his forefathers, rotund figures with high foreheads and benign expressions, and at the oil-paintings of several species of bird and of antelope and tiger in their natural habitats.

We climb the flight of stairs to the second floor and walk along the corridor. Ahead of us, the door of one of the laboratories opens inwards and a man and a woman come out. They're in their mid-twenties and wearing long white coats.

'Hi, Charlie,' the man says. He's wearing glasses with gold wire frames.

'Hi, Matt,' I reply. 'This is Sophie Gresham, my wife, and this is Jem Baldock.'

'Matthew Nairn,' he introduces himself, smiling at Sophie and then at Jem.

'I'm Ali Aherne,' the woman says, her radiant face framed by tresses of blonde hair.

'I'm taking them to meet Bertha,' I say.

'You're in for a treat,' Ali tells Sophie.

'Can't hang about, Charlie,' Matt says, looking at his watch. 'We're giving a report in a couple of minutes.'

'See you later,' I reply, making way for them to pass by, and when they've hurried away I tell Sophie: 'They're on the *Drosophila* project.'

'The *what* project?'

'*Drosophila melanogaster* – the common fruitfly. The genome of that creature with its four chromosomes is offering up endless insights into the patterns of nucleic acid bases and the strings of amino acids they code for and consequent protein structures. We're discovering to our amazement that the same network of five genes that build up the body segments of the fruitfly also create body segments in beetles, grasshoppers and other insects which grow into quite different creatures. They create similar segments in the brains of human beings too. We're finding that we have much more in common with insects and animals than we ever supposed.'

I lead the way again to the far end of the corridor, and when we get to the room on the left there I knock lightly on the door.

'Is this Bertha's room?' Sophie asks.

'Yes,' I nod.

'She's a bonobo chimpanzee and you're knocking on her door?'

'*She's* the bonobo – not *me*. She's learning our customs and manners, being acculturated every moment of every day.'

The look in Sophie's eyes tells me she's realising at last that I've been serious all along about Bertha's status as an individual, about her right to respect and consideration.

'You're treating her like a person,' Sophie says.

'That's how she's learning to *be* a person, by being *treated* as one – just as human infants learn to become persons. That's why the Zulu people in South Africa say: "A person becomes a person through other persons." Biology is only the foundation. As we all know, to become a person takes social experience, inputs from others, guidance, advice.'

'Why doesn't she answer?'

'Bertha, it's Charlie,' I call out, knocking again. 'Open the door, Bertha. I've brought the visitors I told you about.'

The three of us stand there in silence, waiting for a response, but nothing happens.

I knock a third time and wait. Still no reply. 'This is unusual. Bertha's very quick off the mark – full of interest and energy.'

'Maybe she's not in the room,' Sophie suggests.

'There's a way to find out.'

I reach for the door-knob, twist it, push and step into the room. Sophie follows me in. I beckon Baldock with

279

a movement of my head. The look of distaste on his face seems to be carved in stone, but he steps inside anyway. There are two large windows, both permanently locked; the one in the north wall overlooks a corner of the Scholars' Garden in Peterhouse College, the one facing west gives a clear view of the River Cam; there are a dozen or so punts floating on the water and tugging at their moorings. The morning light is streaming through the windows, brightening the peach-and-white colour scheme of the walls.

Sophie takes in the details of the room. She studies the three framed photos on the wall opposite the west window. One is of an individual bonobo facing the camera full on with an arm raised overhead, as though waving. The second is of a bonobo with two human companions, a black man and a white woman who are both clad in khaki shirt and trousers, and the third picture is a shot of two other humans on their own, both men, both white, one in a T-shirt, the other wearing suit and tie. Fixed to the same wall there is also an unframed poster-size enlargement of one of Flame McGovern's photographs of bonobos in the rainforest of the Congo. It's a portrait of a family group in a clearing under a canopy of trees; they are eating sections of an oval-shaped fruit, two of them almost out of sight up on a branch veiled by hanging foliage.

Sophie turns from the pictures and looks at the low bed with its white pillow and pink duvet. She takes in the low chair and the desk with several picture-books on it and a sheet of drawing-paper coloured with streaks of crayon, and glances at the black DVD player with twin speakers in opposite corners and a jumble of CDs on the floor.

Sophie steps to the desk, reaches down and picks up the sheet of drawing-paper. She studies for a long moment the jagged streaks of colour made with crayon, then looks at me.

'Did Bertha do this?' she asks.

'Yeah, by herself.'

'What's it supposed to be?'

'Streaks of colour – can't you see?'

'What was she trying to draw?'

'Flame McGovern says she was copying the rainbow in one of those books there.'

Sophie looks down at the books, then up at me again.

'This drawing looks like it was done by a human child,' she says.

'That's what *I* thought when I first saw it. It doesn't have to be good to be human. Most humans don't draw particularly well. The point is that Bertha has seen Flame McGovern drawing with crayons on a sheet of paper, and has begun to emulate her actions. She's learning from example, the way human children learn.'

'Smells funny in here, doesn't it?' Sophie says. 'A bit like a dog smells when it's wet.'

'Not really like a dog, Sophie. It's a distinctive smell, once you get used to it.'

'A bonobo smell, you mean?'

'Yeah. The smell of Bertha's fur and body heat.'

'Just that? Nothing else?'

'What else?' I ask, then catch her drift. 'No – nothing like that. She's been toilet-trained. She goes to the lavatory when she needs to.'

'She's a chimpanzee and she goes to the lavatory,' Baldock mutters incredulously.

'That's right. And she always flushes the toilet afterwards – and always washes her hands in the basin, the way she's been taught.'

'Who taught her, Charlie?' Sophie asks.

'Flame McGovern mainly, with occasional back-up from other colleagues. Flame has a feel for what is possible, based on her observations in the rainforests of Africa and Indonesia. She has a sense of the pace at which new things should be taught.'

'So where's Bertha then?'

'She knew I was coming to see her with two visitors. I expected her to be here, in her room. Come, she can't be far away. She's free to move about the house when she isn't having facetime with her teachers or having her daily bath.'

We step out into the corridor, I pull the door shut and walk to the next room along.

'This is Flame McGovern's base when she's not away on fieldwork,' I explain and knock on the door.

'Who is it?' a clear voice calls out.

'It's Charlie Venn. I've brought the visitors I told you about.'

'Come in, Charlie.'

I open the door, step inside and, when Sophie and Jem have entered, introduce them to Dr McGovern. She's wearing a tight-fitting boat-neck top and pink tapered hipsters. She shifts to her left arm the bonobo infant she's holding and extends her right hand to Sophie.

'I'm so pleased to meet you at last,' she says in her noticeably Scottish accent, her face beaming. 'Charlie has told me so much about you.'

'I'm glad I could finally make it,' Sophie replies as they shake hands.

The look in my wife's eyes when she glances at me is a mixture I've never seen there before, of surprise and admiration and a somewhat stricken look, as though she's accusing me of keeping a secret from her until this very moment. But she regains her composure enough to smile back at the strikingly beautiful primatologist whose hair gathered together in coils on top of her head is so gingery red, so shot through with natural lights of the sun, that it sometimes looks as though she's wearing a crown of fire. Hence the name her parents chose for her on the day she was born: Flame. I've discovered that the name occurs rather more frequently in Italy in the diminutive form: Fiammetta, meaning *little flame*.

Sophie can't seem to decide what to look at: Flame's lovely face or her figure or the fiery corona of her hair, or at the little bonobo ape she is pressing to her left breast.

'I'd been afraid to come, I must admit,' Sophie says. 'I felt my world would be turned upside down.'

'By a talking bonobo, d'you mean?' Flame asks.

'Yes, by something too extraordinary to take on board without capsizing in some way.'

'And yet here you are,' Flame says with a smile that lights up, not just her blue eyes, but her whole face. 'And you don't seem to me to be floundering – far from it.'

'You're very kind, Doctor McGovern.'

'Please call me by my first name, which is Flame. And this,' she says, moving the baby bonobo who is wearing a diaper, what the Brits call a napkin, from her breast and cradling it in her arm, 'this is Benny. If all goes well, Benny and Bertha will mate one day and start their own family. Meanwhile, *I've* started the first-ever chimeric genealogy. I've given Bertha and Benny the surname Beacon. Bertha Beacon and Benny Beacon: those are the names I've registered in my dossier. These two individuals are leading the way into the post-human future, so Beacon is an appropriate name, don't you think?'

Sophie nods, then reaches out and strokes the baby's fur with the back of her hand. 'I'm Sophie,' she says to the baby. She turns, motions with her arm and tells Flame, 'And this is Mister Jem Baldock.'

Flame extends her hand to Baldock, but he doesn't respond. Instead, he clutches his Bible with both hands and presses it to his chest.

The primatologist glances at me as though asking why I've brought somebody who lacks the basic courtesies. I hope she doesn't blame *me* for Baldock's boorishness which I know won't faze her in any way at all. She's independent, talented, vastly experienced in her line of work, and her beauty has in it something of the feral warmth and earthiness of the creatures she spends so much time getting to know and understand. One can only guess at what she's like in bed. Carnivorous, most likely, and deep down, ultimately, insatiable. But she's never made a pass at me, not once, and I don't fancy the idea of lying in a sleeping-bag in sodden grass surviving on military rations in primal parts of the world. She often flies home to Edinburgh where I have a gut feeling her boyfriend lives. I have my own woman who meets my every need, even if she *has* occasionally made me feel disgruntled and out of sorts and been the cause of very bad dreams. And I have her where I want her: in the midst of civilisation, in a large bed with a firm mattress, and standing with me under a steaming shower as soapy suds slide down our luxurious skins.

Even though I am merely a research scientist, I do know how to count my blessings.

'D'you know where Bertha might be?' I ask Flame.

'She's in her room, as you know – next door along.'

'We've just come from there,' Sophie tells her, 'it's empty.'

'Really? Are you sure?'

'Definitely,' I reply. 'I told Peter Lynn we were going to see Bertha first and you afterwards.'

'In that case,' Flame says, a look of concern coming into her eyes, 'something is amiss. I knew you were coming and took Bertha to her room myself, with clear instructions to wait there.'

'Does she always do what you tell her to?' Sophie asks.

'She always has.'

'But not this time, clearly.'

'Charlie,' Flame says decisively, completely forgetting again, it seems, that I was the person who offered her this position at the institute, that *I* am the director of this transgenic project, not she, 'you go upstairs – check all the rooms there. I'll search this floor. Sophie, you go down to reception and tell Peter Lynn that Bertha's missing. Tell him I said he should look in every room, every hallway and lobby as a matter of the greatest urgency. If Bertha's gone missing—'

'She can't be missing,' I chip in. 'She's too important. Too much depends on her.'

'Let's go and look for her,' Flame says. She strides across the room with Benny the baby cradled in her left arm, opens the door, hurries along the corridor and disappears into the first entranceway.

I race up the steps taking two at a time and barge into the labs one after the other, then into the library, the seminar rooms and lavatories, asking colleagues in their white coats where and when last they saw Bertha our experimental bonobo chimp. Nobody has a clue where she is. I look in every room again on the way back, the sinking feeling in my stomach a counterpart to the nauseous images in my mind of me standing in front of colleagues in Cambridge, Massachusetts trying to explain how we 'lost' Bertha and with her our competitive edge. I see myself standing in a hotel in New York City trying to placate the ChimeroGene investors and somehow reassure them that we'll 'make it up', we'll 'catch up', we'll still be ahead of the game.

'You're a schmuck, Charlie Venn, that's what you are – a loser in disguise,' I hear my American associates saying out loud. 'We were in a position to impose our style and price structure on the gene-swapping industry. We were on the brink of cleaning up to applause from the disabled multitudes and the fitness freaks and the endless millions who want to be prettier and more handsome, who want almond-shaped eyes and a nice nose and a butt that's perfectly shaped – and you threw it away, you all-time sad sack, you nebbish without the slightest nous. Get out of my sight, you unspeakable craphead.'

When I get down to the reception area on the ground

floor, Peter Lynn the porter is standing with arms akimbo in front of Sophie.

'This has never happened before,' he's saying to her. 'We've always known where Bertha was – every minute of the day. It's strict policy.'

Sophie sees me and I see dismay all over her face.

'You don't look well, Charlie,' she says. 'You'd better sit down.'

'I can't sit down – not now,' I reply, feeling weak suddenly, drained, washed-out.

'Where else can she be?' Sophie asks.

'Have you looked in the storerooms and the laundry room?' I ask Lynn.

'I have,' he says, 'and in the kitchen, the boiler room and the airing-cupboard under the back staircase. I can't imagine where that monkey's got to.'

'She's not a monkey,' I shout at him. 'You're so forgetful, so dense. She has no tail. She's a bonobo chimpanzee, also known as a pygmy chimpanzee. Don't you understand that yet, you dozy git?'

'My apologies, Doctor Venn. No offence intended.'

'Charlie,' Sophie says.

I turn to her. 'Yeah?'

'You're very pale, Charlie. I don't like the way you look.'

I'm about to reply when I hear a click, a distinct clicking sound, in my head, on the top left side. I touch my fingers to that part of my head and press my scalp gently.

'Did you hear that?' I ask Sophie.

'Hear what?'

'The sound in my head – a loud click.'

'No. I didn't hear anything.'

'Like the sound of someone cracking a finger knuckle.'

Sophie's eyes are wide open.

'Are you well enough to look outside?' she asks. 'D'you think Bertha might be outside?'

'You're brilliant, d'you know that?' I tell her. 'If she can't be found indoors, she must be outside.'

I grab Sophie's hand and run with her across the black-and-white marble floor to the front door and out down the stone steps, wheeling to the right when we hit the unpaved area where she parked her car. We race towards the side of the house as fast as the two of us can run.

We cut across the lawn at the side of the house and suddenly see the water of the River Cam gleaming in the autumn sunlight. It's September; the new academic year only starts next month, so the students haven't arrived yet. But there's a group of teenagers in a punt, local kids probably; they're laughing and calling out to their friends in another punt closer to the terrace of the Anchor pub. The fellow poling them along is wearing blue jeans and a heavy white jersey; he's standing on the till at the back of the punt, his feet apart, legs bent slightly at the knees, a perfectly balanced pilot transporting his friends towards Mill Pond and the Silver Street bridge beyond.

'Charlie,' I suddenly hear a high-pitched voice calling. 'Charlie, where you been?'

The grating voice is coming from the opposite direction, from the south, nearer to the point up to which the river is still known to some people by its ancient name, the Granta.

'Charlie,' the unmistakeable voice calls out again, 'why you slow?'

'Look, Charlie,' Sophie says, pointing across the water beyond a group of gliding swans at a clump of reeds. 'Is that Bertha?'

It's a bonobo all right, and at first sight it seems to be suspended a metre or so above the reeds. But that's an optic illusion created by the fact that the lower part of the pole that Bertha is clinging to for dear life is concealed by the reeds and the upper part by her own furry body. Bertha is literally stuck up a pole. One can only surmise that she decided to go punting herself after being taken on the river by Flame McGovern and after seeing from her upstairs window so many people doing it so often with such apparent ease that she wanted to have a go herself. She must have become separated somehow from the punt when she pushed the pole too deep into the mud.

'Charlie, get me back.'

'I'm coming Bertha. Don't move. Don't shake the pole.'

'Quick, Charlie. Quick.'

'Sophie, don't take your eyes off her. I'm going to get a punt and pole across to where she is. Okay, darling?'

'Okay, Charlie. But you'd better hurry.'

I race along the bank of the river to the terrace of the pub where lots of punts are floating side by side on the glistening water. There's usually a bulky teenager in charge, but I can't see him or anyone else to pay, so I step on to the nearest punt, undo the rope from its rusty metal ring and lift the pole carefully. I steady myself and push the pole down into the soft mud, remembering to hold tight and never let go. I steer to the left, keep turning, and head upstream, and I suddenly recall the sensation that passed through me when I first navigated these waters some eleven years ago, before I met Sophie. I remember the challenge, and the pleasure of meeting the challenge, and I think I understand what it was that motivated Bertha to take a risk and find out whether she too was able to do the Cambridge thing.

33

'Promise me you'll never go off on your own again,' I say to Bertha when I've brought her back to safety.

'Promise? What's promise?' she asks. Her high-pitched, grating voice sometimes sounds to me as though her vocal cords are made from a mixture of metal and animal tissue. She's holding my hand and looking into my eyes as I squat in front of her on the riverbank behind the institute.

'It means you do what you say you will do.'

'Flame bring me crayon. Flame said she bring me crayon.'

'That's right, Bertha. You're an intelligent girl. Flame promised to bring you crayons and she kept her promise.'

'I like punt,' Bertha says. The lips of her large mouth move over her big squarish teeth in her forward-sloping face whenever she speaks, and she keeps eye contact when doing so. Because her eyes are a light orangey red where ours are white, Bertha looks to those who don't know her as though she's in a fever. And one soon learns to ignore the pseudo look of surprise created by the ridges above her eyes; it's the result of bone structure, not psychology.

'You've been watching people punting from your window.'

'I want more punt.'

'Not on your own, Bertha. Flame took you once. I'll take you again. We go punting together from now on. Anywhere you want to go, you tell Charlie. What must you do?'

'Tell Charlie.'

'I was very sad when I couldn't find you, Bertha. Don't make me sad again.'

'What's sad?'

'Sad is...sad is,' I turn and look up at Sophie standing a short distance away listening raptly to our conversation. She's gone a whiter shade of pale. She's flummoxed. I could knock her over with a feather. Behind her and to one side is Jem Baldock in his dark suit and tie; I'd clean forgotten about him. His mouth is gaping, his Bible cradled in his left arm. 'What is sad, Sophie?' I ask my wife. 'Bertha doesn't know what sad means.'

'Sad is when you don't have faith in the one who loves you,' Sophie says and steps closer. She squats so that her face is on a level with Bertha's and mine. 'Sad is when you lack the courage to be better. Sad is when you think nothing can be new.'

She reaches out and touches Bertha on the arm and puts her other arm around my shoulder. There are tears in her eyes. She tries to smile at me. She tries to be nonchalant. But the emotion wells up and tears escape and slide down her cheeks. She sobs and sniffs and wipes her wet face with the back of her hand.

'Sad,' she says to Bertha, 'is when something makes you cry.'

'You sad,' Bertha replies.

'Yes, I'm sad.'

'What you sad for?'

'I didn't believe Charlie. I didn't believe there was going to be a new world, very different from the old world. But now I see the proof – Charlie is an explorer of the unknown. Charlie's heart isn't chained to the past. He knows the past isn't all there is for us. Charlie is a brave man. He shatters taboos. He's striving to raise people to a higher level of health and understanding. Charlie is the best kind of freethinker – a true *zindiq*. He isn't afraid; he follows through with action.

Without people like him, we'd still be mouthing mantras in monasteries and burning people who disagreed with our ignorance. We'd still be riding camels in the blistering heat with sand on our teeth and in our eyes, instead of driving sleek cars with power-steering, air-conditioning and remote central-locking.'

Bertha can't follow that chain of thought – no way. Bertha doesn't have the knowledge. She lacks experience. Her vocabulary is still meagre. She's too young. She knows no history. She looks at me, then at Sophie, then back at me.

'Charlie not sad,' she says.

'No,' I agree. 'Charlie is not sad. Charlie is happy. Charlie is very happy.' I lean over and kiss Sophie lightly on the lips. 'And soon Sophie also will be happy.'

Sophie smiles at Bertha. Bertha looks at Sophie. Sophie looks at me. Then:

'I'm so happy to meet you, Bertha,' Sophie says. 'Charlie talks about you every day. You won't go off on your own again, will you?'

'I tell Charlie.'

'Yes, tell Charlie. Always tell Charlie.'

I lift my arm and beckon to Baldock. 'Come over, Jem. This is Bertha I was telling you about. She's been naughty but promises not to go off on her own again.'

Baldock steps forward a few paces, then stops. He's in an anguish of doubt and confusion. He can't decide whether to reach out or draw away. He stands immobile on the grass, his frame rigid, while the purply pink blotches of his complexion keep shifting and coalescing in a picture of sorry irresolution.

He suddenly looks like an effigy. He reminds me of those ancient philosophers who thought the abacus was the fastest possible calculator, the ultimate in computing power, who believed that bows and arrows were the last word in missile technology because, haughtily, they were convinced that human inventiveness had ended in their time. Baldock is a persona from the distant past impersonating with his suit, buttoned-down collar, tie and shiny black shoes the outward guise of modernity. His eyes are seeing what his heart still refuses to believe. He's from a totally uncool epoch that is so *passé* he might as well be dead and gone.

He refused to respond when Flame McGovern extended her hand in welcome. He's holding back again, despite my call to him to join Sophie and me in our trans-species rapport, our chimeric communion. The love he talks about is an in-grown thing; it is withered, decayed. The god he keeps quoting is pathologically self-centred. Perhaps it isn't surprising that Baldock can't grasp the new etiquette and that, instead of walking abreast of us into the more robust biological dispensation, he prefers the platitudes of an obscure passion and the hauteur of having all the answers about everything without having done any research.

I give him another opportunity to be civil.

'Bertha, that man there is Mister Baldock. Go to Mister Baldock and say hello.'

Bertha lets go of my hand. She looks at Sophie, then turns and scurries in her knuckle-leaning mode of locomotion across the grass towards Baldock. She stops in front of him.

'Hello,' she says, her head tilted up to see his face.

Baldock recoils. His blue eyes are ablaze with disgust and loathing. He grabs the Bible from the crook of his left arm and holds it with both hands in front of him like a shield.

'Protect me, O Lord,' he cries out in prayer, 'from this sin that would assail me. You are the fountain of all hope and goodness, Lord. Strengthen my certainty that you are the source of all truth.'

Poor Baldock. His rusted gaze, cobwebbed and dusty, sees nothing new anywhere, not even Bertha and all that her being promises. It's a life-threatening prospect, suicidal, for him actually to *see* the world as it is and so many people in it endowed with powers of re-invention.

He begins to back away from Bertha and from us at the riverside. He holds the Bible in front of his body as he retreats on the grass, glancing neither left nor right. Then, when he feels he's far enough from the danger to turn his back on the beast, he wheels away and runs along the side of Audley Hall. We watch him dash down the long lawn towards the pedestrian gate and the safety of Trumpington Street.

Bertha comes loping back to us, pressing the knuckles of her hands down on the grass as she moves fluidly along.

'Gone,' Bertha says. 'He gone.'

'*You* won't soon be gone, will you, Charlie?' Sophie asks.

'What d'you mean? Gone where?'

'When everyone knows about your work and you're famous – Doctor Charles Hadley Venn, gene-transfer specialist – *you* won't leave me then, will you?'

'What's come over you, Sophie? Why would I leave you?'

'For someone more scientific. Someone you don't have to keep convincing about the value of your work and whose attitude doesn't give you bad dreams. Maybe you'll go when you meet someone whose faith in the future is deeper than mine has been. Someone really clever and beautiful, like Doctor Flame McGovern.'

'Flame McGovern? Are you kidding?' I reply, but the look in her eyes tells me she's dead serious. 'What are you on about? It's *you* I love, Sophie – you and no one else.'

'Are you sure you aren't in love with her?'

'What?'

'With Flame McGovern. You couldn't take your eyes off her when we were up in her room.'

'I can't believe my ears. *You're* the one who couldn't take your eyes off her. Are you jealous, Sophie?'

'Of course I'm jealous. I want you for myself. I don't want to share you with anyone.'

'You don't *have* to share me with anyone. What d'you think I am – a bar of chocolate?'

'Come here,' she says, grabbing the hair at the back of my head in a sudden fit of passion. She pulls my face up into position and kisses me hard and long on my mouth. She kisses me as though we're alone in bed, her tongue directing the fire of her flesh to my innards, re-kindling *my* fires and re-establishing her sovereignty over the whole of the territory known to all and sundry as Dr Charles Hadley Venn, molecular biologist from Boston.

'I'll never stop loving you, Sophie,' I tell her when I get my breath back. 'There's no way I ever will.'

'I'm going to make it even harder for you to do so.'

'What d'you mean?'

'I'm going to love you to death,' she says with that coquettish smile of hers. 'I'm going to kill you every day.'

'Oh, Sophie, you know how I love dying.'

'It's going to be murder in the cathedral from now on. You'll regret you ever left me.'

'I'm not leaving you, Sophie. Stop talking like that. I want to live with you for the rest of my life. We're going to have children, remember?' I add, glancing at Bertha resting on the grass. 'We're going to raise our children together and take them travelling.'

'The sooner we start, the better.'

'D'you mean that, darling?'

She nods: 'Yes, I mean it.'

'What about your writing?'

'What about it?'

'Your routine is bound to be disrupted with kids around.'

'I know. But I'm dead sure now. I'm going to switch to modern fiction. Bertha renders historical romance vapid. I'll divide my time. I'll plan everything properly. Doris Lessing says she always had to write in short concentrated bursts because of pressures. That's what I'll do too. You'll

294

be there to help me, won't you, Charlie?'

'Hand on my heart, I give you my word,' I say, placing my palm on my breast. 'I'll always be there.'

'Let's shake on it,' she says, pushing out her hand. 'We're equal partners for ever.'

'Equal partners for ever,' I confirm, grasping her palm and squeezing it gently.

She squeezes back and then, looking me straight in the eye, scratches the middle of my palm with the nail of her index finger: the secret invitation to sex.

'You're a rude girl, Sophie Gresham – I have to tell you that.'

'Tell me something else,' she says.

'What?'

'Whether or not you agree with me.'

'About what?'

'About the sound of Bertha's voice.'

'What does it sound like, d'you think?'

'It sounds a bit like Stephen Hawking sounds when he speaks.'

'Stephen Hawking, the cosmologist?' I ask. 'The author of *A Brief History of Time*?'

'The very same. He uses a voice synthesizer or simulator – whatever it's called – to make his utterances audible and intelligible.'

'That's right – because of his motor neurone disease. He's almost totally paralysed and talks by selecting words on his computer screen and clicking a hand-held mouse.'

'It's a very machine-like voice, isn't it? It's what those science-fiction daleks sound like on TV's *Dr Who*.'

'I know what you mean, Sophie. It's a kind of disembodied recording interposed between Hawking's brain and the person listening to him.'

'Metallic, the resonance of iron – that's what Bertha's voice has in common with Hawking's.'

'You're right – the similarity is striking. But it's Bertha's *genes* that have been manipulated, via her parents, not her vocal cords. Hawking lost the ability to speak long ago. What a conversation it would be.'

'Between Hawking and Bertha?'

'Yeah. It's not impossible. Hawking is Lucasian Professor of Mathematical Physics – he was based in an office not far from here, just around the corner in Silver Street, until they moved to the futuristic pavilions of the Centre for Mathematical Sciences off Clarkson Road.'

'It's a bizarre spectacle, isn't it?' Sophie says.

'What is?'

'Hawking slumped in his electric wheelchair pontificating in a robotic, software-generated voice about the origins and nature of the universe from the debris of his paralysed body.'

'He's an excellent example of mind over matter. His spirit hasn't succumbed to the disease. People say he has a keen sense of humour and is fun to work with.'

'The poor man.'

'What d'you mean – the poor man? He has the deepest intellect and an imagination unconstrained by convention. His book was one of the biggest sellers of all time, even though most people gave up trying to read it after a few pages – if they tried at all.'

'He can just about move a finger to operate his hand-held mouse. He barely has the strength to swallow liquids when they're spooned into his mouth, yet he fancies he knows the mind of God.'

'The mind of God is a metaphor – you said so yourself, Sophie. Remember? It's a collective noun for all the laws of physics, chemistry and nature. What a pity the word God is so saturated with human ego, so full of me, me, me.'

A pensive look comes into Sophie's eyes. 'You've been talking about the chemistry of love for years, Charlie,' she says, 'but I had no clue what you were on about. Your eyes were way ahead of mine, out of sight on the frontiers of love – until now, until I met Bertha. And it's only now that I appreciate just how penetrating Shakespeare's vision was when he had Hamlet say on the castle's battlements: "There are more things in heaven and earth, Horatio, than are dreamt of in your philosophy".'

34

I'm wet all over.

A soft warm rain is falling on me, drenching me with drops of water filled with the sun's heat that slide down my skin sensuously. It's like the gentle drizzle that inundates the streets of Singapore, glistening on the bell-shaped hibiscus, on the pigeon orchids and the flame-of-the-forest flowers with a vividness that vies with the colours of the lantern festival celebrated by the Chinese in September.

I'm lit up. I'm aglow. An incandescence is coming down on me. A lovely sensation of praise and reward is covering me from head to foot. It is immersing me in a soggy delicious pleasure, filling me with a joy so complete it makes me judder and writhe and sigh in that soft precipitation, that warm drenching rain bringing the sun's lustre to my loins and bringing me, all of a sudden, to contented wakefulness, opening my eyes from a happy dream to behold in the morning light streaming through the window a dome of hair covering my pelvis, a dishevelled mane with hairdresser's highlights moving up and down between my thighs, making slurping, spitty sounds.

It's Sophie, I realise.

She's sucking me. She's sucking my flesh. She has my erection in her mouth. Her mouth is full of me. I'm in her throat. It's warm in there, wet. Sophie my lover, my wife, is giving me the best morning call I've had in months. She's blessing me with the ecstatic sensations of a blowjob.

Sophie doesn't want us risking sexually transmitted diseases and bringing bad vibes into our bed and possibly death throes. She says that pleasuring me is *her* responsibility, no one else's; it is part of our relationship, part of the oath we took. She doesn't want anyone else getting in on the act. She'll meet all my needs, she says, even if she has to learn how. No matter how lewd or kinky my request, she'll give me satisfaction. And she does; she always does. The only thing I still don't get from Sophie is Chinese food. But we buy that in restaurants, or ask our cook Margot Lane to prepare some.

As I thrill to the sucking sensations and writhe in joy, my head turning this way and that, I notice a sleek, unfamiliar lampstand on one side of the room and see a framed painting on the opposite wall which I don't recognise at all. Then I remember: we aren't at home. We aren't in one of our own bedrooms. It's our tenth wedding anniversary. Sophie always wakes me up like this on our anniversary – and on my birthday, and on New Year's morning, and on the Fourth of July. I get a blowjob four times a year. Any more frequently and there'd be diminishing returns of pleasure, Sophie reckons. We went to a jazz club last night to celebrate our tenth anniversary and we're in a hotel suite overlooking the Round Pond of Kensington Gardens on one side and the shops and restaurants of Kensington High Street on the other. We're on a huge bed strewn with multi-coloured cushions.

I look down my chest. Sophie's face is out of sight. Her face is in my groin, hidden by her mass of hair which rises and falls as she gives me head.

Sophie is drawing her teeth along my stiffy. She's scraping my flesh, gently. She knows how to please. She's gnawing me now with pursed lips. Her lips, so full, so kissable, are kissing my cock. Oh those lips. So desirable. So supple, designed by her genes specifically to please. And so proactive: sucking strongly, drawing me out of myself, ex-static, disembodied, yet clamping me close, surrounding me with sweet sensations.

I've kissed those lips about ten times a day for ten years and still they excite me, still they bring feelings of sexual ravishment.

Sophie exhales through her nostrils; I feel the draughts of air on my wet skin. I hear the earthy sounds of her effort under the dome of hair. She's catching her breath. I feel her tits heaving. Her mass of hair rises away as she releases me from her mouth.

Her tongue takes its turn. Articulate tongue, *au fait* with foreign languages and many a *mot juste*, now a lascivious tongue pronouncing pleasure phonetically with forceful licks along my flesh, fluent also in the language of love. Licking with the flat of her tongue, licking long licks, licentiously.

Her warm mouth immersed me in moisture, her saliva seeped into my senses and made me dream of rain.

A rainbow is rising now from my loins, making me judder with joy. Sophie's licking has let off a lustre of gratified longing.

She lifts her head up and looks at me. What a beautiful woman she is. Her loveliness makes emotions well up in me. Her eyebrows naturally perfect. Her eyes clear. Her chin just above the head of my dick. Thick liquid like a gluey lipstick is leaking from her mouth. A clump of her hair is sticking to the left side of her lips. The way she looks and the way I feel confirm a fellatious fact – that I've just ejaculated. Like a glutton for the good things in life, Sophie has been licking my plate clean, filling her mouth and swallowing essence of Charlie Venn.

'Happy anniversary, darling,' she says, smiling deeply at me. 'Thank you for agreeing to marry me ten years ago when I asked you on that plane coming back from Paris. And thanks for taking me to that club last night. I loved every minute of it. What a horn that man blows.'

Her coquettish smile which I know so well, alluring and rewarding at the same time, seems plastered in place;

a trickle of the glue is sliding from her lower lip to her chin. She's on all fours. She's an animal, a beast of prey lapping up what she likes. She makes me grateful that I'm animal too, made of flesh and bone and racing blood.

'Yeah,' I smile back. 'What a horn, a jazzman through and through. I knew you'd like it. Happy anniversary, Sophie.'

'How are you feeling, Charlie?'

'Happy and deeper in love than ever.'

'But not yet satisfied. You're in the mood for more,' she tells me.

She knows I never come without making her come first. She knows that her pleasure is an aphrodisiac to me, that it makes me horny, that the more she comes, bathing my flesh in the juice spurting from her innards, the more strength I find to keep loving her. She knows that what's good for the goose keeps rousing the gander.

She's looking into my eyes lovingly, holding my dick between her fingers and thumb, pressing it intermittently, squeezing it, stroking up and down its slippery length. She knows how to make me hard and hot. She's been doing it for years. She's my wife. She's my in-house therapist. She's intelligent: she knows who'll be the beneficiary when I'm risen up and roaring again.

'You're in Oliver Twist mode, aren't you, Charlie?' she asks with a smile. 'More is what you want.'

'More of you, yes. Please kiss me, Sophie.'

She lets go of my drenched dick, places her knees at the sides of my legs and crawls on to my chest. She holds my cheeks with her sticky hands, lowers her head and kisses me passionately, smearing my lips with the mixture of saliva and semen glueing her mouth. The smell of sex and perfume fills my nostrils as we swap a secretion that once was mine and now is mine again. My wife compounds my joy. She doubles it. She gives me back with interest everything I give her. That sort of money is her *métier*. She has an excellent brain for the techniques of love.

'I get the impression again that you like me, Sophie.'

'It's the same delusion, Charlie,' she smiles, 'of loveability.'

'Must be. It's a delusion I wouldn't swap for anything. There's no place on Earth I would rather be than where I am right now.'

'Oh yes there is.'

'Oh no there isn't.'

'Want to bet?'

'Sure I'll bet.'

'What shall we bet for?'

'Whatever you say, Sophie.'

'You'll do whatever I say if I win the bet?'

'That's right – whatever you say.'

'And the bet is?'

'That there's no place on Earth I would rather be at this moment of my life.'

'There's a place you've often said is the best place in the world,' she replies.

She lifts her torso away from me and I see the cleavage of her lovely tits, their nipples pointing slightly apart. I notice the curving lines of her waist flaring out into the lush spheres of her arse. Her navel too is visible from where I'm lying with my head on the pillow; it's a little dent dead centre above her bush of pubic hair. The lustrous mass of wavy hair on her head is hanging down to her shoulders; it swings forward as she looks down between her thighs and encloses my erection in the palm of her hand.

We're physical, Sophie and I.

Flesh, heavy breathing, ejaculated semen. Our orgasms would have filled barrels. We can't understand how a woman can get away with faking an orgasm: the semen makes the man's cock sticky: and if she comes again it fills her cunt so that his dick is like a dipstick in the most delicious lubricant.

We agree: a guy has got to be pig-ignorant about pussy and its dynamics not to know when a woman is faking it.

I've lost count of the times Sophie has said she's glad she isn't a ghost. Despite the novel she wrote about a ghost rising daily from a moat to knock on the drawbridge, she's glad she herself is made of flesh and blood. She's glad she isn't a spirit or a wraith floating above the graves of a cemetery, insubstantial and transparent, able to pass right through tombstones and trees.

'Ghosts have no resistance,' she says. 'You wouldn't be able to fuck me, Charlie, if I were a ghost. There'd be no satisfaction whatever. And if *you* were a ghost, Charlie, your zol which I love so much when it's thick and hard – it would be useless. My hand would pass right through it when I tried to grip it tight and get you in the mood.'

That's what Sophie's pillow-talk is often about: the practical details, the nitty-gritty, of being biological. She has never actually put it in so many words – 'being biological' – but that is the class, the philosophical category, to which much of her post-coital conversation belongs.

Sophie calls a spade a spade. When she's darting about the squash court in her sticky T-shirt and there's a pattern of moisture on her hotpants, it is caused by sweat pouring from her hot muscles, she knows; it isn't some 'dainty glow' of delicate provenance, not a fake appreciation of facts packaged in a pretty little euphemism. She refers to her favourite flesh in straightforward terms: she calls it my 'dick', my 'cock', my 'balls', my 'tackle', my 'hard and handsome harry', my 'most excellent member', and some nights, when she doesn't want to sleep at all, my 'saturnalian slave'.

I've never heard Sophie call the things we do in bed and elsewhere 'sexual intercourse'. Instead, she says we 'fuck' each other indoors, we 'screw' each other, and some nights and days we spend 'banging', 'shagging' and 'humping' in the open air. Likewise, Sophie talks about the semen pouring from her 'pussy' which she mops up with one of our soft, absorbent love rags always handy under the pillows. She keeps a love rag in each of her handbags too. She acknowledges the congenital smallness of her 'quim' – 'I was born that way' – which makes each of our encounters an ecstatically 'tight time', lubricated by the liquid that leaks from me when I'm roused and ready for her.

Sophie doesn't mince her words when we're talking in bed. She speaks plainly. Her language is earthy and to the point. It's a free language without any corsets on the grammar or girdles to give a virtuous impression of her sexual propriety. Her phrases and expressions don't come clothed in foundation garments; her verbal messages never hang from suspender belts.

That's another paradoxical thing about my wife. That's the contradiction between Sophie my lover and the Sophie Gresham of public literary fame, whose historical romances and short stories are chock-a-block with self-repressing evasions and cluttered with the sort of circumlocutions that squeeze the vigour out of our language. The characters in her stories hardly ever say openly what they mean; they hardly ever come out upfront with their agendas. They always speak guardedly. They're always looking over their shoulders to see if a priest is watching, or the squire in the house on the hill, or a potential mother-in-law who emphatically insists that no wife of her son's will ever speak out of turn or even hint at an improper suggestion.

There is no chance on Earth that the main characters in Sophie's stories are anything but cultivated and superior. They flaunt their airs and graces, tactically and strategically. And neither the women in their bonnets and voluminous skirts nor the gentlemen in tophats and tails on the brink of inheriting fortunes from their fathers would ever burp or break wind through the other orifice.

Yet Sophie herself farts in bed. Her farts can be quite

loud. Some of her farts go clamouring on until they peter out in a moist burble. When I pretend to chide Sophie for her noisy, *unfeminine* habit, her come-back is quick.

'It's *your* fault, Charlie Venn,' she says. 'You've been lying on my gases.'

Or: 'They're sounds of celebration. Don't complain. They're whoops of joy for what you've filled me with, for the way I feel. Come here, let me kiss you, you clever conjuror.'

She's kneeling astride me now, this woman who farts occasionally.

'I love you, Charlie,' she says, holding my stiffness steady and fitting me in, slotting me in, pushing herself closely down on me, gently, slowly, until I feel and recognise and am thankful again to encounter the succulent moisture, warm and utterly benign, that is the herald of a different, delicious domain.

I know already that Sophie has won the bet.

This is the place supreme.

I'll do whatever she asks. I owe her so much.

'I love you, Sophie,' I reply. 'Thank you for being so kind despite my preoccupation at the lab.'

Sophie is so thoughtful, it's easy to see why she'd hate being a ghost.

Ghosts have no sex life.

Sophie would hate to be a ghost, even though ghosts are a higher form of life, according to hackneyed religionists. Sophie is happy she has a body that gives her so many joyful sensations. She is blissfully free of any sexual neurosis. She feels no anxiety about feeling good. Nor do I. We've never felt we're doing wrong when we do the things we like.

Sophie sometimes talks in bed about how religion has punished people for thousands of years for having sexual desires, for being conscious of the pleasure, the therapeutic peacefulness, which their bodies can bring, for acknowledging the raciness of flesh and blood. She's done a great deal of historical research for her romances and short stories, filling endless books with her handwritten notes. She does far more research than she ever uses, immersing herself in the details and atmosphere of the period mainly to boost her confidence.

It was religion, Sophie says, that branded sensuality a sin. It was religion, she explains, that made so many adults, grown men and women, snigger about their own sexuality. Religion made them grope guiltily in the dark because sex was defined as 'dirty'. Sex was said to be foul, despicable, by clerics in the *haute couture* of heaven's dispensation, cloaks and cassocks rich in colour, who screwed every country girl who came their way in cloisters blocking out the sun, bishops banging buxom wenches, thousands of them over the centuries who were frightened of being denounced as witches if they didn't comply, didn't spread their legs and offer up the tasty food which their god in his mercy had made available.

The monkey business was so rampant; the fornication and promiscuity among senior officials of the Church so prodigal and routine, Sophie says, the hypocrisy so unrestrained, that Pope Innocent in his *De contemptu mundi*, 'Contempt of the world', castigated the clergy who 'embraced Venus at night and worshipped the Virgin Mary in the morning'.

'Among the more profligate libertines, but by no means the only one,' Sophie says, 'was Rodrigo Borgia. As Pope Alexander the Sixth from 1492 to 1503, he had scores of mistresses, at least three illegitimate children, and was famous far and wide for the elaborate orgies he organised. In the name of God. Amen.'

For lesser mortals, however, all stirrings in the loins were condemned as the lascivious work of Lucifer. Religion revelled in its role as the unflagging agent of repression and psychic persecution. Sex was seen, not as healing togetherness, not as a well-spring of joy or a consummation of love between individuals, but as proof of evil and a sign of having succumbed to filth and sin.

'We are warned,' Sophie says, 'in St Paul's letter to the Philippians, that our lowly bodies will perish and, in his first letter to the Corinthians, that God is going to destroy our stomachs.' So God is a butcher as well as everything else he's supposed to be.

If a man had a wife, then he and she were dwelling in a joyless brothel. Why? Because marriage was said to have the same basis as harlotry.

'Those who have wives should live as though they had none,' Sophie quotes St Paul as saying in his first letter to the Corinthians.

And if a man was married, he wasn't allowed to embrace his wife on Sundays, Wednesdays and Fridays – which meant no sex for nearly half the year. Nor was he allowed to mount his wife during the forty days of Lent or the forty days preceding Christmas or for three days before receiving communion.

'It is a good thing for a man to have nothing to do with women,' Sophie quotes St Paul again, from his first letter to the Corinthians. 'Wretched loneliness is the ideal, we are taught. Nothing is better than being locked away in our cold, isolated, pining selves, for it is best, St Paul says in that same letter, if all people remain unmarried. D'you get the message, Charlie? D'you see where all the sexual frustration, hypocrisy and insanity come from, and the deep, over-compensating impulses to paedophilia and pornography?'

'I think I do.'

'Religion used to preach self-inflicted pain and tortured egoism. Its references to love were just empty words. On those few days and nights when a man *was* allowed to fuck his wife, he had to do so only in the most unsensual way – in the so-called missionary position – and get the dirty deed done as quickly as possible.'

'Why the hurry?'

'Because pleasure and satisfaction were to have no place in the foul act. The act was for procreation only. Both the man and the woman had to be covered in heavy night-clothes from neck to feet with small openings only for their genitals. That way they wouldn't be able to touch each other more than necessary, or feel the soothing warmth of each other's body. And the reason for this unfeeling sex?'

'Search me. *You* tell me.'

'Because flesh and blood cannot enter the kingdom of God.'

'Says who?'

'That same man, Paul, in the first letter he wrote to the Corinthians. Flesh and blood were despised. The female genitals were particularly vilified; they were referred to in Latin as *pudenda*, which literally means "shameful things". And the vulva was considered to be so coarse and disgusting that it had to be covered with a patch of hair, which, in German, is still called *Schamhaar* – shame hair.'

35

The windows of our hotel suite overlook the Round Pond in Kensington Gardens on one side and the shops and restaurants of Kensington High Street on the other, and in the warmth of the sunlight streaming in from both directions on our tenth wedding anniversary my lingering thought is how fortunate I am to be sharing the bed with Sophie. We've enjoyed each other repeatedly to celebrate the occasion and are having a long lie-in. In our relaxed, sexually satiated mood, Sophie tells me what she's discovered in her research about religion.

It occurs to me as she talks that, in all fairness, we can't blame St Paul for his misrepresentations of the human body. We have the benefit of hindsight, whereas he used to be, according to the Bible itself, a blasphemer and a violent man. We have much more knowledge than even the most learned scholars in the past, people whose style of understanding was steeped in ignorance and superstition. So the right thing for us to do is be magnanimous. We should forgive St Paul for his vilification of the human body, his dire castigation of flesh and blood. He didn't know better. He didn't have a clue two-thousand years ago what a magnificently complex phenomenon the human body was with its skeleton, spinal cord, muscular and nervous and endocrine systems, its ligaments and tendons, all controlled by a brain weighing about one kilogram and containing approximately 100 billion neurons connected to 200 trillion synapses forming circuits: the neural network *par excellence*, integrating everything into a single coherent conscious person.

St Paul knew next to nothing about human anatomy. He didn't know that our buttocks, far from being proof of our primitive origins, only came into existence about two million years ago when the bipedal hominids known as *Homo erectus* achieved the upright stance and began walking on two legs when they left the forested parts of Africa and started to inhabit the open savannah in search of food. The buttock muscles then took on a new structure and spherical shape, and the hands of this species, our forebears, being freed for other uses, had a transformative impact on the human brain and on the nature of the connection between the skull and the spinal column.

Beautiful, sensuous backsides, lovely buns, have resulted from our superior posture and are intimately linked with the complex development of our superior brains which have more than doubled over the last two million years to around 1,350 cubic centimetres. The body beautiful, far from being a sinful relic of the past, was one of the earliest signs of our transcendent future. People all over the world, in all cultures, find the arse, the butt, the bum such an alluring part of the human anatomy because its shape, its benign rhythmic geometry, is not bestial at all or primitive, but the physiological correlate of our brain power. It was determined by evolution and the force of gravity when our primal ancestors started walking on two legs across the open plateaux and grasslands of our birthing continent.

No other species on this planet has a round, curvaceous posterior protruding permanently from the spinal column, protruding with such erotic appeal, and no other species is numerate or literate or capable of music, poetry or even the vaguest abstract concepts. None other can really, truly smile or laugh.

In my brain is my butt and in my butt is my brain: a maxim easy to remember for those who insist that knowledge come in the form of soundbites or simplistic jingles.

It turns out from Sophie's research that if, due to sex starvation and the delirium built up by unassuaged longings, a man had a wet dream, a 'noctural emission' from dreaming of sex with someone friendly and forthcoming, he had to jump out of bed, kneel on the stone floor and reel off seven penitential psalms. Then in the morning he had to recite another thirty psalms. If he had an erection, he had to suppress it, look down on it as despicable, confess abjectly and beg his god for mercy.

'Masturbation was no way out of the maddening process,' Sophie says.

'Why not?'

'Because masturbation was a sin greater even than harlotry.'

'According to?'

'According to Thomas Aquinas,' Sophie explains. 'It was Thomas Aquinas who called woman "a failed man". He was so clever, so far ahead of his time, that he taught that rain, hail and wind were the work of demons. He hated women so much that he taught that a devil could change into a man and fuck a woman by becoming an incubus.'

'A what?'

'An incubus.'

'What the hell's that?'

'It's a form of a male that lies on top of a woman and makes her pregnant. And the devil could also become a succubus – lying *beneath* – and be made pregnant by a human man. That's the kind of rubbish religion propagates,' Sophie says. She pauses in thought for a while; I notice the shine of her hair in the sunlight. 'That was how monsters were believed to be born,' she continues presently, 'by sex across metaphysical barriers, sex between a horny devil and a lustful human woman, or between a guy who hadn't got it off in ages and a devil lying under him disguised physically as a woman. It was congress of this kind that gave birth to monsters with the heads of animals and the tails of fish and which had to be fed on special, requisite food.'

'What kind of food was that?'

'Can't you guess?'

'No, I can't.'

'C'mon, Charlie, have a guess. Show me what insight you have into religion.'

'I just know it's blind, whether intentionally or not. How'm I supposed to know what sort of food demons have to be fed? You're the one who's done the research, not me. You're the one who knows about this special cuisine. So it's for *you* to tell *me*.'

'All right then. Human children. Human children had to be stolen from their parents and carried away to be cut up into pieces and fed to the demons.'

'What a horrible idea. I wonder if Baldock's heard of it.'

'He won't let on if he has. Evangelists pick and choose only the bits of religion that make them feel superior. You can ask him this afternoon when we get to Chesterton for Danny's resurrection ceremony. As for women,' Sophie adds, lying beside me in the big hotel bed in the morning of our tenth wedding anniversary, 'they were beyond redemption. Women were the devil in disguise. Women were scheming temptresses destabilising men's integrity with their good looks, their long hair, the shape of their tits and the way their backsides wiggled when they walked. Women were so full of wickedness that they couldn't contain their evil essence which consequently poured forth from between their legs every month in a filthy red slurry that smelled to high heaven.'

Sophie pauses again and her silence continues for a long while. I feel rather than hear her breathing. The moment is split down the middle. She's lying on one side of it. I'm on the other. We're kind of compartmentalised. We're each in the cocoon of a separate consciousness, each with a different take on historical time and old wounds that bleed for different reasons.

When I turn my head on the pillow to look at her, I see that her lips are in a pout, her nostrils are flaring, and tears are sliding from the corner of her eye down the side of her face.

I lift myself from the pillow, turn towards her and dab the tears with my lips. I try to kiss them away. I place my lips on her mouth and kiss her softly, lingeringly. She lies motionless a while longer, distracted, her mind in thrall to a cameo beyond my ken. Then at last she responds. She kisses me back in a delicate, friendly way, her hand touching the back of my head, her tear-stained face and sticky eyelashes exonerating me from the cruelty she's been talking about.

It turns out that Jerome, the man who undertook the Latin translation of the Bible, known as the Vulgate, had no doubt whatever. 'Woman,' he said, 'is the gate of the devil, the way of evil, the sting of the scorpion, in a word, a dangerous thing.'

Tertullian, another 'father of religion', was equally convinced, Sophie says. 'Woman,' he declared, 'is the gate through which the devil enters.'

'All the authors of the Bible, every last one of them,' Sophie says, 'hated women. So it's not surprising that there were no women rabbis and that not one of the twelve disciples of Jesus was a woman – not even as a heterosexual alibi. In the Islamic religion, even though the Qur'an and the *hadeeth* clearly state that women are equal to men, with the same rights and responsibilities as men, and are equal in God's esteem, nevertheless women in Muslim countries have lower status than men. There are no female imams, nor do females lead the congregational prayers. Those who try, like women converts to Islam in America, are run down, denigrated by the religious authorities in Saudi Arabia and their imams abroad speading the Wahhabi word.

'According to various Christian texts, woman is the source of all evil. Period.

'Woman it is who catalyses sin – *concupiscentia* – which reaches its peak in sexual desire, that is, in the "*libido...qua obscenae partes corporis excitantur*": the desire in which the indecent parts of the body are excited.'

Sophie says that is the reason why women had to be kept under lock and key. The entrance to their sex had to be sealed off with a metal contraption tied round their waists and smothering their crotches. Women's word of honour wasn't good enough. Women couldn't be trusted not to make free with their sexual favours. They couldn't be trusted in the Muslim community, which Muslims call the *ummah*, either, where even today a woman's word is found wanting, unreliable. A woman's testimony is only half as valuable as the testimony of a man – it takes two women to counter the word of one man.

According to Sophie's research at University Library, even today women are sometimes murdered by fundamentalist men who suspect them of experiencing sex outside the 'fortress'. The word in classical Arabic is *hisn*, which is, she explains, a cognate of the word for 'marriage' – *ihsan*. Marriage is seen by Muslims as a fortress.

But Wahhabi interpretations of the Qur'an, put forth in the 18th century by a reformer called Muhammad ibn Abd-al Wahhab, who lived from 1703 to 1792, are so severe as to amount to a gross distortion. Wahhabis consider all other interpretations and sects as heretical and their members liable to public execution.

'This chimes in with the Salafi view of Islam which is also extremely conservative,' Sophie says. 'The Arabic root-word *salaf* means "forefathers" – their ancient attitudes and behaviour are supposed to be emulated strictly and everything in the Qur'an taken literally.'

The Wahhabis and Salafis both chose to close their minds

to the world. Their narrow attitudes, their humourlessness and exaggerated piety, and their fear of openness and change made them the exact opposites of the *zindiqs*, those vibrant freethinkers of Islam's early centuries who drank wine, loved poetry and science and whose irreverence and audacious ways of re-conceiving the world contributed so much to the culture and experimental spirit of the West.

Freethinking, Sophie says, is very much closer to the spirit of the Prophet Muhammad's teaching that 'the ink from the pen of the scholar is more worthy than the blood of the martyr', that Muslims should 'seek knowledge from the cradle to the grave'; that it is learning which deepens and transforms a person spiritually and raises him or her to a higher level of consciousness. This raised consciousness, they believe, brings humans closer to divine consciousness and enables them to see themselves more clearly as 'God's vice-regents on Earth', Sophie quotes the Islamic phrase. People should do all they can to deepen their understanding and to beautify the world bequeathed to us by God, not pillage and steadily destroy it.

But the Wahhabis emphasise only the Qur'an's negative verses, the ones about dire punishments, about conflict and war, and they suppress the verses about friendship and generosity.

Sophie says that *surah* 107 of the Qur'an, which is said to be an early Meccan revelation, is called 'Small kindnesses'. 'It reads clearly, with no ambiguity whatever.' She quotes the words to me in translation which, she points out, lack the rhyme and metre of the Arabic original:

'Have you observed him who betrays religion?
He's the one who repels the orphan
And urges not the feeding of the needy.
Ah, woe unto worshippers
Who are heedless in their worship,

Who rush to be seen at prayer
Yet refuse small kindnesses!'

Islam was hijacked and badly twisted by the Wahhabis, Sophie argues, pretty much in the way that Christianity was twisted by the Inquisition which saw the will of God in the merciless burning alive of thousands upon thousands of innocent men, women and children all over Europe. Likewise, the unspeakable cruelty of the Taliban in Afghanistan and Pakistan to their womenfolk has nothing whatever to do with godliness or divine guidance. It is sadism through and through, unrestrained by any notion of sympathy or fellowship. It is what enables young British boys to bomb innocent people going to work on the London Underground, Sophie explains. It shows total ignorance of the Islamic principle of *taqleed*, which condemns blind, unthinking acceptance of religious doctrine.

'Such dogma utterly ignores a key teaching of Islam: "*Le ikraa fi'deen*" – no compulsion in religion,' There should be no compulsion in religion. People should believe because they are convinced, because their hearts accept, not because of external pressures.

'The trouble is,' Sophie adds, 'there are verses in the Qur'an, in the *surah* titled "The Pilgrimage", for example, which contradict this teaching about no compulsion. Those other verses say that "garments of fire" will be prepared for people who disbelieve, and boiling fluids will be poured on their heads; and hooked rods of iron await them too on the Day of Judgement. And Allah says in *surah* 17, verse 8: "We have appointed hell a dungeon for the disbelievers."'

It is one of the Qur'an's insoluble contradictions, Sophie says. 'Seek knowledge, from the cradle to the grave', but also: 'Those who disbelieve and deny Our revelations are destined for hellfire.'

Muslims are urged in *surah* 29, verse 46 to be kind and

compassionate, to converse courteously with 'people of the book' – *ahl al-kitab* – meaning Jews and Christians, but at the same time they are exhorted in *surah* 9, verse 23, Sophie says, to turn against their own parents and siblings 'if they take pleasure in disbelief rather than in faith'. God seems to urge war even against one's own family.

Sophie lifts the duvet, gets off the bed and steps across the room to the food trolley where the remains of our breakfast is reflected in the mirror on the wall. She picks up the pitcher of water and pours herself a glassful. 'Want some?' she asks, raising the glass. I shake my head. She drinks the water, then comes back and joins me in bed again.

'The women are supposed to behave in Islamic ways,' she says, kissing me on the mouth and running her fingers down my chest. She turns and gazes at the ceiling. 'Yet they put on make-up. They have elaborate hairdos in the seclusion of their homes. They wear designer clothes and skin products – Prada, Gucci, Versace, L'Oreal, Lancôme, you name it – under their all-concealing *abayas* and *jilbabs*. I saw it with my own eyes in Jordan and Egypt. Their lipstick and eye-liner are concealed behind the veils called *niqabs* that make them look sinister in these times of terrorist attacks – they can see us, but we can't see anything of them. Their *hijabs*, headscarves, are quite elegant, I think, but who can blame security officials here in the UK for wondering what those women are carrying under their voluminous *burkas* and *jilbabs* – sticks of dynamite, rocket launchers, Kalashnikov rifles?'

'That's paranoid, Sophie.'

'Perhaps,' she replies with a grin. 'Those individuals might even be male suicide bombers disguised as women,' she suggests, 'as has happened in Israel where they have to fight a hugely unequal war.'

Nearly all Muslims in their teens and twenties in Britain were born here, Sophie says. They went to school here, got their GCSEs and A-levels here and some went to university and got their degrees here. A few have joined the British Army, the Royal Air Force and the Royal Navy. Many of the men support their local football teams, and the women are into fashion. Yet some of them, 'a small aggressive minority', Sophie says, are in thrall to a vengeful ideology of tit-for-tat. They are the ones who feel insecure in their Muslim identity. That might be why they wear clothes in public that proclaim what they think is their Islamic identity – except that the clothes tend to be Saudi – the *abaya* and *jilbab* are Saudi garments, Sophie points out – or Pakistani national dress, or Bengali kit, or Indonesian gear, which are cultural/national items that have nothing to do with religion as such.

'Another way in which these few beleaguered Muslims try to reinforce their sense of their religious identity,' Sophie tells me, 'is by sprinkling their everyday speech with Arabic words and phrases.'

In the middle of a conversation in fluent English, she says, they'll slip in words such as *alhamdulillah* and *mash'allah* and *insh'allah*, and *iman* which means faith, *salah* which means prayer, and *khutbah* (sermon in the mosque), *dhikr* (remembering God and mentioning him in daily life), *taqwa* (fearing Allah and revering him), *deen wa dunya* (religion and the lures of the world), *ghayb* (the unseen world of angels and spirits), *jihad un nafs* which means the spiritual struggle against one's own baser instincts such as greed, envy, anger, malice, and *tajweed*, the chanting art of Qur'anic recitation.

One can see confusion also in the Muslim men who, though sticking to the dietary prohibition about eating pork, ham or bacon, which are also forbidden to observing Jews, quite willingly drink whisky and wine and gamble on horses at the racecourse and at the roulette table in casinos – knowing full well that drinking liquor and gambling are *haram*, strictly forbidden. That's one of the pitfalls of being Muslim but also British, Sophie says.

'If in their Salafi and Wahhabi zeal they really want to be like their uncouth Bedouin nomadic ancestors whose belief in slavery was such a central part of their culture that it was abolished in Saudi Arabia only in the 1960s,' she wonders, 'why don't they go back to living in tents made of goatskin and shitting behind bushes, as their forefathers did? Why don't they shun all things modern including sanitation, antibiotics and appliances powered by electricity?'

Why indeed?

I turn on the pillow, prop my head on my hand and look at her lovely face. I smile at her and kiss the bridge of her nose. 'Understanding Arabic has certainly given you insights I would never have guessed at. But there's something you still haven't told me.'

'What's that?'

'D'you remember the day we first met – your Graduation Day?'

'What a silly question. I'll never forget it.'

'You approached me out of the blue in Old Hall and explained why Doctor Lorna Lambert couldn't make it. You said she was drinking tea with alumni from China in the president's office, and we continued talking. I asked you why Islamic countries had become so backward when once they were the scholars, the poets and scientists, the beacons of progress in the world. D'you remember, Sophie?'

'Of course I do.'

'You said you'd tell me when you knew me better. We've known each other ten years now, very much in the biblical sense.'

'Haven't we just?' she smiles. 'Now's as good a time as any, I suppose.' She presses her thigh against mine under the duvet, rests a palm on my tummy, and proceeds to give me the lowdown.

The Arabs' intellectual traditions and cultural honour were lost during their five centuries of subjugation by the

319

Ottoman empire, Sophie explains. By the time of the First World War when the Turks were allies of the Germans and Britain via T.E. Lawrence, known to many as 'Lawrence of Arabia', was encouraging the Arabs to rise up against their Turkish masters, the Arabian peninsula was divided into *vilayets*. *Vilayets*, Sophie says, were Turkish administrative districts that were run by officials who'd become corrupt.

The Arabs, though they all spoke Arabic, were not a united people, Sophie explains. Their loyalty was to the tribe they belonged to and the tribes spent much of their time in *ghazzus*.

'What are *ghazzus*?' I ask.

'Violent raids on one another. Their purpose was to loot property, steal herds of camels and goats and carry off any women they could lay their hands on. Inter-tribal robbing, looting and killing was in fact the norm.'

Sophie says the Hashemite Abdul Aziz Abdurrahman al-Sa'ud, the Hakim of Nejd, was known as Ibn Sa'ud. He was a fierce fighter and chief of the Sa'ud tribe who were deadly enemies of the Rasheed family whose sheikhs ruled the Shammar tribe. The Howeitat tribe were the enemies of the Ruwalla, one of the Wahhabi tribes affiliated with Ibn Sa'ud.

'Then there were the Bani Sakhr,' she counts off on her fingers, 'the Shawam, the Agail, the Qanasil, the Harb, the Billi, Juheina and the Ateiba tribes.'

The tribes were all devoted to their blood feuds passed on from generation to generation. They were constantly sub-dividing into bands of marauders bent on plundering and avenging the murders of their family members. It wasn't unusual for travellers traversing those vast expanses to come across corpses decomposing in the sun, on hills, in the valleys, on the edge of an oasis.

In September 1924 Ibn Sa'ud's Wahhabi forces attacked the Hashemite summer palace at Taif and massacred the inhabitants of that town. The following month Ibn Sa'ud's fighters took control of Mecca. In January 1926 Ali, the brother of Iraq's King Faisal, was deposed as King of the Hejaz region by Ibn Sa'ud who then seized that territory. A new kingdom under him began to emerge. Concessionary agreements to search for oil reserves were signed in May 1933 with the Standard Oil Company of California, and later with Texaco, Exxon and Mobil. This yielded vast amounts of disposable petro-dollars which enabled the royal family to finance the Wahhabi brand of backwardness far and wide.

Simple pleasures were forbidden, Sophie tells me. Music was banned. Women were more tightly controlled. It was common for the sheikhs to have as many as fifty or sixty concubines, many of them snatched in raids, whom they handed over to other men as pawns in inter-clan negotiations after they'd used them sexually. Free speech was an early casualty of the new dynasty. Newspapers, magazines, radio and, later, television were all rigorously censored in the country that was named after the dominant Sa'ud tribe – Saudi Arabia.

Sophie's voice is usually quite low, but it has become huskier from all the talking. She gazes pensively at the ceiling, then says: 'It's as if the Arabs in the police states of the Middle East today with their plush hotels, skyscrapers and gleaming shopping malls are a completely different people from the *zindiqs*. Those cultural pioneers who developed mathematics, developed astronomy, divided day-and-night into twenty-four hours and each hour into sixty minutes, who pushed medical science forward and wrote love poetry with such concise, such ravishing perception – wow! Listen to this,' she says, pauses and recites by heart:

'A twisting curl
Hung down to hurl
My heart of bliss
To the abyss.'

36

Sophie gets out of bed again and, stark naked, steps across to the shower room of our hotel suite. She opens the door and enters the area where the walls and floor are covered in emerald green- and gold-patterned tiles. The tiles become a bright sheen when Sophie switches on the light. She doesn't bother to shut the door, so I see the wisps of hair in her armpits when she raises her hands overhead as water jets down on to her from the shower-head. She turns around with her arms up and I get a view of the curving cleft of her shapely butt glistening with drops of water and then of her thick patch of pubic hair. It is so erotic, that private hair, protecting the entranceway to ecstasy.

As I gaze at her lovely body being pelted with water and see wisps of steam begin to cloud the shower room in the morning of our tenth wedding anniversary, I am amazed afresh at my good fortune and lapse into a daydream about Sophie's charms.

The next thing I know Sophie is emerging from the shower room with a towel round her waist. Her fulsome breasts are on display, each nipple pointing slightly outwards. Her hair is hanging in damp clumps down to her shoulders.

'So what would you like me to do?' I ask her, patting the bed, inviting her to come and lie down again. 'You won the bet. Your wish is my command.'

'Well actually, there are *two* things I'd like you to do,' she says. She knees herself on to the bed, twists her torso and rests her head on one of the pillows as she stretches out on the duvet. Her damp hair wets the side of my face and ear.

'Two things?'

'Is that being greedy?'

'Not at all. I said I'd do whatever you asked, so fire away.'

She sits up, arranges a couple of pillows against the carved headboard and sags back comfortably. The smell of her gel-fragrant flesh fills my nostrils as she itemises her requests.

'First of all,' she says, placing the index finger of her right hand on the little finger of her left, 'I want us to attend Danny Mullins's resurrection ceremony this afternoon with an open mind – even though you still consider it an outlandish request.'

'I don't understand, Sophie. Baldock pleaded with me to bring you – and I'm bringing you. Isn't that enough?'

'Not really.'

'Why not?'

'Don't go there to gloat, Charlie.'

'I don't want to go at all. Baldock's request that we go and help bring a dead boy back to life is the most ridiculous thing anyone has ever asked me to do. I'm only going because *you* said you wanted to see fundamentalists in their element. I have no intention of gloating or even taking the thing seriously.'

'That's what I mean – you *should* take it seriously. Promise me we'll follow the contours of whatever happens.'

'What d'you mean?'

'Let's not go there with foregone conclusions. Let's see how the occasion works out.'

'I know exactly how it's going to work out. Danny Mullins was certified dead several days ago. One important conclusion to draw from that fact is that he will stay dead – the laws of chemistry make no exceptions. That doesn't mean I'm gloating or being blasphemous.'

'But you could help me find out why people feel the need to resort to primitive beliefs when they're in difficulties. As

I said, it could be the core idea of my first modern novel. If we aren't going there to learn something, we shouldn't go at all.'

'I'm only going because *you* want to go, Sophie. I'll keep my eyes peeled and my ears cocked as usual – I can't say fairer than that, can I?'

'I suppose not. I'd have gone on my own, but it was *you* who saw Danny just before his head hit the pavement, not me. So according to Baldock it's *you* who'll be contributing to the actual resurrection.'

'There isn't going to *be* an actual resurrection – regardless of what Baldock said.'

'But there'll be many other people present, people who *do* believe in the power of prayer and who knew or saw Danny while he was alive.'

'They're in for a major disappointment. They're going to be shattered when they find they haven't forced their god to break the laws of chemistry, no matter how many angels they bring as back-up. What's the second thing you'd like me to do?'

'Secondly,' she replies, counting off on her wedding finger, the finger with the gold ring I gave her exactly ten years ago, 'I want you to take me along when you go to the ChimeroGene shareholders' meeting in New York next month.'

'How I'd love that! Oh Sophie – you aren't kidding, are you?'

'I'm perfectly serious.'

'Why've you changed your mind? You usually spend the time at exhibitions when we're in the States, especially the Frick in Manhattan and the Metropolitan Museum of Art. You've told me so much about the medieval armour at the Met and its endless paintings.'

'Because I want to take more of an interest in what you're doing, Charlie. I told you I'd make it up to you, and the sooner I start, the better. Now that I've met Bertha, I want to keep in touch with the vibrations you've been trying to alert me to, the scientific passion that's going to transform the world once again. To be honest, I got a bit of a shock in Flame McGovern's office.'

'Sophie, you don't know how happy you're making me. It'll be my pleasure to show you around Manhattan properly, the way I've shown you around Boston. But remember, Ground Zero still hasn't been sorted out, four years after the attacks on the World Trade Center. We made a point of not going there because we didn't want to gawp, but perhaps it'll be okay to have a look now. The whole area around Liberty and Vesey Streets was closed to visitors last time we were there. Weeds had been growing on the site.'

'I'm not sure even now whether I want to see that hole in the ground. It's so full of bad memories.'

'What sticks in my mind are all those friends and relations at the family-assistance centre on the Hudson river waiting to get death certificates for people whose bodies were never found, people who were either crushed to dust or vaporised. The Red Cross hospital ship *Comfort* was moored at the jetty there, but what comfort could there have been for those bereaved New Yorkers?'

'The poor people,' Sophie says with a pensive look in her eyes. 'How desperately they tried to find their loved ones.'

That was when New York City fell into a frantic kind of communication, I recall, a longing to make contact by means of low-tech messages flapping in the breeze. Walls and shop windows and fences and lamp-posts and subway trains and phone booths were plastered with photos sellotaped in place, and flyers with details of missing persons handwritten by distraught individuals searching for them – their wives, their mothers, husbands, boyfriends, sons. And the question everyone kept asking their fellow New Yorkers, the mantra of that time, was: 'Where were you when it happened? What were you doing?'

'I'd like to get to know other parts of Manhattan, though,' Sophie says. 'It's such a vibrant city. And the people were much more polite and courteous than I'd expected. Let's spend more time there, Charlie. Last time we stayed at a hotel on the Upper West Side. Let's try some of the hotels and restaurants in Greenwich Village this time.'

'Whatever you say, Sophie. There's plenty to see and do.'

'And then Boston, I'd like to see Boston again. I had no idea until the first time you took me there how reminiscent of old England parts of it were.'

'The amazement was all over your face. You kept saying "this bit is so English – are we really in America?"'

'Harvard University too, with its ivy-clad buildings, was an eye-opener.'

'Not really surprising, when you come to think of it. John Harvard was a Cambridge man, after all, an undergraduate at Emmanuel College in 1633, before he migrated to America. He left his estate and library to found the university named after him on the north bank of the Charles River. D'you remember, Sophie – the whales we saw in the bay when I drove you down to Provincetown?'

'I'll never forget those whales. They were so sleek and unafraid. They kept circling the bay, diving with their tails in the air then surfacing and racing one another.'

'And the leaves falling all around us as we enjoyed our bowls of clam chowder.'

'So many shades of red those leaves were, so many tints of yellow and gold. They kept swirling about in the cold wind gusting from the sea.'

'I can't wait to show you the Big Apple properly, Sophie. There are so many clubs and eating places to try. There's bound to be a worthwhile gig at the Village Vanguard on Seventh Avenue.' I keep eye contact and ask in a lower, more intimate tone: 'D'you mean it, Sophie? Seriously? Will you really come to the meeting? Nearly everyone there will be a venture-capitalist. It's a consortium of big money, ChimeroGene – their purpose is to fund research that will make even more money.'

She smiles: 'Yes, I'll come to the meeting – if you still want me to.'

'Of course I do. I have to give the investors a kind of pep talk – how it is they're getting in on the ground floor of an entirely new industry by backing our skills with their money. They know why they're involved, of course – they're business people, hard-core realists. But they like to be praised for the intelligent move they're making by betting on strands of DNA. It's going to be kind of tricky for me – I have to enthuse them, acknowledge their far-sightedness, but take care not to get too technical. A little technical is what they expect, so they can think of their money in a profitable scientific milieu, but not so detailed that they lose track of the bigger picture. I haven't figured out yet which aspects to emphasise and which to avoid. We don't think the time is right yet to take Bertha to New York. We're saving her for maximum impact later.'

'You'll work it out, Charlie, you'll see. You'll have it sorted by the time we touch down in Manhattan.'

'When we do take Bertha, Flame McGovern will look after her, of course. Bertha has become very close to Flame – they have a terrific trans-species rapport. We'll go by plane. Bertha will probably want a seat by one of the windows. She'll just love it when a flight attendant comes along with the drinks and asks what she'd like.'

Sophie smiles warmly at me. She puts her arm around my neck, pulls me over on to her and I feel the cool dampness of her hair on my face as she kisses me on the mouth. She kisses me long and hard. I can *feel* it: her lips are again taking an oath. Her lips are telling my lips that her lips are mine alone.

I should be happy. I *am* happy, ecstatically so.

But my happiness makes me feel vulnerable.

Do I really deserve so much pleasure and intimate friendship? What have I done to deserve it? I've tried to figure it out but still can't. Isn't ten years of joy a long enough innings for anyone? Perhaps George Gershwin and his brother Ira had people like me in mind too when they wrote their lovely song 'Someone to watch over me'.

Last night, to celebrate the tenth anniversary of our wedding, we sat under the metal-pipe ceiling of the Bubbling Cauldron jazz joint in a cobbled courtyard at Camden Lock digging my fellow American Johnny Griffin giving hard-bop renditions on tenor sax of standards such as Cole Porter's 'In the still of the night' and Thelonious Monk's 'Bemsha swing'. The British rhythm section – piano, bass and drums – was gutsy and superb. Something about Griffin's cascade of spiky notes, music not anodyne in any way, reminded me in places of the broiling, earthy sophistication of John Coltrane's *A Love Supreme*. That legendary outpouring of African-American devotion on tenor sax, especially the 'Pursuance' and 'Psalm' movements, makes one hold one's breath; it is complex, engrossing, fervent yet cool – glorious highs of musical expression.

Although there've been many superb instrumentalists in the history of jazz – pianists, drummers, trumpeters, trombonists, guitarists, the magnificent Ray Brown, Charles Mingus, Jaco Pastorius on bass – one is inclined to agree with Ornette Coleman's judgement that 'the best statements Negroes have made of what their soul is have been on tenor saxophone'. It's so easy to concur with that sentiment. One simply has to think of Coleman Hawkins, Lester Young, Ben Webster, Wayne Shorter, Sonny Stitt, Hank Mobley and Eddie 'Lockjaw' Davis, among others. Each has his distinctively ravishing verve. To say nothing of Monk's tenor man Charlie Rouse on such knock-out numbers as 'Well you needn't' and 'Straight, no chaser' or of the deeply talented Joshua Redman who's been thrilling listeners and wowing audiences ever since he won the Thelonious Monk Tenor Saxophone Competition. To say nothing of Sonny Rollins, still endlessly inventive in his seventies when Sophie and I witnessed him bring down the jam-packed house at a gig at the Barbican in London celebrating the fortieth anniversary of Ronnie Scott's jazz club. Or Dexter Gordon, the single biggest influence on John Coltrane's playing. Coltrane's rendition of Ellington's 'In a sentimental mood' with the magnificent Ellington himself the accompanist on piano: that 1962 recording is a pleasure Sophie and I have savoured again and again over the years.

Duke Ellington: probably the most prolific and best-loved composer of the 20th century. He composed on buses while the rest of the band were asleep and they were speeding through the night to the next gig where the new number would be ready. He composed in traffic. He composed on trains, always leaving space within the structure of the sounds for his instrumentalists to ad lib, to extemporise, to explore the harmony and excavate fresh riches from it. And Ellington's collaboration with the prodigious composer from Pittsburgh, Billy Strayhorn, on the iconic melody that became the band's signature tune, the quintessentially American 'Take the A train': what music! So distinguished, so abundantly stylish, urban and cool, conclusive evidence reinforcing the truth of Duke's teaching that 'It don't mean a thing if it ain't got that swing' (*doo wop do waah, doo wop do waah*).

How falsely rustic in our times popular music would have been, how twee and tight-assed, but for the boiling hard-edged ebullience of bebop. It lifts you out of crapville. It jumpstarts *joie de vivre*. You know in your heart and head that you ain't dead. The volts undo the bolts holding you down. You fly when those horns cut loose. Your juice starts to bubble and all the trouble caused by the honkies and their donkeys across the colour line – why, it makes you pine for a dream to come true, for a better day to dawn, shorn of all shallowness and callowness and the need for greed to set the tempo and the speed. Don't you dig it? It ain't cool to pig it.

Sophie and I loved sitting so close to the musicians last night, having our requests for particular numbers performed and getting a waiter to take a tray of drinks to them. It's akin to the satisfaction we find in the inimitable Nat King Cole whose warm, relaxed, well enunciated singing style is still instantly recognisable, *the* iconic balladeer, with a voice like rough silk. But Nat's earlier reputation as a cutting-edge jazz pianist leading the King Cole Trio is even more enduring. Sophie and I have all those tracks, digitally remastered, in our eclectic CD collection.

When she moved in with me so we could go looking together for a house of our own to buy, Sophie brought her collection of Gramophone, Naxos and other classical-music CDs. The first track she had me listen to was Bruch's Violin Concerto No.1 performed by Yehudi Menuhin; it held me fast. She then acquainted me with Vaughan Williams's 'The Lark Ascending' and Elgar's 'Pomp and Circumstance March' and the deeply felt Cello Concerto performed by Jacqueline du Pré with the London Symphony Orchestra conducted by Sir John Barbirolli. Sophie told me du Pré was only twenty years old when she turned in that extraordinarily mature performance which was recorded by EMI; it made her name internationally and became the definitive interpretation. There was no sign yet of the multiple sclerosis that would cut short du Pré's illustrious musical career so cruelly and kill her when she was forty-two. There can't have been a more heart-breaking case, Sophie said, of disease crushing the human spirit so pitilessly in its prime.

It was Sophie who introduced me to the strong, compelling voice of Edith Piaf. An album of Piaf's songs recorded at the Paris Olympia was the first gift Sophie ever gave me; she said she treasured it and wanted me to have it. The distinctive passion of the orphaned 'little sparrow' was deeply affecting, even though I didn't really understand the French words so drenched in love and loss. Her singing always puts me in mind of the great blues performer Billie Holiday, despite being in an obviously Gallic vein. It is hard to express the emotional links I find between Edith Piaf singing about a woman's happiness in 'Heureuse' and Billie Holiday's 'You go to my head'.

Sophie and I often listen to our music as we lie side by side after making love. Sometimes it's Chet Baker performing on trumpet and singing one of the romantic numbers from the Great American Songbook, such as 'I get along without you very well'. Sometimes it's one of the Beatles classics. Or the complex excitements of Courtney Pine's 'Brotherman', Lee Morgan's legendary trumpet-led 'Sidewinder', or those magnificent aching sonorities of Andalucia called *flamenco cante*.

My mind clings to the colours in Sophie's hair from the red, blue and yellow lights shining on the bandstand last night, a trace of gravy smudging her lovely lips as we eat the food at our table and drink the wine and revel in the joy of being with each other.

I remember again how open-hearted Sophie has always been to me in our ten years together. Her refusal to come to the institute to meet Bertha was the only exception – and that is now in the past. She says that henceforth she'll come to the institute frequently to have facetime with Bertha; they'll both be on a learning curve, she says.

This is our tenth wedding anniversary. Sophie meeting the other female in my life, the other female I'm engrossed in – Bertha, our genetically enhanced bonobo chimpanzee – has at last banished the tension between my mind and my body. Sophie, Bertha and I are going to be a *ménage-a-trois* without compare, an ensemble tuned in to harmonies deeper than any the world has ever known. Bertha is turning out to be like Hanuman, the monkey god in *The Ramayana* who helped Rama get back his wife Sita after she'd been mystified and abducted by the demon king Ravana and taken to his lair on the southern island of Lanka.

What better way is there to respect the one you love, the one who gives you so much joy and pleasure, the one whose companionship comprises the main constant in your life, than to free her mind from ancient chains?

Perhaps the lousy dream I've been having from time to time will now stop recurring. I wish it would: the dream in which I lose Sophie to someone else who meets her needs more deeply than I am able to, who keeps demonstrating that I am simply too shallow for her. In one version of the dream, I see Sophie in her white hotpants and sticky T-shirt playing squash within the red parallel lines on the walls. She's playing energetically as usual, darting about with her racket poised to strike the ball, a blue sweat-band round her forehead, her long hair swinging about in a pony-tail, her feet moving fast in white socks and tennis shoes. It's not *me* in the squash court with her, however. It's some other guy, whose face I never get a look at and whom I therefore wouldn't recognise in my waking hours.

In the misery of my dream, the red lines on the walls of the squash court begin to crack and leak. The red lines begin to drip. First little globules of the red paint break away and roll down the walls. Then bigger ones trickle down, until pretty soon great gouts, not of paint, but of blood, are sliding down the walls and plopping onto the shiny wooden floor. Sophie and this guy are blissfully unaware that they are playing squash ankle-deep in blood, blood which in my dream I know without any doubt whatever is *my* blood. And when I look up to see if anyone else is witnessing this carnage, I'm suddenly outside and the whole sky is oozing a vermilion that vies with the brightness of the sun. I'm covered in thick, sticky blood; its smell makes me retch and bend over to puke. I can't find my way home because all the street-name signs are blank. I feel like an outcast in this dream, mocked and maligned despite my best intentions. I have a map in my pocket to untold treasures, a genetic paradigm shift, but nobody wants to know. When I break out of the dream in a feverish sweat, it's such a thrill to find Sophie in bed beside *me*. She covers me in soft kisses and calms me down by humming a soothing melody in my ear.

How I wish these bad dreams would cease. What I hate most about them is that they are so closely related to my feelings for Sophie. I love her and my love brings forth these nightmares. Surely love should bring *happy* dreams? Surely the joy in one's heart should release visions of vivacity and enthusiasm, images of good fortune and positive vibes stretching all the way to the horizon? Love should inspire optimism, surely, not endless permutations of dread and disaster lurking around every corner?

What are my dreams trying to tell me?

That Sophie isn't the one for me, after all, despite the ten years of happiness I've enjoyed with her, fraught though some of them have been? Can dreams be so perverse? Can they change the meanings of feelings, sensations and perceptions the way lawyers in courts of law change the significance of evidence so that it points in exactly the opposite direction to what everyone took for granted? Perhaps dreams aren't reliable indicators of one's inner life. I'd prefer that to be the case. I certainly haven't been enjoying the idea that my emotions are where my nightmares originate, that I am a masochist relishing the pain visited upon me by my own brain when I'm fast asleep.

Now that Sophie has come over to my side, come to the lab and met Bertha, perhaps I won't have bad dreams any more. Perhaps this is at last the end of my sleepless nights.

Sophie's meeting with Bertha has had another effect, apart from filling me with joy. It has made me feel devious, underhand. It makes me regret that in my long months and years of frustration, of wondering whether my wife and I would ever get to team up more tightly, I secretly penned a little poem inspired by the tension between us which she has now at last resolved so happily:

> I'm in science, she's in the arts,
> My target's the brain, hers is hearts,
> My works change the world in all its parts,
> Hers are at best melodious farts.

37

Sophie and I haven't been to the Chesterton part of Cambridge before and we're surprised to see as she drives her Jaguar along Chesterton Road how tawdry the parade of shops is compared to the historic parts of Cambridge. The shopfronts are grimy; the sagging sign above one of them says *Simon's Pastry Parlour.* We see two plate-glass windows that are broken, shards of glass strewn across the sidewalk. Some of the walls have spray-painted graffiti. One sign in faded letters that look a few years old says *The endtime cometh,* another proclaims *Nations will disappear like Sodom and Gomorrah.*

We can't be much more than a mile from Trinity College, Gonville and Caius, Clare and the other wealthy institutions with their huge endowment funds, billionaire bequests, private clubs, formal dinners and uniformed servants, but we might as well be in a depressed part of the country where the rigours of the economy take their toll in very stark ways.

'Run-down, isn't it?' Sophie says, driving slowly along the kerb.

'The shopping parade is. It might've been a storm that smashed the windows, but look at the houses – they're quality, solid.'

'Which street are we looking for?'

'Garfield Road,' I say, glancing at the card with the street lay-out sketched on the back which Baldock gave me. 'We have to turn left into Matthew Lane after Chesterton Avenue, go through Stephen Cross Square, pass Mark Jones

Place, then right into Garfield.' I hold the card up so Sophie can see the street plan; she studies it and nods.

'Quite detailed, isn't it?' she says.

'Baldock didn't want us to have an excuse for not turning up.'

'I wonder what they're like.'

'Who?'

'Danny's parents – Ceri and John Mullins.'

'Grief-stricken, probably. Danny was only twelve years old when that van knocked him off his bike and he died in hospital. He was a gifted chess-player. He put his mum and dad in the limelight, brought them a kind of fame. They're bound to miss him badly.'

'Did he have any brothers or sisters?'

'I don't know. Probably not – Baldock didn't mention any other children. We've just passed Chesterton Avenue, Sophie. Here – this is Matthew Lane coming up. Turn left here, then go to the end of Stephen Cross Square, pass Mark Jones Place, then first right into Garfield.'

Sophie glances in the rear-view mirror, flicks the indicator on and as she makes the sequence of turns we notice how crowded the streets are with cars and vans and pick-up trucks. There's no parking space left that we can see. Motorcycles and push-bikes are slotted in the gaps between the four-wheel vehicles. White lettering on the side of a blue van says *Only Jesus Saves.*

Sophie drives slowly up the crowded street which is flanked by double-fronted two-storey Edwardian houses, semi-detached dwellings in 1930s style and the odd plot with a small block of flats lying at the back of a paved courtyard. Some of the houses are separated from the sidewalk by unkempt hedges, others by low walls enclosing narrow strips of garden. Instead of trees in the street, there's a forest of television aerials jutting up from the rooftops, and quite a few of the houses have satellite dishes fixed to their front walls.

336

'Where'm I going to park?' Sophie says. 'I can't leave the car in the middle of the street.'

'Turn right here – this is Garfield Road, where the Mullins house is.'

Sophie flicks on the indicator, steers the car round the corner and we see similar houses with similar hedges and low garden walls and parked vehicles taking up every inch of space on both sides of the street. We know almost immediately which house is the Mullins residence because of the crowd of people spilling out of one of the gateways and milling about on the sidewalk, between the cars and on the tarmac in front of us. The sounds of singing voices are coming from the open windows; it's a religious melody being belted out passionately, to which the men and women outside are making their sonorous contribution. It is God's Alliance in full throat.

'We've come to see Danny Mullins,' I call out to a man in a check shirt with sleeves rolled halfway up his arms and a blue baseball cap on his head. 'Where's a place to park?'

He smiles and comes round to my side of the car. The brass buckle of his broad leather belt is a cameo in relief of Christ's crucifixion.

'Bless you for coming, brother,' he says, bending down to my open window, 'and you too, sister. The good lord has got the word around.'

'We got the word from Baldock,' I tell him.

'Jem Baldock?'

'Jem the steeplejack.'

'A good man, Jem is. He's got God in his heart.'

'I got a look at Danny Mullins just before his head hit the sidewalk.'

'You saw the accident?'

'Yeah – in Silver Street, in front of the River Gate entrance to Queens' College. I'm the person who called the ambulance.'

'You've got to get into the house quickly, brother,' he says, moving the peak of his cap closer to my face, 'and get yourself up to Danny's bedside.'

'Where shall I park?' Sophie asks him.

'Parking's not important. We can't let parking blow Danny's resurrection. Leave the car here and get into the house.'

'Here?' I say. 'In the middle of the street?'

'Why not? Anyone else coming this way today will be coming for the same reason. Please, brother – get out of the car and get into the house quickly. You saw what no one else here saw. I'll clear a way for you.'

He steps to Sophie's side of the car and makes his way through the crowd across the street towards the house.

Sophie glances at me. 'Let's do it,' she says. She switches the engine off and pulls the key out of the ignition. 'Remember what you promised me.'

'What did I promise?'

'That we'd follow the contours of whatever happens here today. That we'd come with an open mind.'

'How open? So open that our brains fall out?'

'Don't jump the gun, Charlie. Don't put your preconceptions on parade.'

Sophie opens her door and gets out of the car. So do I. The house is semi-detached, its pointed gable matches the one alongside, but the brown walls and beige-coloured window-frames clash with the white-washed walls and blue window-frames next door.

There are quite a few young people in the crowd in front of the house singing aloud with their eyes shut and their outstretched arms held high. There's nothing fuddy-duddy about this gathering; the women are young, attractive, with long hair and lipstick on their mouths. Some of them are wearing jewellery – necklaces, earrings, bracelets. Their faces aren't pasty or ascetic. They don't look as though they've been fasting, as though they've been mortifying their flesh with whips or chains. On the contrary, the first thing I notice is how sensuous they are, how obviously aware of their bodies and proud of their appearance. But they are singing about something beyond themselves, singing from their hearts, with a passion to which the men's deeper voices are adding a rich vibrato:

'How can you say there's no resurrection of the dead
When all that's in our hearts soars overhead?
If we die and aren't reborn,
Our faith is useless, shorn
Of the promise that Jesus made
That we'd move out of the shade
Into everlasting light.
So stand firm and fight
The messengers of the night.
For Christ was raised from the dead.
He rose 'spite the blood he shed.
For as in Adam all die,
So in Christ we all fly
Back where we belong,
In heaven's blesséd throng.'

The sounds of the song are ringing in my ears as I take Sophie's hand and thread a way through the swaying, outdoor choir. By turning our shoulders, edging sideways and pushing gently, muttering 'Sorry', 'Excuse me', we reach the kerbstone and then the sidewalk, get through the gateway, cross the small garden and finally make it up the three steps to the front door which is wide open.

The man wearing the blue baseball cap smiles back at us.

'Make way,' he says to the people crowded together in the hall of the house. 'Make way for a crucial witness,' and clears a path for us bodily. 'Follow me,' he says over his shoulder.

'You okay?' I ask Sophie, looking back at her and squeezing her hand as we cross the threshold.

'Never felt better,' she replies. 'It's a whole new genre.'

'It's a resurrection ceremony, Sophie – not a short story.'

'It's my way forward as a writer,' she says. She pulls her hand from my palm, places it on my butt and sinks her claws into my flesh.

38

On our way through the crowded hall towards the foot of the stairs, the singing suddenly stops. The people open their eyes and smile and hug one another. There is manifest joy in the faces of the allies. They're like travellers who've crossed dangerous lands since they last saw one another and are celebrating the reunion.

The vibes in the house are friendly, informal, relaxed. There's no stiff old-style religiosity. There's no keeping still and paying attention to some guy in a long black dress standing at a lectern and telling everyone else the way it is. Boys and girls about Danny's age are offering the visitors plates of sandwiches and handing out glasses of fruit juice. Meeting one another in Jesus is a happy occasion, I realise. Then I see the allies in the front room move away from the centre of the floor and make space for someone to do an individual turn.

A well-built young black man in blue jeans, white shirt and red braces over his shoulders steps forward. His head is close-shaved, his face bony, feet in white sneakers. He smiles to all and sundry, then purses his lips, gathers his thoughts and, bending at the knees, bobbing to his own beat, he comes out in a clear rapping cadence:

'Secularism is junk,
It leaves you drunk
And in a funk,
Scared to make a move
To find the groove

You know will prove
That Jesus is true,
For me, for you,
For everyone
Under the sun.
So don't preen yourself,
Come clean yourself,
Be open and say
I bend my knees and pray
To Jesus most high
Who'll never let me die
Cos I'm the apple of his eye.
Flesh ain't our final fate,
We have a date
With eternal life
Beyond the strife
Of the hustlers and sharks
And Cerberus who barks
At the gates of hell
Where the haughty angel fell
Who sounds the death-knell
Of those who cannot tell
The chaff from the wheat
And are content to eat
Endless junk,
Smell like skunk,
Signalling with their pong
The depth of how wrong
Their perception is.
Please,
Make the move,
Come and groove
With those who prove
That Jesus is the man for all seasons
For the best reasons.

Come now, before it's too late
And you suffer the fate:
Your heart turned cold
For love of gold
And you decrepit and old
While we live vigorous in our Lord,
Wield his eternal sword.
Together, each of us, man and wife,
Enjoying everlasting life.'

There's a moment's silence, then someone calls out, 'Nice one, Jack,' and they all clap their hands and cheer in waves of heartfelt applause.

Jack nods and grins and clenches a fist overhead in a Godpower salute.

'No wonder the churches are emptying,' Sophie says into my ear.

I glance back at her: 'What d'you think of it?'

'I like it. It's fresh, almost raw.'

'It's rap, hip-hop.'

'So? It's people's poetry.'

'Christian poetry.'

'Descendant of John Milton, a rebel Christian you might have heard of, staunch republican against the Church's lust for power.'

'Don't be sarky. Of course I've heard of Milton. *You* got me reading his blank verse. He said paradise was lost.'

'Human paradise, he meant. Oliver Cromwell had failed to bring democracy and Milton, blind, was a target for the king's assassins.'

'Come, brother, this way,' the man in the baseball cap beckons me, waving an arm so I can see him across the throng. He's at the foot of the stairs.

'We going upstairs?' I call out to him.

'Yeah. That's where Danny is.'

'D'you really want to go upstairs?' I ask Sophie. 'There's a dead body that must be decomposing – not my idea of a civilised state of affairs.'

'We gave our word to Baldock. Remember?'

'I remember, but I'm not sure he'll be real pleased to see us.'

'Of course he'll be pleased. He wanted us to witness the longing for everlasting life.'

'That was before he met Bertha. Remember how he backed away, turned and ran with his Bible? He couldn't get away fast enough. He might not be so keen on our company now.'

'He'll keep his word, I'm sure. He struck me as an honest man, sincere.'

'Sincere in his false perceptions. Since when did sincerity make anything true? People sincerely believed the Earth was flat. Catholics sincerely believe all Jews are Christ-killers – it says so in their Bible, hence all the pogroms. Today some Jews believe Palestinians are vermin and treat them accordingly. D'you have to be brainwashed to be sincere?'

'For God's sake, Charlie,' Sophie hisses into my ear, 'we're in the house already. We came because Baldock sought you out in Grantchester and more or less begged you to come here – for the best possible reason: to save a boy's life. We might as well go upstairs. I'm curious. Who knows when I'll get another chance to observe a gathering like this. The feeling is getting stronger and stronger that what I discover here today is going to be the core of my first modern novel. I'm pretty sure I've found the theme, at last – and a way in.'

'You're right, of course. We agreed. We made a deal with Baldock.'

'*You* made a deal with him,' Sophie says. 'So move it.'

I take her hand and push my way towards the stairs. As we snake through the crowd, I suddenly notice the smell of perspiration competing with the smell of perfume, the contradiction of what the body *is* and what people *wish* the body would be. The place is full of vibrant young men and women with blood coursing through their veins, but it's also full of something invisible, something with an upward draught lifting the thoughts of everyone to a higher plane: an ideology that transcends muscle and bone and the notion that bread is all that humanity is about.

Getting to the foot of the stairs is just one stage of our journey. Climbing the steps and getting to the top is another story. My hand feels clammy; it's been gripping Sophie's too long. Holding tight becomes uncomfortable. I let go of her hand and glance over my shoulder. She smiles at me with her pale-blue eyes.

'Don't worry,' she says. 'We'll shower later. I'll wash your hands too.'

The flow of human traffic on the stairs is haphazard. Better progress would be made if everyone going up stayed on one side and everyone coming down kept to the other. Instead, it's a mindless free-for-all, a writhing, twisting kind of motion in which the only way of knowing who's coming down is that they are the individuals whose faces tend to be wet with tears. They've seen something up there, or felt something up there, which they couldn't contain within themselves and which has seeped from them and reddened their eyes.

When Sophie and I finally reach the landing, we find that we're facing the bathroom; its door is wide open. There's a puddle of water on the floor inside and a big man with his bare back to us whose hair is soggy and from whose neck and shoulders water is running down to the waist of his trousers. On either side of him is a man in shirt-sleeves whose profile we can see clearly. The one closest to us is blond and has a bushy beard. The one on the other side has a receding hairline and is wearing glasses. Each of them has one hand on the head of the man in the middle, and the other palm pressed to his bare shoulder-blades.

'How beautiful are the feet of those who bring good news,' the blond-haired man says.

'And the good news is heard through the word of Christ,' the man further back replies.

'I believe in the supernatural powers of Jesus,' says the man in the middle with his back to us, 'utterly and entirely do I believe. Jesus can intervene on my behalf, directly in my life. He can heal me when I'm sick, find me a job when I'm out of work, steer me to a soul mate, clear up my debts, and raise to life again those who have died. This I believe in my very deepest heart.'

There's a split-second pause, then the men on either side of him push his head down and immerse it with a loud splash up to his shoulders in the bathwater. Sophie and I glance at each other while he is bent over with his backside to us in ritual baptism. He is held underwater for more and more seconds, for an unconscionably long time, then his head is suddenly pulled up and a spray of liquid flies everywhere, drops of it hitting my forehead and Sophie's face as we stand side by side in the doorway. Sophie glances at me, then lifts a hand and dabs the water from her cheek.

The man with the bushy beard and blond hair looks into the eyes of his soggy brother in Christ and says to him, loud and clear: 'Thou shalt not make unto thee any graven image, or any likeness of any thing that is in heaven above, or that is in the earth beneath, or that is in the water under the earth. Thou shalt not bow down thyself to them, nor serve them, for I the Lord thy God am a jealous God, visiting the iniquity of the fathers upon the children unto the third and fourth generation of them that hate me; and showing mercy unto thousands of them that love me and keep my commandments.'

I turn to Sophie and take her hand. 'It's a full immersion,

just like the baptism of John was. It's an imitation,' she says. 'This is an occasion to re-commit, remind and to strengthen one another.'

'It isn't just a resurrection ceremony, is it?' I reply, 'It's a house-party on high.'

'Come this way, brother,' Baseball Cap calls out, lifting his arm and pointing to the door of the front bedroom. 'Danny's in there. He needs you urgently.' He raises his voice somewhat and tells the gathering: 'Make way for the crucial witness. This brother here saw the actual accident. He saw Danny in the last moments of his life.'

Five or six heads turn. They stare at me with a kind of awe. Then their bodies separate, pull apart and create an avenue for me and Sophie to enter the room. Danny Mullins, surrounded by several adults in the afternoon light coming through the window, is lying cold and dead on a narrow wooden bed.

The room is full, not only of people, I realise suddenly, but also of the highly aromatic smell of camphor. They must have rubbed Danny's corpse with camphor to conceal and disguise the putrid smell of physical decomposition.

39

'You're a good man, Doctor Venn,' Baldock says, rising from his chair at the side of the bed. 'You're a good man despite your delusions.'

He is soberly dressed again in dark suit and tie. He steps towards me and offers his chunky hand in greeting. I look into his bright blue eyes and there's not a trace that I can see of anger or malice. His blotchy complexion is still purply-red, his lips much paler and well defined. I reach out and clasp his hand. I owe him respect. I really didn't expect him to take kindly to me after the episode with Bertha on the riverbank behind the institute.

'I came because I gave you my word I would come.'

'And you've brought Mizz Gresham, as you said you would. Good afternoon, Mizz Gresham,' he says, turning to Sophie. 'We are very pleased you could come. It's in accord with God's wishes.'

'I always wanted to come – as I told you,' Sophie says.

Baldock turns at the waist and gestures with his hand to the couple sitting near the pillow on either side of the bed.

'This is John Mullins and this is Ceri Mullins,' he says, indicating a man of about forty with brown eyes, a thick moustache and square jaw with a dimple in the middle, and a woman whose eyes look as though she's been crying non-stop for days on end. Her blonde hair explains the colour of Danny's hair in the newspaper photo Baldock showed me, and her sorrow lends her beauty a gaunt, stricken quality. On a small table on the window side of the bed is a chessboard with all the pieces set out, ready for a game to start when

Danny regains his faculties and rises from his pillow. 'And this is Doctor Charles Venn and his wife the author Sophie Gresham. Doctor Venn was pre-ordained in God's wisdom to be passing by in his car when Danny was knocked off his bicycle near the Anchor pub in Silver Street.'

John Mullins rises from his chair.

'It's kind of you to come, Doctor Venn,' he says, extending his hand, and when I clasp his palm, he adds: 'It means a lot to us that you're willing to bring back to Danny the precious moments of his life which you were fortunate enough to witness.'

I don't know how to reply. I don't know what to say. This is a man and wife in the grip of grief. This is not a time to be arguing with them, to have a slanging match about ideology.

'Look at Danny, would you?' Ceri Mullins says from the other side of the bed. Her voice is so hoarse it's barely audible. 'Concentrate on his face for as long as you can. Please, Mister Venn. You're in a position of great power. You can help raise our Danny from the dead. That's what Jesus wants you to do.'

I feel impelled to glance at Sophie, to check her reaction, but something tells me it would be a bad thing to do. It would be construed as an aren't-these-people-silly look, aren't they pathetic?

So what should I do instead? Go figure, I tell myself. Work it out. What's the etiquette?

I do what the mother has asked me to do. I comply with her request, which I know is what her husband wants too.

I move aside the chair Danny's father has vacated, step right up to the bed, lean over it and look down into Danny's face. The smell of camphor is very strong.

Danny's blond hair is close-cropped high above his ears, but there's a clump hanging sideways on the left side of his forehead. His skin is pale, so pale that it has in it a tinge of yellow. His lips are just thin lines. I wonder as I look down into his face if he would have beaten me at chess. He very probably would have. If he could beat a dozen adults at the same time, he could probably pulverise one adult in no time. But over the game I would have heard what his voice sounded like. I would have asked him who his best friend was, and why, and discovered thereby something about his likes and dislikes and drawn an outline of the personality he might possibly have grown into. I would have got some sort of fix on a virtual person. If it's true as the saying goes that the child is father of the man, I would have got an insight into the man whom twelve-year-old Danny Mullins might one day have become.

Danny's face is cold and pale against the white pillow. Looking at him reminds me of the last time I saw him, when he was pedalling his bicycle along Silver Street and I was waiting in my car for the traffic lights to change. When I got out of my car and dashed to him, blood was flowing from his nose and there was a pool of blood around his head. He isn't bleeding now. He seems too pale to have any blood left in him, yet his button nose and pointed chin give him a mischievous, impish look. His pointed chin reminds me of the chin of the tap-dancer Fred Astaire who starred with Ginger Rogers in old movies such as *Swing Time*, *Follow the Fleet*, *Flying Down to Rio*. And Astaire's chin in turn reminds me of the long, sloping chin of Peter Lynn, the man in charge of security at the institute where I work. I'm looking at the face of a dead boy I didn't know when he was alive, and he's reminding me of people I do know.

I remember my mother telling me that doctors and nurses and electricity-supply workers were all at one time other people's children, that without other people's children there would have been no useful things in the world, like paper or writing or photography, because there would have been no one around to invent them. So I'm looking at dead

Danny's face and remembering, not only my own face when I was young, but also the kind of thoughts I used to have in those days. I remember walking between my mother and father to the Little Angel Theatre in Boston to go and see the puppet people living their lives.

I remember walking between my parents when they took me to the Hayden Planetarium, and when I saw photos of the dead body of the man who, despite his alleged penchant for prostitutes and links to organised crime, came across to many in his time as the most charismatic American president of the 20th century; and the corpse of his brother Bobby Kennedy, and the corpse of Martin Luther King, Jr, and the corpse, riddled with bullets, of Malcolm Little, alias Malcolm X, who used to be known as Detroit Red because of the colour of his hair which came his way via the white man who'd raped his grandmother and passed on the genes that coded for his mother's fair skin and the colour of *her* hair.

So much history is in our genes, I think as I stare at Danny's face.

Why do I keep thinking of dead Americans?

Why this sudden morbid fascination?

I wonder about it as I stand at the side of the bed, leaning over the corpse of a boy who used to play a dozen games of chess at the same time, walking in his short pants from one table to the next, glancing quickly at the layout of the pieces and making his move, then stepping to the next game and devastating the opposition there too.

Why am I thinking of Americans who were murdered in the five years before I was born?

Why am I sad that their lives were cut short so suddenly?

It must be, I decide as I keep my eyes fixed on Danny's dead face, because I wish they *weren't* dead, because I wish they'd had the time to pursue their dreams, to carry to fruition their projects which might possibly have ennobled the rest of us.

And in wishing they were still alive, I'm wishing, it dawns on me at the side of Danny's bed, that I could bring them back from the dead. I'm wishing they could live again. I'm wishing I could meet those men, talk with them and take the opportunity to pick their brains.

I'm ensnared, I realise.

I'm a research scientist and here in this house I too am rooting for resurrection.

I'm going round the bend.

That's what comes from consorting with irrational types. You start getting into their grooves. You start pretending it's realistic to be romantic. You start thinking pie in the sky is what the sky's there *for*. You ask yourself why you're a gene-transfer specialist and the answer comes back loud and clear: because my business is the chemistry of love. Improving people's health is my life's work. Curing diseases and disabilities at source is the name of my game. I know in my heart that humankind can move to a higher plane of evolution. I know we can nurture the seeds of transcendence that are embedded in us, by excising at source the genetic mutations responsible for our physical, mental and moral weaknesses, for the epic saga of our suffering.

We can instil human values into human flesh by deploying the incisive, profane means at our command.

It requires patience, however, and painstaking attention to detail. It requires a willingness always to learn, systematic observation and classification of data, and continual improvement of the array of high-precision skills. It demands unwavering faith in the scientific method and excommunication of anyone who tries to cut corners, who panders to gullibility or makes claims that go beyond the evidence.

The chemistry of love has all sorts of compounds in it, including ribonucleic acid and deoxyribonucleic acid. These acids help to make us what we are; they play crucial parts in constructing the identity of every human, animal and plant everywhere in the world. DNA lays the foundations of everyone's personality, makes it possible for us to relate to other personalities, feel solidarity with them. And sooner or later DNA shows people up who want their wishes to come true without any intermediate effort, without an instrumental struggle. It exposes as work-shy malingerers the charlatans and tricksters who go down on their knees because they want gods to do their work *for* them, who refuse to be self-reliant. It exposes the guys and gals without guts who beseech their gods endlessly to help them pass exams, help them win money on the lottery, help them find jobs, help them pay off their debts, help them buy a used car at a good price – help them, in short, so they don't have to bear the burdens of life themselves, or take responsibility for themselves, but be served by gods who are really nothing more than menial *gofers* – go fer this, go fer that and, while you're about it, go tell it on the mountain that you really love me even though I'm mentally indolent and want everything on a silver tray.

I feel I've been standing at the bedside doing this couple's superstitious bidding long enough. I've paid obeisance to their god. I've been deferential to those who are jealous of their impotent beliefs. I feel I've kept my side of the bargain. It's been a strain, though, and a loathing is welling up in me. I feel choked by a mixture of anger and commiseration with Danny Mullins. Danny wanted to go to Russia to play chess there; instead, he was knocked off his bike and died in hospital. Where was the god who was supposed to love and protect him? Where was God and his host of angels when Danny was pedalling his bike along Silver Street and the removals van struck his back wheel? Absent again, as usual. Non-existent.

Recalling the clicking sound in my head at the lab when Bertha had gone missing, I feel weak all at once and vulnerable. I feel pale. I wonder whether I'll sleep soundly tonight. Will the nightmare of Sophie leaving me for someone else return with a vengeance when we go to bed? Is that dream an epiphenomenon of my feelings of insecurity, of my awareness that for years Sophie kept herself away from me in one crucial respect? Is the dream a psychological elaboration of her holding back from me the esteem I craved so much? Will I get any sleep at all? I see myself tossing and turning again, thrashing about beside her, unable to break out of the hold which other people's wilful obscurantism still seems to have on my heart.

I look up from Danny's dead face and see Sophie in the crowded room on the other side of the bed. She's talking with a man in a black cassock whom I didn't notice when we entered; he's wearing a dog-collar too. He looks like a Catholic or Church of England vicar and I wonder what he's doing here. This isn't his scene, surely? This can't be his cup of tea – a corpse surrounded by born-again evangelicals in a room reeking of camphor, not of incense. Maybe he's on a reconnaissance mission, keeping tabs on the religious competition, on the non-conformists. He looks about fifty years old, and he's handsome in that dark-eyebrowed ascetic way of so many men who make a vocation of their god.

Sophie is standing close to this vicar-type, looking into his eyes. He has her full attention. What can he possibly be saying that's holding her so rapt?

What spiel is he giving her that's luring her into the recesses of his mind? I hope she isn't being taken in. I hope her defences aren't down to the extent that she's being seduced by the flannel about a better life after death. I hope she isn't being conned.

That scenario *can* sound seductive when one's guard is down: a host of virtuous people in white togas singing hymns and playing harps endlessly with their ghostly see-through fingers in a place beyond the clouds where, according to

Milton's *Paradise Lost*, 'ambrosial fragrance filled/ All heaven' and which rings with 'blest voices, uttering joy'. This is the Kingdom of God where the door policy is very strict. Flesh and blood get no entry whatsoever because flesh is vile. The Doorman simply won't let you in.

And yet, strange conundrum, there's an area segregated along religious lines known in Arabic as *jannah* (paradise), a zone of exemption set aside by divine wisdom for those in receipt of special dispensation. The air in this un-slum-like ghetto is full of the sounds of erotic breathing, of grunts and sighs of satisfaction. The earthy sounds are emanating from Muslim men with beards who are lying between the thighs of lovely young women and passionately enjoying the sexual favours of seventy-two virgins each, one after the other. The curvy butts of these chaste gifts from God, whom no man or *jinn* has ever touched, are settled on green cushions on the finest carpets in a garden of fragrant flowers fed by sprinkling fountains.

This is each zealot's eternal reward for crashing hijacked planes into the World Trade Center and the Pentagon in the blue-sky morning of Tuesday September 11, a little before, and a then short while after, 9am., US Eastern Standard Earth-time, and for suicide-bombing teenagers at night-clubs in Tel Aviv and for killing holidaymakers in Bali and fellow-Muslims at prayer in mosques in Pakistan and Iraq and passengers in trains on their way to work in Madrid and London, and workers doing their jobs in Istanbul.

Three-thousand miles from Boston in the bedroom of a dead twelve-year-old chess player, I look around me and suddenly feel dreadfully homesick.

I long to be with my parents. I want to be among people who know that dogma and blind faith offer very little guidance in the 21st century. I long for the wisdom of those who value lucidity, members of the US National Academy of Sciences who know that humanity has to be self-reliant, that as a species we only have our intellects, imaginations and moral vision to depend on.

I've had my fill of obscurantism and peddlers of pie in the sky.

I turn and look again at John and Ceri Mullins on the other side of the bed.

'Please accept my condolences,' I say to them. 'It's one of the saddest things in the world when a child dies.'

'Thank you for coming and for looking at Danny's face with such concentration,' Ceri Mullins says, a brave smile trying to break through her stricken features.

She extends her hand across the bed. I squeeze it lightly and try to give her an encouraging smile.

Then I put my hand into my jacket pocket and bring out one of the institute's business cards.

'Here is the phone number of the lab where I work,' I tell her, proffering the card, which she takes. 'If this gathering has succeeded in its purpose, if your son Danny comes back from the dead any time soon, please give me a call. I'll be very interested to hear from you.'

I turn away from them and watch Sophie paying rapt attention to what the vicar-type man is saying. I watch her until, eventually, she turns her head and her eyes meet mine. I motion with my head to the door. She nods, says goodbye to cassock-man, turns and proceeds to leave the room full of mourners.

I realise again that I'm in an alien place and feel I have to get out quickly. I must get away fast. I'm surrounded by individuals who look modern, who seem to speak the same language as I and wear the same sort of clothes, but whose minds are paralysed by a primitive voodoo pinning them to the past. They suddenly look dead to me, all of them corpses, not just Danny on the bed. Something convinces me they're residues, ghoulish relics that belong in graveyards and charnel houses where the rotting bones of by-gone generations are revered, worshipped, kowtowed to for no other reason than that they crumbled long, long ago into an obscure, ancient dust.

Sophie and I make our way past the bathroom where there's water on the floor, then down the crowded, writhing staircase of the house, and more or less fight our way out the front door and through the throng of believers on the sidewalk.

As we head for the car parked in the middle of the street, Sophie stops me by grabbing my arm. She looks at me with dismay in her eyes.

'You've gone terribly pale, Charlie,' she says. 'Aren't you feeling well? What's happened?'

'It's this lot,' I reply, feeling faint as I wave a hand at the born-again brethren all around us.

'What about them?'

'They've got a damn nerve to be so wilfully nonsensical, to impose their stupidity on me like that. I can't believe what I've just done.'

'All you did was keep your promise, Charlie.'

'I kept a date with people proud to be duped, proud to be strung along. I'm a research scientist, Sophie – remember? – focused on the facts of the future. I feel humiliated.'

'You came because Baldock came to the institute with us – that was the deal.'

'I know, I know, you don't have to remind me,' I say in a burst of anger. 'Why d'you always speak up for them? What the hell was that vicar guy saying that you couldn't take your eyes off him? You still find these people credible, don't you? What's wrong with you, Sophie? Aren't I ever going to be able to trust you?'

'Don't start that suspicious crap again, Charlie,' she hisses, tilting her head forward and eyeing me angrily. 'I asked him why so many bishops and priests had affairs with women, got them pregnant in secret, why so very many of them were paedophiles, raping young boys and intimidating them into silence – all over the world, for years and years on end. I asked him why the Church was being taken to court by so many American families, why its officials were so often found to be not just lecherous, but brutal, devious, perverse – *that's* why I kept looking at him, Charlie. I was listening to his answer.'

'What *was* his answer?'

'I listened carefully, but everything he said amounted to evasions, platitudes. He said God works in mysterious ways. He said the flesh is weak. He said bishops too are human beings, forgetting that bishops are supposed to be exemplars of good behaviour and integrity. He came across as a waffler using weasel words. Now get into the car,' she orders me with a wave of one hand while bringing out the keys from her jacket pocket with the other. 'You don't look well. I hope you aren't going to have one of those nasty dreams again.'

'So do I. That's the last thing I need – another nightmare.'

'Try to relax, Charlie. This gig is over – there won't be an encore. Try to take it easy.'

'I'll try. I've got to relax.'

'It's the best thing you can do. I'll get us home in no time. Margot's preparing a cosy, candle-lit dinner for our tenth anniversary. She knows we both like fish. She told me she's doing a starter of crab salad with coconut, tomato, celery, croutons and green beans, followed by baked sea bass with garlic. We'll sip a few wines with the food and chill out in front of the fire, then have an early night.'

'Good idea. That's just what I want – peace and quiet, a nice long sleep.'

'We'll be alone, there'll be no one to bug us,' Sophie says, trying to reassure me, trying to start the unwinding process so that by the time we get into bed I'll be relaxed enough to fall into deep slumber.

*

Despite the wines we sip with our tenth anniversary dinner and the satisfying crunchiness of the croutons in the crab salad, followed by baked sea bass done the way we like it, with a hint of garlic, and the snug atmosphere afterwards near the flames in the fireplace that lulls me into drowsiness as we chat, when Sophie and I get into bed that night I have, instead of a sound sleep, another bad dream.

The nightmare recurs. It gets hold of me yet again. It's about sexual betrayal, sleeping with the enemy – detailed, disturbing, but this time it seems also, curiously, to be about free speech.

The ceremony at Chesterton has surely affected my brain.

I see a guy enjoying Sophie's body, grunting as he does so, her thighs enclosing him in a togetherness that isn't just physical but pulsing with meanings that keep melting and merging in those blurred layers of allusiveness peculiar to dreams. He's lying on her, in her, thrusting, and their coupling personifies freedom of movement, freedom of assembly, the taking of liberties that allow pleasure into life and make it worth living. It's a very American dream concerned in opaque ways with the First Amendment of the US Constitution, the part of our Bill of Rights that guarantees the latitudes without which we would all be enslaved.

The dream is chock-a-block with American imagery. Symbols and tones of voice from my country's iconography fill my mind as I lie aghast beside Sophie and watch her being pleasured by someone else. Perhaps it's because I'm homesick. Perhaps the trips I've been making every year to brief colleagues at our parent company in Cambridge, Massachusetts about the progress of our project in Cambridge, England haven't been enough to slake my patriotic thirst. I might be missing America more than my busy work schedule has allowed me to realise. Who knows how feelings, fears and memories fuse into that internal kaleidoscope we call a dream? Who can distil the sense, decode the messages, from images that accompany a sleep-induced soundtrack?

It's the most unsettling dream I've had since Sophie and I became an item a decade ago. The anger it reveals is frightful. Bitterness is again bubbling. Despite her protestations to the contrary during our waking hours, Sophie abandons me once more for someone else. The dream's meaning lies in a displaced context; it is disguised by the setting that gives it a superficial otherness. But even though the time-lines are jumbled anachronistically and the moods keep shifting, everything is vivid, clearly outlined, and I get a solid handle on what the score really is.

I dream I'm a successful gangster. I live, not in a Georgian house in the charming English village of Grantchester on the outskirts of Cambridge where my lab is located, but in a penthouse apartment in a skyscraper overlooking Lower Manhattan. I have clear views from the windows of my apartment. I see, not only the roofs of the buildings below and the white, sagging headstones in the churchyard of St Paul's Chapel where George Washington celebrated his inauguration as the first President of the United States from his pew in the north aisle, but also Fulton Street fish market where extortion and loan-sharking took place until quite recently under the control of organised crime, and the Woolworth Building with the bas-relief caricature of its owner, Mr F. W., counting nickels and dimes, and, immediately opposite St Paul's Chapel, the gap in the skyline at Church Street between Vesey and Liberty Streets where the twin towers of the World Trade Center stood until the blue-sky morning of September 11 2001, now Ground Zero, the murderous heap of rubble shrouded in dust cleared away for the memorial structures to come.

I'm a mobster at the top of the pile. I'm in control of

all the rackets, including bootleg liquor, gambling and prostitution. On my say-so hoods who encroach on my turf get bumped off and disappear without trace. The police are in my pocket. Corrupt mayors take my money and look the other way. I'm a version of Lucky Luciano, legendary head of the Mafia's Genovese family in New York and boss of the Cosa Nostra syndicate, acknowledged founder of organised crime in the United States who'd quit school in Manhattan's Lower East Side when he was fourteen years old. I'm immaculately dressed in black tuxedo and bow tie, expensive rings glittering on my fingers.

It's that nightmare again, the same one, different only in little details. Makes me feel that *I'm* the one being screwed, again and again. The shine of my slicked-down hair vies with the sheen of the white silk scarf hanging elegantly from my shoulders. I'm *nouveau riche* and vulgar and love every minute of it. All the broads come to my parties: they know the booze flows like water and that I book the very best bands in town, not only at the Cotton Club where Duke Ellington swings. If a pianist won't play at one of my places, I have his fingers broken. If a trumpeter won't gig for me, he won't gig for anyone else: with a punctured lung he won't have the necessary puff.

I'm standing in one of the beautifully appointed rooms of my apartment high above the city, admiring the paintings I've acquired. Money can buy anything, even advice on good taste. A chunk of my wealth is hanging on my pastel-hued walls in the form of works by Matisse, Hockney, de Kooning and a huge three-dimensional Rauschenberg collage incorporating paint, cloth and metal. Alongside the open laptop computer linking me to my operations in all the boroughs is an elongated wire sculpture of a human figure by a guy called Giacometti. It doesn't appeal to me at all, too damn scrawny, but my advisers tell me it's good art, meaning its money value will go up. All the floors of my pad are covered with Persian carpets and the door-knobs are eighteen-carat gold.

I am Charles Hadley Venn, leader of men, master of my turf.

I open the door to the master bedroom and see that Sophie, my woman of ten years, has been two-timing me all along. Sophie's heart has been elsewhere. I see her pelvis pushing up and down, up and down, and wonder if she's forgotten the words of the song we've sung together more than once about not going to strangers when we're in the mood for love but coming to each other for pleasure. I open the door of the main bedroom in my penthouse apartment and Sophie is crying out in ecstasy. A guy is lying between her smooth thighs, fucking her as if there is no tomorrow, thrusting vigorously.

The bed is rocking under their naked bodies. Their clothes are scattered on the floor. Smoochy music's coming from the sound system in the wood panelling.

Sophie is being blessed by a bishop from God's Alliance, by an exemplar of moral rectitude. He is pumping her full of sacred pleasure, consecrating her body with bursts of satisfying joyfulness far superior to the pallid climaxes which mere mortals can attain.

Acknowledgements

Rachel Cross went through an earlier version of this novel with a fine comb and her searching queries and perceptive comments made me re-think and re-write whole sections of it. I remain indebted to her.

I owe much more than a debt of gratitude to Ruth Florence, my wife and contributor of insightful intimations. She and I are well acquainted with four friendly, intelligent, widely travelled sisters, all of them sympatico possibly because each has had her own traumatic problems to deal with. It was from those sisters that I borrowed particular personality traits which I fused with other elements into the character of this novel's Sophie Gresham. Those sisters are all linguists; they all studied Latin and modern languages and lived abroad whilst undergraduates.

Nevill Coghill's modern verse translation of Chaucer's *Canterbury Tales* is the source of the few lines from 'The Miller's Tale' which appear on pages 135–136 of this book. I am happy to acknowledge that the publisher of Coghill's title as a Penguin Classic is Penguin Books Ltd. My best efforts to ascertain the copyright holder of the Rumi quotation on page 137 indicate that it is Coleman Barks who lived in Athens, Georgia, USA and who received an honorary doctorate from Tehran University in 2006.

Enver Carim
Greater London, July 2014

About the Author

Enver Carim was born in Johannesburg, South Africa where he grew up and finished high school. He graduated from Exeter University in England and received editorial training at Penguin Books. As a journalist he met business, military and political leaders in Africa, Asia, Europe and in eight cities of the United States. His PhD thesis is an empirical critique of a Harvard University theory of people's moral development. He ran the London Marathon to raise money for cancer research. His work has been translated into several languages and one short story made into an animated film by the National Film Board of Canada. He is married with daughters and lives in Greater London.

envercarim@yahoo.co.uk

Lightning Source UK Ltd.
Milton Keynes UK
UKOW04f0728211114

241905UK00001B/5/P